S I E N N

OBSIDIAN

AWAKENING

For my husband and children
who taught me love.

This book is a work of fiction. Names, characters, places, and incidents either are the product of the author's imagination or are used fictitiously. Any resemblance to actual persons, living or dead, events, or locales is entirely coincidental.

Edited by Kyle Robertson

ISBN: 978-616-588-112-8

Some things are deadly when broken...

The heart of Obsidian lies in this sentence. Obsidian breaks sharper than any other materials and must first be broken to form a deadly weapon.

This series is, therefore, a story of broken people who have been forged by life into dangerous weapons to survive. It is also a story based on many forms of love and how far we, as humans, will go for love, be it the love of freedom, of an ideal, of pride, of our homeland, of a child, a husband, a wife, a parent, or those closest to our hearts.

The brutality of this story has been written for the sole purpose of proving that violence, discrimination, racism, and slavery have no place in this world, that no one ever truly wins in wars, and no true heroes are ever made in an act of killing. The objective of this book is not to offer hope, it is to show that we all have the strength to prevail in the absence of hope, that even if the world does not improve, we have the power to change it, little by little, if we choose to let go of our hatred and prejudice, little by little.

⁜

'Fate is a condescending, angry, sadistic bitch with few things to do and too much free time. But when Fate decides to strike, you can choose to die broken, or you can break like obsidian.'

— Deo di Amarra

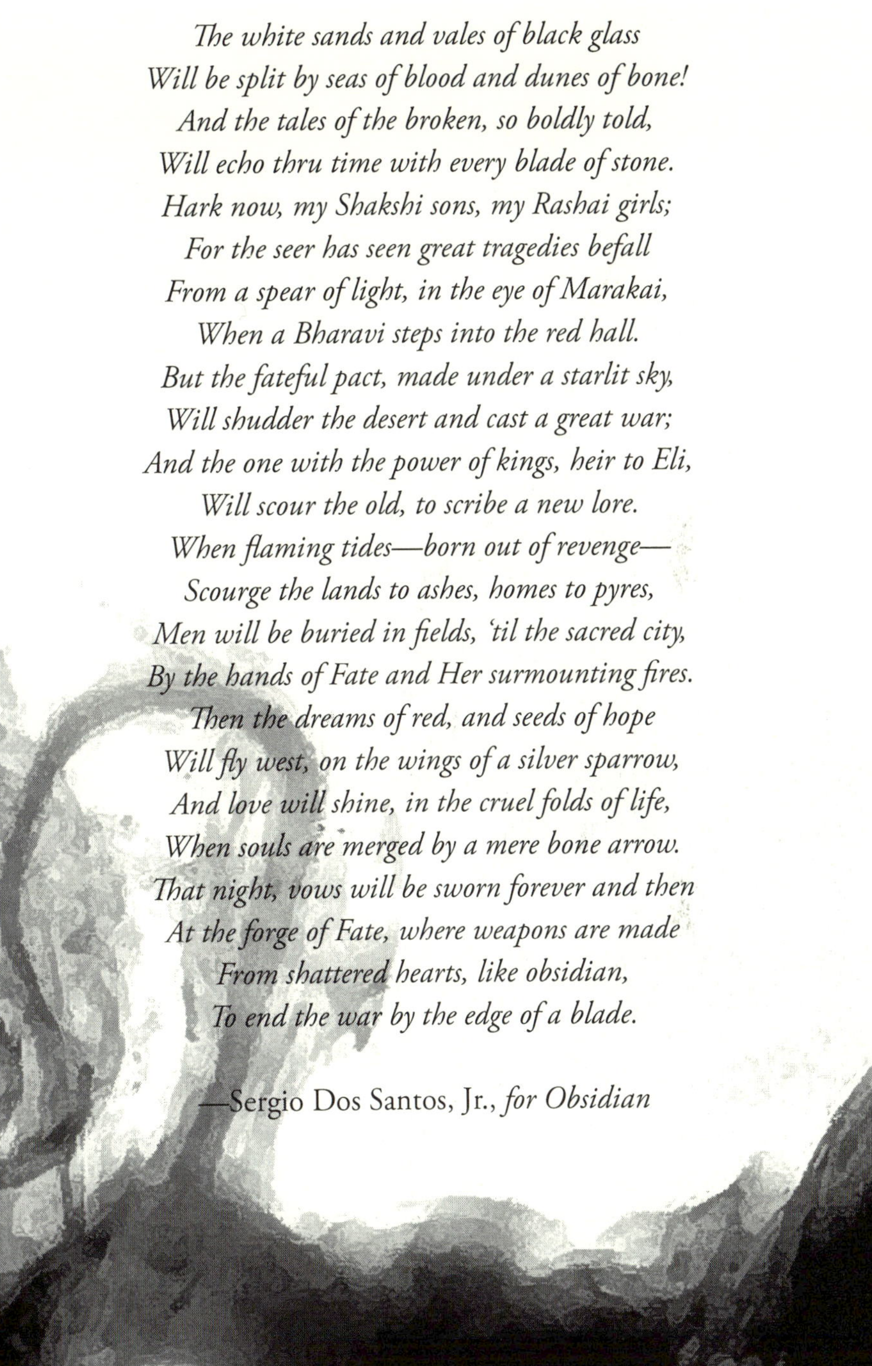

The white sands and vales of black glass
Will be split by seas of blood and dunes of bone!
And the tales of the broken, so boldly told,
Will echo thru time with every blade of stone.
Hark now, my Shakshi sons, my Rashai girls;
For the seer has seen great tragedies befall
From a spear of light, in the eye of Marakai,
When a Bharavi steps into the red hall.
But the fateful pact, made under a starlit sky,
Will shudder the desert and cast a great war;
And the one with the power of kings, heir to Eli,
Will scour the old, to scribe a new lore.
When flaming tides—born out of revenge—
Scourge the lands to ashes, homes to pyres,
Men will be buried in fields, 'til the sacred city,
By the hands of Fate and Her surmounting fires.
Then the dreams of red, and seeds of hope
Will fly west, on the wings of a silver sparrow,
And love will shine, in the cruel folds of life,
When souls are merged by a mere bone arrow.
That night, vows will be sworn forever and then
At the forge of Fate, where weapons are made
From shattered hearts, like obsidian,
To end the war by the edge of a blade.

—Sergio Dos Santos, Jr., *for Obsidian*

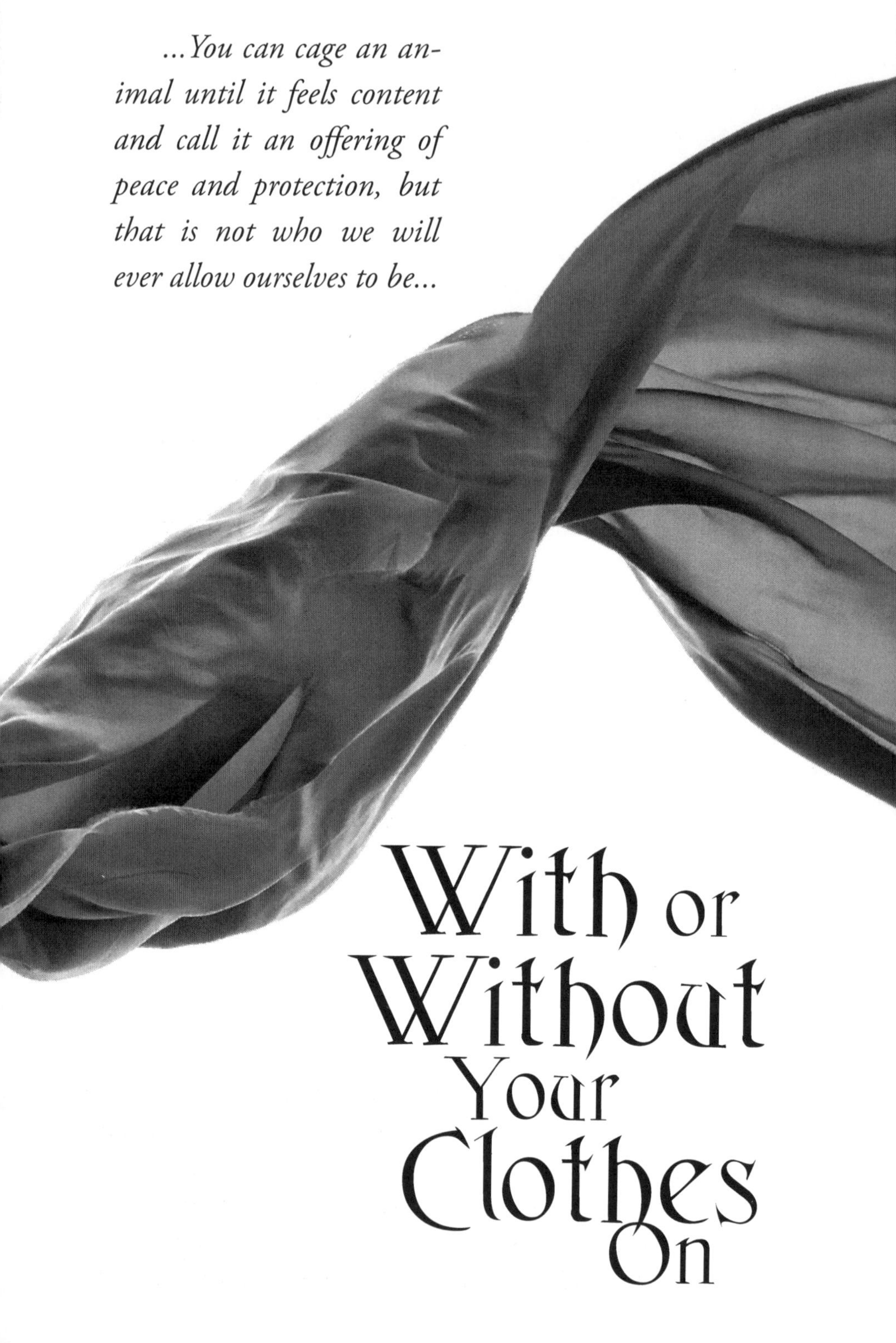
...You can cage an animal until it feels content and call it an offering of peace and protection, but that is not who we will ever allow ourselves to be...
With or Without Your Clothes On

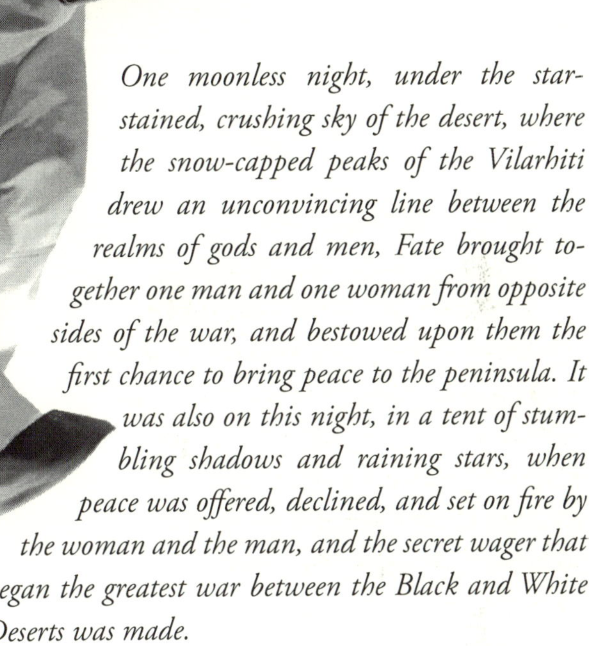

One moonless night, under the star-stained, crushing sky of the desert, where the snow-capped peaks of the Vilarhiti drew an unconvincing line between the realms of gods and men, Fate brought together one man and one woman from opposite sides of the war, and bestowed upon them the first chance to bring peace to the peninsula. It was also on this night, in a tent of stumbling shadows and raining stars, when peace was offered, declined, and set on fire by the woman and the man, and the secret wager that began the greatest war between the Black and White Deserts was made.

⁜

She was nineteen years old when he found her, bound to a post in a military tent, half-naked, and about to be raped by one of his generals. The prince, son and heir to the Salar of Rasharwi, High Commander of the royal army that had successfully wiped out her Kha'gan and three more in the Vilarhiti, was said to be in the middle of a damage assessment report and therefore in a mood to cause more damage when the news about a woman being missing from the prisoner camp had arrived.

The general, who had yet to learn—or had been too ignorant to notice—the supernatural ability of the crown prince's most trusted advisor and right-hand man to be so shockingly accurate on head counts during the chaos of battle, had thought he could keep a girl for entertainment for a few nights before sending her back to her holding pen. The prince, being already on edge from the heavy loss of his army despite the eventual success of his campaign, had stormed into the tent, unsheathed the two obsidian blades strapped to his back, and executed the general with his own hands—something he hadn't done often, judging from the looks on the guards' faces.

He turned to his advisor, snapped a clear and precise command to have every man who might have been aware of such treason executed and made to leave. He stopped, as though there were a calling or an invisible force of some kind that prevented him from leaving, and turned, in an agonizingly slow and calculated manner, to look over his shoulder toward her.

Time inched by like a nervous criminal hoping to escape as the three other men and one woman kept their mouths shut, and seemed to screech before being snatched back into the tent by the prince who, after some deliberation, decided to return to the exact same spot where he'd slain the general.

It took him no time, no time at all, to figure out what she was.

"Why," he said, cold anger rising in his tone, "did no one know there's a Bharavi among these Kha'gans?"

The soldiers behind him shifted their weight, suddenly finding something stuck between their teeth or in their fingernails to be a matter of great importance and proceeding to pick at them in perfect synchronization. Only the man she understood to be his trusted advisor was able to keep his personal hygiene a concern for other times, despite the visible effort to swallow a mysterious object that must have materialized in his throat.

The prince turned to look over his shoulder when the answer didn't come. "Are you all deaf, or am I?"

Those words, spoken in a mere whisper, were enough to mute everyone in the tent in addition to their apparent hearing loss. The advisor, however, managed at long last to swallow the mysterious object and replied, "I will have the men responsible found and brought to you before dawn, my lord."

The young prince, drawing a breath and exhaling loudly as if to make sure it could be heard by his deaf and mute officers, shook his head. "Have their heads on display before dawn along with General Hamir's accomplices and their crimes clearly explained to all divisions," he commanded in an effortless, practical tone, the same way one might have instructed a meal to be prepared or a table to be set. "Take this woman, wash out the red filth in her hair, and bring her to me. I will speak to this Bharavi before nightfall."

The soldiers carried out his instructions with utmost care. They washed out the red dye she'd applied to her hair to hide her identity. The paste, made from a mixture of red wine and the root of a Biba tree, came off easily enough with water, but left a blood-like stain on her clothes. Having been too terrified to touch her after learning what had happened to their general, the small group of soldiers assigned to carry out the task had left her dress on as they emptied buckets of ice-cold water on her hair and decided to deny her a change of clothing.

It had not been a part of the command, one soldier had argued when another suggested giving her something dry to wear. She might be executed soon, he said, and it could be considered a waste of resources, which the prince didn't like. Then again, her soiled garment and state of appearance might offend him, the first man argued. The rest nodded in agreement, but none found the reasoning sufficient to draw a safe conclusion. The issue, from which more arguments ensued for a considerable amount of time, ended up being passed to a higher-ranking officer on duty to judge. The officer, conveniently finding it above his own rank to decide, thought it would be best to bring it up to the general of their division, who in turn decided it was safer to check first with the prince's advisor regarding this complicated problem before issuing a command. By then, twilight had already arrived, and the decision, she overheard from the commotion, ended up being to send her over to the prince's tent in whatever state she was in as soon as possible. The most crucial and clearest part of the command, his advisor pointed out, was, *'before nightfall.'*

And so she was sent to him, still in her tattered, dye-stained garment, dripping wet from her hair, now returned to silver, to her toes. They had, fortunately, given her a blanket to dry herself with, for the reason that the prince would definitely find it unpleasant to have his floor wet and stained.

He was being stripped down by two handmaidens when they brought her in. The armor had been taken off and laid neatly on a bench to their right, leaving only a thin layer of tunic underneath. The black silk, trimmed subtly with gold threads in a simple yet elegant design, clung to his blood-soaked body as if he'd been riding all day in the rain.

It wasn't that far off from the truth, she thought bitterly. The Vilarhiti could be said to have rained blood all week for how many had died defending the valley, and had the fabric been any color but black, it would have shown.

She wondered, watching the girls remove the last piece of clothing from him with exaggerated care, whether this man had been aware at all how much trouble he'd caused. It was becoming clear to her that the first rule around here was to be competent or be executed, even over something as trivial as the matter of her dress. She could see why the Rashai soldiers, usually intimidated by her people's White Warriors during battle, had fought the way they did. They would have been more terrified of this man—this monster—who was leaving no room whatsoever for mistakes.

It might have been why they'd lost the battle, despite so many Kha'gans having united for the first time against a common enemy. She had heard many stories of the exiled prince, sent to the dungeon of Sabha in his youth as a punishment for his mother's crime of infidelity. The boy, who had later been pardoned and reinstated in status after three years of being imprisoned, had made it back to the Black Tower and eventually became the new heir to the throne. There had also been, she recalled, stories of several untimely deaths in the Salar's royal household in the past ten years.

The truth to those stories was being made clear to her now, proven by the numerous scars that crisscrossed the prince's body. He stood with his back to her, stripped down to the skin in the middle of the tent lit by four hurricane lamps. On the back of his left shoulder, the mark of slavery remained visible even from a distance. It would have had to be left there deliberately, in light of the many procedures available to him to remove or alter such a scar. She might have been able to guess why, but she was too afraid of being right to fully shape that thought.

The girls began wiping him down with a cloth, dipped and washed in scented water that smelled like a mixture of sage and mint. The bucket required change with almost every limb they cleaned.

The blood of her people, she thought, washed away so quickly, so effortlessly, as if the massacre and the pile of dead bodies outside could be so easily forgotten. She had seen him in battle. Everyone had. A dark figure atop a black horse, snapping precise, efficient commands in the midst of chaos at the front where the White Warriors had congregated. He shouldn't have survived, and yet he was standing here, alive, with no more than a few flesh wounds.

'We will not win this fight,' her father had said on the first day of battle, watching the two armies clash from a cliff overlooking the plain. *'Not unless we have that man on our side or we find a way to kill him. Pray,'* he'd told her, resting his large hand on her shoulder and squeezing it firmly, *'that he never makes it to the throne.'*

The battle had lasted six days. The Vilarhiti had fallen, lost to the Salasar for the first time in the long history of the White Desert. Four large Kha'gans had been disassembled, their survivors taken prisoner down to the last child. Their horses—the very best in the peninsula—had been rounded up to be used by the Rashai army. All the White Warriors had died one way or another, knowing they must not be taken alive for the secret they had sworn to protect. Her father and brothers had been among those deaths. They had died with honor, with pride on the plain of the Vilarhiti.

All because of this man.

The man who was standing naked before her.

Naked and unarmed.

"What is your name, Shakshi?"

The question pulled her from the dangerous thought that had begun to form in her mind. It had been a while since she had been tossed into the tent, and until this moment, the prince had not acknowledged her presence besides an initial nod to his burly personal guard who'd brought her in. The guard who was still quietly standing behind her with a massive axe strapped to his back.

She drew a breath and straightened. "I see no reason why you need to know."

The two handmaidens, in nearly synchronized motion, made small, startled sounds as though someone had just cursed a god in his own temple. Showing no signs resembling that of his attendees, the prince stilled for a time at her words, and then with the slow, confident step of someone used to dominating every room he occupied, turned, in all his nakedness, to face her.

Acutely aware of the fact that there was a man standing with every inch of him fully exposed before her eyes, she fought the initial instinct to turn away and kept her gaze precisely where it had been. He regarded her for a time, and, as if in answer to her defiance, took a step out of the shadows made by the two handmaidens and into her unobstructed line of sight.

He stood in the middle of the tent, head held arrogantly high, legs firmly apart, and shoulders pulled back to catch the flickering light of the lanterns, inviting—*challenging*—her to look, to see if she had the stomach for it.

It just so happened that apart from being a Bharavi, she had also been an experienced healer, making her no stranger at all to the male or female bodies. She sneered a little at the attempt to intimidate her and proceeded to scrutinize—as she had been invited to do—the figure being displayed before her.

Moderately tall and built to the exact proportions from which a sculptor might choose to render his masterpiece, the prince's hard, compact muscles revealed years of training in both combat and endurance. His skin, burnt by the recent exposure to the sun and made substantially darker than the average Rashai, was covered in enough scars to rival any experienced White Warrior she knew. He wasn't a big man, not remotely close to his giant bodyguard behind her, but she knew without having to see it put to the test that he would be a match for some of their best wrestlers with those broad shoulders and saddle-hardened thighs. The fact that this man who was about to be handed the Salasar and all its power was so well-endowed in every way was hard, depressing evidence of how unfair the gods could be.

In another place, at another time, and given different circumstances, she thought she might have been able to admire such qualities in a man as capable as this. But here and now he was her enemy, the murderer responsible for the death of her family, and the monster she wanted to see dead. She detested him for what he was, for the detached respect and admiration her father had harbored for his enemy, and for the warmth on her cheeks that was not from the heat of the fire.

"So you do speak Rashai," he said at length, looking at her with keen interest.

She resisted the urge to bite her lip. No point in denying it. He had asked for her name in Rashai and she had responded without thinking. "I speak four languages," she replied in Samarran.

He nodded, thought for a moment, and picked up the conversation in fluent Khandoor. "You are schooled, then, in linguistics?"

"No more than in history, geography, and mathematics," she responded, this time, in formal Shakshi. "We are not savages or uneducated camel herders, despite what your incompetent informers might have told you. Do you," she asked, switching back to Rashai, "need me to translate?" She had, after all, thrown in some difficult words on purpose for a chance to see that arrogance subdued a little.

It didn't touch him. Not even a bit.

"What does *jamanya* mean?" he asked with casual curiosity, in the way one might inquire from a cook the ingredients he used.

"*Djemanya*," she corrected in Rashai, out of spite. "Incompetent."

"*Djemanya*," he repeated, this time in perfect pronunciation. She could see him taking a note of the word in his mind, and was sure he would remember it for next time. She was also sure her master linguist would have wanted to adopt him had he been one of their own.

"Leave us." He turned to the girls and dismissed them. They promptly obeyed.

The prince, still clad only in his own skin, took three steps forward to stand before her. He paused for a time, watching her quietly as if waiting for a chance to catch something she might let slip. She forced herself to remain still, holding his gaze, despite the awareness that the distance between his entirely naked body and hers was no more than a hand-width away—her hand, to be precise. The thought of backing away had crossed her mind several times, but only over her dead body would she allow him to intimidate her to that point, with or without his clothes on.

There would be nothing, no one at all to stop him from whatever he wanted to do to her. That reality, too, had always been there in her consciousness, pressing down on her every time she turned a corner. He would do what it took to get what he wanted, to force her to reveal the secret that would bring down the White Desert—the same secret she had vowed to protect, no matter how vile or unbearable the torture he put her through.

The prince leaned toward her and reached out to rest his hand on something behind her ear. She closed her eyes at the sudden disappearance of space between them and braced herself for the nightmares to come.

"Don't worry," he said, tugging on the robe hanging behind her and proceeding to cover himself with it. "I'm not as incompetent as my men, whatever you may think of me."

It came out of her without thinking, thrown together by the shame of having allowed herself to be played by her enemy—the response she would have considered unwise had she been more calm and composed, only now she found she couldn't stop. "You are just as foul and as despicable as your men. That is what I think of you."

The axe touched her neck the instant she finished the sentence. The guard—who was as large as a bear and looked like one—had been quick to respond despite his gigantic size.

"You will bow and apologize before I take off your head, Shakshi!" The tone was raw, etched with genuine anger in every word, as if he'd been personally insulted—or his mother had been.

She kept her eyes leveled on the prince, ignoring the blade at her throat. She had not been raised to fear death or men, and she wasn't going to start now just because her Kha'gan had fallen. Death, in any case, was a gift to be desired at this point in her life.

"I am a Bharavi," she said, "daughter to the Kha'a of the largest Kha'gan in the Vilarhiti. I bow to no one but my Kha'a. You do not outrank me here, or anywhere on our side of the peninsula. If you want submission, seek it on your own land."

The blow that followed sent her crashing against the wall to crumple at the prince's feet. She wiped the blood off her lips with the back of her hand before turning to glare at the giant who'd just slapped her with his massive palm, daring him to finish the job with that axe. It would have been a quick, painless death, and just what she needed had the beast been less sensitive to his master's need to keep her alive. He was, unfortunately, fully aware of such a need, judging from how hard he was struggling not to hack her to pieces.

"That's enough, Ghaul," said the prince with no more than casual amusement in his eyes. "Leave us. I will speak to this Bharavi alone."

"My lord...."

"Do as I say. Or do you find me incapable of defending myself against a girl?" The tone was mild and considerate, one she hadn't heard him use with the others. They must go back a long way, these two. The giant Samarran—she figured from the red hair and the face tattoo—seemed to have held a special status among the prince's subjects and was apparently tolerated much more.

"No, my lord, of course not," Ghaul replied. To her disappointment, he offered a quick bow and headed reluctantly toward the exit.

"And Ghaul." The prince called him as he was halfway through the door. "Have that wound on your arm looked after. We have a long ride tomorrow. You fought well today."

She looked at his arm, saw the blood seeping through the dark fabric, and wondered if the prince had possessed a prior knowledge of that injury or if he was simply that observant. The latter being true could complicate many things for her.

Ghaul, beaming now like a fifth hurricane lamp at the compliment, sketched an elaborate bow and left the tent.

Power, intelligence, a highly disciplined army, and men loyal beyond his post who seemed to consider him a god to be worshipped. She was beginning to understand her father's words at that moment, why he'd considered this man such a threat. If he was difficult to deal with now, what would they do when he had full control of the Salasar?

"Can you stand?" He held out his hand.

She ignored it and rose to her feet.

The prince smiled. "Take a seat." He gestured at a chair by a table where food and drink had been laid. On it were a few flat breads, some cheese, a small serving of local fruits, and a pitcher each of wine and water, both made of plain, unadorned silver.

She swept her eyes around the tent and noticed the practicality of the furnishing. It offered comfort and elegance, but never to the point of being vain. He wore no jewelry besides a signet ring. His hands were those of a man used to wielding weapons on a daily basis. There was nothing soft about this prince who should have been no more than a sheltered, spoiled, over-privileged imbecile had he been raised in the Tower like all the others. Instead, they'd thrown him into prison, given him a reason to fight, and the hell of Sabha had spat out this exceedingly capable creature who had destroyed her home.

"Let us talk then," he said formally, "like two civilized people on equal ground. Or should I say, man to man?"

She regarded him for a time, searching for a sign of mockery in his expression, and didn't find it.

Adjusting her robe to cover the torn dress underneath, she drew herself up straight and seated herself on the opposite chair from the one he'd suggested. He smiled at that, then picked up the pitcher to pour himself a drink.

"Do you take wine?" he asked, but filled another goblet anyway. "It's the finest Samarran we have on reserve. The texture is superb, if a little too intense from being in the heat." He handed her the drink. "It washes down blood rather well. Perfect for the occasion, don't you agree?"

She took the offered cup. "Perhaps," she said. "Is it poisoned?"

He took a seat on the opposite side of the table and leaned back on the cushion, turning the goblet in his hand. "It could be," he said. "But then you're not afraid of dying, are you? That is the Shakshi way of life, is it not? *All lives come to be by the will of Ravi, and through death rejoin her in the land of eternal life and ever-flowing springs.*"

Dark, intelligent eyes stared at her in a challenge as he quoted, in near perfect Shakshi, a phrase from the *Passage of Life.*

"Ah, the prince reads." She raised the cup, sipped it twice, made sure he could see it. "Or is heresy a thing in the Black Tower these days?"

"I'm afraid I'm not pious enough to be considered a heretic for any religion, but my position does require that I show faith in Rashar. As for reading, what was it they say…*One must first gain a place in the enemy's mind before he seeks to gain more*?"

"*And stray not from the path of righteousness,*" she said, taking another sip of the drink. The prince, as it turned out, didn't simply read, but read excessively. *The Secret Journal of Eli the Conqueror* was not a tome that was easy to come by, or one that could be found lying about for a prince to pick up out of boredom. The text itself had also been written in old Khandoor and was considered one of the most difficult to decipher. She wasn't sure what disturbed her more, the fact that he seemed to be everything she would look for in a man, or that he had everything she'd long feared her enemy would possess.

He made a small sound in his throat when she finished quoting the rest of the passage, took his time to reach for a single grape from the plate between them, and rolled it back and forth between his fingers. "I'm impressed," he said.

She smiled and tried not to wince when he bit into the fruit. She could almost feel the cold of his teeth, perhaps also the heat of his tongue. "You should have poisoned the wine," she said. "It's a waste of time and effort to think you can get the location of Citara from me."

He wiped his hand on a napkin nearby and gave her the smile of an adult to a child. "I'll tell you what's wasteful," he said. "The lives of our soldiers who died today. The cost of sustaining a campaign in the desert when it could have been used to build roads and dams and feed a city during a famine. The damage of battles that must be rebuilt. How long have we been at war, do you think? Two hundred years? Perhaps more? How many lives have been lost, how many more will be if this continues?" He paused, took a sip of the drink and placed it back down on the table, leaning slightly forward as he did. "We can end it now, you and I, on this table, over wine. Give me Citara, and I will give your people the freedom to continue living in the desert. It will be as before. No one has to die. Nothing has to change. I give you my word."

She smiled thinly at that. It sounded like a handsome offer, as handsome as the man who'd offered it on the surface, and just as poisonous underneath. "Nothing has to change," she repeated, "except that we bend our knees, allow your people to pass through the desert without fees and settle on our lands without tributes. Let me guess." She paused to sip the wine. "You will take control of our oasis and tax us for our water and all our trades. Our children will be sold as slaves if we refuse, our men killed for breaking the slightest of your laws. Tell me, is this the freedom you intend to give us? To continue living on *our* land?"

"In exchange for peace and protection, yes," he added, matter-of-factly.

"We are adequately at peace and well protected, and would continue to be if you were content with your side of the desert. What you offer is rotten from the inside. I'm not naive enough to fall for your empty promises. You are wasting both your words and your wine."

"Am I?" he asked, not smiling now. The playful, amused expression was gone, replaced by something colder and much more disturbing than what she had seen already that evening. "You speak of peace when your Kha'gans continue to fight among themselves every time an opportunity arises. The Shakshis have been killing each other for centuries with or without interference from the Salasar. This land you are trying so hard to protect has tasted more blood by your own doing than what we have shed in the past two hundred years. We do not wage war on our own people, you do. Who's being naive now?"

It was true, and no one alive in the White Desert or the Black would deny the long existence of conflicts between the Kha'gans. Territory disputes happened on a daily basis, and the Kha'as did nothing but plan to attack each other for power. They were a violent people. She wouldn't deny it, no one would, but it was who they were as much as it had been their way of life for centuries. Right or wrong, it wasn't for anyone to judge, and definitely not for a Rashai who understood nothing of life in the desert.

"It is the price of freedom you will never understand," she said sharply, allowing the anger she'd been holding to slip through, "as long as your people cower behind walls and abandon all their pride for the comfort of the city and the meaningless wealth it gives. You can cage an animal until it feels content and call it an offering of peace and protection, but that is not who we will ever allow ourselves to be. We will fight each other because we are free to fight, and we'll take our chances in these mountains even if it means a lifetime of struggles and conflicts for a life without boundaries. You speak of freedom when you have no clue what it truly means. That is why you have never been able to conquer the White Desert, why you never will. I will have more, if you don't mind." She placed the cup down on the table and pushed it forward. "It does go well with blood."

He stilled for a time, watching her intently from across the table. She returned the gesture, waiting and making herself ready for the next blow.

It never came.

He reached for the pitcher to refill her cup, then his, before leaning back on the chair. "I take it you won't give up Citara even if I vow to kill every living soul among the prisoners here today?"

It was spoken in the most unanimated, practical tone possible, as if they'd been discussing a transaction concerning a sack of grain. She swallowed the lump in her throat at the image of more women and children being executed on that plain, shut her eyes to quiet the different voices in her head, and replied firmly, resolutely, "No."

It would mean more deaths, tremendously more, if the Rashai ever found Citara. The sacred city, the beating heart of the White Desert, was where all the collected tributes were sent, where the wealth of every Kha'gan was kept and guarded. The city traded directly with Makena—the last independent nation in the peninsula, protected from the Salar's army by a treacherous mountain range and the White Desert itself. Makena's riches supplied the Kha'gans. Destroy Citara and one destroyed the White Desert as a whole and for good.

The Salasar had always known this, of course, but for centuries, Citara's location had been her people's most well-guarded secret. Apart from Bharavis and oracles, only the White Warriors who delivered the tributes and brought back traded goods to the Kha'gans were allowed to enter the city. All took an oath of secrecy upon entering the gates. The punishment for breaking such an oath was an execution of three entire generations of one's bloodline.

Everyone chose their own death over that punishment. It was the price and weight of becoming a White Warrior, of wearing the white robe called the zikh, and why her father and brothers, along with all zikh-clad warriors, had not been captured alive. They fought to their deaths or killed themselves before being put to torture to protect its secret location.

She would have to find a way to join them soon before she, too, was put to torture. He would never have it, not from her.

There was a small knife on the table for the purpose. She had been trying, despite her need to reach for it, to not let her gaze linger too long on the blade.

The prince reached over to pick another grape, toying with it as he had done a few minutes ago before putting it in his mouth. "And if I throw you out there as a reward for my men?"

"It would be predictable," she said, "and disappointing." He might kill her for that, if she was lucky.

The prince responded with a chuckle. He rose from the chair and walked over to her side, seating himself on the edge of the table. "You are aware," he said, "that it's never a good idea to leave a man with so few options."

"Or a woman." She raised her chin to meet his eyes. "Understand me. No Rashai will ever set foot in Citara. You will not have the White Desert, in this life or the next. That is my answer. The wine," she said, emptying her cup and placing it down on the table, intentionally near the plate and the knife, "was brilliant."

He smiled, and in the small window of time when he turned back to the pitcher, she leaped off her chair and reached for the blade, making her decision in that split second. The silver tip of the knife gleamed as she plunged it forward, aiming at the spot she knew would kill him in an instant.

Losing none of his composure, the prince slipped out of the way with the ease of a cat and positioned himself behind her. His large, strong hand closed around her neck and slammed her back down against the table as if she weighed no more than a child.

In the same instant, Ghaul burst into the tent, axe raised and ready to draw blood. Still holding her down with an iron grip, the crown prince of Rasharwi raised his free arm and held up a finger. Ghaul lowered his weapon, gave a quick bow, and left the tent without another word.

He turned back to her, eyes flashing with something frighteningly hard. "I could take you." The prince closed his grip around her throat, the searing heat from his hand seeping through her skin and into her bones. "Right here, right now, were I in a slightly different mood this evening."

She struggled to break free, to breathe, her hands clawing desperately at the arm that was pinning her down. It made no difference. He was a rock on top of her and his fingers tightened the more she tried.

"I *have* thought of it, from the moment I heard you recite Eli," he continued, his chest heaving visibly from what appeared to be a mixture of rage and excitement, perhaps also desire. "But I wanted to give you a chance, to talk and discuss in a more civilized manner, to see if we could end this war without being barbaric to each other. Apparently, you disagree."

He took a sharp breath and exhaled, as if to still a need that was threatening to overcome his reason. It subsided, though not completely. His body still stiffened, the muscles on his arm unnecessarily tight despite the small effort needed to hold her down.

"And perhaps you're right," he said. "Perhaps I don't understand your people well enough to conquer the White Desert. Perhaps there is also something I can do about my own ignorance."

In a single, forceful motion, he dragged her down to the edge of the table where he'd been standing, pinning her back to the wood, and holding her in place with his thighs pressing against her hips. The hand around her throat flexed as he lowered his face to her, lips hovering just above her ear.

"I'm not going to kill you, or send you out there to be defiled by my soldiers." The words, spoken in a mere whisper, burned like fire against her skin. "You will live, with me, in the Black Tower, as *my* prisoner, *my* Bharavi, *my* wife. You will bear me a son, and he'll grow, as a Rashai, a prince of Rasharwi, who will return to raid your land in the name of the Salasar. We will see, you and I, if you and your people truly cannot be conquered. I will do this thing, or you can give up Citara, here and now, and no one has to die. This is your last chance. What will it be, Bharavi?"

She gathered her breath, despite the way her stomach turned at the thought of what he intended to do to her, and delivered the words she knew would lead to exactly that outcome. "I would sooner kill my own child than let you have such satisfaction, you unimaginable monster!"

She knew something about what would follow, had expected it when she decided to aim the knife at him and not her own heart in the case she failed. What she hadn't anticipated was how far he would go, how inventive he would be in making her pay for such a mistake.

He smiled in a way that made her skin crawl and her hair stand on end. "Allow me to show you the kind of monster I can become. *Jarem!*"

In the time it took a man to take three steps forward, the same advisor who'd been with him in the general's tent emerged promptly at the entrance. "My lord." The salute was executed in a precise, spotless manner, as if it had been the Salar himself he was addressing.

"How many prisoners do we hold?" He'd released her by the time Jarem entered, and was now pouring himself a new drink as he spoke.

She pushed herself off the table, adjusting her clothes absentmindedly, and realized that her hands were trembling. The prince, now standing a few steps away, watched her from the corner of his eye as he waited for the answer—one she wished she hadn't been there to hear.

"Eight thousand two hundred and fifty-three, my lord."

Eight thousand prisoners. She wrapped her fingers instinctively around the back of a chair for balance. She was going to be sick.

"How many women and children?"

The figures, given to the prince as if he had been reading off a scroll, had also been offered to the last digit.

The prince nodded, sipped his wine and delivered a command as precise as the numbers he'd been given. "Pick one of the women and give her to the soldiers. When they're done with her, have her killed and her head put on a spike. Tell the other prisoners one of them will be killed in a similar manner every time their precious Bharavi disobeys or so much as raises her voice at me. If she takes her own life, or mine, everyone will die, all eight thousand of them. I will have it known it is one of their own who will be responsible for their deaths. I want this done tonight, close by, where she can hear it."

Jarem paused a little, obviously finding the command a cause for concern. "My lord, the Salar may wish to sell a number of these prisoners."

"He can wish," said the prince, smiling sardonically at his advisor now, "or he can buy them from me. The Vilarhiti is mine if I can take it, and so are these prisoners. That was the agreement. They are to be given quarters among the deserters when we return to Rasharwi. I want them untouched and kept healthy for my new Bharavi wife to slaughter. Go. And have someone bring her a change of clothing before she freezes to death."

Jarem smiled, evidently proud of his prince. He offered another perfect bow and left the tent.

Still gripping the chair, she watched him go to execute the command with a nauseated feeling that drained all her strength. Those words, a promise of a life-long torture, of being stripped bare of the freedom she so loved, had taken from her the last valuable thing she'd intended to keep to her grave. All because she had made one simple mistake with the knife that was now lying at her feet. She should have been dead, and now even that much freedom had been taken from her.

They were alone again. Two figures, in a simple tent lit by four lanterns, holding the fate of the peninsula in their palms. He turned, picked up the knife, and walked over to sit on the edge of the table, exactly where he'd been before.

"I'm curious," he said, turning the blade back and forth in his hand, "as to how life is measured in the White Desert. What gives you the right to decide that the lives of eight thousand people—or one—was a worthy sacrifice for Citara, for *your* idea of freedom?"

He flipped the knife over and offered it to her by the handle. "Here's a chance to prove your point. Take the knife, bury it into your own heart or in mine. Decide again, as deliberately as before, how willing you are to spend the lives of those people based purely on what you believe in. Do you think they still want to live, now that they are my prisoners? Isn't that why

I will never be able to take the White Desert? Because all of them would rather die than live without your so-called freedom?" He pushed the knife closer to her hand, daring her to take it. "Show me, Bharavi, how strongly you believe that to be true."

How, she thought, looking down at the knife that was gleaming temptingly in his hand, did one measure a life—or eight thousand of them—against an ideal? None of them would ever return to their homeland now, not after being branded as prisoners of the Salasar. Their lives in the White Desert would be forfeited for them and their children, and for generations to come. In ten or twenty years they would be considered residents of Rasharwi, their knowledge of culture and tradition lost behind the enemy's walls. Their spirit, honor, and love of freedom would be gone like the ashes of their homes that were still scattering in the wind.

In the eyes of Citara and its Devis, they would be considered lost and better off dead. No one would blame her if she killed herself now, for her pride, her honor, for the love of her people and what she believed they represented. It would send a strong message: that they could not be conquered, that Citara would never fall. What were eight thousand lives, against twenty times more, against a thousand years of tradition and generations that would be lost if she failed to uphold their way of life today?

But what if she was wrong? What if all they wanted was peace and prosperity, or a chance to live free from the fear of being raided, of not enough food and water, for their children to grow up safe and sound behind walls? Who was she to decide that they were no longer her people to protect if they became Rashais, that eight thousand lives were worthless the moment they stopped representing her ideals? They were her people now, and they would still be her people tomorrow and the day after. She, too, would never return to the White Desert, not after this. Would that make her less than what she had been the day before? She had no right to decide such things. Not without becoming the same monster she wanted to see dead.

There was no choice left for her, or none that she could see. There would never be again, for the rest of her life. Not after this.

Letting out the breath she had been holding, she closed her eyes and forced herself to look straight at him: to remember the moment, the hour, and the face of the man who had done this to her. She swore, inwardly, that she would live for as long as it took, even if she had to crawl and beg for her life, to see him die.

"I thought so." The prince took the knife away and placed it on the table. "You think I'm a monster, but are we so different, you and I? I'll kill for what I believe in, and so will you."

He rose to his feet, his shadow looming over her bruised and beaten frame. "You think you're better than me, and your people better than mine," he continued, his thick, penetrating voice burning deep into her memory. "I'll show you just how corruptible they can be, how easy it will be for me to crush them just like all the others. I *have* conquered the White Desert, even if only a small part of it, here, today, and I will have more. The Vilarhiti is mine; so are its eight thousand survivors who are now citizens of Rashawi, and so are you. You *have* been defeated, and from this day onward you will live and die by my command. On your knees, Bharavi!"

And that night, on the plain below the majestic snow-capped peaks of the Vilarhiti that had stood strong and unconquered for centuries, she could see it all come tumbling down as she—the last free soul of the valley, the first Bharavi to have ever been captured alive and forced to bend the knee—knelt, in all her shattered pride and honor, to the man who would become the supreme ruler of the Salasar.

"Good," said the prince. "I hope you are now sufficiently motivated to give me your name."

Flight

Mara di Rosso died on a quiet Sunday morning, suspended by a rope from the ceiling in Hasheem's old room, in her father's house.

It wasn't the first time a woman had hung herself in his room, Hasheem had been told. People killed themselves in the pleasure district. These things happened in the Salasar—in the peninsula. Everyone broke, eventually, one way or another. Some broke into weapons, others into pieces. Some lived, some took another life, some died bringing to life monsters and beasts.

The world made room for these things. It made room for change when one wished for change, for courage when one chose to face its consequences, for love and desire when life demanded vengeance, for kindness and compassion when one drew the line between humans and beasts.

Humans and beasts. Hasheem asked himself that Sunday morning, staring at the bruises on her dangling feet, storing into memory the piercing creak of the beam above her swinging corpse, if what he had done or was about to do would make him a beast or a man. If there ever was a time where the line was constant and reliable, when things were as simple as the black and white that separated the lands they lived in and fought for. If he would find the answer in the ending of his life, or the beginning.

⁜

HE WAS SOLD FOR THE PRICE OF A PIG, was the common introduction to the story of his life people liked to hear. That particular line, among the other, more spiced up or entirely made-up ones, happened to be quite accurate.

Five hundred silas was the actual sum. Back then, it was considered outrageously high for a ten-year-old boy. In the world of the slave auction, the starting price for a child that young was just fifty, given they weren't being offered for free as a bundle deal with the mother. Young boys and girls needed more time to train. They also made mistakes, lacked the strength needed for most jobs, and could die young. Not a great investment, unless one were out of means or options.

Some children were, however, the most profitable assets for the pleasure district of Rasharwi. Men could be expected to pay a good fee to break the innocents, and comely children could be sold above market price for such purpose. In the business of pleasure, it was also considered wise to train them young. Children had less resistance, could be taught and shaped into whatever was needed, made to believe it was what their lives were meant to be.

By the hands of Fate or whichever god had sought to curse him out of boredom, Hasheem hadn't been born comely. At ten, his was already a face that made people stare—the kind of face that stood out in a crowd. But more than that, he was a pureblood Shakshi, born, raised, conveniently orphaned, and directly plucked from the White Desert during the raid that wiped out his Kha'gan. As with most purebloods, his typical package of light hair, pale eyes, and dark skin was a rarity in a city full of black-haired, fair-skinned Rashais. An exotic flower, the auctioneer had said, to raise his price.

Beauty, however, was a privilege until it singled one out from the rest to be sent to the private quarters of captains and generals before the auctions commenced. They couldn't do that with girls, whose virginity had a price. Boys, however, didn't lose their value no matter how many times one used them. They also couldn't become pregnant, so they were used with little care, often, and often for free.

They had—not unexpectedly—used him most frequently during those eight months while waiting to be sold in the holding cells at Sabha. By the time Hasheem had been put on auction, there wasn't much he hadn't been through. These things, of course, had value, and pleasure house bidders knew experience and endurance when they saw them. Unsurprisingly, his was the highest price paid for boys that day. The bid had been won by the House of Azalea, the biggest and most profitable pleasure house in Rasharwi.

It was the first time Hasheem had learned the art of trading. You could do that if you listened, observed, and connected the right dots during auctions. You'd learn, for instance, that the value of a product had less to do with what it was and more to do with what it could be, or what you made people believe it could be. Anything could be sold at auction if you could do that well enough, even garbage.

Such a craft was a ticket out of anything, into anywhere. It didn't take Hasheem long to realize that if they could sell him for a better price than he was worth, then there was nothing to stop him from selling himself to a better life than the one they'd thrown him into. One could focus on that, understand that there was nothing to be gained by crying for help, take pride out of the equation, and start getting results. For a slave, crying was a one way ticket to getting you whipped, and those whose only talent was to feel sorry for themselves ended up in the sewers, eaten by rats or things that ate the rats.

Now, there were only two options for a boy cursed with his face in the pleasure district—he could serve the largest number of clients unwillingly or willingly serve just a few by being exceptionally good. The choice was never difficult for anyone in his position. The implementation required the same things any success in life did: *endurance and tenacity.*

Endurance and tenacity were what he had. You couldn't survive Sabha for eight months without growing some of those qualities, along with warts and a supernatural ability to tolerate all kinds of crap and everything in between. He also came from the desert, where death happened on a daily basis and waking up the next morning was what they prayed for at night. By comparison, life in the pleasure district was bearable, even comfortable at times. At the very least the owners tried to keep you alive—most of the time, anyway.

Things became straightforward after that. Reading people was simple when you learned to look at clients as humans, not beasts. Deep down, people always wanted something more than sex when they came to the pleasure district—a distraction, some attention, an opportunity to hold power for once in their lives, a need for release, and, on rare occasions, even love. Give them those, and sometimes, though not often, you could even get paid without having to take off your clothes.

Reading people was what he was good at, and by the end of his career, the fee for a night with him could feed a small village for a week—with pigs thrown in as extras.

They called him the Silver Sparrow. *Silver* for the shade of his eyes. *Sparrow* for the color of his hair. That name, given to him by his owner to elevate his status, had landed him in the paths of some immensely powerful people. One of those happened to be Deo di Amarra, a royal advisor to Salar Muradi of Rasharwi, an entrepreneur with investments in half the businesses in the city, and the master of the most exclusive house of assassins catering only to the elites of the Salasar. The most influential man in the peninsula, some would say.

Deo di Amarra's decision to buy him was made on the first day they met and before it was even over.

The actual trade happened two years later, before which time he continued working for the House of Azalea while apprenticing under Deo di Amarra, or Dee, as Hasheem had come to call him. During those years, he was taught everything from trade, politics, and, most importantly, the art of killing. At the end of the two-year period, a sum of five hundred thousand silas was paid in gold by Deo di Amarra to fully acquire him into his service—the equivalent of the price of a thousand pigs, most people would point out to finish the story.

It was how he became both the Silver Sparrow and Deo di Amarra's first-class assassin, how his worth had gone from one pig to a thousand: endurance and tenacity.

He was going to need both of those things again tonight, Hasheem thought, one evening on his seventh year of living in Rasharwi—trying, as discreetly as he could, to pick a piece of something that might have come off a kidney or liver from his sleeve before it was noticed. Not that identifying it was required. Whether kidney or liver or otherwise, entrails were supposed to stay inside the corpse when the job was done professionally, and professionalism was important to Deo di Amarra. He didn't see himself being given a choice now, not for the crime he had committed, but considering the circumstances he could still try to die quickly, as opposed to dying slowly, painfully, and in as many pieces as possible.

Dressed in a robe of exquisite golden brown bear pelt, arms crossed over his chest next to his priceless desk carved out of a single oak tree, Deo di Amarra stood staring at him with the expression of someone who'd just taken a mouthful of leftover wine and been deprived of a decent way to spit it out.

A bad sign, considering his wine habit.

Not that Hasheem was expecting anything different. If Deo di Amarra wanted you brought in as opposed to killing you on the spot when he found out you'd just dismembered someone on his protected list, it meant he wanted to let you know how pissed he was before you died. Out of principle.

"Ravi's precious cunt," Dee rasped in his native Khandoor tongue, disgust dripping off his face. "That's Makena fucking silk, you ungrateful imbecile. Do you have the slightest idea what that shit costs?"

It cost a day's job at most with Hasheem's normal fee, but one didn't try to argue with Dee, especially when he started swearing. "I wanted to die pretty." He decided lightening the mood might help a bit. Sometimes, you could get away with all kinds of shit if he liked your answer enough.

"Did you now?" Dee's voice, this time, rose to a pitch usually reserved for a cook who'd messed up an expensive cut of meat or spilled a priceless wine. Which, to Dee, happened to be a crime of equivalent proportion to having his most trusted subordinate go off on a killing spree and get himself chased down by half the city over a personal agenda. "Understand me, my prancing little peacock." Dee shot off the desk he'd been leaning on and took a step forward, just in case his apprentice was half-deaf, or perhaps to make sure that happened. "No five-hundred-thousand silas purchase of mine is going to walk out on me or die in anything until I say so. The next time you want to get yourself killed, have the fucking decency to ask for permission or I will make sure you don't die so I can put you back on auction for a tenth of the price, to be used like cattle for life and die eaten by pigs, never mind how pretty you are."

He'd expected that, truly. They were as close as could be as master and apprentice, but everyone who knew him well knew Deo di Amarra put profits before all else, without exception.

To Hasheem's surprise, and for all his seventy-something-word curses in three dialects packed in a single sentence with no punctuation in sight, Dee kept him on his feet, leading him into the study.

The room was warm when Hasheem walked in, telling him the fireplace had been lit for some time. His mentor had known his plan, it seemed, perhaps even before his arrival at the general's estate. Had prepared for it, actually. Probably could have stopped him, too, but hadn't, for some reason Hasheem would rather not know. The evidence of it appeared in the form of clean clothes, a pack filled with supplies, and enough weapons to besiege a fort, all arranged neatly on the oversized desk, along with his Jar of Souls.

The jar was there to make a point. Assassins didn't count their dead. They counted coins, silver, gold, and reputations that made it into the nightmares of people whose names had been written on a piece of paper—a piece of paper small enough to fit in one's palm yet large enough to hold a life. Dee collected those. He had the jar on display in his study for all to see, next to a quill and a stack of blank papers ready and waiting for him to write someone new into that jar.

Hasheem had imagined his own name contributing to its content tonight. Apparently, Dee had another thing in mind.

"You're letting me go?" he asked, still trying to understand how it was even an option. Helping him escape was crossing the line; it would make Dee an accomplice, a traitor. Advisor to the Salar or not, it could get him executed or thrown into prison for life. Killing him was the simplest, safest, most logical solution. He would have agreed on that, might have even advised it. "Why?"

Dee ignored his question, walked over to the nearest torch, and took it down from the wall. "Sit," he said. "Take off that silk."

"Dee," he said, realizing in a flash what the torch was for. "It's a death sentence to tamper with the mark of the Salar." The only way he would live past tonight was for him to run, and to do that, the mark of slavery on his back had to be gone, or wherever he ended up, anyone who saw it would drag him back to Rasharwi. There were rewards for turning in runaway slaves, and someone of his reputation would fetch a sum large enough for a whole village to hunt him down, if not the entire peninsula.

Deo di Amarra snorted. "I know the laws of this peninsula better than you know how to fuck, boy. Shut up and sit down."

It was the end of the conversation. When Dee used that tone, you obeyed.

"Do you remember the passage leading to Sabha? The one I showed you on the map?"

"I do, ye—" Hasheem clenched his fists and forced the scream back down his throat as the flame licked the back of his right shoulder. That could have been better with a warning.

"Behind the second brick from the bottom on your right is the key to the outer gate of the fortress. Put it back when you're done. Do you understand?"

Hasheem nodded, holding back a groan as the fire continued to burn off the brand on his back.

"Once you're out, you'll be in Shakshi territory. If you run into a Kha'gan and they catch you, make up a story, a good one. They'll kill you if they find out you've been branded."

That they would. The Shakshis wouldn't send him back to Rasharwi—they would kill him on the spot. It didn't matter that he was one of them. The Kha'gans had been at war with the Salasar for centuries. They took zero risks when it came to having spies in their lands. In the White Desert, deserters or captured slaves bearing the mark of the Salar were killed on sight without trial.

"Lie low and try to make it to Makena one way or another. You'll be safe there if you can make it. Or you can stay in the White Desert, if they'll take you back."

If they'll take me back.

He might have laughed at that if only the burn on his back hadn't hurt so much. These people had more reasons to hunt him down than the Rashais. For them to take him back would require him to lie. They cut out your tongue for that, if he remembered correctly.

Moreover, this was the White Desert they were talking about, the largest unclaimed strip of the peninsula filled with inexorably proud, code-abiding, unforgiving Shakshis and their White Warriors that made Rashai soldiers piss their pants at the mere sight of their white robes. The *White Desert*, where the heat killed during the day and the cold turned corpses into ice at night, preserving them in perfect condition to be eaten by wolves in the morning. There was no other place on the peninsula as brutal as his former home, which was precisely why the Salasar had never been able to claim it. The Shakshis had survived every day—for generations—in the harshest conditions the land had to offer. Meanwhile Rashai soldiers were fed like pigs, fattened by wine, entertained by whores, and woke up in warm beds stuffed with enough wool to suffocate a sheep.

And he had been living like a Rashai for the past seven years—except for the whore part.

No, he would rather take his chances to reach Makena. Far, yes, but still a better plan than hoping the Kha'gans would take him in as one of their own. He didn't even see himself now as one of them. Couldn't even remember what the tents looked like or how to milk a goddamn goat.

"Which way do I go?" he asked sometime later when Dee was applying a layer of salve on his back. There were several ways he could get to Makena, but all of them would require going through the White Desert. Hasheem had only a vague knowledge of his homeland or the different Kha'gans that ruled it since he'd been taken by the Salasar. It seemed like a good idea to know now.

Dee didn't reply. He finished bandaging the wound, helped him change, and handed him the weapons.

When it was done, after the long, crippling silence between them, the last thing Dee said to him, his parting gift, were two simple words.

"Go west."

Only Tradition

"Kill the horse, Djari," her father said, looking down at her with the eyes of a man more than ready to draw the blade at his waist. "Do it, or I'll have her put down by someone else."

The Kha'a of Visarya was a hard man with a reputation that preceded him, but there was a burning, permanent anger in him now that hadn't been there before. It had been different when her mother was alive. The Kha'ari had, everyone knew, been the only soul in the desert that could bend Za'in izr Husari.

Djari didn't have that kind of influence over her father, nor her mother's gift that had allowed her to move people with words. Her talent leaned more toward causing a fight or a fit of rage in powerful men, like her father.

"I will," she said. "When the time comes." Her horse might never run again, but there was still hope, wasn't there?

"Tonight, Djari." The command, this time, was spoken in the tone of a Kha'a to his subject, not of a father to his child. It was also given in a tent full of chiefs and White Warriors, and she was old enough to know the penalty of disrespecting a Kha'a in front of his men.

Still, she opened her mouth to speak, and immediately closed it at the small gesture of her brother's hand.

Nazir was their trueblood oracle, born with the correct characteristics of one with his amber eyes and silver hair. It meant that he was never wrong. She knew then, biting back her arguments and her tears at the Kha'a's dining table, that the fate of her horse had already been decided, and not by her father.

She left the table without finishing her dinner. Father would punish her for that later, she knew, and intended to accept the consequences of her actions. Wasting a meal would get her starved for a few days. For her display of defiance, he would take away more of her freedom. It wouldn't be the first time she had to endure it. At some point, one could get used to such things and find living with consequences better than living in fear.

Tonight, she needed time to deal with the impending loss, and the consequences were acceptable. Lady had been her mother's horse. For three years she had taken care of the mare, had washed her, fed her, and even helped her deliver a foal over the summer. *How*, Djari had asked herself a hundred times in the past three days, *could she end such a life and live with herself afterward?* So far, she didn't have the answer.

It would be the first time she had to take a life, and she had long wished it would be an enemy's, or at least in self-defense. One could live with some justification for causing death when it had to do with vengeance or self-preservation and expect a measurement of forgiveness from oneself or others. But there was no justification for killing in the name of mercy, not to her. Living, no matter how painful, was the embodiment of hope, and hope was what they needed to end the war, to carry on their traditions, and to offer peace to the next generation. She would choose to live, even with every joy and freedom taken from her. She was already living that life, had been from the moment she was born a Bharavi. Joy and freedom were for someone who didn't have to carry the lives of thousands, for someone who wasn't daughter to a Kha'a.

If she could live with that, why couldn't her mare?

The dagger in her hand gleamed like newly-polished silver. It felt heavier now than when she had held it a few days before. 'A blade must be wielded with purpose, or it will become a burden,' her sword master had said. She could understand that saying a little better now, for how heavy it had become.

She opened her hand and closed it again around the hilt, her palm slick with sweat from having done so many times over the past hour.

"You don't have to do it yourself," a voice sounded from behind, gentle and comforting, the way her mother's had been. "No one will know."

When he'd come into her tent, she couldn't tell. Nazir always seemed to be able to appear out of thin air, like all the other impeccably-trained White Warriors at camp. It was one of the first few lessons they were taught and tested on—to track and kill in silence. Things they would never teach her.

"*I* would know," she replied, without looking up from the dagger.

Nazir sighed and seated himself at an arm's length away. She didn't have to look up and see the expression on his face to know those brows resembling her mother's would be knitted watching her then. He'd always found her difficult. They all did. She never understood why.

"It's only tradition, Djari," he paused, taking time to choose his words carefully, "not an expectation for everyone to follow through."

She looked at him then, her chest filled to the brim with anger that had been accumulating for days. There might not be a written law that said she would have to kill her own horse, but for generations, it had been deemed the responsibility of every Shakshi to execute one's own prisoner or animal when the time came. How much of a coward did Nazir think she was, to believe she would hide behind such an excuse, to think she could have lived with it? Even their father had expected it of her.

"I am a daughter to a Kha'a, a Bharavi of Visarya, and the future Kha'ari of a Kha'gan. It *is* expected of me." Djari drew herself up as tall as she could, hoping she looked a little like her mother then, wishing she remembered her right. "If we do not uphold tradition, no one will."

Those had been her mother's words. They had been the Kha'ari's explanation when Djari had asked why her hair had to be braided this way and that, or why she could only choose a Khumar or a Kha'a to marry. They were the ruling family of their Kha'gan. Whatever happened to the Visarya—good or ill—was their doing.

"You're only fifteen," Nazir said. She thought she heard pity in that voice, but he'd always been quick to hide such things. "There's plenty of time and opportunity for you to carry that weight on your shoulders. It doesn't have to begin now."

"I'm turning sixteen," she said. "In two years I'll marry into another Kha'gan. You will not be there with me. If there's a weight I have to carry,

I might as well begin to carry it now."

A shadow rolled over Nazir's face, as always when the issue of her marriage was brought up. She didn't like seeing it. Sympathy wasn't what she needed. She needed strength, cooperation, and maybe some appreciation for what she had to do. Marrying to strengthen the Kha'gan was her duty as a Bharavi. She had been raised to accept larger responsibilities than fulfilling her own desires, the same way Nazir had been raised, and the same way everyone who was born into power should be raised: to protect their people. There would be so much more than this she would have to sacrifice, so many more lives she would have to end if Nazir's visions about her had been right, and her brother had yet to be proven wrong. To assume that she would have a problem carrying such a weight, or would try to run from it, was an insult.

Nazir sighed. "Being able to kill won't make things any easier, Djari."

"No," she said. "But it will make me harder." She would need to be harder, and stronger. "If I am going to ask people to kill for me in the future, I have to understand what it means."

The hurt that appeared in her brother's eyes had nothing to do with the issue of her horse, Djari knew. There were things he wouldn't tell her about her future, no matter how many times she'd pressed for it. Something about that future scared him, which gave her all the more reason to be prepared. "I'm sorry," was all he said.

"You might have told me she wouldn't heal three days ago." She decided to confront him. There were always meanings in how Nazir chose to do things or not to, and that day was no exception. "Why didn't you?"

Nazir drew a long, unsteady breath and looked away, his gaze lingering somewhere far out toward the dark horizon. The wind blew in through the opening of her tent and tugged gently on his white robe. She saw him wince a little, and knew for certain that it hadn't been from the cold.

Nazir had been like that once, the morning of the day their mother had left camp and never returned. For hours, he'd stood in the same spot, watching the caravan disappear behind the valley like it was the last time he'd ever see it. No one had understood why until the news of the attack arrived two days later. She'd never seen him so vulnerable as he had been then. Being the only son, Nazir had been born a Khumar, the future Kha'a of Visarya. It was a role he'd always filled to perfection in both duty and appearance. That morning, he hadn't looked like one. He'd looked like a boy, a brother, a son—the same way he looked now.

"It wasn't the right time," he decided to reply.

"The right time for what? What did you see?"

Nazir pressed his lips together and straightened. Djari knew it was the end of the conversation. A kind and doting brother he might be, but on this, and especially this, Nazir drew the line as crisp as the white of his zikh.

"There are certain privileges to not knowing that makes life worth living, Djari," he reminded her. "My vision is not for you or anyone to carry. It is my burden and mine alone."

It *was* a burden. Djari had known this for some time, having observed him more closely as she grew older. Nazir knew what the world required of him as an oracle, and what price his rare, gods-given gift of foresight would exact. It was his fate to bear witness to what was coming, to live with the premonition of blood to be shed and battles to be won and lost, to stand tall knowing the time and manner of his own death—and that of his loved ones. A burden he insisted on carrying alone.

She remembered asking him once what it felt like to have those visions, to know things before they happened.

'*Like having lived your whole life by the age of ten,*' Nazir had replied.

She'd stopped thinking of it as a privilege after that, and had always tried to forgive him afterward when he refused to share those visions with her. She knew her brother, however, and she had her intuition. There was a reason he'd decided to hold back Lady's fate until today, and guilt was why he had come.

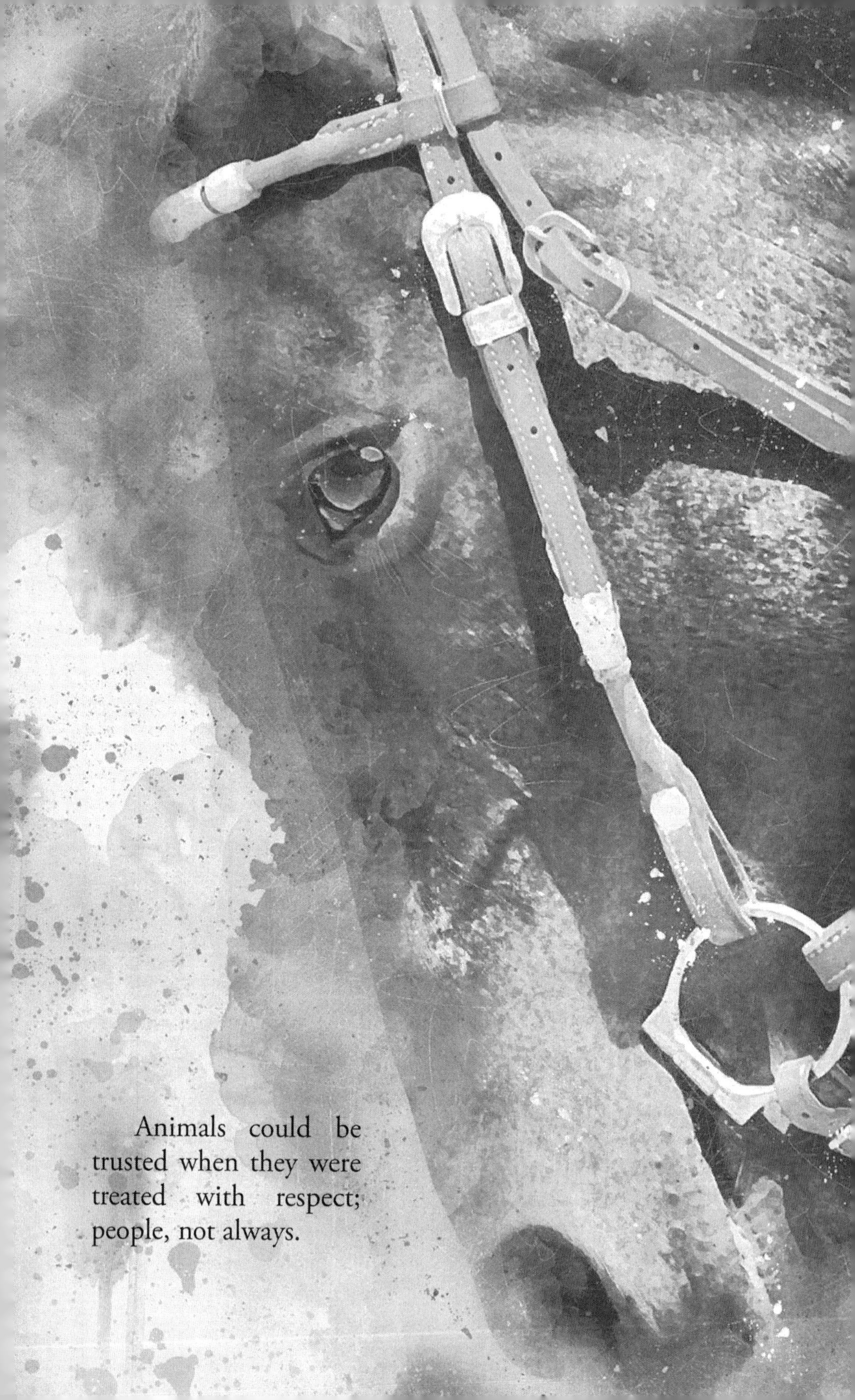

Animals could be trusted when they were treated with respect; people, not always.

A Poor Excuse

The torches had all been put out by the time she reached the stable. They'd stopped lighting fires at night years ago to lessen the chance of giving away their location. Raids had become more frequent and successful since Salar Muradi had taken over the Salasar, and his intention to conquer the White Desert had neither been a secret nor subtle. It had also been by his command that her mother's caravan was attacked. The Vilarhiti had been lost, for the first time in the history of the White Desert, during his campaign. The best of their horses had been taken, and now only a handful of Vilarians remained for them to breed. Life hadn't been this hard, her mother had said, not since that man had taken the throne.

She paused at the entrance for her eyes to adjust to the dark: a poor excuse, Djari admitted, as she continued to linger by the door. For years, she'd been coming out to check on her horses during the night, sometimes to sleep in one of the stalls with them, and light had never been needed for her to navigate the place. Horses were great listeners, in the way that none of the girls or boys who always seemed to tiptoe around her had ever come close. She spent more time with them than with people. Animals could be trusted when they were treated with respect; people, not always.

Something moved at the far end of the stable. Someone must have forgotten to secure one of the doors again. The last time that had happened, they had spent the whole day looking for the missing colt. Djari sighed and picked up the rock that had been keeping the main gate ajar, hoping to close it before the horses could escape. The shadow moved again, this time revealing a shape she knew was too small to be a horse.

Has Father sent someone to put her down already?

He might do that to punish her. Her father could be creative in delivering punishments when he needed to be.

Djari drew a breath and made her way slowly into the stable, dread coiling in her stomach at the thought that she might be too late. Halfway down the aisle, she could see the silhouette of the person more clearly, and this time a different kind of panic seized her.

The man—she figured from the size and build of the figure—was wearing black. Black was the color of the Rashais. The color no one wore in the White Desert.

She reached for the bow on her back and paused halfway through the motion. In this silence, she wouldn't be able to draw an arrow out of the quiver without being heard. She could call for help, but at this range, she wasn't sure she could outrun the man should he try to grab her. Backing out of the stable without being noticed was possible, but there were six of their most precious horses in these stalls, one priceless Vilarian belonging to Nazir among them. By the time help came, the man could be riding one with too far a head start for them to catch up.

Father is going to kill me for this. The thought crossed her mind as she drew out the dagger. It didn't, however, compel her to seek alternatives.

Holding her breath, she closed in on him, gripping tight on the blade that suddenly felt too large and heavy in her fist. Short-range weapons were something she had not been given enough lessons on, and she struggled to recall everything she had been taught as she took ten paces toward the stranger. He appeared to be unarmed, at least from what she could see.

The intruder, to her surprise, had Lady cradled in his arms, and appeared unaware of her presence. Her mare looked unexpectedly calm in his embrace, but people of the desert would kill a human before a horse, if it ever came down to choosing one. Unlike people, animals were always useful.

She drew one more breath and delivered her warning, keeping herself at a considerable distance. "Step away from the horse. Now."

He stiffened at the sound of her voice, and she congratulated herself for it. "Turn around and state your business."

The stranger raised both hands in the air at the threat, his movements careful and calculated—too much so for her comfort. He turned toward her with the slowness of someone who had the situation in his grip, threatening her without holding a single weapon.

From behind the long, disorderly web of hair, a pair of intense bluish-gray eyes peeked out from the dark, looking down at her from a considerable height. He took a small step forward, allowing himself to be seen in the low light from the window. A sliver of moonbeam caught the left side of his face and lit up the bridge of his nose along with the top of his cheekbone.

The stranger couldn't be much older than she was, judging from the mass she could now make out at a closer range. He had a face she would describe as too pretty for a boy and too harsh for a girl. The kind of face that provoked and didn't allow people to forget.

A beauty, she thought, too hard to be put into words, too severe to be looking at for too long, lest one forgot to breathe. And yet there was an air of deadliness, a layer of something venomous about him, that sent a shiver down her spine as she continued to stare.

"I'm only looking for shelter," said a voice smooth enough to coax a snake. His expression changed swiftly from careful to pleasantly surprised when he saw her for the first time, obviously having just realized her size and age.

It pissed her off to no end when people did that.

Djari stepped forward and pressed the dagger under his chin. The intruder was no Rashai nor mercenary, now that she could see him more clearly. Those raiders from the east had black hair, dark, deep-set eyes, and pale skin. The boy's hair had been golden brown, and those ghostly gray eyes might very well be lighter than hers. If that wasn't enough, his hard, prominent cheekbones and dark honey skin matching her own made his origin more than obvious.

The stranger was textbook Shakshi to the tips of his fingers; the kind they called a pureblood even. What a Shakshi boy of superior bloodline was doing in a Rashai robe and creeping about her stable at night was a question that needed to be answered immediately.

"You're one of us," she said.

"I am," he responded with a slight raise of his chin, exposing his neck defiantly to the weapon in her hand.

Shakshi to the tips of his fingers, Djari thought, *complete with that irrepressible pride and arrogance.*

But then again, so was she. "Then you should know that we give shelter and food to our own travelers." She dug deeper with the tip of her blade, drawing blood. "Only thieves and murderers creep around unannounced. I will ask again. What is your business here?"

The intruder, betraying no emotions whatsoever to the fact that she'd already cut him, made no attempt to explain himself. He stood in silence, jaw tight, and feet planted firmly on the ground, staring back at her.

Intimidation is half the fight. She remembered her sword master's teaching and decided to take a step forward. He remained precisely where he was, rock-solid and back straight as an arrow, as if she hadn't placed herself at a highly convenient distance to slit his throat.

"We don't have to do this. I will be gone in the morning." The words had been soft, spoken easily as if from an adult to a small child, if with some caution. He expected her to turn a blind eye to avoid a fight. A fight that she was sure to lose.

A grave mistake, and one she would make sure he never made again.

"You are addressing the Bharavi of Visarya and daughter of the Kha'a." Djari drew herself up as tall as she could, never mind the fact that he was a head taller than she was and therefore the effort was useless. "You have broken our law and will be brought to trial in the morning." She sucked in a breath and yelled at the top of her lungs, "*Guards!*"

The stranger sighed and shut his eyes for a moment. When he opened them again, they turned almost white. She gripped harder on the hilt of her blade and moved into an offensive stance. He might be larger and taller than she was, but she was the one holding a weapon, which should give her an advantage. Shouldn't it?

It should, had she been trained—or at least taught—well enough to notice and anticipate the slight shift of his weight and the way he angled back his shoulder. Before she realized what was happening, the dagger jumped out of her hand and flew across the room to land somewhere she couldn't see. He dropped quickly as she turned to look, and knocked her to the ground with an elbow to her ribs.

Still doubled over from the pain, Djari saw him open the door on the opposite stall and climb onto a horse.

No. Not Springer.

She scrambled to her feet and ran to block the exit. This was her brother's stallion, a pureblood Vilarian bearing the symbol of the Khumar. To have him stolen, on her watch no less, was an unspeakable disgrace to the Kha'gan. She would die before she let that happen.

She could have died, had she been any slower around horses. But years of being around them allowed her to drop to the ground just in time, when Springer leaped out of the stall and missed her head by a hair.

Rolling on the floor, Djari cursed herself repeatedly. How many suicidal things could she possibly have done in a single night? She should have run to the door and closed the main gate, but by the time she'd thought of this and managed to get back on her feet, the stranger and her brother's horse had already made it out into the night.

Through the windows, she could hear the sound of the guards heading her direction. It was too late. She knew this with accuracy. She knew all the horses better than any stable boy in camp. Springer was the fastest of them all, and by far. They would never make it in time to even catch a glimpse of the intruder galloping at full speed on their second-best horse, especially with that much of a lead.

Djari paused for a few breaths, ignoring the panic that was nipping at her heels, and made a decision. Winter stood alert and ready to her right, if a little agitated from the commotion. The young stallion they'd acquired a few months ago liked to race Springer and hated the sight of the older horse in front of him. He was the best chance she had, and would have to do.

Securing the bow and quiver snugly on her shoulder, she leaped onto Winter and kicked him into a full gallop. By the time she was out the door, the boy had gained at least a hundred and fifty paces on her. Djari followed at full speed, calculating the distance between them as she tried to close in. Ahead of them was the entrance to the Djamahari mountain range, a maze of narrow passages impossible to navigate at night. On the other side of that was the Kamara Kha'gan's territory, whose boundaries they couldn't cross without starting a war. She would lose them one way or another at the speed he was riding, unless she did something about it.

A hundred and ten paces... no, twenty, Djari corrected herself. It was still too far. But at that point, she could already hear Winter's breaths growing heavy. She had been riding him at killing speed, and knew he wouldn't last much longer at such a pace.

One hundred and ten.

It would have to do.

Letting go of the mane she had been holding, Djari shifted her weight to steer Winter with her knees. She unslung the bow from her shoulder and reached for an arrow, nocked it on her bow, and waited.

One hundred paces.

She held her breath and listened for the sound of Winter's hooves striking the ground once more before they all lifted in the air.

Now. The arrow flew toward the target, cutting through air with a piercing sound that told her the release had been clean. This would be her first kill, Djari thought, if it struck him where she wanted, and not her brother's horse. She would never forgive herself if it hit the horse.

Despite her lack of training in close combat, she had been training in archery since she was four. No one at camp could land an arrow as precisely as she could. No one had ever come close for the past three years.

Even then, shooting a target from hundred paces or more wasn't something she could always accomplish on horseback, especially without a saddle, at night, and on a moving target. But experience had granted her the ability to tell if her arrow would fly true from the moment she loosed it, and that night she knew for certain that she hadn't missed.

A Rock With Ten Men On It

Hasheem barely had time to look over his shoulder before the arrow struck. The girl, who had seemed so harmlessly small and thin in the stable, was no longer what he thought she was. She was riding at his heels the way no girl should be able to ride, on an unsaddled horse three times her size. The moment she drew back her bowstring and straightened her spine atop the stallion was when he realized he would never make it to the Djamahari.

And he didn't. The arrow, despite the ridiculous distance between them, struck him from behind on the deadliest spot, as if she'd driven it in by hand at close range. Had it gone through the way it should, it would have pierced his heart right in the middle and come out cleanly on the other side. By sheer luck, or fate, or whatever it was that had been keeping him alive this long, it didn't, and he fell off the horse with an arrow halfway in his back, still breathing and alive. For the time being.

The next thing he saw was her standing over him with another arrow already nocked to her bow. She looked at him and the embedded shaft, then frowned as if she'd missed her target. From her expression, she seemed to be contemplating whether to shoot him the second time or wait for the dozen or so guards now riding toward them to finish the job. When the stallion he'd stolen trotted back to her, she snapped back to her senses and decided the horse was more important.

He could have said something then that might have given her the urge to finish him where he was, knowing the consequences of being captured and brought to trial. For some reason, he didn't, and would always wonder from time to time afterward if that had been the right decision or the biggest mistake of his life.

They took him back to camp instead of killing him on the spot. She rode in the middle of the procession, surrounded by five White Warriors who guarded her like they were escorting a chest of gold through a lair full of bandits, never mind the fact that there seemed to be no other living thing in sight. It made sense in a way. Bharavis were becoming rarer and rarer even out here, deep in the heart of the White Desert. These silver-haired, yellow-eyed, so-called direct descendants of the moon goddess Ravi were the only ones who could give birth to oracles, and having an oracle could mean winning a war.

And he'd struck her, Hasheem realized, on top of everything else. The punishment for that, if he had to guess, would probably be close to being skinned alive and left to die on a spike.

They threw him into a tent, bound him hand and foot, and tied him to a post, all with the arrow still sticking out of his back. At least it was warmer inside, and they'd been thoughtful enough to give him a blanket. Then again, they wouldn't want him to die before the trial in the morning. Desert people, Black or White, treasured their codes and honor like water. He was beginning to wish the arrow would kill him before they had a chance to finish him off or move on to other means. But they would have thought of that too, wouldn't they?

They *had* thought of it, apparently, because some time later the girl who'd shot him—the young Bharavi of Visarya—returned to make sure that didn't happen. She had changed into the form-fitting white gown of a healer. Her near-white hair had been tightly braided and gathered away from her face. He could see now, more clearly in the light made by the small fire in the tent, those otherworldly yellow eyes shared by all Bharavis.

It wasn't the first time he'd seen one. Having lived in the Black Tower for years, he had seen the Salar's Bharavi wife a few times from a distance, but this was the first time he'd seen one up close. She was prettier than average, like most Shakshi girls and boys tended to be, but there was a hardness to her that made one appreciate her beauty the same way one might admire a well-made, carefully sharpened sword rather than a flower or a piece of jewelry. Then again, no person in their right mind would equate anyone who could shoot that way, girl or boy, with something so delicate.

She looked at him from where she was standing and frowned upon the realization that his arms had been tied behind his back in a way that made it impossible for her to tend to his wound.

"I'm afraid you'll have to cut me loose if you're here to remove the arrow," he told her.

She looked over her shoulder toward the door, where the guards were sure to be standing, and hesitated. There were others outside who could do this for her, of course, which would have been more appropriate. Hasheem, however, would much prefer to not be handled by those White Warriors right now if he could do something about it.

"You know," he said. "I *could* take that knife strapped to the inside of your arm and hold you hostage." The idea was rather tempting, knowing how far they would go to protect a Bharavi, but not wise. "But I wouldn't live past tomorrow with this wound on the run. Believe me, I'm not stupid enough to try." At least not while an arrow was still sticking out of his back.

She looked at her left arm and then at him, her eyes narrowed thoughtfully. They were truly beautiful, he thought, if in an unsettling way.

"You'd be dead before you took ten steps from this tent," she snapped before walking over to sit behind him. "There are five armed guards outside to shoot you down from every direction if you try. Don't move." She took her time trying to loosen the knot, lost patience, and began to cut free the rope around his wrists instead. She knew how to use the blade; he could tell from how quickly the bonds came off. Hasheem thought then of the girls he knew in Rasharwi, how most of them wouldn't even be allowed to carry a weapon—or learn to ride bareback for that matter—and decided he would have to stop regarding her as one or be content with dying badly.

Which brought him to the dilemma he was facing. "How many laws did I break?"

She had been trying to cut his robe open to get the wound. Her hands paused for a moment at the question, as if she needed time to count. It wasn't a good sign. "Three."

"And the punishment for those?"

"Depending on the motive, you may be lashed or have your toes removed for the intrusion. For stealing, your hand would be cut off, but since it was a horse, it would likely be your arm. For attacking a Bharavi…" She paused for a moment. "It's decapitation."

No chance at dying pretty, then. "In that order?"

She nodded. "In that order."

Better than being skinned alive and left to die on a spike, at least. "I suppose there's no chance you might be willing to keep that last bit between us?" By then he had come to the conclusion that her discipline might be more difficult to move than a rock with ten men on it, but it was worth a try.

"I could also have your tongue removed for suggesting that I lie."

A rock with ten men on it. Perhaps even twenty. "You might want to write that down," he said. "Or they might forget to remove something tomorrow." The list, truly, was getting rather long and appeared to be growing by the minute.

"It will be me who will have to remove them tomorrow."

Now that he hadn't anticipated. "Because I struck you?"

"Because I shot you," she said, matter-of-factly. "You are now my prisoner, my responsibility to execute. That is the custom."

A highly fucked-up custom. He had to restrain himself from saying it or she might find yet another body part to remove tomorrow. Surely there had to be some kind of age restriction on these things that wouldn't allow a girl to hack off limbs and heads of prisoners. But considering her pride and discipline, she might find it offending if they didn't let her.

The way she breathed with some difficulty revealed many things, however. "You haven't done this before, have you?"

Silence, and then a heavy sigh. "No," she admitted. An honesty there he could admire. "I wouldn't have to if you had died," she added, regrettably.

"It would have solved all kinds of problems, yes." On both her part and his. Who would have thought his death could be so useful, or convenient. "Believe me," he said in a tone that was more apologetic than he should have sounded, given the fact that they were discussing the very subject of his death, or at least the manner of it, "I'm beginning to regret that very much right now."

In truth, it would have been merciful, poetic even, to have been shot to death with an arrow to the heart by a Bharavi while riding on the back of a beautiful white Vilarian horse. If only the arrow had gone through the way it should have. By some divine intervention, it hadn't, though according to her, the fault seemed to have been his. "It was a good shot, by the way." A good shot was a good shot, whether or not one was the target, and a compliment always worked in softening people, didn't it?

It didn't. Not on her. For some reason, his experience as the highest-paid escort in Rasharwi was utterly useless with her. Then again, he'd never had to entertain a Bharavi.

"It was a perfect shot," she said. "You should be dead."

"Forgive me," he said, trying not to smile too widely. Small, and fifteen at best if he had to guess, the girl had more conviction and pride in her than some men twice her size and thrice her age. "I had no intention to offend. For what it's worth, you will have another chance tomorrow."

To his surprise, she didn't respond. He wondered what her expression would be like, sitting behind him at that moment, what she would look like if her color were high when she was surprised, entertained, or flattered. He also realized he was unreasonably agitated by the thought that he might not live long enough to see any of it.

"You're not afraid," she said at length. It sounded more like an observation than a question.

I'm done being afraid, he wanted to say, but it would require an explanation and she might find it not to her liking. There was, apparently, an unlimited number of ways to offend this girl, and he was acutely aware of the possibility of her using a blunt blade on purpose to cut off his limbs tomorrow. "Is it not considered an honor to be killed by a Bharavi?" She would like that, wouldn't she?

Again, she did not.

"There is no honor in death." Bitterness there. Perhaps also scars. "It's useless and wasteful."

Not always, he wanted to say, but thought it wise not to argue. Death had opened doors for him in Rasharwi, and in the desert where resources were limited, dying meant fewer mouths to feed. They'd kill him tomorrow for that reason, first and foremost.

Her hand paused the moment she finished removing the bandage around his burn wound. Hasheem wondered then, if the stories—the lies—he had prepared to tell even mattered at that point. His penalty was already death, whether or not she believed his stories.

"How did you get this burn?"

'*Make up a story. A good one,*' Dee had said. Lying wasn't difficult. He had survived this long with a lot more than lying. But that night he simply didn't want to. Not to her.

"What is your name?" he asked in return.

It must have been an inappropriate question, but she gave it a consideration and replied, "Djari."

"Djari." It was a pretty name. Every man should know the name of the person who would be taking his life, shouldn't he? "Don't ask your victims too many questions if you have to kill," he told her. Knowing too much complicated things when one had to end a life. Walking away from the body of one's enemy was easy; knowing he had been a father, a son, or a lover was not. This was his gift to her, if he was to be her first kill. One good deed before death seemed like a good idea, even though it probably wasn't enough to save his soul.

"You have done this," she said thoughtfully. "Killed."

"I have."

"How many times?"

How many times had he killed? Ten? Twenty? Fifty? Or had there been more? He thought for the first time of the deaths he'd caused in the past seven years. The soldiers who'd raided his Kha'gan. The inmates who'd attacked him at Sabha. People Dee had wanted dead. The general just two nights before, and the city guards that had pursued him afterward.

The very thought angered him. *How many times?* she'd asked, as if he would have been proud to name the number or consider it some kind of an achievement. The Rashais did that. Soldiers told tales of warriors they'd killed, villages they'd burned, girls and boys they'd raped and slain. Stories to wet their appetite before dinner, to entertain at campfires. "Do not," he snapped at her before he could stop himself, "mistake me for the scum and murderers who count their dead."

The hands that had been busy with removing the bandage paused for a moment, followed by a long breath she held for a time. "Then what are you?" she asked icily, obviously not pleased with the tone he'd just used. "If not scum or a murderer? What were you doing in our stable?"

The sudden display of hostility didn't surprise him. He had tried to chastise a Bharavi, the equivalent of a princess in the White Desert, whom he had also discovered to be proud to a fault. It just so happened that when it came to the issue of pride, he was also notorious for being just as bad. "Trying to survive," he replied, for the first time with spite in his tone. That was, in reality, his only crime committed around here, or anywhere.

"Would you still try, given a choice?" A voice sounded from the doorway, smooth as silk and slippery enough to rival it. Hasheem closed his eyes to the fact that they were no longer alone. He knew this man, knew the words to come before they would be spoken.

Not again.

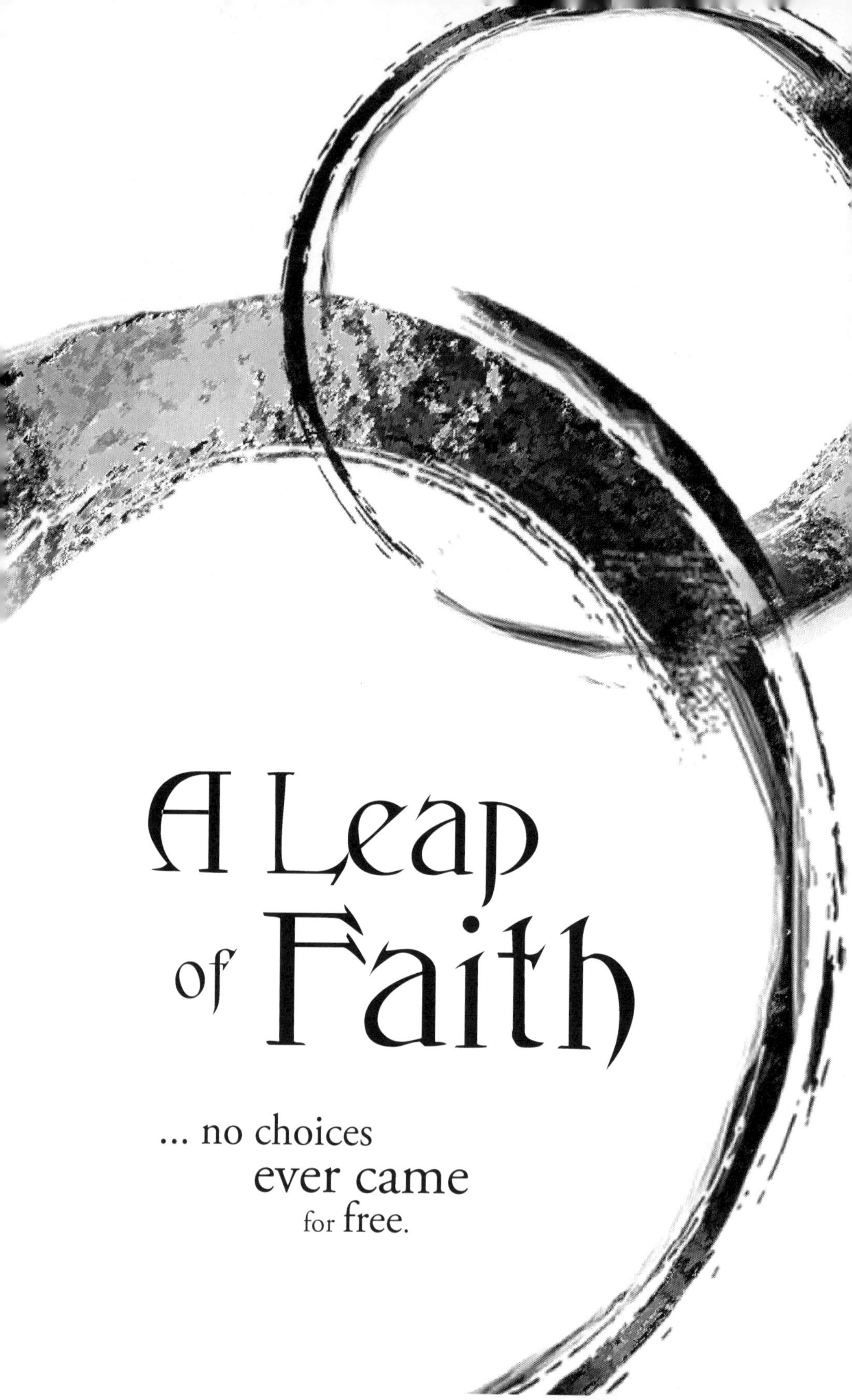
A Leap of Faith
... no choices
ever came
for free.

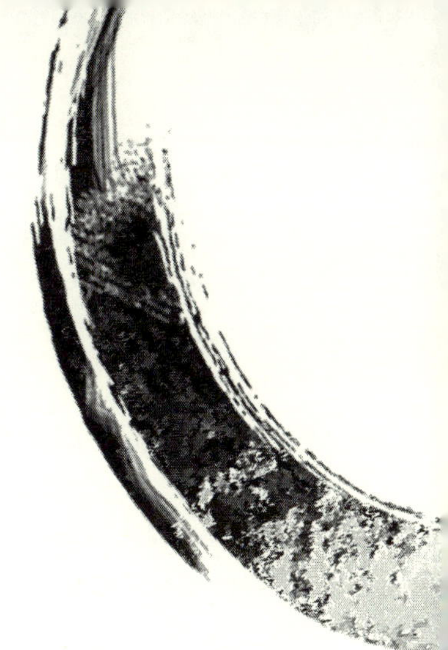

"Would you still try, given a choice?" The speaker, a young man, tall, lean, and elegant almost to the point of looking delicate, must have been standing there for some time listening to their conversation. An undeniable air of authority filled the tent the moment he allowed himself to be noticed, giving Hasheem a sudden need to relocate himself.

He had come to know this man by experience, and had been expecting him to appear at some point. There had been one like him everywhere in his life. In the dungeon, the brothel, the slave quarter, or one of Dee's hidden chambers. Every time, just when he had settled for death, Fate always sent someone to offer him a choice to live, but no choices ever came for free.

"And you are the man who would give me that choice, I presume?" Hasheem asked in his most sardonic tone. It was about to begin again: the games, the punishment, the reward. The chains around his wrists and ankles. He'd known this dance for a long time. A price would be named soon.

The man crossed over in three smooth, flawless strides and stopped in front of him, looking down from his considerable height. He was wearing a zikh, the signature white robe given to the most elite class of Shakshi warriors, and had kept the hood on so that only a part of his face could be seen. The way Djari had fallen into complete silence told him that this man, whoever he was, outranked her in more ways than one.

There were only a handful of people who outranked a Bharavi in the White Desert, as far as he knew.

"That depends," the man said mildly, "on how willing you are to consider my proposal."

"A proposal." Hasheem sneered at the irony of things. He hated being right sometimes. "And what," he said, "would you have me do, may I ask? Clean your stable, kill your competition, or fuck your guests? I happen to be highly proficient in all three."

The arrow in his back was suddenly snapped in half, and Hasheem, nearly yelping at the pain, looked promptly over his shoulder.

"You are in the presence of the Khumar of Visarya," Djari said, with murder in her eyes. "You *will* mind your manners, or I will add your tongue to the list of things to remove tomorrow."

It would explain a lot, Hasheem realized, looking at the young man who was standing calmly over him. This was the Khumar, heir to the Kha'a of the Kha'gan—the highest ruling figure of the tribe. He might not be the most powerful man on that strip of the desert now, but he was the one next in line, and bestowed, apparently, with enough authority to change and corrupt the most notoriously strict laws in the peninsula.

A proposal, the Khumar had said. Anything could be bought, even among the most disciplined, code-abiding people on earth. *There are no monsters bigger than the worst of men*, Dee used to say. There really weren't. The world was the same, everywhere, whichever side of the desert you were on.

"Good," he said, ignoring the throbbing pain in his shoulder. "I was beginning to wonder who I would have to fuck to get out of here."

Behind him, Djari took hold of whatever was left of the arrow shaft and twisted. It took everything he had to not howl at the pain. He didn't have to turn around to know those yellow eyes would be attempting to burn a hole through his skull right about then. And if her sense of duty toward her Khumar hadn't been enough to make her want to shoot him again for his blatant display of insubordination, the love and respect she seemed to harbor for this man would certainly do the job. That, for some reason, was pissing him off more than anything else.

"My sister has a temper. For that, I apologize," the Khumar said as he gestured something to Djari, who obediently removed her hand from the arrow. "I will, however, advise against the use of such words and tone with the Kha'a. Many have lost their tongue for less."

He didn't doubt it, but he was way past giving a damn about losing limbs, especially when death was already at his doorstep. "Assuming that I choose to live past tomorrow," he said. It was going to be *his* choice this time whether or not he let himself be put in chains again.

The Khumar smiled. He could see the resemblance between the two of them now, looking more closely. They had the same yellow eyes, the similar straight nose, and the high, well-defined cheekbones. There was a special meaning to that, something about a man who shared the same characteristics with a Bharavi that he couldn't remember. It didn't matter. He was about to die in any case.

"Assuming that you are who I think you are, I believe you will like my proposal," continued the Khumar with the same presumptuous, silky-smooth voice that had been getting on his nerves since the man entered the room. He sounded like he knew things people didn't, and was certain of it in ways that no one should have the right to be.

"You don't know me."

The gentle, seemingly harmless smile turned swiftly into a poisonous, disturbing one. "Don't I?"

The next Kha'a of Visarya took two measured steps forward to stand before him, looking down from an imposing height with a calmness that stilled the room. Sure, steady hands moved slowly to push back the hood from his head, revealing the long, near-silver hair matching that of Djari.

"You lost your family when you were ten," he began in an unanimated tone, as if reciting from a text or a scroll. "It happened on a Raviyani night. They came with fire, in the dark, burning first the eastern side of the camp. Your entire Kha'gan was destroyed, burned to the ground as you watched. I think," he said, leaning closer, "that is why you haven't tried to return to the desert ever since. Or am I wrong?"

Hasheem swallowed as a torrent of images rushed through his head. They *had* come with fire, with torches and on horseback. The tents had gone up in flame, one by one—a giant burning snake slithering through camp, leaving trails of fire everywhere it touched before the main cavalry had charged in. Then came the screams of horses and people, rising above all the sounds in the desert as they began to slaughter the men and round up the women and children.

It was among the memories he managed to bury in the furthest corner of his mind, now dragged out of hiding by this man—this stranger—who seemed to know every detail of that night. It wasn't possible, not even imaginable, that he could know these things. Those who did had all died or still resided in Rasharwi.

The Khumar lowered himself to the ground to stare levelly at him, his eyes glowing a ghostly shade of amber. "You killed a man, not too long ago," he continued. "That's why they're hunting you. Why you're on the run. That burn," he glanced quickly at Djari, "was no accident."

Hasheem opened his mouth to speak and found he couldn't. Long, elegant fingers reached over to cradle his head from behind, holding him in place. The Khumar leaned forward, his lips brushing the side of his ear, and whispered in a tone that made every hair on his body stand on end. "I know what you have done, what you had to do to survive. I've seen the faces of the men you've killed, and those you wanted to see dead. Have I said enough, or would you like me to go on?"

If there had been a part of him that thought the Khumar was harmless in any way, it was gone as soon as he'd finished the sentence. This was someone who knew all his secrets, his past, and every crime he'd ever committed. Hasheem suddenly realized what he was. He should have known the moment saw that silver hair. "You're an oracle." His voice was trembling now, despite all his efforts to hide the fact that he was frightened out of his wits.

"The only one you will likely see outside of Citara," the man said, smiling again as though nothing had happened.

Hasheem realized then why Djari had been so protective of her brother, so respectful of him. No one had seen or heard of an oracle outside Citara since the hunt that had begun more than a decade ago. Salar Muradi had ordered an extensive search for them, and still offered a large sum for any information that would lead to their capture. To everyone's understanding, oracles, pureblood or imposters, had already been butchered to the point of extinction.

Hasheem, having been caught in the middle of that same hunt which had killed his family, had never truly understood the need for it until now. The late oracle of his Kha'gan, a pureblood with blue eyes and light copper hair, had only been able to see the arrival of a storm or perhaps an unseasonal rain. The man sitting in front of him was something else. This was a trueblood oracle whose visions and foresight could bring down the Salasar, the kind that had forced Salar Muradi to order a wholesale slaughter of the White Desert to get rid of.

Shocking as it was, the revelation had also told him something else with regard to his own situation.

"I'm never going to leave here alive, am I?" It was too much of a risk, now that he knew what he knew. Whatever alternatives the man had been meaning to offer him, it did not include the possibility of him leaving this Kha'gan..

"I'm afraid not."

"And the alternative?"

"You can stay," the oracle replied, "and become a part of this Kha'gan."

"I see." He allowed himself to smile a little too widely this time. "As your prisoner or your slave, may I ask?" How many times could one possibly jump from one set of shackles to the next in the pursuit of freedom before eventually finding it—if one were to do so at all?

The same gentle smile returned, though this time with a hint of something else that hadn't been there before. It might have been uncertainty, or guilt, or even pity; he wasn't sure. "As Djari's sworn sword and blood. If she will take you."

Behind him, Djari stiffened.

"*My* sworn sword and blood?" she repeated.

"If you will take him," said the Khumar again. The coldness in his voice disappeared when he spoke to his sister, Hasheem noticed. "He is your prisoner, Djari. You can let him die, or you can speak for him. It is a choice you alone must make."

She grew quiet for a time, considering her options, despite the absurdity of it all. When she spoke again, it was with unmistakable conviction. "You trust him to be my sworn sword and blood? Is this what you have seen in your vision, Nazir?"

The Khumar shook his head and smiled, almost apologetically. There was much love between the two of them that was visible for anyone to see, and neither tried to hide it. "I see nothing beyond this point, Djari. I'm only a messenger. I don't know if he is meant to live or die, or why the gods have sent him to us. All I know is what you decide today will shape the fate of the entire peninsula. It is your judgment that I trust, as the one who has been born to bring an end to the war."

To bring an end to the war. Hasheem found himself holding his breath at the revelation. These words, spoken by a trueblood oracle, could be considered a prophecy. And he, after all this time, had been sitting in the same tent as the one who would bring it all to an end—the raids, the bloodshed, the war that had been going on for hundreds of years.

And his life had been tied into it, according to the Khumar. A few moments ago he might have dismissed it as folly, but how was he supposed to dismiss anything this man had to say, having heard what he had about his own past from another's mouth, having seen what he could do?

"And if I choose wrong?" Djari asked, uncertainty in her voice for the first time.

"Then it is meant to be," he replied. "Perhaps we are meant to lose the war or become a part of the Salasar. Perhaps there are other ways to find peace. I don't know. But there are always signs everywhere. If you look for them, you may see the will of Ravi."

Had there been signs? Hasheem wondered. Was there a pattern, a coincidence, that had led him to this point in his life? He'd never considered himself to be pious. When one had been through what he had, the promise of prayers being answered seemed like a joke. But sitting there, in front of an oracle, knowing what he knew now, it was difficult to not question whether there had been a purpose to all this, or if every loss, every suffering he'd been through, had simply been a part of a grander design.

'*Go west,*' Dee had said, for a reason he refused to share, just before Hasheem left the city. He'd never considered that a gift of foresight might be one of Dee's many abilities. Why, he'd often wondered, had he been singled out from the other slaves, to be bought and trained by one of the most brilliant men in Rasharwi? How was it possible that he had survived to this day, given what he had been through? "Why," he said, "am I not dead?"

The tent fell into silence. Nazir Khumar looked past him to Djari, waiting for an answer. She took a breath, and, without further hesitation, plunged the tip of her blade into the arrow wound and began to cut it open. His mind went blank at the unexpected jolt of pain. He could have used a warning, or at least a gentler hand, but she seemed to be concentrating on digging the arrow out quickly, not digging it out safely at that point.

The arrowhead came off, miraculously, with him still alive and breathing. After a moment of pause, Djari rose and strode to where she'd left her belongings. She picked up her quiver and emptied it onto the floor between him and Nazir. The arrows, beautifully crafted and identical, had all been tipped with small, gleaming black stones.

Obsidian. He knew that stone, could recognize it from anywhere. The iconic Black Tower in Rasharwi was made almost entirely of it. '*You should have died,*' she had said. Now he understood why. Obsidian broke sharper than any other material could be forged by hand. These arrowheads could penetrate two men and still come out clean on the other side.

It had barely gone halfway through him.

"This is bone," she said, holding up a white arrow point still covered with his blood. "Somebody put a bone arrow in my quiver."

There are signs everywhere. The Khumar's words still occupied his mind as he looked at the rest of the arrows scattered on the floor. One out of twenty-four. Even if someone had put that arrow in her quiver on purpose, what were the chances that she would have picked it without looking? Hasheem closed his eyes and exhaled the breath he had been holding. "Explain to me," he said, "what I have to do."

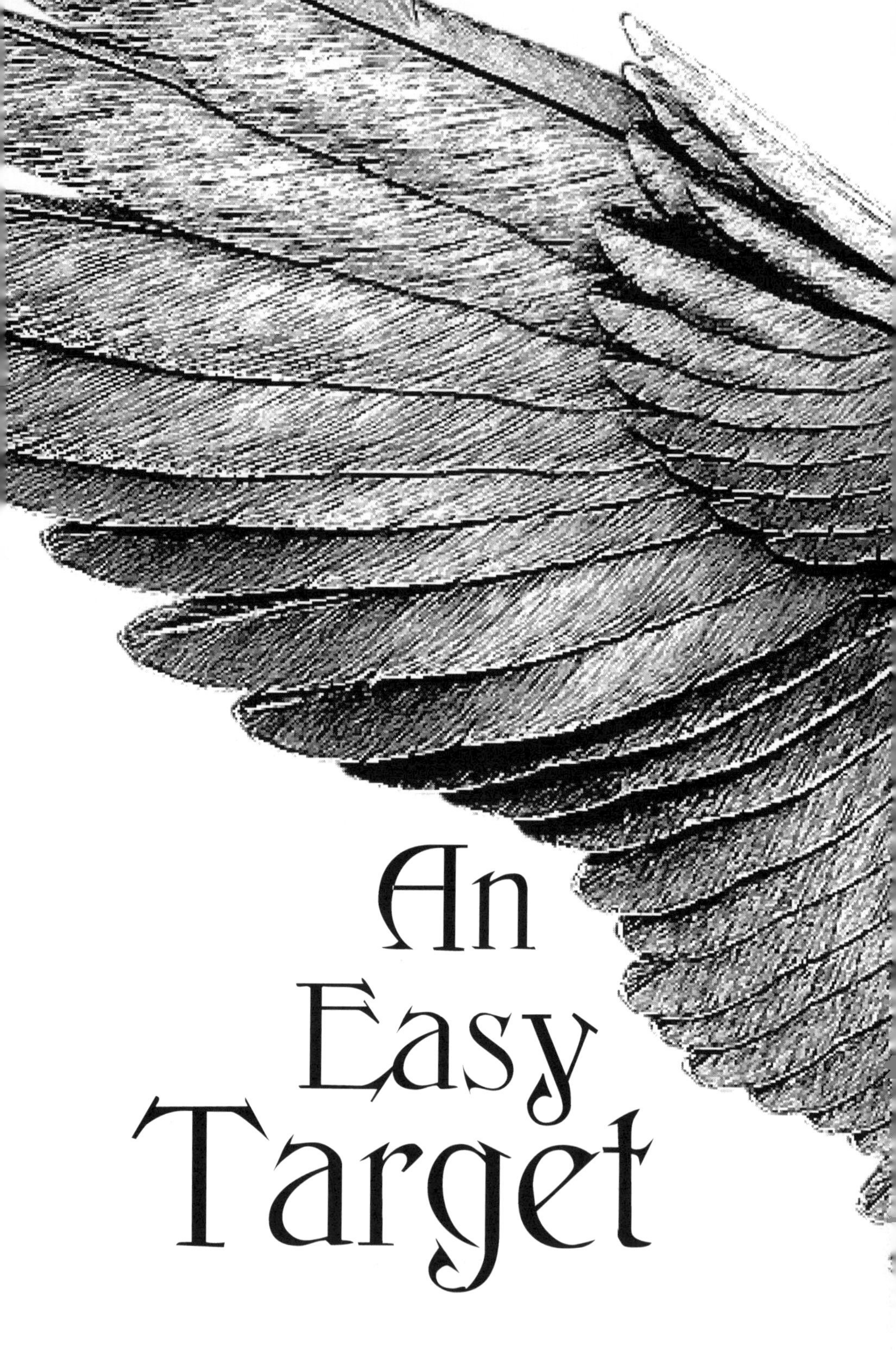

An Easy Target

Lasura shifted his weight on the nondescript bay colt as he waited for the trackers' return, trying to find the best position to save his behind from this torture device of a saddle. He had been trained on military and traditional Shakshi ones, both of which offered more comfort for a long ride. This afternoon's journey might not have been considered long, but after two hours, the only thing that soothed his backside at the moment was imagining the prick responsible for its creation being made to sit on it for three days with his dick tucked underneath him.

Next to him, Azram seemed to be suffering no discomfort on his white stallion, or he was suffering but was too used to enduring such an instrument of torture. Azram's saddle—complete with gold studs and decorative stitchings, as if the pain of sitting on hard, embossed leather wasn't enough—was a display of status more than anything else a saddle was supposed to be. Status was everything in the Black Tower. As far as Azram was concerned, no son of the Salar should ever be seen riding on anything less, especially as a part of his grand entourage. And so, thanks to his kind regards and thoughtfulness, Lasura had also been made to ride on this princely thing that was going to make him sore for the next two days.

At least his didn't come with studs, he thought. You had to be thankful for the small things in life, especially if you were born a half-blood son in a city full of Rashais. Prince or not, the Shakshi part of his blood—a priest of Sangi had decided—was something to be cleansed with leeches and discarded in holy fire. Since life in the Tower required one to survive by agreeing with whoever had the power to put leeches and set dogs on you, he'd agreed with said statement and advised that salt should be added somewhere in the process, just to be sure. There was no point in fighting these things. No one cared what happened to a prince of Shakshi blood;

it only mattered that he remained alive, since dying required permission from the Salar. His father had made that clear.

Azram's summons had come without a warning shortly after midday. The instructions had been precise, demanding him to show up at the royal stable within the next half-hour—an amount of time that didn't allow one to do much, considering the distance from one point to another in the Black Tower and the steps to be climbed between them. He'd simply put on a robe and a pair of riding boots, grabbed himself a bow and a half-empty quiver, and went. The mounts had already been picked and saddled by Azram's stable boys when he arrived, and there had been no time for him to have the horse or the saddle changed to his liking—not that he thought Azram would have allowed it in any case.

It had been done deliberately, though, if not meticulously planned well in advance. The obvious difference in his more subtly-designed saddle and Azram's extravagant black and gold one was there to differentiate, to bring attention to the *right* son. One of the first things Salar Muradi had done the moment he took over the Salasar was to toss out the rules of succession and made it his right to name whichever man he saw fit an heir, royalty or not. With rights to the throne being fair game, one did what one could to gain the attention of the Salar by trying to stand out one way or another, and discrediting competition was the oldest trick in the book for humans anywhere, of any race, age, or rank.

Only Lasura had never been in competition, not where the throne was concerned. It was generally understood that whatever set of candidates the Salar might choose from as his successor would never include one of Shakshi blood, half or whole. Until two years ago, he had simply been a convenient and satisfying subject upon which all other sons should urinate for the sake of target practice, but the day the Salar decided to ask him along to one of his hunting sessions—something no other sons had so far been given opportunity to do—his status in the Tower had gone from public toilet to a dressed up goat dragged along for the most popular sacrifice.

Which was likely why prince Azram, the only son of the Salahari, had demanded that he join the hunt that afternoon in the Black Desert outside of Sangi, where the Salar was expected to pass through on his way back to the capital. Many advantages could be gained from this event if things were to go as planned. A fox hunt that deep in the desert, if successful, would give him a chance to offer their father a rare and exquisite trophy as a welcome home present. It would also prove Azram a capable hunter and a friend to his father's favorite son, giving him a chance to be included in future hunts where other sons might not. Hunting sessions were the only opportunities to spend the entire day with the Salar to get to know him or be acknowledged by him—the most direct path to the throne, so to speak.

Or the quickest way to be thrown off it, in Lasura's opinion, should it be your inconcealable shit that he acknowledged.

A brilliant move for the prince, nonetheless. So brilliant that Lasura wondered if it had been his or the Salahari's. Azram, with his wrong choice of saddle and garment to prove it, would have never been observant or thoughtful enough to come up with such a plan. It would be interesting to see if he could carry it through. No one in the Black Tower had been able to predict with any certainty whether an attempt to impress the Salar would end up being considered impressive or manipulative. The latter usually meant being thrown off the Tower that same evening, prince or otherwise.

Had Azram been any less arrogant, he might have thought about seeking the so-called favorite son's advice on how to do this right, and Lasura might have even given said advice if only for the sake of saving his behind from the agony of this goddamn saddle. He could, in a manner of speaking, offer said advice out of the kindness and purity of his heart, but he decided watching Azram humiliate himself with his own ignorance was more enjoyable.

Which was exactly why he'd neglected to mention the suspicious shadow behind a rock he'd picked up before the trackers had been sent out. The Salar, being an excellent tracker himself, enjoyed tracking his own game. He brought with him only a small party to any given hunt, or none at all when the ground was considered safe. It had given Lasura enough opportunities to observe and learn these skills from his father, to the point where he could now aid the Salar in spotting prey.

To observe and to learn were all the opportunities he had. To his father, wisdom and skills were to be acquired through experience and keen observation, and those who failed to acquire them by these means were considered a waste of time to teach. He was as far from caring as a father could be, but removing himself as an influence was also how he tested the capabilities of his sons. It would, however, be a serious mistake for any of them to think he wasn't watching everything they did. Very few things escaped his notice, whether or not he chose to address them.

Perhaps he should have said something about the shadow, Lasura thought, shifting his weight again on the saddle. The trackers had been gone for a long time. Azram would surely try this again if the hunt were to fail that day, and Lasura wasn't looking forward to yet another outing on this horrible thing

To his relief, the two trackers returned to inform Azram about the young males they'd spotted in the canyon just east of them.

Azram snapped a command for the guards to secure the area as he prepared to pursue them on foot. The Black Desert was a region filled with boulders and obsidian-covered hills, making it near-impossible to hunt on horseback without risking injuries to one's horse. They would have to sneak up to the foxes to shoot them. Lasura had expected this, and was glad to be out of the saddle more than anything else.

The foxes were feeding on a rabbit when they arrived: one a deep-red, medium-sized male with a splash of orange along its back, the other an exquisite silver of similar build, both sporting rows of clear, characteristic black rings around their fluffy tails from tip to rump. Rare and difficult to hunt, the pelt of these ring-tailed black foxes was a luxury only royalty and the elites of Rasharwi could afford. A pity, Lasura thought, given how beautiful they were alive, and how ugly the men who wore them dead on their shoulders often were.

The foxes could be considered easy targets, as long as they could remain unnoticed and hit them with their first shot. Lasura prepared his bow as one of the trackers handed Azram his, an arrow nocked and ready. From what he knew, Azram was a decent archer, and at that range even he wouldn't miss.

Lasura, however, would be expected to do so. An easy enough thing, and one he didn't mind doing. Hunting for sport wasn't really his thing, especially not when it was being served to him on a plate. The Salar sometimes returned with no kill at all. It was always the difficult climb, the effort taken in tracking down an animal, or the test of how close he could get to any given prey without being noticed that excited him.

He and his father had spent three days tracking a mountain cat once in the high forest of Cakora and came upon a den full of cubs. The mother had turned to face them, her eyes blazing gold as she readied herself to attack. The Salar had smiled, lowered his bow, and ended the hunt. The creature had been '*too magnificent to die by an arrow,*' he'd said. Those who'd accompanied him on that hunt agreed that the Salar's mood coming down that mountain had never been more pleasant. They would also agree that it had also been the case on the way up. He'd grinned like a boy being given a new toy every time they lost track of the cat. It was one of the most memorable hunts Lasura had experienced with his father, which, in turn, was making that hunt with Azram more boring than having to babysit a rock—if not also unsatisfying where skills and pride were concerned.

One tracker gave them a hand signal, telling them to be quiet and ready. He would have to wait for Azram to shoot first out of etiquette before shooting the second fox ceremoniously and failing. The two trackers also had their bows to hand, in case Azram's arrow missed the target. It was generally understood, of course, that while the trackers were expected to finish the job, Lasura was never to bring down Azram's fox, or it would be considered an insult of epic proportions. The same act, done by a different man, could mean entirely different things for men of power.

Azram's first shot hit the silver fox in the shoulder rather than the neck. Still able to move freely, the injured fox leaped up onto the rocks and began to scale the canyon. Lasura loosed his arrow at the remaining target around the same time the two trackers shot theirs to finish Azram's kill. The silver fox fell to the ground with two more arrows in its neck. The red fox got away, as expected.

Azram turned to him, grinning as if the two arrows in the neck had both been his, ignoring the real one that had left a hole in the best part of the pelt and therefore ruined it. "I thought I'd left the easier one for you."

"Indeed you did," Lasura lied. "It was a difficult shot." It wasn't, really.

"Father will be pleased." Not with that hole in the middle of his pelt, he wouldn't.

"A pity he couldn't have two." Azram shrugged and climbed back on his horse. The dead fox was collected by the trackers, who then removed and took back their arrows after returning Azram's to his quiver. Princes didn't get their hands dirty or their clothes soiled, according to Azram. Lasura wondered what he'd say if he saw how dirty their father got during a good hunt. "Come, he should be close to Sangi."

At least he has enough sense to watch the time, Lasura thought as he picked up his misfired arrow and climbed back on his colt. They were, after all, heading toward an even more difficult target, if not the most dangerous one.

With the Birds in It

They spotted the Salar's company coming out of the valley a few hours before sundown. The entourage of eighty men had two riders a short distance ahead to clear the path and two rows of guards flanking left and right of the five wagons that presumably contained gifts from the governor of Khandoor. The Salar made a trip to all four provinces surrounding Rasharwi at least once a year. Once independent kingdoms that now belonged to the Salasar, their governors needed to be kept on a short leash to discourage any plans of an uprising. There was always an uprising somewhere in the Salasar no matter how long they'd been conquered or how many privileges they were allowed. '*People are like spoiled children,*' his father often said. '*Give them an apple and they'll tell you it's an orange they need.*' It was a big peninsula to rule, a responsibility more enormous at times than the power that came with it. Lasura had never quite understood why anyone would want to sit on that throne.

Ahead of the wagons was Salar Muradi in black uniform, one identical to the guards that surrounded him. His mount—a magnificent black Vilarian stallion—was dressed with the same military saddle as the rest of his men's. To his immediate right, Ghaul rode sturdily atop his massive Samarran horse, alert and ready, as always, to kill any living thing that came within two steps of his Salar. A royal carriage followed not too far behind. It would be empty, as always, dragged along only to deceive those who might try to assassinate the Salar of Rasharwi.

It would have to take a truly ignorant assassin to attack the carriage; Lasura humored himself with that thought, watching the company coming nearer. The current Salar of Rasharwi was a figure that filled rooms and doorways. Even with his giant guard removed from being the center of attention, anyone who'd ever been in his presence could still spot his father again from a crowd ten times as large.

And that presence was causing Azram's horse to fidget where they stood—or to put it more precisely, Azram was causing his horse to fidget from the anxiety of approaching someone from three hundred paces away. Azram, for all his eagerness earlier that afternoon, looked like he was trying not to sit on a spear someone was poking up his behind.

Ghaul snapped a command, and the two riders in front came forward to check on Azram's party. Once their identities were confirmed, one rode back to the main company to inform the Salar, and the other stayed behind to signal a change in situation, should that ever occur.

Azram urged his horse forward as the Salar's company reached them and offered their father a princely bow—something Lasura had never truly accomplished. "Welcome home, Father." He gave one of the trackers a signal to bring forward the kill. "We were out hunting in the area and saw you coming out of the mountains. I've caught you something."

It had to appear as a coincidence; the Salar had always been suspicious of those who went out of their way to please him. Lasura doubted the event would be seen as a coincidence by his father, but sometimes one could get away with at least putting up an effort to conceal such things.

The tracker brought the dead fox over to the Salar. Ghaul steered his horse between the two and reached for it in his place, handing the kill to another soldier. His father, who had yet to say a word, took a glance at the animal, and then at both his sons. The silence that ensued made all the horses nervous. The first word from the Salar always felt like a death sentence, for the reason that sometimes it literally was.

"I see," said the Salar, with a grin that made Lasura wish he had something to cover his head with. He had come to know that smile, that look in his eyes, and what it was his father was truly seeing. *At least he seems amused more than insulted.* "Only one?" The address, for some unnerving reason, was directed at Lasura.

It wasn't a difficult question to answer, but when it came from his father, everything became more complicated. Lasura considered his choices for a moment. On one hand, he could tell the truth and risk damaging Azram's ego; on the other, he could lie and risk insulting the Salar's intelligence. He might just be able to avoid both, however, if he chose his words carefully. "My aim was a little off today." It wasn't exactly a lie. His aim had been off, whether or not it was deliberate.

The Salar studied him for a time. Lasura held his gaze, despite the urge to relocate himself somewhere underground. Above them, an eagle was soaring, whistling a distinctive, high-pitched sound Lasura could readily identify from his time spent hunting in the desert.

His father looked up at the eagle, then at him, and nodded. "The bird, Lasura."

It was one of the signals he used during hunting sessions—a quick glance at the prey, and a characteristic nod to give permission. Lasura unslung the bow from his shoulder, nocked an arrow, and made his aim without delay. It would have to be done swiftly, if at all.

He didn't want to shoot the bird, especially one as rare and magnificent as the spotted eagle of the Black Desert. But a command from the Salar was a command, and between his life and that of whatever it was his father wanted dead, Lasura chose his without much hesitation. Clearing his mind to focus on the target, he drew a breath, calculated the timing, and released the arrow.

It missed by a hair.

He looked at his father, hoping that it wouldn't be seen as a calculated attempt to fail. The Salar nodded. "Again."

He fitted another arrow, recalculated the speed and distance of his target, and released. This time, it went through the chest, and the eagle screeched a piercing cry before it fell to the ground. He released the breath he'd been holding, feeling a mixture of relief and pity for the magnificent creature. More relief than pity, if he were to be honest. There were, after all, several things he could imagine happening should the Salar regard his failed first attempt to be deliberate, and probably as many he couldn't.

It hadn't been deliberate—he was smart enough to know how well his father could see through an act. The first shot had truly been a mistake. He hadn't shot at a flying target often, except during the tournaments he was required to enter and lose. His skills in archery had been taught by Shakshi warriors in gray, handpicked by his mother, of course, and they only hunted for the meat, or sometimes for the fur as a necessity to stay warm. To the Shakshis, killing birds was seen as a waste of both animal and arrow, and so they never practiced on such a target. He also remembered his father saying something of the sort, but there was, as always, a purpose to that last command. Every act had a purpose when it came to Salar Muradi. Deo di Amarra, his sword master and tutor in many things, had taught him that very early on.

"The next time you want to kiss Azram's princely behind," said the Salar, "do so when I'm not around."

Lasura swallowed. A lesson taught with the life of a precious bird. A message for both his sons. Next to him, Azram shifted uncomfortably on his horse as if feeling the saddle for the first time. His brother opened his mouth to speak, but seemed to have decided just in time to not die prematurely and closed it.

For Lasura, it required an acknowledgement. "There won't be a next time," he said and stopped himself from dropping his head too apologetically. That, too, had been known to irritate the Salar. Anything in excess irritated him. "May I have permission to retrieve the bird?"

The Salar nodded. "You may."

Guiding the horse with his legs, he trotted to the eagle that had fallen a short distance away. When he was close enough, Lasura leaned over to the side to pick up the bird without getting off or slowing down his horse—a show of competence in horsemanship he wouldn't have done in front of Azram on other occasions. His father, however, having seen him done so many times, would be expecting it, and he wasn't going to make the same mistake twice in one day.

The bird had been a fully grown female, judging from the colorings of its feathers. Now that he was closer, Lasura could see the dead rabbit still clutched in its talons.

A female carrying food back to her nest, he thought. *A nest full of chicks in it.*

Without thinking—a deadly, careless, idiotic thing to do in front of the Salar—Lasura looked up at the mountain behind them and saw his father turning the same direction. Their gazes returned moments later to meet, and a wordless exchange of understanding passed between them.

A hint of a smile appeared at the corners of his father's lips. "You think you can get them." A statement, not a question.

Lasura drew a breath and began to consider the consequences. "I'll miss the reception," he said. "But I can try."

"You can ride back with me to the reception and fatten yourself on wine and suckling pigs, or you can go get them." The Salar pulled his horse to the side to continue his ride back to the Tower. "If you choose to go, you come down with the birds or you don't come down. A man does not try. He does, or he dies doing. What will it be?"

A difficult choice, considering that he might still die after successfully getting the eaglets, this time by the hands of his mother for the crime of trying to please the husband she preferred dead. On the other hand, choosing the reception could make him a son no longer worthy of accompanying him on hunts, which would, in turn, lower his status in the Tower and allow all sorts of crap to come back into his life. Either way, he was fucked, not that he wasn't used to being in that position.

He gave his father a pained smile. "May I have a change of saddle?"

The rare, resonating laugh that followed would be heard and remembered by the company of more than fifty men and the two young princes for a long time afterward. Words would be exchanged in the Tower (they always were) regarding how the Salar's half-blood son had found a way to entertain his father, and while he would likely be showered with attention and gifts from the lords and ladies at court in hope of a quick promotion, he would, unfortunately, also be made to suffer adequately for these things by the other princes and their mothers when he returned. *If* he returned.

"And I was so looking forward to seeing you limp coming down from that thing," said the Salar, chuckling, before turning to a soldier nearby. "Get him a new saddle and a flask of water. Ghaul, my cloak." He made a gesture and Ghaul, who had been holding on to the bear pelt cloak for the Salar, handed it to Lasura. "I want it back. Do you understand?"

"With the birds in it, I know," he replied, taking the one thing that was going to mess up his life in the most elaborate way possible with his free hand. He was now officially the only one in the Black Tower the Salar saw fit to allow to wear his cloak, and he was about to climb one of the most treacherous mountains in the region to get him a nest full of priceless, young, and trainable spotted eagles no Salar had possessed in the past few hundred years. How many piles of shit could he possibly step into in one day? All because he'd allowed himself to lick Azram's behind and take an easy way out.

Knowing his father, it was probably or precisely because of it. Lasura looked up at the mountain with all its deadly cliffs ahead of him and let out a heavy sigh once the party had left.

He would either die tonight unless he remembered all his training, or he would survive only to kiss life as he knew it goodbye for at least the next decade.

A Great Kha'a

"You are certain about this?" asked the Kha'a of Visarya, taking the offered wine from his only son.

Nazir looked at his father with the usual sense of anxiety crawling in his stomach. Za'in izr Husari was said to have been a strikingly handsome man in his youth. Now, in his late forties, the lines of aging on his face deepened every time he frowned, adding to the intimidation the old scar running down the left side of his cheek already delivered. To Nazir, his father appeared more striking than handsome, and the evidence of time and hardships over the years only made that fact more severe.

"My visions are never certain," Nazir replied uncomfortably. The things he saw weren't always clear, and most required interpretations one could rightfully call a blind guess at times.

"Spare me your diplomatic presumptions, Nazir." The Kha'a seated himself on a cushion behind the low table as he spoke. Nazir did the same on the opposite side. Nobody sat or stood higher than the Kha'a, as per tradition. "You are the Khumar, and my most trusted advisor. It is your opinion that I need, not information. Are you certain?"

Nazir swallowed, trying to keep his composure despite the reprimand he'd just been given. The Kha'a of Visarya had never been a subtle man, especially not to his son. His father was a seasoned fighter: a battle-hardened, self-made Kha'a who had risen into rank from a mere commonblood family. Someone who had obliterated three rival Kha'gans and taken five more into his own. He had done it first with an unimaginably small army of two hundred men, which had grown into more than five thousand in the past twenty years, not counting those in the Kha'gans under his rule. Za'in izr Husari was a legend, a name that opened doors and passages for those who followed him, a disaster waiting to happen for those who didn't.

A nightmare for a son to live up to, he often caught himself thinking. Not bitterly though, never that. Nazir loved his father and had always found himself looking up to him, sometimes with a mixture of fear and respect, most of the time in awe.

"I am," he replied, this time with more conviction. He was going to be the next Kha'a of Visarya, the most powerful Kha'gan in the west, and he would have to learn to wield and hold power. His father had never allowed him to forget it, even in small things, and when Nazir had been too young to understand what was being asked of him and why.

The Kha'a nodded. "And Djari knows what this means?"

I believe so, were the words that came to his mind. He checked himself just in time. "She does."

He *had* told them everything—the boy and his sister—of what it all meant should they agree to do this. To be someone's sworn sword and blood was to swear an oath to serve and protect the person beyond all reasons for life or until that oath was undone. The boy would live and die under her command, regardless of the obligations to his family or his Kha'gan. The punishment for breaking such an oath was the same as a White Warrior breaking his over the location of Citara—an execution of three generations of one's bloodline. In exchange, he would be under her protection and be subjected to her judgement alone. No laws could touch him so long as he remained her sworn sword and blood, not without Djari's consent. At the same time, no laws could interfere if she chose to treat him poorly. It was, in a way, akin to throwing him back into slavery, but it was the only way he would live past tomorrow.

To Djari, however, it meant that her life would be on the line for everything the boy did. One took full responsibility for one's sworn sword—such was the cost of having one. The problem was that she was a Bharavi, a daughter of a Kha'a, while the boy was an orphan with no family for them to execute should he ever break his oath. The stakes were too unbalanced, too high for Djari and their Kha'gan as a whole. While it would be her sole decision whether or not to accept that oath, the Kha'a had to be informed. *You are insane,* was what he'd expected his father to respond. In too many ways, it was insanity.

"Has she agreed to this?" asked the Kha'a, thoughtfully.

"She is thinking," Nazir replied. "I told her she has until morning to decide." Neither of them were going to sleep tonight, for sure.

The Kha'a nodded, sipped his wine, and said, calmly, "Then we will wait for tomorrow."

"You approve?" He had expected some kind of concern, even a flat-out rejection of the idea, and had prepared quite a speech for it.

Za'in Kha'a finished the wine and placed the cup on the table. Nazir filled it dutifully and waited.

"Did you wait for my approval when you gave them that choice?" asked his father, his eyes pinning him to the ground the same way he might have done with a spear.

Nazir, aware of what was expected of him, took a breath and made himself stare right back at his father. "No."

"And you have done this knowing the stubbornness of your sister?"

Nazir swallowed at how easily his father could see it. Something had told him it must happen, regardless of his father's approval, and he had, in a way, done it to make sure it would be too late for anyone to interfere, even the Kha'a. "I have," he admitted.

"Then it doesn't matter if I approve." The Kha'a smiled and leaned back on the cushion, sipping his wine. "Djari will do exactly what she wants. That bloody girl always does, and Ravi is always on her side to accommodate. You know this as well as I do."

There was pride in his expression. There had always been pride whenever he spoke of Djari. The Kha'a loved his daughter dearly, despite the way they always clashed against each other. Stubborn, decisive, and utterly fearless, Djari was her father's daughter as much as Nazir was his mother's son. She would have made a great Khumar, if only she had been born a boy. She might still make a great Kha'a if customs allowed it.

"You're not angry with me?" He didn't do that a lot—allow his insecurity to show—especially to the man sitting across the table, who would see it as a weakness to be crushed immediately. Perhaps it was the magnitude of his decision that had given him the need to seek some kind of approval, or perhaps it was his father's strange mood this evening that made room for it.

The Kha'a leaned forward and picked up the pitcher to refill his own cup, then did the same for his son. It was the first time he had ever done so, and Nazir, aware of the significance of such a gesture, found himself drawing back the cup reluctantly. Fathers didn't do that for sons, especially when one's father was Za'in izr Husari.

"Do you think," the Kha'a said, looking at him, "that I have been hard on you because I want your obedience? Your submission?"

He took a sip of the offered wine and returned the gaze. "I think … that you want me to be a capable Kha'a."

"And what do you think is needed to be capable Kha'a?"

He thought for a time before voicing his answer. "Strength. Discipline. The courage to do the right thing."

"You would make a great Kha'a." His father nodded. "And be dead within a year."

Za'in Kha'a rose from the cushion and gestured. "Come," he said, and gestured for Nazir to follow him out of the tent.

The cold hit him as soon as they stepped outside, made worse by the persistent wind that rushed through the valley, howling as it went. Nazir tugged on his robe to shield himself from the cold. Next to him, his father stood unruffled in his worn-out gray tunic. The Kha'a of Visarya had never liked wearing his zikh, and would only put on one for the sake of ceremony when necessary. *It gave away too much,* he had said. Za'in izr Husari thought about these things; he was a fighter, a warrior before all else.

"Look at our people." He gazed at the tents scattered around the settlement. They had been coming to this site every spring and summer for three years now. In the winter they would move further south, where the ground wouldn't freeze over. "Why do you think they sleep so soundly without guards around the valley?"

Nazir knew the answer to that question. He'd always known. "Because of you." No one attacked Za'in izr Husari or his people at night, except maybe a Rashai army whose presence would be known days before they could even get close. For the Kha'gans, it was a matter of pride. If you were going to kill a legend, you'd want it known and talked about for generations to come and with honor attached. Only a coward would attack him in the dark and risk disgracing his entire bloodline.

"Because I have done the unthinkable," the Kha'a replied, his expression hard as a hammer. "I killed my Kha'a and took over the Kha'gan. Me, a commonblood, born into a family of camel herders. Now, I rule over half the western region of the White Desert. My wife was a Bharavi, my son is a trueblood oracle, and my daughter holds the fate of the entire peninsula in her hands. Some will tell you that what I've done is an inconceivable act of treason, and others will say I'm a tyrant, but that is why they fear me."

There were some who would forever call him a traitor, and nothing more, Nazir knew. There were always men and women seeking to spit on those who rose above their station, or above them. "Some people find comfort by seeking faults in what they can't achieve."

"In what they lack the courage to." His father nodded. "Nazir, I am what I am because I've never waited for anyone's approval. You do what you must for the survival of your family, your people, even if it means breaking a thousand years of tradition, even if it makes you a tyrant. That is what makes you a good leader. People will follow you for doing what they can't accomplish, for risking what they wouldn't dare, for carrying the weight they believe they can't carry."

The Kha'a turned to face him. They were of similar height now, if still much different in substance and hardness. "Our people don't need you to do what's right. They need you to do what you must to protect them. What you did today told me you are capable of foregoing my approval to do what you must." His large, calloused hand clapped Nazir twice on the cheek endearingly. "You are much wiser than I am and have been given a gift that is far beyond what I can do. I need you to become the leader that knows what needs to be done and won't hesitate when the time comes, even if it means killing me. Do you understand?"

Nazir suddenly felt the need to breathe, and no matter how many times he did, it never felt enough. There seemed to be an unlimited number of things his father could still surprise him with. After all this time, he had focused on earning his father's approval, but it was his support, his foresight as an oracle that the Kha'a had needed, not a son to fill his shoes.

Even if it means killing me. He thought about that for a time as they stood, side by side, watching the peaceful night being unravelled by the gradual onset of dawn. A subtle, golden light drew a faint line at the horizon, separating the pitch black sky now streaked with purple and blue from the white dunes that seemed to go on forever. The stars blinked out of existence one by one, like dancers in white taking turns to bow out from the stage. He could feel the warmth of the new day on his face as he stood, and that of his father standing next to him.

"Is that why you killed the last Kha'a?" Nazir asked.

His father, grinning a little wider than usual, shook his head. "No," he said. "That was for your mother."

Nazir allowed himself to smile at the rare display of amusement from the Kha'a and the love he still harbored for his Kha'ari. "She was one hell of a woman, wasn't she?"

"She was." The Kha'a fixed his eyes somewhere in the distance, his expression softening considerably. Nazir couldn't remember the last time his father had allowed him—or anyone—to see such vulnerability in him, and would alway remember that night for years to come.

They stood there for a while, sharing the quiet moment without another word spoken before he was excused. Nazir took one last look at the Kha'a before he turned to go, and once more found himself flooded with an overwhelming sense of awe for the man he called father. Za'in izr Husari was a sight to behold and remembered. A figure so large and terrifying under the stars, whose shoulders seemed capable of bearing even the weight of the sky. He often wondered if everyone felt that way about their father. If there would ever be a day when he didn't feel so small against such a man.

⁂

SUNLIGHT BLED through the line of the horizon, painting the dark sky with new bruises of red and purple as dawn approached. Za'in izr Husari closed his eyes and breathed in the cool air of the morning, thinking of the conversation he'd had. It was no small thing he had done tonight, no trivial decision he had made. And it *had* been his decision to make, despite what he had told his son.

He could insist on seeing the boy dead tomorrow. He could even have him killed tonight. No one would question his honor for having a stray—a thief—killed without trial. It would be wrong, with regards to their code of conduct, but it wouldn't be the first wrong thing he'd done, and hardly the worst. When the lives of thousands—or just your daughter's—depended on your decision, codes and laws meant very little to Za'in.

But Nazir had done this thing. His only son, who had always been fearful of his father—or at least his opinion of him—had decided to go to Djari first with a clear intention of muscling him into accepting the inevitable. It was Nazir's first rebellious act that marked him as an adult; a man who'd decided to step out of his father's shadow. One did not say no to such things, being a father, and he was a father before all else. His children didn't know that, of course. There were damages one could do to one's children for appearing too much of a parent.

Or too little of one, their mother would have said. She would recognize such a balance. Women were sensitive to these things, and Zuri *had* been one hell of a woman. She had been a loving mother, an understanding wife, a Kha'ari much loved and admired by her subjects. The light of his life.

She was also the reason behind all his life-changing decisions, even suicidal ones. Young, long-limbed, and beautiful, Zuri had been a Bharavi promised to the last Kha'a. A woman so far out of his reach that it had forced him to do the impossible—the inconceivable. She had, once again, gone far out of his reach, and this time it was beyond his ability to close that distance. He could try to kill the man who had made it so, of course. It would give him a sense of purpose, if nothing else. Vengeance was easy to hold onto and fight for.

It could also destroy a man.

Za'in was aware of the risk he was taking. He had always known of the madness that surrounded revenge, how fast it could consume and blind a perfectly wise and reasonable man. He could destroy the entire Kha'gan, or march them all to their deaths in the pursuit of vengeance if he was not careful.

But he had Nazir, his only son and a trueblood oracle. The power that boy possessed was the assurance he needed. Nazir would know when to stop him. It was why he had to be hard on his son—too hard on occasions, he knew. When the time came, Nazir would have to be able to do it without hesitation. Or with one, if necessary.

Still, he wondered if he'd revealed too much of himself tonight. There were weaknesses that came with being a parent, with loving another's life more than your own. He would have to fix that tomorrow. Nazir izr Za'in was a trueblood oracle and his Khumar. He must be these things before all else.

So must Djari, for what she was destined to be.

A shiver ran down his spine at the thought. He'd never quite come to terms with it since Nazir revealed his vision. She would bring an end to the war, he had said, but by way of salvation or destruction to their people had not been clear. He had been raising her as well as he could, to make sure it would be the former, not the latter, but parents were humans, and mistakes were sometimes made unawares.

She was like him though, his daughter; too much like him for her own good. Djari had been a strong, stubborn baby from birth. By the time she was three it had taken several guards to keep her from venturing too far away from camp. The girl, curious, adventurous, and virtually fearless, could never be kept still for any amount of time. Intelligent children were all like that, his mother had said. But intelligence was never a problem. The problem had always been her tenacity, or too much of it. Djari was a rock, an immovable object once she set her mind to a task. No amount of punishment or chastising had ever been able to discourage that girl.

Intelligence and tenacity. His skin pricked at the thought. One could create a hero or a monster from that combination. There was never much distinction between the two to begin with, if any. Djari was his daughter in this more so than anything else, and he knew how much of a monster he could become. How many times he *had* become just that. The thought scared him, and Za'in had never been afraid in his life. It would have helped if Zuri had been alive. She would have known how to deal with it.

Or would she?

He wanted to laugh at his own folly. Djari would do exactly what she wanted, the same way he would have. More than this, it was going to be her decision that would shape the fate of the peninsula, if Nazir's vision had been right. Who was he to interfere or get in the way?

It was not his role to play. There was an ache in that reality as much as there was pride. Children grew to succeed their fathers everyday, even one who was Za'in izr Husari.

I'm getting too old for this. He smiled at that thought and went back inside, pausing to rub away the pain in his knees along the way. Even the cold was getting to him now. He wondered what his wife would have said to all this, if she would find him old and brittle, and realized he already knew the answer.

'You have won yourself a Bharavi,' she had said, many times. *'Is that not enough?'*

No Stranger

"I see Djari has gotten herself a handsome new horse," Zabi iza Nyema said after taking a step back to look at Hasheem, grinning widely. Djari's grandmother and mother to the current Kha'a was a handsome woman with strong features, made stronger by the numerous lines on her face. They were laughing lines though, Hasheem could tell, and she smiled a lot with her eyes. *Nan'ya,* Djari had called her. It was how grandmothers were addressed in the White Desert. Hasheem realized he'd forgotten that word, and what his own nan'ya had looked like.

Earlier that morning, iza Nyema had insisted he be taken to her tent as soon as the oath was done. He needed some cleanup before dinner, she had said, wrinkling her nose as she sniffed his clothes. Hasheem didn't blame her. For the past four days, he had been sleeping in enough barns and stables with the animals to smell like one. Iza Nyema had ordered him to be wiped down three times to make sure he was clean enough to join the Kha'a's dining table. She'd also sent for a healer—a proper one this time—to check on his wound. He was especially thankful for that part, considering the fact that his relatively small arrow wound had turned into something a lot more substantial—thanks to Djari and her knife—on top of the burn that hadn't yet healed.

"Now, let's see what I can do with that hair," she said, sitting him down for a braiding session. All Shakshis kept their hair long and braided, at least in the White Desert. Hasheem had never braided his. In Rasharwi, it reminded people of the White Warriors and often made them nervous.

to Pain

There were also strict protocols with braiding, he'd learned. Different styles defined different status in the Kha'gan.

Status in the Kha'gan.

The thought gave him a chill. It still felt unreal to him, thinking back on the events that happened earlier this morning. He was a part of a Kha'gan now, had sworn himself to a life of service and protection to Djari, tying himself to her in ways that could be considered more binding than being someone's slave. And she had chosen to place that trust in him, knowing what it meant, despite everything that happened the night before, or the fact that he had no family for them to execute if he were to break that oath.

Or she trusted her brother. He was aware of that, too, as the better explanation.

Still, it shouldn't have been possible, or allowed, even if the Khumar himself had come up with the idea. The chiefs had said as much when Nazir brought him before the council and told them of Djari's decision. The Kha'a, whom Hasheem later learned was none other than the legendary Za'in izr Husari, simply sat quietly on the dais, arms crossed over his chest, and listened to his son with an unreadable expression. When Nazir had finished, he turned to Hasheem and asked, '*Why?*'

It was the only question asked that morning, and the tent's entire complement besides himself, consisting of ten high-ranking White Warriors and one Bharavi, had turned to look at him for an answer. A simple question, truly, but also one most difficult to address given the circumstances. They had expected him to have agreed to this in order to survive, mostly, and while it wasn't completely wrong, it would have been the wrong answer, especially for Djari, who had stood up for him and agreed to take on such a risk.

But there had been no doubt in her eyes then, not that he could see. There ought to be none in his for the sake of her, Hasheem had decided.

And so he had turned to the Kha'a and revealed the truth about the attack on his own Kha'gan seven years ago, then lied about how and where he'd survived. A merchant family in Khandoor had taken him in, he'd told them. Their caravan had been burned down four days ago on a journey across the desert by bandits. It was where and how he'd gotten the burn, and also why he'd tried to steal a horse. As to why he would take such an oath, he'd told them the truth, or at least what he believed to be true.

The Kha'a had listened, thought about it for a moment that felt like a century, and then nodded. The chiefs' protests erupted immediately after, only to be silenced just as swiftly with a few words from Za'in. Hasheem had never seen grown men—fully clad White Warriors at that—being put in their places that way.

Then again, it was Za'in izr Husari on that dais, a man whose reputation alone should suffice to silence even crying babies. This was, after all, the man who had slaughtered an entire raiding party of two-hundred Rashai soldiers with only fifty White Warriors. Sarasef of the Black Desert himself, another legend of equal proportions, was said to have avoided raiding the western Kha'gans because of izr Husari.

One didn't mess with a man who gave Black Desert mercenaries second thoughts, and Hasheem, having seen the legend himself in the flesh this morning, didn't doubt those stories. When you were trained to a certain point, you learned to measure an opponent before a fight. As far as his ability to measure such a thing went, Hasheem concluded that he would likely die in fewer than three moves crossing swords with this man.

Which was probably why the majority of that council had left the tent with no more than a discreet glare at Djari's new sworn sword. It didn't, however, change the fact that Hasheem had managed to make an enemy out of at least eight zikh-clad warriors after just one day of being there. For all he knew, his troubles had only just begun. He would have to start learning about each and every one of those chiefs soon, if he hoped to survive.

"You're going to break a lot of hearts," Iza Nyema said. She had finished the braid and was now beaming like an artist highly content with her creation. She'd given him two small braids above either side of his ears, running in parallel toward the back of his head—a symbol of someone who belonged in the upper circle of the Kha'gan. To honor Djari, he supposed. "If only I were sixteen again," she added.

"If only." He returned the smile, out of habit more than anything else. "You would have broken mine."

It wasn't far from the truth. There was an air of something warm and comforting about this woman, like a morning ray of sunshine, that would have attracted him a great deal.

Iza Nyema paused for a moment and regarded him thoughtfully. In her eyes was a different kind of light now—a sharper, colder one that suddenly put him on guard. “Be careful, boy,” she said, patting him softly on the cheek, her fingers cool against his skin. “I’ll break a lot more than that if you ever wound Djari.”

He didn’t doubt it. This was the woman who’d raised Za’in izr Husari. If there had been warmth and comfort in her, it was not without strength and ruthlessness at the core of it.

“With all due respect, iza Nyema,” he told her, “it was your granddaughter’s arrow that struck me last night and her sword that will likely end my life when the time comes. If anyone is to be wounded in this, it would be me.” He could not, in truth, imagine himself or anyone wounding Djari, or imagine her allowing herself to be wounded—not emotionally anyway. Physically...well, he had just sworn to make sure that didn’t happen, hadn’t he?

She gave him a faint smile, but one that didn’t quite reach her eyes as before. “And what,” she said, trailing her fingers down the side of his face and tilting his chin up to face her, “would you do if she were to wound you? Are you the kind who fights back, or one that runs?”

It was then that Hasheem came to understand the true reason why he had been brought to her tent. Zabi iza Nyema, old and frail as she was, was not without venom. He was being measured, tested, and subtly warned all in one sitting.

“I am no stranger to pain,” he told her. “Whether I fight or flee, it will not be the cause.” Pain had never been a factor for him. He was used to being wounded, abused, and thrown into a hopeless situation with nowhere to run. Those things had never dictated his choices to live or die in Rasharwi. Or to kill.

“Then what would?” she asked, green eyes matching those of her son narrowing sharply. “Your pride? Your integrity? The love of your land? What *do* you want, Hasheem?”

What did he want? It was a good question, and one he’d never asked himself. Hasheem considered himself to be proud, but never to the point of being willing to live or die for pride. Integrity was something foreign to him—one couldn't survive in Rasharwi holding on to anything resembling that. He had no love for his land, couldn't even remember much of it, and even vengeance had not been on his mind when he decided to survive no matter what the cost.

It had been none of those things that forced him to endure all the pain and the pride-swallowing events of his life. There had, however, and now that he thought of it, always been a small yearning, a faint flicker of light that seemed to have guided him through those ordeals. He realized then that even after all this time, he was always looking for something, always trying to survive to reach somewhere. A place, perhaps, where there would be no more need or desire to run. He looked up at her then, surprised at the answer he'd discovered just now. "To find ... my place in the world."

"And where," asked iza Nyema, "is your place in the world?"

There was a correct answer to that, one he wasn't supposed to stop and think before giving her. Considering the oath he'd just taken, to reply with anything else would have been wrong. But it wasn't what she wanted from him, not a grandmother who loved her grandchild. "I can't answer that," he told her. "Not right now."

She smiled again, and this time it did reach her eyes. "Good," she said. "I would have put something in your tea if you'd said what you were expected to say. Come. We must be at the table before the Kha'a."

"I don't need to cage a beast.
I need to find a way to use it."

My Favorite Son

The city of Rasharwi came alive at night, to the sound of bells from the four sanctuaries of Rashar. It began at sunset with the silver bell at the temple of Sabha to the west of the city, followed by the southern sanctuary of Suma, and then the northern bell tower at Suri before the golden, most elaborately ornate bell of Sangi Sanctuary east of the city joined the procession, ringing above the lesser three to finish announcing the departure of the sun god for the day. The four bells would be rung simultaneously until the last light disappeared, during which time the residents of Rasharwi would illuminate their streets and homes in preparation for the end of day prayer. In the morning, the ritual would begin again, starting at Sangi, to announce the return of Rashar at sunrise.

At the heart of the city, protected by the four strongholds of Sangi, Suma, Suri, and Sabha, stood the Black Tower of Rasharwi. The iconic royal residence of the Salar owed its name to the natural mountain of obsidian out of which rooms and halls had been carved. Standing twice as high above all other structures in the city, the intimidating beauty of the Black Tower had been considered one of the most famous and distinguished landmarks of the continent for centuries. It was often said among travelers and pilgrims alike that life in the Salasar was not complete until one witnessed the majesty of the Black Tower and prayed to the sounds of the four great bells of Rasharwi. It was the strength of the continent, the power around which all things rotated, the place where histories were made and the fates of men were decided. The center of the universe, in a sense, for those who resided in the Salasar.

At the very peak of the Tower, in a chamber carved on the very edge of a cliff to accommodate an unobstructed view stretching far beyond the walls of Sabha toward the glowing ivory mountains of the White Desert, stood the man who held the power over the rise and fall of cities and empires. The tall, straight-backed, square-shouldered man in his mid-forties showed no signs of age beyond the streaks of gray among his otherwise coal-black hair and the fine lines that seemed to have added more wisdom than years to the hard features of his face. Standing dangerously near the end of the balcony with nothing between him and the plunging depths below, the Salar of Rasharwi appeared to have been carved out of a rock—a solid statue that could not be moved or swayed by the wind that rushed through the opening. His eyes, deep set and a piercing shade of blue, focused somewhere in the far distance as the last light of Rashar began to fade from the horizon and the city lit up in its place down below.

Jarem izr Sa'id, commander in chief of the royal army and right hand man of the Salar, tugged lightly on his fur-lined robe as he stood in front of the desk, waiting to be acknowledged. Depending on his mood and what occupied his mind, the paralyzing silence the Salar required before acknowledging the subjects he had summoned could last anywhere from a few breaths to the time it took one to climb the Black Tower on foot. Clarity of thoughts was important when one ruled an empire, and ideas were too precious to be destroyed by meaningless interruptions. Cities had been built or sacked from these moments of silence, and men had been thrown, understandably, off that open balcony for breaking them.

"I'm listening, Jarem." The command had been smooth and lacking emotion. As always, he didn't turn from the balcony. One did not usually get to observe his expressions during report sessions, not until decisions had been firmly made, and by then he would have already finished putting aside all emotions relating to it.

Jarem took a step forward, sketched a bow, and began the ritual of reporting the important events that occurred in the Salar's absence. These visits to the four strongholds and the provinces beyond them usually lasted four to six weeks at a time, longer if there were problems to be dealt with, during which time Jarem would be put in charge of overseeing Rasharwi, making sure everything was in order, and that his projects progressed as planned. Upon the Salar's return, Jarem would be summoned to make sure he was up to date with the information that would allow him to seamlessly resume command.

It was the first thing the Salar did when he returned to the Tower, on the same day, and before any reception or activities of leisure would commence. He would be here, still in his dust-covered riding tunic, as he was now, to listen to Jarem's long and detailed report and store every word into memory. Salar Muradi was always working, thinking of solutions to things, or planning something with that incredible mind. Jarem often considered his own discipline and work ethic to be spotless, but compared to his Salar, his qualities seemed very small.

He hasn't changed at all, Jarem thought, watching the figure standing on the balcony with hands behind his back, casting a large, almost unearthly shadow on the stone floor. The boy he'd brought back from the dungeons of Sabha more than thirty years ago had looked like this when he arrived back at court. The young prince, still in his prison garment, hair long and wildly tangled, face and hands filthy with mud and gravel from labor, had stood exactly this way looking up at the Black Tower, as if he'd owned the place and had just returned home from a long absence. *'I want to see,'* he'd said, eyes gleaming like a blade freshly honed as he looked up at the balcony he was standing on now, *'what it looks like from up there.'*

It hadn't taken long for Jarem to decide in whose hands he wanted to lay his life and loyalty. From then, he and Ghaul—the prince's cellmate who'd been taken out of Sabha with him—had worked tirelessly to pave the way to the throne for the man who had become the Salar of Rasharwi.

"Anything else?" asked the Salar when he'd finished his recitation, still looking out somewhere toward the mountain.

Jarem grimaced at a thought that occurred to him, but decided to investigate a little more before voicing it. "No, my lord."

The Salar's hard, unreadable face turned to look over his shoulder. "You hesitated."

Jarem swallowed at the way those eyes studied him, as if to catch a secret he might let slip. It stung a little. Three decades of being by the Salar's side and he was still considered a liability. Jarem knew he was trusted only as far as his competence went. His loyalty had been tested again, and again, and again, and was still being tested now. But Jarem also knew it had been his disinclination to trust even those closest to him that had made Salar Muradi so indestructible. A sense of pride swelled in him at that thought. He was a soldier more than anything else he had become, and there was no honor greater than being able to serve a man like his Salar.

"I have yet to verify the facts," Jarem said, and saw the approval in those eyes.

"Give me the rumor, then." The Salar turned to fill his goblet with the red Khandoor wine he'd brought back and gestured for Jarem to do the same.

Jarem offered a slight bow and poured himself one. "There's been an assassination attempt on Sarasef."

The Salar grinned and sipped his wine. "So, Saracen has decided to make a move?"

"Apparently. The Rishi is now split between the two brothers, or so I've heard, but I have yet to verify the details regarding the alliance on either side."

The two brothers had been at odds for years, even before Sarasef took control of the Rishi—the Black Desert mercenaries currently working with the Salasar. The fact that the younger brother had been chosen by their father as the new grand chief had created the conflict, and both Jarem and the Salar had been observing where it would lead to for some time. "This may be a good time to take the Black Desert if you wish to do so."

They had, after all, been paying a heavy sum to these mercenaries who ruled the outskirts of the Black Desert surrounding Rasharwi every year for the past decade. The mercenaries had been making a living from independently raiding Shakshi settlements and merchant caravans for as long as they existed. They shared an alliance with no one—or anyone willing to pay the price. The Salar, having seen an opportunity to increase the tension in the White Desert without sending his own soldiers to their deaths, had opted to support their cause by offering a ridiculously high price on raided goods and prisoners taken by them. In return, the Rishi stayed clear of royal properties and citizens of Rasharwi, while the Salar turned a blind eye to their crimes elsewhere. Jarem had never liked the idea of paying more than market price to these bloodsucking mercenaries, and had always found them too much of a threat to be left unconquered. It would have been better, he'd always thought, to take the region and disband the tribe altogether—and now, with their internal conflict, it would be a good time to do so.

"What would I do with the Black Desert?" The Salar shook his head, smiling. "It's nothing but a useless, barren land full of rocks and vultures." He swirled the wine in his hand, sniffing the aroma before taking a sip. "The only valuable thing that damned place produces is its mercenaries, who are doing a fine job raiding the Shakshis for us."

"At a price." A ridiculous price for that matter.

"Everything has a price, Jarem. Raids cost money, whether it's carried out by our soldiers or by hired help."

"They do, my lord. But perhaps less of one if we own them?"

The Salar chuckled. "And force the Rishi to fight for our cause? You might as well try to tame a grown eagle while at it. They are what they are because they operate to serve their own interests. I don't need to cage a beast. I need to find a way to use it."

Jarem had to admit the Salar had a point. The Rishi had worked independently for centuries, its warriors bound together less by loyalty to their grand chief and more for the promise of continuing wealth. In many ways, they weren't so different from the Shakshis, except they were more of an unruly brotherhood than a Kha'gan, whose strict rules and well-defined social structures formed a highly functional society. Sarasef and his tribes would be most difficult to subjugate without crushing them altogether, which would be considered, as the Salar had put it, killing a highly valuable beast. Then again, the only way to utilize it... "You want to bind them somehow to our cause," he said, trying to catch up with the brilliant mind behind those sharp eyes.

The Salar nodded. "We need to form a long-term alliance with the Rishi, creating a profitable relationship for both parties, and convince them that it is in their best interest to do what we need done. This conflict is the perfect opportunity to interfere."

It *was* the perfect opportunity, Jarem thought. They could lend their support to one of the brothers and tie the grand chief to the Salasar. "Are we backing Sarasef or Saracen?"

"Saracen is an arrogant, ignorant fool. He would never last more than a year leading them."

Jarem smiled and sipped his wine. His Salar had always been a good judge of character, even when the encounter had been brief. "So we offer Sarasef what he needs to deal with his brother, but how do we make sure he won't brush us aside the moment he secures his leadership?" They were, after all, thieves and murderers who were as likely to stab their benefactors in the back as they were willing to trade with the Salasar.

"We can give him an army, on the condition that it stays to ensure the alliance afterwards."

That they could do, Jarem thought. A large enough army stationed near their lair would make Sarasef think twice before breaking a contract. Only... "Sarasef will need some kind of assurance that the army won't attack them from the inside." No Rashai soldiers had ever been allowed to enter Rishi territory. It was going to take a figure of some importance held as a hostage to make Sarasef even consider it. "We could offer him a wife. One of the princesses, perhaps?" Marriage always worked to strengthen an alliance, and from what they knew, Sarasef was an intelligent, logical man who used his head as much as his blade.

The Salar shook his head, his expression thoughtful. "Sidra and Majira are not yet ten. They won't last in the Black Desert, and Sarasef will never consent to a marriage contract on paper." He took another sip of his wine. "We *can* send a prince to be fostered. How old are Raoul and Nareen now?"

"Fourteen and fifteen, my lord," Jarem replied. "You approved their marriage to the daughters of the governors of Khandoor and Cakora last year. It may create some tension if you send them." The alliance between the provinces and Rasharwi needed constant nurturing. They could deal with one or two uprisings at a time, but more would be a problem. Jarem didn't think anyone would raise an army against the Salasar, not while

Salar Muradi ruled, but he preferred to act in precaution rather than find solutions to active problems, and had taken steps to bind these provinces to them long ago by suggesting the right marriages to the Salar, including his own.

"And Azram is not an option." The Salar frowned.

"Not without a protest from the Salahari, which will create a problem with Samarra." The Salar's official wife may not hold much power in the Tower, but her father, the governor of Samarra, was one of the most powerful figures in the peninsula they wanted to keep on their side. To send a grandson he'd been working to put on the throne to be held hostage would be close to lighting a fire in a room full of hay.

"That's all the sons I have?"

Jarem shifted his weight at the answer that suddenly came to mind. It would need to be said, and would solve all the problems at hand, but it revolved around something that had been deemed sensitive and untouchable for a long time. It was, however, his job to give his Salar the best possible advice, Jarem thought, before deciding to risk it. "There is Prince Lasura, my lord."

The half-blood prince was their perfect solution. He may be half a Shakshi, but he was a son nonetheless, and also one with no use whatsoever otherwise. No governor would marry his daughter to a prince of Shakshi blood, and Lasura was generally excluded from holding any position of power in the Salasar. Prince Lasura was expendable, as far as Jarem was concerned. The only problem was that the Salar seemed to be favoring this son as much as he favored the mother. Seemed to, because no one would claim to know the truth in his head unless they were willing to risk theirs being hacked off.

The silence that ensued told him he'd hit a nerve. Jarem felt a bead of sweat trickling down the side of his forehead and wondered if he should remove the evidence of his anxiety. He suddenly recalled the sound the last captain of the royal guard had made on his way over the balcony after having suggested that the Salar's lowly Shakshi wife be placed in a different wing of the Tower as befitted her status. Then again, that had been a different matter involving a quarrel between royal wives in the Tower. This was a matter of state. The Salar would understand, wouldn't he?

"Lasura is a half-blood," the Salar said, turning back to the balcony at an angle that made it impossible for Jarem to observe his expression. "He will not hold much value as a hostage."

Jarem had expected this and knew it might be true. Still, it was worth a shot. "He is also known as the favorite son by the favorite wife of the Salar. There's value in this."

"Is he now?" The tone was light and considerably thin.

"He's the only one you've taken with you on your hunting trips, my lord, and you've rarely summoned any other wife but Lady Zahara for the past two decades. The other princes and their mothers are beginning to feel it and have made several attempts to win the prince over to their side. His influence is growing and may upset the balance in the Tower." He paused and drew a breath, knowing he was on dangerous ground here. "I'd rather not say this, but..."

"You think they're my weakness."

Jarem swallowed. "I doubt they are," he said, and paused a little to arrange his next sentence. "But it would be better that no one else draws such a conclusion."

Sending the prince to Sarasef would not only show them otherwise, it would remove a big piece of interference from the Tower, weaken the power the Salar's Shakshi wife held, and at the same time keep her in check by separating mother and son. It would send a strong message: that the Salar had no favorites, at least not one so important that he couldn't sacrifice them for the greater good.

"Unless, of course, that is your intention," Jarem added. It could be. Salar Muradi rarely did things without a reason. For all the time Jarem had served him, he'd never allowed emotions to cloud his judgement. Jarem would hate to think a mother and a son would be able to accomplish that now, and hoped it had been a part of some plan that had yet to be revealed to him.

The Salar turned back to face him, deep blue eyes studying his face closely. "And what do you think is my intention, Jarem?"

Jarem felt the hair on the back of his neck stand at the question. One of the things Salar Muradi didn't forgive was people making assumptions, trying to read his thoughts and manipulate him to their advantage. It wasn't the first time Jarem had been tested, but he would be lying if he said he wasn't nervous every time it happened. "I am still waiting for you to tell me, my lord, because I can't seem to see it."

A hint of a smile that appeared on the Salar's lips told Jarem he'd passed the test.

"I will think about it. If he makes it down the mountain."

"He'll make it." Jarem smiled as well. "I'm so sure, in fact, that I would suggest delaying the reception until he returns with the birds to give him a big entrance. Sarasef may turn down a half-blood son, but he won't turn down one bearing the gift of a young spotted eagle." For some reason, he had a feeling it would take a lot more than falling off a cliff to kill the Prince, and definitely more to kill his mother.

"I didn't know you had so much faith in him."

"He reminds me of a boy I met decades ago. Tough as a pair of old boots, that one," Jarem replied in his most serious tone.

"Is that so?" The Salar raised a brow. "Is he still around, I wonder?"

"Very much so, my lord," he said, raising the goblet in his hand in a salute. "I believe he will be for a long time yet."

A rare grin graced the handsome face that had altered little with time. Every once in a while, Jarem would see a glimpse of that carefree boy in the man upon whose shoulders the fate of the peninsula now rested.

"Go ahead and delay the reception. Find di Amarra. I will have a talk with him on this when Lasura returns."

"Di Amarra, my lord? You want him to accompany the prince?" Jarem didn't like that one bit. Deo di Amarra might be the Tower's most valuable advisor and strategist, but he could also be considered the most dangerous to utilize where security of the Salasar was concerned. The man had climbed his way up from a blacksmith's workshop by the age of twenty-four, established his own house and a highly successful chain of businesses with connections in every province, and made it to the Salar's inner circle all in the single decade since he'd first set foot in the Tower. Competence in one's men could make a ruler, but an excess of it, as with all things, could break one. You couldn't pet a deadly snake and disregard its venom, and di Amarra happened to be one of the deadliest snakes in the Salasar.

"Sarasef will kill both Lasura and whomever I send with him if he turns down the offer, or he will take them hostage. As would I." The Salar sipped his wine and turned back to the balcony, fixing his eyes somewhere in the distance. "If there is one man who can negotiate his way out of certain death, it's Deo di Amarra."

It was true, Jarem realized only then. An offered hand to a proud man could be considered an insult. Not only that, but there was also a chance of them being held and used as leverage. This was an ambitious move with its own risks attached, and he had to admit there was no better candidate to propose such an alliance than di Amarra.

"For that, I am certain he can." He gave his Salar a slight bow. "I will make sure he arrives the moment the prince returns. Will you require anything else, my lord?"

"That will be all, Jarem." Salar Muradi waved his free hand to dismiss him. "But do send for my so-called favorite wife while I wait for my favorite son."

The tone was full of mockery, of course. The Salar would never truly admit to having favorites.

"Speaking of wives," Jarem said as he placed the emptied goblet back on the table, "may I suggest you summon Lady Amelia first, my lord? Her father has been inquiring of late as to when he should be expecting a grandson. I believe you have yet to summon her since the night of your wedding."

The Salar's hand that held the goblet paused just before it reached his lips. He asked, in an expression that was more surprised than irritated, "You will tell me now which wife to bed first and when?"

"Only when it concerns matters of state, my lord. That is my job." It was in his job description as an advisor, of course. Marriage and extension of one's bloodline were matters of state for any ruling monarch. "Also, we are, as you can see, a little short of princes and princesses."

"And so I am expected to breed," said the Salar. "How very thoughtful of you."

"A son from a young wife every once in a while sends a good message to your enemies, my lord."

"Does it now?" The Salar smiled. "And what message would that be?"

"That neither your appetite nor your hunger have been satiated," Jarem replied. "A man who no longer conquers women conquers no man. They need to know you are still the man who defeated them and that you will do so again, and again, and again should the need ever arise, my lord."

A small chuckle rose from his throat. "Well, then, send her up. I'll give her a son," the Salar said. "Send for Zahara as well. I doubt one will be enough for my hunger or my appetite, when you put it that way."

An Extension of You

The Kha'a's dining tent offered enough space to hold twenty men, its furnishing offering sedated elegance, yet also extravagance in the finer details—a contrast to the Kha'a's appearance that told Hasheem someone else had chosen the pieces. At its center, a low-legged wooden table lined with a strip of gold and silver-bordered fabric could easily hold twelve guests, but had been set for six. One large, equally handsome embroidered cushion sat waiting at one end of the table for the Kha'a, who had yet to appear. Immediately to its left sat Nazir, and then Djari. Iza Nyema took the place opposite her granddaughter and left the place immediately to the right of the Kha'a empty—presumably for the Kha'ari, whom he had yet to meet.

His place was beside Djari, iza Nyema had explained. It was to be so from now on, everywhere she went, at any time. He would take a tent next

You are an extension of me,
my own flesh and blood.
That is where you now belong in my life.

to hers, attend the same classes, and guard her during all activities unless she deliberately excused his presence. Nighttime would be an exception, but any private activity—iza Nyema had stressed—was to happen in his tent, where he could still guard her effectively, and nowhere else. Only he should know that the walls didn't keep in sound very well, she'd added with a grin. He'd smiled at that and told her he didn't think he would be needing that information anytime soon.

Nazir looked up at him when he entered, raised his brows in surprise, and then gave him an approving nod. The serving girl, a dark-haired, hazel-eyed commonblood with freckles on her nose blushed all the way to her ears when he offered her a smile. Djari simply looked and acknowledged his presence, apparently unimpressed with his cleanliness or the change of clothing. She smiled very little, he'd come to notice, and always carried herself like an adult despite her age. A fifteen-year-old girl—he'd found out from iza Nyema—who looked like she had the weight of the world on her shoulders. He wondered if all Bharavis were that way.

The Kha'a entered the tent some time later, alone. He had anticipated the Kha'ari to have arrived before or at the same time, had been looking forward to seeing the woman who had raised Djari and Nazir. The seat, however, remained empty while the meal was served, despite the place being set up to the last silverware. From time to time, he would see Djari glance at the empty plate and then look away from the table, as if it reminded her of an unwelcome memory.

They spoke of small things and he listened quietly, taking care to not show too much interest except when asked a question. Surprisingly, there

had been no questions asked about his past, and he wondered if Nazir had already told them the truth. If he had, none of them seemed to mind. Except maybe Djari. She sat through the meal without a word spoken, picking at her food absentmindedly and barely eating. He couldn't tell if something else was disturbing her or if she was displeased with him. She was difficult to read, and he considered himself highly adept at reading people.

"I assume you have been trained to fight?" The Kha'a took a sip of his wine and glanced briefly at his son.

Have I been trained? Hasheem thought. Assassins were taught to kill swiftly, discreetly, preferably from a distance. Fighting an accomplished warrior head on, fair and square, would be another story. It would have to be explained carefully.

"I can use a sword, and a dagger." *And all kinds of cutlery, a piece of jewelry, a quill, a scarf, his bare hands, and poisons.* He decided to omit all that from the answer, including the piece of paper he'd had to use once. "I am...adequate with a bow." Compared to what Djari could do, adequate was considered the correct word for his own skill, if not poor.

"And the rest?" asked the Kha'a. "How good are you?"

How good was he? He was Deo di Amarra's gold ring assassin. Back in Rasharwi, that was as high as one could go in status where deadliness was concerned. In front of Za'in izr Husari... "I'm not sure," he concluded. If a fifteen-year-old girl could shoot like that, to these people, he could be average at best.

"A modest answer," the Kha'a said, with an approving nod. "We'll find out tomorrow. You will train with Nazir, and we'll get you some weapons to carry."

Djari shifted uncomfortably at that. She parted her lips to speak—to protest if he had to guess—and then pressed them back together.

"I will not be training with Djari?" He was treading on dangerous ground, questioning the decision of a Kha'a. Then again, as the only one in the Kha'gan who could not be executed even by the Kha'a without Djari's consent, he might as well use the privilege. Still, it was wise to not make an enemy out of powerful men, and boundaries must always be carefully observed to survive in any situation.

Nazir raised a brow and looked at his father. Izr Husari regarded him for a moment and sipped his wine before he replied, "Djari's training in combat has been limited, and she will no longer need them now that she has a sworn sword."

Djari, this time, held nothing back. "You can't take away my training. Not for this." The tone she used was what he would consider a crossing of boundaries, even for a Bharavi.

Her nan'ya winced at that, and Nazir looked like he'd suddenly developed a headache.

Za'in izr Husari was a big man by any standard, and when he drew himself up to square his shoulders, he seemed twice as large. "The next time you use that tone with me," he said crisply, the long, prominent scar on the left side of his cheek gleaming like a blade in the candlelight, "I will have your tongue removed and marry you to a Khumar who doesn't need his wife to speak. I am waiting," he took a sip of his wine and placed it down on the table, "for an apology."

It wasn't about to come easily, Hasheem thought, looking at the young girl sitting next to him who seemed to have every intention to make Za'in izr Husari wait. She met her father's gaze with a mixture of rage and hurt in her eyes, chest heaving from trying to control her emotions. He glanced down at her hands, saw them clench tight around her dress, and contemplated whether it would have been appropriate to offer her some comfort. Before he could decide, Nazir reached for her hand and squeezed it discreetly under the table. She closed her eyes then, drew a long breath and released it before she gave her father what was due. "Forgive me," Djari said, staring at the food she had barely touched, not at her father this time. "It won't happen again."

The Kha'a nodded, his shoulders relaxing the moment she apologized. Hasheem wondered if Djari had noticed the tension, and if Za'in had already chosen which role he would prioritize between a father and a Kha'a if the situation called for it. There was always a price to power, as with everything else.

"You engaged an intruder despite my orders to stand down and call for guards in the face of danger," her father began in the tone one would expect from a judge to an accused prisoner. "You deliberately disobeyed me by pursuing him beyond the boundaries of our camp, where you have been forbidden to venture. Your training has made you arrogant and foolish. It will be taken away until you learn your place and understand your responsibility. Do you find my judgment unfair?"

Djari listened quietly, staring at a spot on her plate. Might have burned a hole in it if she could. "No," she replied, not quite defiant, but definitely not as submissive as she should have sounded.

"You are a Bharavi; your life is not yours to do with as you please. It is the property of the Kha'gan, me, and the Khumar you will marry. I expect you to remember this and act accordingly. Do I make myself clear?"

She mumbled a response, eyes still fixed on the table. They were dry, despite being visibly red.

"You will soon be the Kha'ari of a Kha'gan," snapped izr Husari, his voice cutting through the silence like a whip. "Sit up straight and act like one. Do you understand?"

Djari straightened, raised her chin almost in spite, looked straight into her father's eyes, and replied, "I understand, Za'in Kha'a."

A retort of sorts, deciding to address her father by name and title. In many ways, Hasheem could see where it all came from. For someone born into the ruling family, Djari had clearly been raised to see it more as a burden than a privilege. She was not being allowed much room—if any at all—for being young and naive or for freedom. A contrast to the overprivileged women at court in Rasharwi.

Not a Kha'gan to be defeated easily, Hasheem thought, if the sons and daughters of the Visarya had all been raised this way. He was beginning to understand a little more now as to why the White Desert had never been conquered, just watching the two of them that night.

Three, he corrected himself, taking another glance at Nazir, who had been sitting there observing them quietly, thinking—or seeing—something he wasn't about to disclose. Perhaps also working to rearrange everyone's lives to his liking ten—even twenty—years in advance with his gift. One would have to be unreasonably brave or unfathomably stupid to not be afraid of Nazir. And he *was* afraid of the oracle, perhaps even more than the Kha'a.

"You are dismissed," said the Kha'a to his daughter. "And for the last time, Djari, get rid of the horse."

Djari stood quickly, decided to give her father no response, and left the tent. On the table, her food was left nearly untouched. It was the only mutual decision made by both of them that night—Djari's to not finish her dinner and the Kha'a's to starve her for it. A clash of stone and metal, Hasheem thought, wondering how long this had been going on.

"Since her mother passed away," iza Nyama explained when he asked the question later that night. He'd also found out the empty seat *had* been for the Kha'ari, who had been killed in a raid years ago, deliberately set up and left empty at every meal as per instructions of the Kha'a. A reminder of what they'd lost, she added.

A reason for revenge was what it truly was, if one were observant enough.

Revenge would mean a fight against the Salasar, against Salar Muradi. A fight that would take every Kha'gan to unite if they were to attack Rasharwi, or an army large enough to draw the Salar himself to lead his force into the desert. It had happened before in the Vilarhiti, and the mass slaughter that followed was still talked about in bars and taverns. Salar Muradi was a legend in his own right. A hard, unforgiving man, who knew how to fight, *to win*. For the Kha'a to exact his revenge would take a force of epic proportions, and the command of a leader with equal capabilities.

A force of epic proportions brought together by Za'in izr Husari, Hasheem thought, *backed by a trueblood oracle, and led by a girl who was born to end the war.*

It was possible, he realized, with a shiver running down his spine as he walked back to his tent afterward, that he had just become a part of something much larger than he'd ever imagined. He could see himself fighting by her side, cutting down Rashai soldiers in battle, even dying doing so, and immediately knew it would feel more right than anything he'd ever done in his life.

What do you want? Iza Nyema had asked earlier that afternoon.

The answer was becoming clearer to him now, even if he still couldn't reply with certainty. There was a sense of purpose, a yearning much stronger than survival that was taking over his life at that precise moment. Something was changing. He could feel it in his bones, in the tightness of his chest, in the blood that was rushing through his veins and the heat it left behind.

A cool breeze brushed softly against his cheek and brought with it the faint, cool scent of sage and mint that grew around the valley. He paused to look at where he was—something he hadn't done since he'd arrived. The night was clearer then, and even with the full moon, the stars could be seen far across the desert. He noticed for the first time the golden, smooth-as-silk dunes that seemed to stretch far beyond the horizon, the large, oddly-shaped gleaming white rocks that gave the White Desert its name, and the curved natural wall of alabaster that loomed over and around the campsite. Somewhere in the distance, a woman was singing a lullaby to lull the little ones to sleep. She seemed to have been singing for some time, only he hadn't been paying enough attention to hear it.

It was achingly beautiful, in the way that it shouldn't have been possible for him to have missed it so completely. There had also been, he now remembered, so many beautiful things in Rasharwi he'd never stopped to appreciate. Everything seemed to have rushed by him in a blur for the past seven years he'd been struggling to survive, and somewhere along the way he seemed to have lost focus on where he was heading. That night, he could see it all again with startling clarity—where he had been, where he was, and the choices that had been laid out before him. For the first time in a very long time, he knew for certain the path he wanted to take, where he wanted to go, and he was trembling at the anticipation of what tomorrow might bring.

Something moved in the distance. He looked and saw Djari walking alone in the dark, her near-silver hair tossed and tousled by the wind that rushed through the valley. She appeared to be coming back from somewhere to her tent, and stopped for a moment when she saw him before resuming her steps. There was a blade in her hand, the same one she'd assaulted him with. It was dripping with the same blood that stained the entire right side of her white tunic. Her eyes, made unnatural and otherworldly by the moonlight, were glowing a frightening shade of gold.

He was beginning to understand, then, why Bharavis and oracles were believed to be direct descendents of the moon goddess Ravi. The Shakshis sorted and ranked their own kind by how closely one's features resembled that of oracles and Bharavis—the truebloods, as they called them. Hasheem's golden-brown hair and grey eyes had given him the status of a pureblood from birth, the kind more likely to produce another Bharavi or oracle than the mixedblood or the commonblood Shakshis when the right match was made. Hasheem had always thought it to be superstition, and considering that Za'in izr Husari—a commonblood by appearance—had produced both a Bharavi and an oracle, he was willing to bet on it being a myth. Djari did, however, under that silvery light of the full moon, look like someone not of this world.

She paused when they were close enough to speak. He could see the smear of blood on her cheek and its crimson stains on her hair from where he was standing. Hasheem remembered then that the Kha'a had mentioned the killing of her horse. It would have been her first time ending a life, if he remembered correctly from their conversation.

"Will it always be this hard?" Djari asked. There was a tightness in her voice, an unsteadiness to her breaths. Her eyes, he noticed, were dry and startlingly clear.

Would killing always be hard? Some question to ask an assassin. The first time was always the hardest. It ended more things than the life taken. The next time only added to it, and so would the next, and the next, and the next. He could call it a kindness to comfort her with lies, but for who she was, what she was destined to be, the fate of the entire desert might depend on the answer he gave her tonight. A terrifying thought, that, a power he had never desired, a task he must try to do right. "Harder," he replied, "if you allow it to be."

"And if I don't," she asked breathlessly, "allow it to be?"

"Then it gets easier over time."

Djari looked down at her hands—stained completely by the blood of her horse—and then back at him. "Do I want it to be easy?"

A question he was both glad and sad to hear. "Enough to do what you have to," he said. "Never to the point of being effortless." The time would come when she would have to end—or be responsible for ending—thousands more lives, and not just those of her enemies if her brother had been right. Only the arrogant or the naive would see the grandeur of war and not its carnage. She would have to come to terms with hard decisions and seeing herself as a monster from time to time. She would have to kill, in cold blood, and be able to sleep through the night to kill again. She would also have to draw a line, or risk becoming the tyrant she wished to defeat.

Not an easy burden to carry, even for a grown man, or one as experienced and hardened as her father. A burden he could share as her sworn sword and blood.

"I could have put down the horse," he said as mildly as he could. "If you had told me to."

Djari's expression hardened. "If I had told you to?"

The sharpness in her tone gave him the urge to defend his proposition. "I swore to serve and protect you this morning. My life is yours by right to command." He had, after all, agreed to tie himself to her, to put the chains back on his wrists and ankles. It had been a choice he made without regrets, and she should know he was content with his decision.

"And what does that make you?" she asked. "My slave?"

His turn to frown. "I have agreed to this willingly. There is a difference."

"There isn't." Djari's voice cracked like a whip—like her father's. "You are no more than my slave if your life is my right to command, whether or not it was offered willingly. I am no Rashai. We do not take slaves in the White Desert or find it flattering to be offered such service. What have I done for you to find me so lacking in courage, in honor, to believe that I am capable of accepting such things?"

"I didn't..." he stammered at this most unexpected response, trying to figure out where and how he had offended her.

"I didn't take you in this morning to have your life at *my* command." Djari stepped forward, placing her foot down as deliberately as her words. "I took you in for your skills, your ability, your sword. I need you to be what I am not, to be my eyes and ears when I can't see, to fight my enemies and stop me when I cross the line. I need a weapon to win this war and an ally I can trust, not a slave or a pack horse." She drew a breath, took her time as if to find calm, and succeeded. He had a feeling she succeeded in everything she tried. "You are an extension of me, my own flesh and blood. That is where you now belong in my life and what you have sworn to be. Do you understand?"

Something came down inside of him at that moment. It shattered and crumbled, revealing a red, raw place no one had been allowed to enter or touch. In his mind was an image of her standing among the rubble she'd created, claiming space, settling down, planting a presence as permanent as the damage she'd caused.

My own flesh and blood. Somewhere, someone had said that to him. He remembered it now, along with the hand that stroked his hair, and the kiss on his forehead that followed. There was a time when he was a part of something, when he had a place to call home, when he wasn't alone in the world. For a long time he'd forced himself to forget it ever existed, convinced himself that it would never be whole again. And Djari had come into his life and said what she'd said, giving him the only thing he'd needed and looked for: a place to belong.

A suffocating tightness wrapped around his heart as he thought of a response. He had an urge to kneel, to offer her his heart, his life, everything he still had that was worth giving. But Djari would take none of it—he knew that now—not in the way he was prepared to give. She was bigger than that.

'I think that I have survived to do exactly this,' had been his answer to the Kha'a that morning, when he had been asked why he would agree to be her sworn sword. It was clear to him now, watching her that night, feeling her presence slowly filling every dark and empty corner of his life, that this was where he was supposed to be, what he had survived to do all along. He had a vision then, of the arrow she'd let loose the other night, and realized, belatedly, that it had never missed his heart.

"Then let me be an extension of you," he said breathlessly, without thought, without consideration of consequences. "Take me with you to battle so I can be your weapon and your shield. Allow me to be the monster you can't become when you have to be. Next time let me kill the horse, or we do it together, you and I. Don't do this alone." He held out a hand, realized it was trembling, and didn't care.

She looked at the offered hand, drew an unsteady breath and then answered his gaze with an expression that might have matched his own had he been able to see. "Together?" Djari asked, uncertainty in her voice. She seemed to be, Hasheem thought, as overwhelmed by all the events of that day as he was.

"Together," he replied.

She stilled for a time and then reached out with her hand. Small fingers, roughened by the bow, true as the arrow she had meant to pierce his heart, wrapped around his so unwaveringly as they stood face to face, joined in an understanding that was to be his and hers alone. Their fates were tied now, more permanently than the oath he'd taken that morning, than what it demanded them to be.

You are an extension of me, my own flesh and blood. That is where you now belong in my life.

Hasheem would not realize until later on, despite the fullness of his heart that night, that there would be a time when such a place he'd been given in her life would not be enough.

The Summons

There was a crease on her dress. Zahara grimaced as she smoothed it out quickly. She must have been curling her hand around it when she watched him approach the Tower. Such a detail would not be missed. She knew this from experience and always made certain there would be none present when she was summoned. He enjoyed being able to read her as much as she dreaded being read by him. The man whose door she was standing before enjoyed many things, despite the grimness he displayed to the world at large. One had to be close enough to see it, or be the object of his entertainment to understand.

Next to her, Amelia was busy doing the opposite. Just shy of eighteen years old, the youngest daughter of Zubin izr Mafouz, Rasharwi's most influential banker, had both her hands wound tight around the silk of her priceless crimson dress. Her expression was a strange mixture of stress, anticipation, and fear that wouldn't escape anyone's notice. It wasn't the first time Zahara had seen such a reaction from those who'd been summoned to this room, man or woman. The Salar had that effect on people, especially on those who hadn't been called often to his private chamber.

It had been a little over two months since the wedding. Amelia had been brought into the Tower only days before her husband's departure to Khandoor. He'd left almost as soon as the reception was over, and Zahara knew for a fact that he'd yet to bed her. Which explained why the girl was as anxious as she was.

Amelia had, to everyone's knowledge, been looking forward to this moment, however. Being izr Mafouz's daughter, everyone expected Amelia to become the new figure of power in the Tower and not a mere addition to the Salar's existing collection of wives, be it for her father's or her own ambition. Such power required capturing her husband's interest to raise her status above that of other wives, perhaps even the Salahari. The effort to put her youth and beauty on display in the most extravagant way possible, therefore, had been done with no expense spared by her father from the moment she set foot in the Tower.

The effort had tripled the day she'd first knelt and kissed the signet ring on Salar Muradi's finger. Zahara could still remember, watching from behind the throne with his other wives, how she'd blushed from her ears down to the cleavage she'd intentionally exposed through her dress's plunging neckline the moment she'd laid eyes on him. The fact that he was more than twice her age hadn't seemed to bother her any more than it bothered the other young women at court.

For one thing, not only had Muradi been a strikingly handsome man in his youth, he also happened to be aging like fine wine. For another, even at forty-two, he was still just as strong and capable as any young man at court; more so, in fact, than all his sons from how frequent he trained. The ruthless, unforgiving reputation that should have given any girl second thoughts seemed to be giving him an edge that drew attention like a well-cut ruby. That said, the very fact that he had power—immense power—would have eclipsed all his flaws in any case, had he possessed some.

It just so happened that he possessed none, which was why Amelia wasn't the first young girl to have fallen head over heels for him at first sight. Zahara, of course, had an entirely different view on this issue. Having one's entire family slaughtered in a single day by the same man who married you tended to distort one's perspective to a certain degree.

Amelia's infatuation with the Salar had grown from ambition into something more personal, and had caused quite a stir in his absence. Over the past two months, she'd managed to interfere with not only the housing arrangements of the royal household, but also the balance of power in the Tower. Alliances changed and loyalty faltered when enough coins were involved, and coins were what Amelia had in near unlimited amounts. So far, she'd managed to win over the Salahari's favorite jeweler, and every new batch of silk from Makena now went to her before his other wives for the first pick. Her servants outnumbered that of the Salahari's now, and the high-ranking officers at court surrounded her like flies, hoping to gain favors from the Salar through his promising new wife and access to her father's gold. All the while, Jarem, who'd been in charge of the Tower, watched and did nothing, as though finding this influence a profitable one. The Salahari and his other wives, as anyone might have expected, had turned their attention and talons from his Shakshi wife to Amelia instead.

Which would have been a good thing for Zahara, had the Salar not summoned her to his chamber instead of his new, young, promising wife on their wedding night—an insult that had landed Zahara on Amelia's list of people to eliminate in the process.

Since then, she'd suffered everything from minor humiliations to having parts of her living quarters turned into the girl's personal space whenever she saw fit. Amelia knew what she was doing, had both the drive and the means to never stop until she had what she wanted—and what she wanted the most was undivided attention from the man who ruled the peninsula.

Looking at their reflection on the pair of gold-plated doors before her, Zahara could see the possibility of this being accomplished. The girl was tall, slender, and well-endowed, with fuller hips and a noticeably slim waist. Her long, jet black hair—the complete opposite of Zahara's silver—curled neatly on either side of her half-exposed, shapely breasts, offsetting the smooth, alabaster skin that could be said to glow in the dark—a complexion considered undesirable and sickly in the White Desert, but celebrated in Rasharwi.

Any man would appreciate the things Amelia could offer, and the Salar seemed to have realized that now, having summoned her as soon as he'd returned. In a way, it would be a good thing for her if the girl could indeed capture his attention. She would then be excused and forgotten, left to her own devices to live out the rest of her days without having to endure his attentions. He might even allow her to relocate to one of the Shakshi quarters in the city if she were lucky.

If only life were that simple.

Zahara sighed at her own childish thoughts. By now she knew better than to expect such a miracle. The moment she became no more than one of his boring wives, her life and that of her son would be expendable. They wouldn't last in the Tower for more than a season, having been a pebble in the Salahari's shoe for the past eighteen years, and Lasura in all the princes' for nearly as long. The two of them were the excess of the Tower, kept there only because its master demanded it.

It couldn't be allowed to happen; not if she was to save her son and keep the promise she'd made a long time ago. His interest in her had to be kept going. His desire to conquer and reconquer a Bharavi—a living symbol of the White Desert he'd yet to claim—had to be stretched and rekindled for as long as she needed to stay alive. Her future and that of her son hung on his decision tonight, and whether Amelia's plunging neckline would get the job done. Most men succumbed to desire when enough flesh was displayed and the woman proved inviting. Sometimes just the invitation was enough.

The man Amelia was trying to catch, however, wasn't most men. Anyone who had been close to the Salar knew he liked to hunt and preferred his game challenging—the kind that pushed him to the limit and extended it afterward. Which was why Zahara had chosen a high-collared, traditional white gown that bespoke her origin—to remind him of what he still couldn't get his hands on.

Or she could be wrong.

It wasn't unreasonable to think a man might decide to enjoy a wife he hadn't unwrapped for the rest of the night and disregard his own summon for the old one, especially when the new wife was young enough to be his daughter. The order in which they would be summoned was also important, if both things happened.

The door to the inner chamber clicked open. Ghaul, who'd been guarding the entrance, turned to watch two handmaidens carry a basket full of worn clothes from the room. He must have just finished his bath, Zahara thought, registering the familiar fragrance of sage and mint that escaped through the open door. She'd come to hate how much that scent could unnerve her over the years and was often amazed that she hadn't gotten over it by now.

"The Salar has called for you, my lady." One of them turned to Amelia and curtsied as she spoke. "The Lady Zahara is to wait here for the summons."

A numbness spread through her then, like being stripped naked and left to stand in the snow. It had, at long last, come to this after eighteen years of enduring endless, pride-swallowing torture. She'd been aware of the possibility of being cast aside for some time, having reached an age no longer considered young, but nothing was ever enough to prepare one for it, especially when so much was at stake. The pain she felt was shocking, considering that her heart wasn't a part of what had been afflicted, or shouldn't have been.

"Of course." Zahara nodded and stepped aside, putting on her best mask of indifference as Amelia flashed a victorious smirk before entering the chamber.

Where he would be standing now—in nothing but the black silk robe he always wore after a bath, grinning, she was sure, in amusement at the thought of her being made to wait by the door as he entertained himself with his younger, more eager bride, believing that he'd found a brand new way to torture her all over again for the mistake she'd made eighteen years ago.

And it was working. Oh, it worked beautifully, tremendously. The defeat, the humiliation, the searing pain of being put aside like a toy he'd grown tired of rushed through her veins like a paralyzing venom, on top of the frightening knowledge that the reality she'd long feared was knocking on her door.

"You might want to sit down," Ghaul said as he closed the door. The satisfaction on his face unmasked and unrestrained. "It may take the whole night."

She resisted the urge to glare at him, despite the need to find an outlet for the rage she was feeling. Ghaul despised her. She had known this from the first day they met, when he'd struck her down in that tent. Tonight, her patience was running thin, but she wasn't going to give him the satisfaction of thinking he could get under her skin, on top of what his master had just done.

"It usually does," she said, smiling back sweetly. "The Salar's appetite can be..." She paused, drew a breath as if recalling a certain memory too explicit to be put into words, and waited for it to reach his imagination. "...quite exhausting in bed."

It never ceased to amaze her how the trick still worked after all this time. Ghaul, flushing like a boy seeing a naked woman for the first time, suddenly found threats to observe with vigor in every object that existed, from the carpet to the Khandoor vase by the door as though they hadn't been there in the same places for the past twenty years. He would retaliate for that at some other time, she was sure of it.

For how much Ghaul despised her, she might have even thought him jealous if the Salar had also been taking boys and men to bed. Then again, there were many forms of jealousy. Ghaul was the most trusted man among those closest to the Salar in the Tower, and she shared that position now: not as the most trusted one, but definitely as the one closest to him where time spent in his chamber was concerned.

A position that was being threatened at this moment, Zahara thought, grimacing as her mind wandered off to imagine what might be going on in that room.

To her surprise, the door opened before she'd finished her thought. Zahara looked past Ghaul's gigantic form to see the slender figure of Amelia limping out from the chamber, her neat curls now disorderly and tangled, tears pooled in her bloodshot eyes that had moments ago been bright and clear. She looked like she'd been through a raid. Like a girl who'd just found out there were real monsters in this world.

It dawned on Zahara then that whatever he had done behind those doors, desire or attraction hadn't been a part of it, and that she'd been wrong in her initial interpretation of the situation. She knew that look, and had seen it a hundred times before on the faces of her people and in her own reflection, time and time again in the past eighteen years—the look of something that had been broken beyond repair.

Upon seeing her, Amelia straightened and squared her shoulders. The soft, youthful lines on her face had become harsh and weathered now, as though she'd been gone several years since she'd disappeared through that door.

"He is expecting you," she said through gritted teeth, refusing to shed any more of her pride, especially in front of another woman.

Another life changed over the course of one night; or in this case, in less than an hour. Zahara recalled then how a single event could strip a child so completely of her innocence, how quick the world could be in punishing the naive and the ignorant. Amelia would always remember now, and long after, that there was a hardness to living, that things wouldn't always turn out the way she wanted.

Had she been a different woman with a different past, she might have tried to offer some comfort to the girl, but comfort and compassion wasn't something either of them should be relying on to survive—not around this man. In a way, she was glad Amelia seemed to know this now, and had refused to show a need for it. She had, after all, been born and raised in Rasharwi.

'There is only **NOW** and what you do next. That is how a leader is made and change is accomplished,'

My Entertainment

Stepping into the outer room, Zahara paused for her eyes to adjust to the sudden absence of light. The space was dimly lit, with only one hurricane lamp to illuminate the dark walls. Expecting to find him in his bedchamber through the inner door, she walked past the round table and paused to note the spilled wine on the white tablecloth. A goblet lay on its side by her feet, its contents emptied onto the floor, painting a blood-like trail on the priceless carpet. She picked it up and placed it back on the table, pushing away the image her mind conjured as to how it had gotten there. It was always better not to know.

A shadow caught her eyes and drew her attention to the window. The moon, full and high, cast its golden light through the window, where a dark figure lounged carelessly on the windowsill as if unaware of the certain death its height promised should one were to slip and fall. As always, he sat daringly with his back against the frame, one leg extended lazily on the ledge, the other hanging loosely outside the window. The silver goblet in his hand glinted in the moonlight as he turned it back and forth absent-mindedly. The wine had been gone a while ago, she could tell. He had a tendency to leave it unfilled and nurse the emptied cup for a long time when his mind was occupied by something important.

Zahara headed to the window and replaced the empty goblet in his hand with a new one she'd filled. He took it in silence, keeping his eyes fixed somewhere in the distance as she waited for him to initiate the conversation. It occurred to her then, as it had many times before, how easy it would be to reach out her hand and end the life of the most powerful man in the peninsula and, at the same time, how powerful a few words spoken could make a task so seemingly simple near impossible to accomplish.

"Does it ever bother you," he drawled at length, sipping from the cup she'd given him, "when they expect you to breed?"

The melancholy in his voice surprised her. She'd expected him to be in a different mood, to goad her over Amelia, and grin victoriously at the result. Instead, he'd asked her this, and he sounded almost tired.

"No more than being kept for entertainment, I assure you," she replied. She may have been born a Bharavi, and had been expected to do nothing more than to breed more Bharavis and oracles, but whatever her previous life had required, it was still far better than the life she was leading now.

He turned and regarded her appearance for the first time that night. The white gown she wore would be noted, of course, so would the moonstone necklace around her neck—the same one she'd been given on her eighteenth birthday, as per tradition, to eventually bestow upon the man she chose to marry. It was a symbol of sorts. One that told him she had not surrendered, not completely. The knowledge always rekindled his interest, and her defiance excited him. After a long absence, Zahara knew it was what she needed to maintain her status in the Tower.

A grin appeared on his lips soon after. "Is that what you think you are? My entertainment?" he asked, with a noticeable edge to his tone. "Am I so susceptible to pleasure, Zahara?"

She resisted the urge to swallow, knowing he would catch it in an instant. Reluctance made him suspicious, and indecision seen as a sign of dishonesty. Assume too much, and one became a liability; too little, and one appeared incompetent. Salar Muradi of Rasharwi allowed only competent, intelligent people to occupy his attention, and if she were to stay in that circle, her answers to these questions of many meanings had to be intelligent ones.

"You like to play with your food. You always have, my lord," she replied with practiced sweetness. "In that sense, I do find you susceptible to pleasure, yes."

His mouth quirked into a smile, the same way he'd always done when he was pleased with her answer. "How very observant of you."

She gave him a pointed look. "One has to be to stay alive around you, my lord. Ask Jarem."

He rose from the window and took a seat on the chair facing her, sinking his weight into the velvet cushion. The front part of his robe hung loose and disarrayed on his body, revealing a generous amount of skin below his collarbone. She wondered if he'd bothered taking it off when he took Amelia. The man sitting in front of her had never been one who enjoyed quick, casual pleasures. He took time, always, to savor every little thing he could take from rendering his opponent defenseless, tasting every hint and note of his victory the same way he tasted his wine, in both sex and war. Whatever he'd done with the girl, considering the pace at which it had been executed and his mood at the moment, didn't please him.

"Jarem will tell you that I'm old and not as unforgiving as I once was."

The mood tonight was indeed strange. There seemed to be a weight that was pressing on him, judging from the stiffness of his shoulders.

"Jarem will tell you what you want to hear and offer to produce you an heir if he could. Perhaps more willingly than Lady Amelia. You know this."

He made a sour face at the mention of her name, as if dealing with an aftertaste of something he needed gone. "She wasn't unwilling."

"She was crying on the way out." Zahara poured herself a drink.

He sneered at that. Guilt was not something that fit him or a thing one could force him to wear. *'There is only now and what you do next. That is how a leader is made and change is accomplished,'* her father had said to her brother one night. Muradi was a ruler before all else, and the entire peninsula could change at the end of his sentence, or at the beginning of one. Guilt had no place in his decision-making.

"As a result of her own false presumption, I assure you."

"For expecting her newlywed husband to be gentle and affectionate when he beds her, my lord?" She didn't like Amelia, but that statement still bothered her.

"For expecting more than what was on the contract," he replied with a stone-cold expression, one he normally used when discussing business and matters of state. "I agreed to take her as my wife and give her a son in exchange for a loan from her father at a small interest rate. A son he plans to put on *my* throne so he can manipulate it to grow his profits and eventually take control of the Salasar. I see no reason why I should be required to shower her with gentleness and affection when they're out to suck my blood, father and daughter both."

Put that way, he did have a point, Zahara thought. The projects he'd been putting into action to build dams and better roads in Rasharwi had been draining the Tower's gold reserves, forcing him to take out a huge loan from Zubin izr Mafouz to support them. The marriage must have been Jarem's idea of minimizing the interest, judging from how much it was grating on his patience.

"So you hurt her on purpose."

"I don't like being muscled."

"By using me as a weapon," she said pointedly.

"You sound angry."

She *had* been angry, and still was, but now for a different reason. "You will forgive me, my lord, if I don't enjoy being used."

"I thought you might have appreciated it," he said, and took a sip of his wine as he regarded her expression, "considering what she's been putting you through these two months."

That startled her. "What has Jarem told you, my lord?"

He watched her quietly for a time, considering, of course, how much she needed to know regarding his awareness of things that had happened in the Tower while he'd been away. It was in these moments that she could measure how much he trusted her, how far he was willing to discuss things when she chose to press for it. When his eyes flickered to something else on the table, she knew the answer to that instantly.

"Enough."

She'd always known that his walls weren't going to come down easily. Eighteen years of being in this room and she'd barely made a dent in them, Zahara thought bitterly.

"And you wish me to believe you've done this to humor me? Truly, my lord?" She wasn't born yesterday, or naive enough to even consider that a possibility.

"Why not, Zahara?" he asked casually. Only his eyes told an entirely different tale. They fixed upon her like a hawk waiting for the right opportunity to strike, its sharp, deadly talons opened wide and ready. "Surely you are aware of how everyone considers you my favorite."

This is it, Zahara thought. This was the weight that had been pressing down on him when she'd entered the room. The very idea that he had a favorite was a threat, a spark he had to put out immediately and decisively. She should have been killed that night to put an end to it and to set an example, but he needed her alive to prove the point he'd made eighteen years ago. He *could* throw her into a dungeon and treat her as a prisoner, the way she deserved, but she also knew he was enjoying her company too much to dismiss her entirely.

Now, he was presented with the problem of having to show them she wasn't one, and he was testing her now as to how much she was aware of her power over him, how far she might go to manipulate him with that knowledge. To see if he should let her remain as close as she had been.

It must have been Jarem. That man could always dig up something to make her life difficult.

She looked straight at him and smiled, praying that he wouldn't see how much the subject was unnerving her. "*Everyone* is usually wrong, my lord."

"*Are they?*" The tone he used sent a chill down her spine. His deep, penetrating eyes pinned her in place like a spear to the throat. "Have you not been trying to hold my interest after all these years?" He turned the wine in his hand as he observed her every move, every expression. One breath held, one twitch of her eye, or one small sign of discomfort would all be noted, she was certain. "After all, you have picked that dress for a reason, have you not, Zahara?"

She *had* picked it for a reason, Zahara thought, and suddenly regretted her decision. Had she known Jarem would bring this up to him she would have chosen to react differently. Deny it, and he might find it an insult to his intelligence. Tell him the truth, and she would be accused of trying to manipulate, or believing that he *could* be manipulated. Her reply, if she were to survive this conversation, had to do more than convince him that she wasn't a threat as Jarem had proposed her to be.

Or she could do something else entirely, based on how well she knew this man.

"Of course, I did," she said. "Is it working, my lord? I hadn't noticed."

I am trying to cross the line. Are you afraid?

Something changed in his expression then, as if he'd just been reminded of something he'd forgotten, and Zahara knew in an instant she'd hit the mark.

Keeping his eyes on her, he drew a long, sharp breath as he uncrossed and recrossed his legs in the opposite direction, and then exhaled with the uneven, ragged sound of someone who'd unexpectedly been brought to the height of pleasure. The outlines of his muscles grew alarmingly tensed underneath the silk robe, and all the while his predatory blue eyes stared at her with the same intensity they had on the first day they'd met.

"Is it working?" He repeated almost breathlessly, tasting each word as if they reminded him of a rare delicacy. "I wanted to rip it to shreds and take you by that window the moment you came in."

To Win My Heart

She turned her gaze to the pitcher, picked it up, and proceeded to refill his wine, hoping he wouldn't notice how unsteady her hand was as she poured its contents into the cup. A mistake she immediately regretted. An opening for him to surprise her when he reached over and took her wrist without warning. Zahara jolted at the sudden contact, spilling the wine in the process, and bit her lip. He would have caught that, seen through her, gained satisfaction from it. A loss on her part she'd remember. A victory on his.

The evidence of that was written clearly on his face, in the small sound he made in his throat, and the way his eyes trapped her where she stood. Zahara willed herself to hold that gaze, despite the way his hand around her wrist tightened, or how hard those fingers were digging into her skin, as if to leave a mark. She knew that hand, every crook and dent in it, how those callused fingers felt on her body, and what they could do.

"Come here, Zahara." The tone was uncharacteristically gentle, and so was the hand that tugged on her arm, pulling her toward him.

She stepped around the table to where he'd commanded her to be, positioning herself within reach and yet half a step too far for him to catch the rhythm of her heart. For everything he would take from her, there were things she would not give, no matter how much torture awaited her in this room.

He rolled her arm gently to expose the underside of her wrist, brought it to his lips and lingered there, not touching, not yet, to sniff at her scent the same way he might have done to catch the aroma of an exquisite wine before tasting. "How is it possible," he asked, trailing his nose further up her arm and back down to where he started, "that a girl half your age couldn't excite me with her cunt the way your scent did when you entered the room?"

What is it, Zahara thought, *that gives this man such a contrast within him?* By then, she could withstand all his torture and unforgiving ways effortlessly enough, but not quite his vulnerability when he decided to let her see it. And he was vulnerable tonight, enough to give her an uneasy feeling in her stomach. She hated those moments, those words, hated them for what they could do to her.

"And yet it was enough for you to finish the job," she said in an attempt to change the mood, the way things were heading. "What was it that stirred your desire then, my lord? The thrill of discovering her spirit or of breaking it?"

He smiled, to himself, to her, amused at the answer he was about to give. "The thought of you listening outside my door." He planted a kiss on the inside of her arm, brief enough to last no more than a heartbeat, long enough to leave something behind.

"Cruel." She scowled, more at the heat from his lips that lingered still on her skin than the words spoken.

"To her?" He kissed her again, this time on a spot closer to her palm. "Or to you?"

The place he'd touched her felt tender. It stung like ice, like fire on an open wound. "Do you ever pick just one, my lord?"

He stilled for a time, looking straight at her, into her, reading her thoughts and considering something. She had come to know that look, that gesture he let slip when he decided to take a risk, to do something out of character. "And if I tell you that I can?" he said, not smiling now, not anymore. "Choose one?"

It was a question that aimed to wound, an attack of sorts at something too deep, too precious in her heart. A proposition that threatened to end her if she so much as considered it. She brushed it aside immediately, feigning indifference, ignorance. "To be the subject of your torture, my lord? I'd pity the woman." The woman would not be her, not for what he'd implied, this she silently swore by the loyalty to her land and whatever was left of her pride.

The grip on her hand tightened. He said softly, greedily, "To win my heart, Zahara."

To win my heart.

One simple sentence, delivered like a spear pressed hard against her chest to demand her complete surrender. This was his response to her being his favorite, the path he'd chosen to deal with the problem. It was simple, simpler than throwing her into the dungeon and ridding himself of the entertainment, or to pretend that she was no longer his favorite. The solution, of course, was for her to lay her heart at his feet, and in doing so eliminate herself altogether as a threat.

She steeled herself against that possibility—*that impossibility*—and offered him a reply. "I wasn't aware that you possessed one, my lord."

The blade she'd wielded hit the mark. She could almost see when it struck from the way his jaw tightened and the way his breaths altered. There was an open wound in the man whose hand now tangled with hers, red, raw, and dripping blood.

"You wouldn't be here if I didn't have one," he said with a deadly calm. Another blade delivered in answer to her own, sliding with precision between her ribs, into her heart. "You have known this for a long time. From the first day we met, Zahara. You know what I want."

You know what I want.

And she had—known it—for a long time. From the first day they'd met. In the flickering light of the lanterns, the excitement in his eyes when she'd recited Eli, the tension, the fire that had been set alight behind every word of their conversation at that table. And then, in the years and years of being in this room, sharing his bed, being touched and touched again by his hands, his words, his unquenchable desire to have her, to conquer and reconquer her more than once, and one too many times. She had known what he wanted from her, just as well as how much he'd wanted to destroy such a desire, how many times he'd tried.

Now he was offering her a truce, a chance to change her life, the life of her son, and the fate of the peninsula, to be the one and only one to wrap her hand around his heart, to have this power to change and make a difference.

I can choose one.

Four simple words that told her everything could be undone. She had only to reach out and take it, to answer the call she'd known was there, the one she'd buried in the deepest part of her heart and kept hidden to deny its existence. It would be so simple, so effortless to say the words that would rewrite the history of what happened from then on, to take this life-changing gift she'd never imagined would be offered.

But there were things she would not—could not—surrender, for lives or reasons or loyalty to her land.

"You took everything from me," she told him, a decade of lingering rage, of caged, controlled anger etched in every word she spoke. "My home, my family, my pride, my integrity, my freedom, my right to live as a person, as a *human being*, and you will ask for more?"

She pulled away, putting an end to their physical contact, placing a distance between them. She would toss this offered gift to the ground and crush it with her feet if she could. It would be an act of treason, but one she was willing—even needing—to kill for if only to draw herself a line. "There are things you cannot have in this world, and my heart is among them." She spelled the words, carving them into his memory, into hers. "It is beating to see you die, never for you to claim."

He looked at her quietly then, and in the finality of that punishing silence, she had a vision of something breaking, of a sky falling down upon the world and into a deep, dark pit with no way out. He rose from the chair and took a slow step toward her, standing over her with his imposing height and impossibly large shadow made by the light of the night's full, achingly white moon.

"Do you know," he murmured, looking down on her from above, "what they do to prisoners that can't be sold in Sabha? How the guards find entertainment to pass the time, besides sticking their cocks where they don't belong?"

He lifted a hand to touch her hair, pushing it back behind her ear. The touch was tender, in the same way a butcher might stroke an animal to relax its muscles before the slaughter.

"Every other month they'd pick ten prisoners, boys and young men who could fight," he whispered, the words so light she would have missed them had he not pressed them against her cheek. "They're put in teams of two, given weapons and one week to train, then force you to fight until only one pair remains."

Large, unforgiving hands wrapped around the back of her head, holding it in place. Outside, a baby was crying somewhere down below, its wails brought up on the wind that rushed into the chamber.

"In the trials, they kill you when your partner dies, so we'd watch each other's backs, tend to each other's wounds, make sure the other one could fight the next day." His fingers clamped down around her neck, digging deep enough to reach her bones. "Then they pit you against each other. Your partner, the one man who's taken care of you for the past four weeks, your one and only friend in that pit of hell, until he is killed, or he kills you."

She could feel his lips on her earlobe, his hot, burning breaths scalding her skin as he spoke. "I was held in Sabha for two years, and in those two years I'd won the crown eleven times. The twelfth man who now stands outside my door is the only one I didn't kill from the trial." He pulled back to look at her then, to make sure she saw it on his face, in his eyes—the hurt, the burning, killing desire, his relentless, unforgiving fire to punish those who'd inflicted a wound. "I don't have a problem killing what is dear to my heart, Zahara. I never have."

The baby was screaming now, its cries cutting through the silence like the shriek of an eagle. She closed her eyes to the words she knew were coming, to the heat of his lips as they grazed hers, speaking them. "You could have been an exception. You and Lasura. I would have given you the world, the freedom you wanted, even put your son on the throne and given him control of the Salasar. I *have* thought of it, and offered it to you tonight. You are right, there are things I cannot have in this world." His words grated on her skin, leaving scars.

"I live to crush those things, Zahara. That is who I am. You have one week to say goodbye to your son. I'm sending him to raid your home."

A Dream of Red

Hasheem's nightmare came almost every night for the past three weeks since he'd been accepted into the Kha'gan. She could hear it from the proximity of their tents—the muffled groans and whimpers of someone running from or seeing something too terrifying to imagine. Most of those nights she had stayed awake, tossing and turning on her own bed as she listened. It would take someone without a heart to sleep through such things, Djari thought, especially for someone like her who had been through the same ordeal at night, no matter how long ago it had been.

It had been awful, those dreams of her mother being tortured, hurt, left to die in the desert like a worthless carcass waiting to be picked by vultures and eaten by foxes. Her mother, the sweetest, kindest soul whose hand had been gentle when she'd braided her daughter's hair or dressed her husband for battle. Those careful, thoughtful words she'd used around people to move and bend them to her cause, to calm and comfort even her father during his most impossible fits of rage. A delicate being, a beautiful face, a Bharavi, won and loved by Za'in izr Husari, by her children and people, dragged behind a rock by Rashai soldiers, made to weep and scream.

Soldiers, the survivors had said. No one would tell her the details of what they'd done to the Kha'ari of Visarya. She had been given no opportunity to see her mother's face before they'd buried her. But she had seen her father's when he brought his Kha'ari home that day.

It had been enough.

So had what Za'in izr Husari decided to do afterward to villagers, to

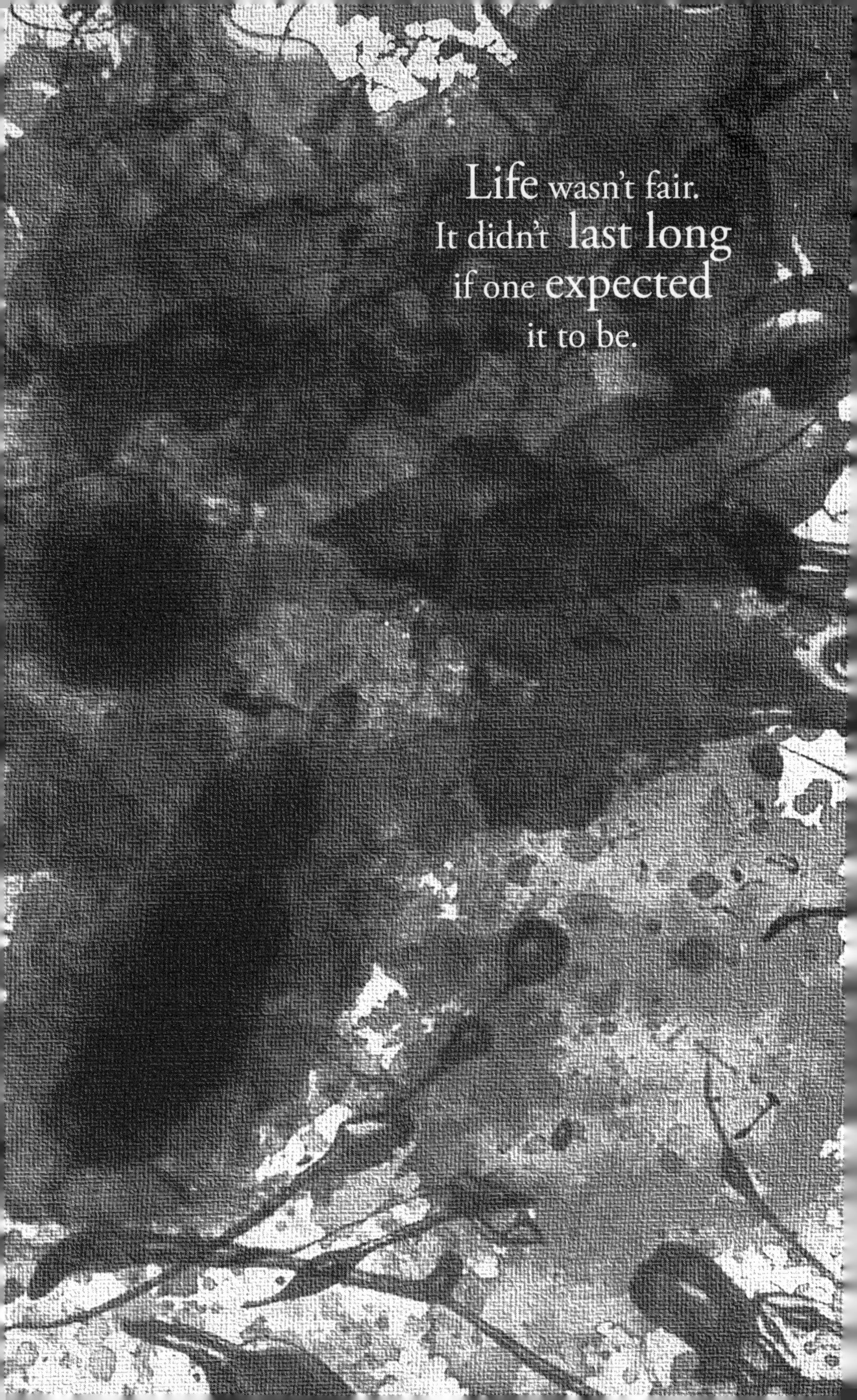
Life wasn't fair.
It didn't last long
if one expected
it to be.

the men, women and children along the outskirts of Sabha, been enough to tell Djari what the Rashais had done to his Kha'ari.

Some approved of his choices, others didn't. Everyone had, however, learned that there were lines one couldn't cross with people and things one couldn't take away from a man—or a woman—without consequences, sometimes to those who deserved it, other times to those who didn't. Life wasn't fair. It didn't last long if one expected it to be. Some wounds didn't close until one sought some kind of retribution. The scars remained though, and so did the nightmares. Djari had some for the death of her mother, and others for what her father had done to the Rashais.

The desert had been painted red. There had been blood in the sand, on her father's swords, in the crease of his skin just below his eyes, running down toward the scar that had turned crimson on one side, and dripping off his chin on the other. The white of his zikh had disappeared, soaked almost completely by blood, its excess dripping endlessly onto the already drenched shoulders of his horse. At the horizon, the flame rose high above the wooden roofs, reaching up in unison with the cries of babies and the shrieks of mothers toward the clouds as the day bled into night, staining the sky deep red the same way the dead had stained her father's zikh.

Red was what she saw in her dreams. She hated the sunset, hated it for the memories it threatened to bring and for the future it promised. Za'in izr Husari had brought both his son and daughter along to witness his retribution: to remember, to etch into their memories and carve on their hearts a scar that would dictate every action in their lives and every decision they would make afterward. She remembered her father's face that day, how tight his jaw had seemed, how much sorrow had been painted so clearly on it. Za'in izr Husari had never been a monster, but that day he decided to become one. It was a seal made from the blood of innocents, a promise that from then on there would be no line between him and his retribution, even if it meant breaking the world and his children along with it.

It did break her, and probably Nazir. That nightmare repeated itself often, sometimes with her in her father's place, in his garment, covered in the blood she'd drawn or ordered drawn. There was no guarantee that she wouldn't make the same mistakes. She was her father's daughter, after all.

Tonight she might also be making one, Djari realized as she stood by her sworn sword's bed. She had come into his tent on half a thought. She did that a lot—putting things into action before she finished thinking. A terrible habit that was going to get her killed one day, Nazir had said. A prediction she had yet to agree with.

On the bed, Hasheem lay tangled in his sheets, his fists wound tight around the blanket. Beads of sweat formed on his forehead despite the cold night air that seeped into the tent. He appeared to be crying or yelling something, only the words never made it past his lips. It sounded like he was drowning—or choking—on his own scream.

She placed a hand on his shoulder, hoping to stir him awake from the bad dream. Hasheem's eyes snapped open the moment she made the contact, giving her no time to yelp when his hand shot up to grab her by the throat and flung her down on the bed. His knees trapped her between them. The hand around her neck pinned her in place. A dagger's point flashed in one of her eyes, ready to drive it through the socket.

Djari whimpered and clawed at his arm, trying to push away the hand that held the blade to her cheek. Hasheem's eyes turned almost white as he tightened his grip, his expression an unrecognizable mask of someone she hadn't met.

I am going to die tonight, Djari thought as her consciousness began to drift away and her grip on what was happening loosened.

Something caught Hasheem's attention before she ran out of breath. It froze him on the spot, twisted his expression into what seemed to her a mixture of shock and terror, like someone who'd just walked into a room full of corpses, like her father the day they'd brought back her mother's body. His eyes began to clear, returning to the warm shade of gray she had come to know. The moment he recognized her, Hasheem jerked his hand free and backed away toward the far end of the bed. He was shaking visibly, she noticed, and gasping for air as he watched her gather herself up.

"Did he—" Hasheem bit off the words, swallowed, and began again. "Did I hurt you?"

He? The need to cough and fill her lungs interrupted that thought. "No," she croaked. "No. It's alright." Her throat still ached from the pressure of his hand, but it would heal soon enough.

Hasheem's shoulders sagged like a man suddenly depleted of all his energy. He covered his face with his hand, perhaps to hide from her his expression, perhaps out of shame or frustration, she didn't know him well enough to tell. It was still trembling, that hand. "Don't do that again," he said. A plea, she thought, more than a warning. "I could have killed you."

He could have—would have—had he not recognized her soon enough. He had recognized her, though, and that was important. "But you wouldn't," she decided.

Another breath, another sharp exhale. "You don't know that." He shook his head. "You don't know me. What I've done... What I can do... It isn't safe."

She had a feeling he was angry with her or with himself, she wasn't sure which. It startled her a little. Hasheem had not struck her as someone quick to anger. He accepted everything with the patience and calm of a man thrice his age, as if he'd been through every insult, every offense, and in the process had learned to live with it.

It didn't, not in the least, mean that he could be walked over and treaded upon. There were boundaries with Hasheem that made everyone approach him with caution, behind which lay something he intended to keep hidden or guarded at whatever cost. Djari didn't know what it was, but she might have been given a glimpse of it tonight.

She decided she wanted to know more, needed to know more.

"Then tell me," she said. "Tell me who you are, what you've done. I deserve to know." He had told her nothing, not a word about his past, and Nazir hadn't revealed any of it when she'd asked. They had known each other for almost a month, had spent almost every waking hour in each other's company, and yet she knew nothing about him besides his name. It had been sitting in her chest like a rock, a tree that was beginning to grow roots, that agitation of being locked outside, in the dark.

He stilled for a time, watching her from the other end of the bed that seemed a world away. When he turned to look at the door, she knew she wasn't going to get an answer from him, not tonight. That stung like a wound, and in more ways than one.

But there were also wounds in her sworn sword, she could see them just as clearly as her own. Injured people, like horses, she thought, needed time to heal, to trust. She knew horses and how to gain their trust.

"I hear you," she said. "Almost every night. Your nightmares." She paused, recognized her question to be somewhat intrusive, and asked it anyway. "What do you see?"

He looked up at her but gave no answer. Hasheem did that a lot—responded to unwelcome questions with deliberate silence, holding on to thoughts and secrets with a clear determination to never let her touch them.

When will you trust me? She wanted to ask it, but didn't. He wouldn't answer that either, not now anyway. They were still somewhat tip-toeing around each other, learning limits and boundaries, with her constantly pushing them and him standing his ground, never allowing either of them to cross the line. Hasheem was always careful, unassuming, and gentle with her, however, the same way he was gentle with horses. She liked how he handled horses.

"It helps to talk about it with someone." She had a feeling it wouldn't work, but she was also impossible in her own way. "I had them too when my mother died."

He made no reply, but she knew he was always listening. Her sworn sword was a good listener.

"It went on for months," she continued, "until nan'ya let me sleep in her tent and gave me this." The charm bracelet made a small sound when she raised her arm to show him. "My mother used to wear these on her ankle. I would hear her coming from far away. It reminds me of her presence. Calms me down." A memory returned to her as she spoke, and Djari found herself smiling a little.

"When we got into trouble, Nazir used to say that rescue was coming the moment we heard her charms jingle. By that point, Father would stop scolding us and leave." It only took a smile, a gentle touch on his arm from his Kha'ari to settle Za'in izr Husari. She missed her father in those moments. They would never come again. "I guess that's why it helps me sleep. Do you have anything like that? Something that calms you down? Makes you happy?"

Hasheem's silence continued and Djari realized she might have pushed her boundaries a bit too far. You had to know when to back out with horses, to read the signs before damaging that trust further. "I'm sorry." She sighed and rose from the bed. "I didn't mean to pry. I'll go now."

He reached for her arm and held her back. She stiffened at the contact. Hasheem was careful with women. He stood at a calculated distance, took great care to observe people's boundaries and minded them. Tonight, he'd crossed that boundary he'd drawn himself, his large hand now closed gently around her wrist, making it seem childishly small.

"I've been meaning to ask," he said, for the first time after that long silence. "That arrowhead. Is it the one you shot me with?"

She looked down at the bone arrowhead dangling from her neck and realized all of the sudden what she'd missed. "This is what you saw?" Her heart skipped a beat at the possibility, at the revelation. "What brought you back?"

He didn't reply. He asked, gently, quietly, "Would you mind if I had it?"

Another pause in her heart, then a beat resumed, picked up in strength, in acceleration. "Why?" *Tell me this, at least.*

He smiled at her then, but only with his eyes. He could do that; smile at someone to make them feel like the only one in the room—in the world—with the way he looked at them. '*It leaves a mark,*' a girl at camp had said about his smiles, his eyes. It was doing that to her now, at this moment.

"You wanted to know what calms me down. What makes me happy," he said. The hand that held hers loosened and shifted. She could feel the roughness of his thumb on her palm, tracing the lines on it. "I *am* happy and calm, Djari," he told her. "Right here, right now."

She could feel it so clearly then, the weight of his presence settling itself on a newly discovered part of her, claiming a place in it.

"Because of me?"

He nodded. Smiled. "Because of you."

She sat back down on the bed next to him. The tent grew quiet and still. In the silence of the night, she could hear nothing but the sound of her own breathing, falling in rhythm with his. His fingers stopped moving on her hand and stayed there. He was, she realized, fully aware of the discovery of something new that had materialized in the small distance between them, waiting to be addressed. A question. A revelation. A risk.

A risk she wanted to take.

She said, before finishing that thought, "Is this when you'd kiss a girl?"

He sucked in a breath. His eyes never left hers, didn't waver when he said, "Sometimes."

And there it was, an opening, the unlocking of a door that tempted her to peek inside. She drew herself up, caught his eyes. "And this time?"

An unfair question, a step in a direction she shouldn't go. She had known and decided she would go, in any case, on half a thought.

He hesitated. "It isn't my choice to make, Djari."

It wasn't, she knew. "And if it were?"

A moment of pause from him. Then the hand around hers shook a little. "Yes." He seemed to wince at his own answer. "I believe I would."

The door was wide open in front of her now and she had only to step inside. She would take this risk, but not before addressing another. "You know who I am."

"I do."

"I will marry a Khumar of my father's choosing."

A breath drawn, and released. "I know."

"You know the line." It couldn't be crossed, not for anything, at any time, now or ever.

He smiled then, a little ruefully. "I know the line."

She nodded, made her decision, and took the offered gift that would be the first and possibly the last that was her choice, her desire to take, not her father's.

"Kiss me."

⁜

LATER THAT NIGHT, lying on her bed, staring up at the roof of her tent, Djari wound her hand around the string on her neck as she thought about what had happened. She could still feel his hand around her wrist, the lightness of his touch, the breaking of something inside of her caused by the simplest contact that only lasted a few seconds.

Kiss me, she'd told him, had demanded it of him to offer her this, despite all the risks they would have to take.

And he had given it to her. A brief, careful, and considerate kiss. A casual yet delicate gesture that sealed and carved something permanent she would bring with her to her new Kha'gan, through her new life with the man she would call husband, to her grave.

She would turn sixteen in a month, and there had already been letters from other Kha'gans asking her father for her hand in marriage. Before she turned seventeen, her father would make the decision, and by eighteen she would be old enough to marry. Her husband would be whomever he chose, from whichever Kha'gan that benefited them the most. The chosen Khumar or Kha'a would claim her then, as soon as possible, to seal the contract. When they had enough force, her father would lead their army to war. She would be expected to give her husband a son—another oracle—as soon as it could be done.

She might die from that, or she might live. Her freedom would die the day he claimed her, along with any choice she could make on her own, that much was inevitable. Her obedience would be expected—demanded—and she would obey. She would do that, for the lives of thousands that depended on her to play that role.

But the kiss she would keep, in a place where no one could take it away from her. It was a choice she'd made, on her own, no matter how unfair or how cruel it had been on her part.

Cruel, because he was in love with her. He'd let that slip tonight, on his face, in his eyes, in the kiss he'd given her.

It would stay with him too, for as long as he was by her side, no matter how many times he would bed another woman. Many had come to his tent in the past few weeks and there would be more. She would have to learn to live with these things, and so would he.

But the kiss would stay.

She closed her hand around the bone arrowhead, felt its edges dug into her hand as she squeezed it tight. She'd hoped to keep it as a reminder for when she married into another Kha'gan. But she had him now, as her sworn sword and blood, and it was enough. It had to be enough.

She smiled at that thought, and decided she would give him the necklace in the morning.

No Way Out

Raviyani, the full moon celebration in honor of the goddess Ravi, was coming up in three days. For more than a week, the entire Kha'gan had been busy with preparations for the event. Life in the White Desert revolved around Ravi and Raviyani; all chores and activities were carefully scheduled to avoid interfering with prayer time at moonrise. Resources were put on reserve for Raviyani every month. It wasn't uncommon for families to live on the barest minimum for weeks to make sure they had enough food to go around on this single night.

Having been taken from the White Desert as a child, Hasheem couldn't remember how it had been celebrated in his own Kha'gan, and he found himself watching the scale of preparation involved for the event in complete bewilderment. The Kha'a and Nazir had been bombarded with enough requests and questions that they were forced to make decisions even at meal times. On a busy day, the lines of people waiting to see the Khumar and Kha'a wrapped themselves twice over around their tents.

The main camp, usually well-spaced and quiet, was now tightly packed with supplies and people preparing for the feast and the entertainment. Women occupied themselves with preparing food and new garments for the special evening, while the men gathered to set up the fighting pit, clearing space for the Kha'gan to come together. On the training ground, warriors in gray gathered in large numbers to prepare for the duels and games that would be the main events of the celebration. New White Warriors, he'd been told, were given their zikhs on this night, and marriages were proposed and accepted—or declined—only on Raviyani.

But the heart of the evening, the event that made it the busiest, most highly-anticipated celebration in the White Desert, were the games. There would be competitions in (but not limited to) archery, wrestling, swordsmanship, horseback riding, hand-to-hand combat, and other forms of fighting that differed from Kha'gan to Kha'gan. The zikh-clad champions with the most wins for each year were then sent to compete in the Dyal—the biggest annual competition, held in Citara. To the Shakshis, being a Dyal champion was the highest honor a White Warrior could have. It could make one a Khumar, a council member, or at the very least elevate one's family to elite status in the Kha'gan. The warriors, both Whites and Grays, trained for these competitions like their lives depended on it, and practice duels ran nonstop every day on the week leading to Raviyani.

Which was, unfortunately, one reason why Hasheem found himself in the ring one afternoon, crossing swords with the man he'd been trying his best to avoid running into for the past three weeks.

Zozi izr Zahan, firstborn son of the chief of the southern camp and right-hand man of the Kha'a, was considered one of the most promising young men in the Kha'gan. Just one year older than Hasheem, Zozi had been the undefeated champion in the duels held on Raviyani among the Gray Warriors for two seasons to date, and had even been allowed to join the Kha'a's council when possible. His father, Zahan izr Abari, being one of the most influential figures on the council, had not been subtle about securing the future of his son as soon as he had a chance to be trained in Kha'gan politics. From everyone's unspoken understanding, Zozi was the best candidate for the position of Khumar should Nazir fail to father a son, or should an untimely death find him before he could. Becoming the next Khumar, however, required both the votes from the chiefs and for Nazir to name him his successor. In short, he desperately needed to be in Nazir's favor and hadn't been shy in its acquisition.

All this shouldn't have had anything to do with Hasheem, had Zozi considered the fact that he was an orphan with no family to execute and therefore conveniently excluded from the possibility of ever earning a zikh—which, in turn, made him no competition in any way one chose to look at. But the fact that he dined at the Kha'a's table at every meal and shared every lesson with Djari seemed to draw enough attention to lodge him as a pebble in Zozi's shoe, which had resulted in a number of unfortunate, life-threatening events finding their ways into Hasheem's schedule for the past three weeks.

While having his saddle strap cut halfway just before a race or his quiver replaced with defective arrows were childs' play compared to what he'd been through in the Tower and Sabha, one thing history had taught him was that petty insults could always escalate into being stabbed in the heart while one was asleep. Consequently, Hasheem had made it a priority to avoid Zozi like his life depended on it, including removing himself from all the places where they might meet and rearranging his plans to make sure they didn't run into each other.

That morning, thanks to Nazir, who'd decided out of the blue to express an interest in seeing him engage in a duel with Zozi, Hasheem had been given no choice but to comply. One didn't say no to a Khumar, not in front of his people here in the White Desert, and expect to walk out with one's limbs intact.

And so Hasheem stood watching Zozi izr Zahan draw his double blades out of their scabbards, wondering whether he would actually live to experience his first Raviyani as an adult if he so much as gave the man a scratch.

Luckily for him, giving his opponent a scratch happened to be more of a challenge than not.

Zozi izr Zahan, still a warrior in gray, was a remarkable fighter, more so and on an entirely different level from the fashionably-trained high-borns and princes of the Black Tower. His footwork was ridiculously light, his offense well-placed and proficient, his tactics difficult to read and evade. Zozi trained with two blades, and they moved at a speed that was twice as quick as the other Grays wielding just one.

Those blades weren't light either, Hasheem realized, wincing at the bone-shattering impact climbing up his forearm every time he had to block an attack. In fewer than ten moves, his shoulder was beginning to feel numb from taking on consecutive blows. Hasheem knew it wouldn't be long before he got himself cut by one or both of those blades, and from the looks of it, he was pretty sure Zozi had intended every wound he might cause to be embarrassingly deep and preferably fatal.

Soon enough, and with no surprise to anyone, he was knocked off his feet and sent sprawling on his back, staring at the tip of Zozi's blade from the ground.

The crowd cheered as he pushed himself up, and Zozi turned a full circle to take in his compliments. He swept his eyes over the audience, noting every face that failed to acknowledge his achievement, and came to a pause at Nazir, who stood there with his usual unimpressed I-know-something-you-don't expression. To make the matter worse, the Khumar, who happened to be the one man Zozi needed to impress the most, was looking, in plain sight, not at him, but at his sister's overprivileged sworn sword. It definitely didn't go unnoticed, judging from the way Zozi was already staring daggers at him when Nazir offered a hand to pull him off the ground.

Hasheem thanked the Khumar and brushed the sand off his tunic before inclining his head in Zozi's direction in a show of respect. It wasn't acknowledged, not in the way Zozi traditionally did with other opponents. He fixed his eyes on Nazir in the same way a jealous wife might have glared at a cheating husband, and Hasheem, being Nazir's unwilling center of attention, had a vision of himself as the mistress that got stuck in the middle.

Bloody marvelous.

"It was a good effort." Nazir smiled and nodded, not bothering to take a glance at Zozi, who was still waiting to be noticed. "But you just cost me two silvers."

Hasheem sighed at that. One of these days, he was going to die from Nazir's choice of placing bets. "He's too good a fighter. I could have told you before you put coins on it."

"Is that so?" The grin on Nazir's face was an unsettling one, and Hasheem didn't want to start guessing the many hidden meanings there. He hadn't engaged in many conversations with the Khumar since the night he'd sworn his oath. Nazir had been keeping his distance, watching him from the corner of his eye as if he hadn't decided yet what to do with this new addition to the Kha'gan.

Or he had simply been taking time to measure him for something. It was possible. Anything was possible with Nazir izr Za'in.

"Come." Nazir's eyes flickered past his shoulder. "Before Nakia brings you water. She's already halfway here. That girl will cause more problems for you than winning that duel."

Resisting the urge to turn around and look, Hasheem took the advice and let Nazir lead him out of the training ground. "Why her?" he asked when they were out of earshot of the crowd.

"She's the Chief of the Treasury's daughter. Her father's vote is the most influential among my father's council members. Long story short, Zozi needs to marry her if he wants to be named the next Khumar," Nazir explained without slowing down the pace, to make sure no one would overhear them talking about the subject, he supposed. "And she intends to bed you before this Raviyani is over."

That, Hasheem swore inwardly, *would be a problem.* A big problem. He parted his lips to ask how Nazir had found out about her rather personal motives, decided it could be seen as overstepping his boundaries, and closed them.

That much, apparently, had been enough to give it away.

"You want to know how I came by that information."

Hasheem sighed. *Fucking oracles.* "If you don't mind my asking."

Nazir gave him a sidelong glance, one that ventured a little deeper than he was comfortable with. "You're not the only one with access to the women's circle," he said, "and had you been more involved with things around here, we wouldn't be having this conversation."

The chastising of his ignorance had been subtle, yet obvious. "I wasn't aware my involvement was required." The only reason he'd survived Sabha and the Black Tower had been because of a deliberate decision to not get involved beyond what was necessary. Invisibility had its uses when it came to self-preservation, that much was common knowledge in Rasharwi. His might be a famous name in the Salasar, but it didn't appear on people's path as a pebble to stumble upon.

Nazir frowned. "You are Djari's sworn sword. What you do reflects on her reputation, mine, and my father's who've put you here, and subsequently the well-being of this Kha'gan. Which brings me to the question," he said, turning to face Hasheem, "What happened last night?"

Hunting down oracles, Hasheem thought, had to be the most intelligent decision Salar Muradi had ever made in his life if this was the extent of their awareness. "I don't—"

Nazir raised his hand in a warning. "Before you insult me with your false ignorance, understand that I've been taking care of Djari since she was ten. Something's changed. What did you do?"

For all his subtlety, Nazir could be damningly blunt when he wanted to be. It occurred to Hasheem then why he'd been singled out that morning, and also the fact that he wouldn't be able to get away with denying it or changing the subject.

Then again, one couldn't survive the Black Tower without acquiring certain skills to escape from a pit full of vipers. "With all due respect, Nazir Khumar," he said formally, lowering his head in a show of obedience, "I am, as you say, Djari's sworn sword and blood, and as such my position demands discretion when it comes to her. It isn't a question I can answer without her permission, as much as I would like to."

The smile that came from Nazir wasn't one from a man who'd been pleasantly surprised, but one from someone who'd been right about something and was enjoying it immensely. "An answer befitting an apprentice of Deo di Amarra," he said. "A pity for someone who insists on being invisible. Do give my regards to your mentor when you see him again."

Hasheem swallowed. How much exactly did this man know about his past? *Or his future?*

"If," Hasheem replied, watching Nazir's reaction carefully, "I see him again."

Nazir smiled and made a point to not correct him. "Meet me at the stable before dusk," he said, changing the subject. "I'm having dinner with the chief of the northern camp. You're coming with me." And with that, he walked away.

Hasheem sighed. It didn't leave room for negotiation; not that one could say no to a Khumar's direct command, especially if said Khumar happened to know all your secrets. He'd given up trying to think about what Nazir was planning to do with him for some time. You couldn't do that and hope to be right, unless you knew what he knew.

Go west, Dee had said. He might have pissed off his mentor one too many times, but surely this was going a bit far where payback was concerned.

My Grand Design

"What do you think about Khodi?" Nazir asked on their way back from dinner with the chief of the northern camp, gazing lazily at the large moon that hung low on the horizon. He was referring to the chief's firstborn son, who'd joined them at dinner tonight.

The meal, as casual as it had seemed, had been held for several purposes. Large Kha'gans were separated into camps ruled by chiefs who operated under the command of the Kha'a. A good relationship with these chiefs allowed the ruling family to keep things under control. To the chiefs, dining with the Khumar offered a chance to introduce his sons and other family members to the next Kha'a. To Nazir, it allowed him to check on problems and address them. Why Hasheem had been dragged along, however, was about to be revealed through this rather dangerous question.

Dangerous, because where he came from, having a wrong opinion of someone could kill you.

"He seems...brave and honorable," Hasheem replied, thinking of the young man who'd appeared every bit the perfect representation of what a White Warrior should be, right down to the missing wrinkles on his zikh.

"He is," Nazir said. "But what do you *really* think of him?"

"That would depend," he said, half stalling for time to decide how to respond, half trying to read where Nazir was going with this. Opinions changed under different circumstances. It was all a matter of perspective, and until he knew Nazir's motives, it wasn't safe to offer his freely.

"On what?"

"On why you need to know." Hasheem half expected a chastising of some sort for his response, or for the very least a dismissal of the question. People in power rarely explained themselves, and Nazir's thoughtful silence that followed surprised him. So did the nod of agreement.

"Fair enough." Nazir glanced at the main camp they were heading toward and reined in his stallion, falling into step with Hasheem's mount that had been following close behind to give them time. "I will need my own council when I become Kha'a."

Hasheem shifted uncomfortably. It was a piece of information he'd rather not be given. Things would change quickly and substantially around camp should one word of it get out that Nazir was searching for candidates to fill his future council using these casual dinners and gatherings. No one would have guessed that he was already preparing for it. The Kha'a was still in his prime and the Khumar still young, too young to be thinking of such things.

Unless, of course, he knew something they didn't.

"In which case," Hasheem said, wondering whether he should be impressed at how competent this young Khumar was or be more afraid of him, "the man is arrogant and a fool, and should never be allowed to handle big decisions." It was a leap of faith he was taking, but one no larger than Nazir's for revealing his own agenda.

The corner of Nazir's lips lifted into a grin. "Out of curiosity, why?"

Hasheem smiled at the question he'd guessed would follow. Asking why was a sign of intelligence, and he had come to know how well-equipped Nazir was in that department. "He took too much space at the table and adjusted the zikh too many times. A man who cares more about his appearance than the fact that you'd actually brought me along as an opening for him to make a move is a liability." Another thought came to him. "The younger brother, I'd say, is a different story. That one would make a good strategist. If you want my opinion."

"Khali?" Nazir raised a brow. "How so?"

"He wanted to know who braided my hair."

Another thoughtful silence. A nod. "And knowing would tell him how close you are to my family. That's why you didn't tell him."

"He'll find out tomorrow," Hasheem said, "when he sends someone to deliver a jar of that fig jam you like so much. He did give the order to refill your plate twice."

"*Before* I finished the jam. Both times," Nazir added. "Khodi is too ambitious, too full of himself, but easier to move and control. With Khali…" His brow furrowed. "I'm trying to decide if he's too good to be left out of it, or too dangerous to be kept unwatched."

It occurred to Hasheem then that Nazir didn't need his insights on either of them at all. There was, he figured, only one explanation left for asking him these questions. "You're testing me. Why?"

The grin on Nazir's face widened, but whether from being impressed or being right, he couldn't tell. "Djari will need someone who knows politics when the time comes. And I want you on the council."

Hasheem blinked, twice. "Me? On the council?" *He couldn't be serious.* Being knowledgeable in Kha'gan politics to support Djari made sense, but sitting on Nazir's council was going a bit far, if it were even possible.

"Why not?"

"I'm an outsider. A stranger to the Kha'gan. My experience—"

"Is more valuable than my father's entire council combined," Nazir finished the sentence. "You survived for more than half a decade in Rasharwi after pulling yourself out of the gutter and into the inner circle of the Tower. You understand politics, know every corner of Sabha and the Black Tower inside and out. You *know* everything we need to win this war. With all that skill and insight—" Nazir turned to him, catching his eyes. "—you don't really think you're here to keep my sister entertained, or do you?"

It took Hasheem a while to process the magnitude of information being dumped on him over the short ride back to camp, and he wondered how long Nazir had been working toward this night.

"That's impossible. I can't get a zikh." The entire council was made up of White Warriors, if he recalled correctly.

"Owning a zikh is not a requirement," Nazir replied, as if the issue had been proposed, thought about, and resolved a long time ago. "And I may be able to get you adopted when I'm Kha'a. You'll get your zikh then. If that is what you want."

If that was what he wanted...

He didn't want to become a White Warrior. He never had. The idea of being bound by another oath was as unwelcome to him as going back to the pleasure district. Djari might like that, however. He could already imagine her grinning from ear to ear to have a zikh-clad sworn sword, and that might just be the only reason he'd do it if he could. Still… "They'll never accept me on the council." These people would have to accept his authority to do that, be content with letting him lead, and he was an outsider, a stranger who didn't even grow up in the desert. As things stood, it was hard enough to get past one day at camp without someone trying to trip him out of spite, literally.

"Oh, they will," Nazir said, "when you start winning duels at Raviyani and quit pretending to fail at everything—including finishing Zozi in fewer than three moves. All for the comfort of being invisible."

He stared at the Khumar. "What makes you think I'm pretending?"

"Now you insult my intelligence."

I am, Hasheem thought, sighing, *going to have to be more careful with this man.*

"I happen to enjoy the comfort of being invisible," he admitted. That much was true. He knew all the stakes, what it would take for him to fit in and become accepted, but being a real part of the Kha'gan and holding such a power was to commit himself to things he'd been trying to avoid. He'd had a Kha'gan, a family, a few friends, someone he'd come to care about. They would all be gone, all of them. He wasn't looking forward to going through that again.

"It will never last, and you know it," said Nazir. "You were born for so much more than what you are now. That rock you are hiding behind isn't big enough for you. That," he said crisply, finally, "was a *vision*."

Hasheem closed his eyes and tried to swallow that revelation. It meant that he had no choice in the matter if he were to believe in the accuracy of Nazir's gift—which, unfortunately, had so far been accurate to the tiniest detail.

"It's big enough for now," he told Nazir. A man could at least try to stall fate even if he couldn't change it, couldn't he?

For him, it wasn't even his decision to make. With power came responsibilities and sacrifices, lest one use it entirely for personal gain. You became a tyrant or a martyr, never something in between when your decisions affected the lives of others. He wouldn't be able to live with himself being the first, and one would have to still be able to make sacrifices for the second. "With all due respect, my answer is no." It needed to be made clear. "I have agreed to be bound by one oath only. I will not make another."

Nazir let that sit for a while. More, Hasheem thought from looking at that relaxed expression, to give him time to prepare for what would follow than to accept the decision. "There may be time," he said, the words dragged down his spine like a knife, splitting it open, "when that oath requires you to take another."

When, Hasheem wondered at the hopeless hilarity of it all, *will I stop running into shackles?* He knew exactly what it meant, how easy it would be for someone like Nazir to make it happen. It would take just one word to Djari and it would be done. "And you would go that far to bend a man to your grand design?"

"For the love of my land?" The reply came readily, deliberately; the clearing of a half-drawn blade from its scabbard. "Absolutely. So," Nazir added with certainty, with precision, "would Djari."

A knife in the heart that, left there to remind him of what exactly he'd sworn into. "Of course," he said. "And you bothered telling me this why? So I wouldn't make too much of a fuss when you need something done? When *both* of you decide which strings to pull and when?"

Nazir's expression changed into something colder, and Hasheem had a vision then of a ghost being roused involuntarily from its resting place. "Believe me," he said, "if I wanted to pull those strings, you'd still be in someone's bed right now doing what you do best behind closed doors to get me what I need. And you'll do it," he added, pulling his lips back into a grin that made one imagine a full row of sharp, white teeth underneath, "if I only propose to tell Djari every little thing you don't want her to know."

And so it began again: these games of politics, of power, of control. For a moment, he felt as if he was back in Rasharwi, in the Tower. How much of a fool he was to have thought that he could care about something without paying a price for it, or that people were different on the other side of the desert. "Of course. That is why I'm here. Why you've suggested that she take me as her sworn sword and blood. Tell me" he said, realizing something just at that moment, "did you even hesitate when you switched the arrow to bring me into this, or when you decided to put me back in shackles, knowing what you knew?"

He wasn't sure what bothered him more—being used by the enemies who had burned down his home, or by the people who were *supposed* to be on his side. They were beginning to look the same to him the longer he stayed around here. Except Djari, who should have been the only one with the right to move him at will, but had never wanted to.

Nazir drew a breath, as if to still something within, and then released it with a heavy sigh. "What should matter to you is not whether I hesitated, but that I have *chosen* to tell you this tonight despite the power I possess to do otherwise, and to give you a *choice* no one has ever given you."

A gust of wind rushed by them from the south, pushing back the hood of Nazir's robe and revealing the straight, silvery strands of his hair that looked identical to Djari's, except that Nazir's was almost white and carried with it an air of something eerie and terrifying, especially at night—like a being that was not of this world, and belonging nowhere.

"You can choose to be a part of this and make something out of it, or you can wait for fate to drag you along screaming. That is why we are going to my tent to have a civilized conversation over a drink," he said with a playful grin, "where I hope my irresistible charm and the promise of good wine will be enough to seduce you to my cause. What do you say?"

Hasheem stilled, considering the proposal he hadn't seen coming. In a way, Nazir had a point. There had been no need for the oracle to hold back from pulling those strings or to tell him the things he had tonight, including his own secrets and plans for the future. He was trying to play nice—as nice as his position and duty would allow. Still, there existed a feeling, a small hunch in the pit of his stomach, that this could be nothing more than Nazir's unfailing ability to wrap people around his finger.

"And if my answer is still no?"

"Then we will drink and talk," Nazir said, leaning forward to give

Springer a few pats on the neck. "I can also use a friend who doesn't want to kill me to become Khumar. I was hoping you wouldn't say no to that at least."

For a moment that ended too soon, Hasheem thought he saw a glimpse of vulnerability in Nazir's eyes. There was always a sense of bleakness in the air around him and Djari, a feeling of isolation that hung around them like shadows. He'd had the same feeling watching the Salar lounging alone on his balcony from the bottom of the Tower, or Za'in izr Husari standing outside his tent looking up at the stars when everyone else had gone to sleep.

It's always colder on the top of the mountain, someone had said. The truth was, where isolation was concerned, he was no stranger to the feeling, even if for completely different reasons and circumstances.

"I can't say much about your charm," he told Nazir, "but I'm not one to turn down a promise of good wine."

"She's nervous." Djari grimaced as she ran her hand along Twilight's neck, feeling the mare's pulse.

The horse was fidgeting a little, not to the point that would have alarmed him, but Hasheem didn't question Djari about her horses, not when she spent half her days in the stable and slept in it several nights a month.

"I can take Bruiser."

She shook her head. "Bruiser won't be able to keep up with Nazir, and he gets jumpy in a big crowd." She hesitated a little before arriving at a decision. "Take Summer."

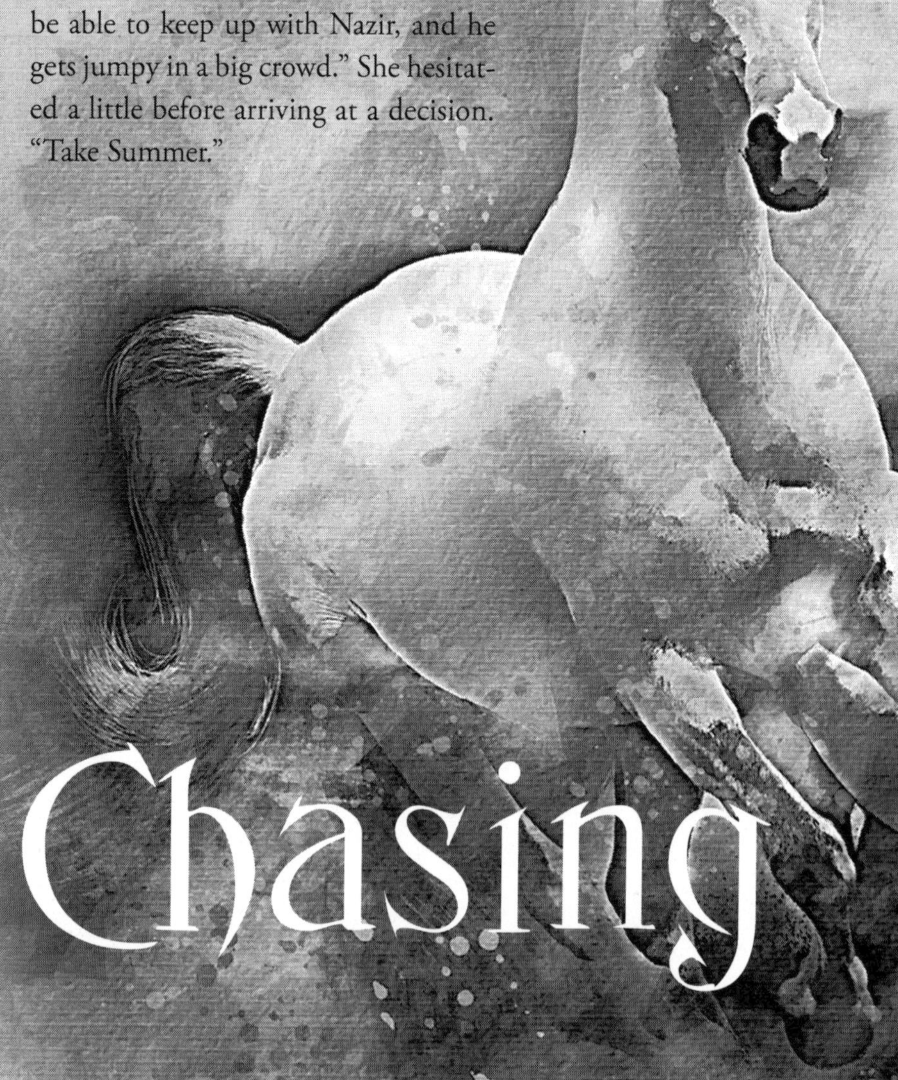

Summer was Djari's colt, her personal mount and their second-best horse next to Springer. If he took Summer... "Who will you ride?"

"No one," she said. "I'm not coming."

The answer surprised him, and not in a good way. He had expected to accompany her on the ride. This was a ceremonial hunt, done on the afternoon of the same day before each Raviyani to bring back desert gazelles as holy offerings to Ravi. From what he'd been told, there would be over a hundred riders participating in the event. She would have been with a big crowd, and safety shouldn't have been a concern. "You can't or you won't?"

"I have...things to do," Djari said, keeping her eyes on Twilight, her lips stretched into a thin line and pressed tight together.

Hasheem knew that look. She did that whenever her sense of duty forced her to make a decision she didn't want to make. "Then I don't need to go," he told her. All things considered, it made no sense for him to be there without Djari.

"You have to," she said. "If Nazir wants you there, then he has a reason. Besides, it's your

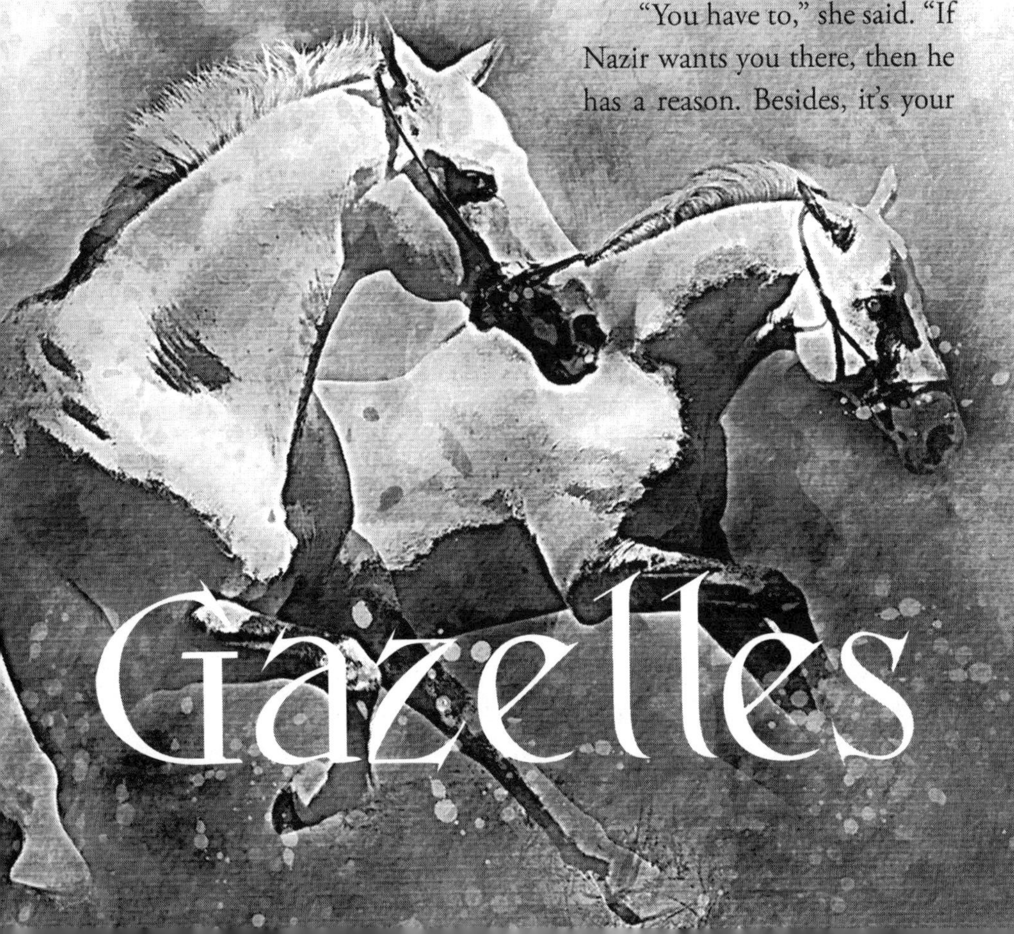

first Raviyani. You'll enjoy it."

Hasheem doubted he would. Hunting had never been an enjoyable sport for him. There was nothing thrilling about chasing down helpless animals, not when he'd been that animal too many times. But whether or not he would enjoy the event wasn't the problem. The problem was that Nazir definitely *had* a reason to want him there, which was precisely why he was having second thoughts about this whole idea. One never knew what an oracle could be seeing—or planning.

The sound of someone entering the stable drew their attention to the gate. Down the corridor toward the entrance, Nazir appeared in his spotless white robe, followed by two stable boys carrying a ceremonial saddle. The Khumar's zikh had been freshly pressed, Hasheem noticed, and over it hung a sash of blue and gold—the symbolic colors of the Visarya Kha'gan. His hair, neatly braided in the White Warrior style, also had blue and gold threads in it. He carried a dagger, a sword, a bow, and a quiver full of arrows, all of which were gilded or painted in the same colors.

Hasheem drew a breath at the unsettling sight that was entirely new to him. Nazir was in his most formal attire, which implied that the hunt held a lot more significance than he'd originally thought. The Khumar of Visarya was far from a man of excess. He wore the zikh only sometimes. His everyday sword was unadorned and ordinary and his boots were always stained from heavy use. They were brand new today, Hasheem noted. Nazir was making a statement with this, or he wouldn't have appeared that way.

Next to him, Djari was blinking in surprise. Apparently, she hadn't seen him in that getup many times either.

"He's letting you lead the hunt today?" she asked, stepping forward to take a good look at her brother.

Nazir smiled. "He told me he's too old to be chasing gazelles."

She shook her head, then reached over to straighten the sash for him. "You know he isn't."

Nazir's smile was gentle. It always was with Djari. "I know he isn't."

They exchanged a look, and an understanding seemed to pass between them. It was in these moments that Hasheem could see the strength of their bond, how much love there was. Words weren't always needed with them. One look from Nazir or one gesture of his hand could make Djari pause in the middle of an act, or continue. He had come to enjoy watching them and often wondered if his bond with Djari would ever come close. There had, inevitably, been an awkward atmosphere between them since that night. It was going to take a while, he knew, before things went back to normal.

"Are you nervous?" Djari asked with a touch of concern, perhaps even fear. He wondered why, especially when this appeared to be Nazir's first time leading the hunt. The Kha'a was obviously making room for Nazir to secure respect and acceptance from the Kha'gan. If anything, it should have been a cause for celebration. Unless there was something else about the event he didn't know.

They would see him too, next to Nazir. Hasheem shivered at the realization. Not a comforting thought, given the proposal he'd declined the other night.

"A little," Nazir said before turning to him. "Not as much as this one, I'm sure."

Hasheem rolled his eyes. "Who wouldn't be, seeing you in that?"

Djari raised a brow, probably to the way he was speaking more casually with her brother now. They had ended up talking and drinking until quite late that night. He didn't exactly find Nazir to be his new best friend, but it did break the ice a little.

Nazir snorted. "You just wait until nan'ya gets her hands on you tonight. She was sorting out ribbons this morning."

He swore, and Djari laughed. It was worth wearing ribbons, Hasheem thought. She didn't laugh very often.

Nazir went to Springer's stall and stood by to watch the men saddle his horse. They did so with unusual attention to detail, checking every buckle twice and smoothing the blanket underneath, making sure the borders were perfectly even on both sides. It was the first time Hasheem had seen them put so much effort into dressing up a horse. This was truly no small matter for the Visarya, and it was giving him a bad feeling in his stomach.

"Take Summer," Djari repeated, handing him the saddle that had originally been prepared for Twilight. He took it, this time without question. Springer was being saddled, and his horse had to be done before the Khumar's.

Djari held the reins as he mounted, rubbing down her horse and giving it a few soothing words as she did. She checked his stirrups and then handed him the bow and quiver. "Keep up with Nazir," she said, not smiling now. "Stay close to him. It will be more difficult if you fall behind. Accidents happen during the hunt."

He nodded, taking the reins from her and patting Summer on the neck.

"The first shot is Nazir's. After that, it's fair game," she continued. "Bring down the adult males only. Never the females."

He didn't like the sound of that. Of any of it, actually. "What happens if I bring down a female?"

"Don't do that." She winced at the question. "They won't let you hunt again for a year if you kill a female. More, if she has a baby in her womb. Also, you'll probably die if you fall off the horse or if you accidentally kill someone. Make sure your way is clear before you loose your arrow."

Hasheem resisted the urge to sigh and curse audibly at Nazir as he listened to her instructions and warnings. Not all of it made sense to him, and he was beginning to wonder if his previous understanding of hunting had been a complete misinterpretation of the word.

"Any more ways I might die from this?" *Go to the hunt*, she'd said. *You'll enjoy it,* she'd said. The definition of enjoyment, Hasheem decided, was definitely different in the White Desert.

"Whatever you do," Djari said, and looked him in the eyes. "Don't hurt my horse."

That he didn't have a doubt about, and told her as much. You could be forgiven for many things with Djari, but you didn't mess with her horses and expect to get away with it, which made him even more nervous about being on her favorite colt.

He waited for Nazir to mount up and head out of the stable, then followed a few paces behind. Outside, a band of riders in equally formal attire was waiting. Fourteen warriors would accompany the Khumar to the hunt that day. Fourteen men, each one hand-picked by Nazir to ride out with him. They were the candidates for Nazir's future council, Hasheem noticed, all wearing a zikh, except for the two Grays among them. Hasheem had expected Zozi to be there, as a gesture of respect toward his ambitious father. The other Gray, however, took him by surprise.

A surprise because the older brother wasn't there.

Next to Zozi, Khali sat atop his white stallion with the ease of someone who'd been invited to join the leading party a dozen times, only Hasheem knew for certain he hadn't. The chief's younger son, physically small and more lithe than muscular compared to the other Grays in general, didn't seem at all intimidated by the White Warriors around him despite being the youngest in the party. Leaning back leisurely on his saddle, Khali's half-amused, half-uninterested expression could easily pass him off as a lazy, unimportant young man who was simply there to pass time.

If one were ignorant enough to pass him off as such, of course, Hasheem thought, watching those pale green eyes turning from one face to another, seeing how they noted the smiles, the braids, the zikhs (and the wrinkles on them), along with the tiniest details in the way someone sat his horse or how tightly a man held his reins. The same thing Hasheem had been doing, looking at him.

Those eyes came to rest on Hasheem. He answered the gaze with a blank expression and a polite nod of acknowledgment. Khali stared for a moment, took a glance at Summer, and then smiled. The fact that he was riding Djari's horse had been registered, of course, and would certainly be used in the future.

Too good to be left out, or too dangerous to be kept unwatched. Nazir had been right and appeared to be putting that to the test. Someone as intelligent as Khali could offer much if he was willing, and needed to be kept close if he proved otherwise. The big question was, would the boy be any less dangerous under watch?

'An excess of any quality is always dangerous,' Dee had said. *'Too much intelligence in one's men can mess up your plans just as well as too little.'* By the logic of that statement, Deo di Amarra was someone who should be put to death immediately. He'd said as much to his mentor on one occasion, to which Dee had laughed and replied, *'I am stupid enough to want to live,*

so there's that.' He wondered sometimes if the Salar was wise to be keeping Dee so close. Or if Nazir was to want to keep Khali close.

Nazir snapped a command, and the fifteen warriors began their ride toward the hunting ground, to be joined by the rest of the young men of Visarya along the way. *Fifteen White Desert warriors and a stray*, Hasheem corrected himself, and sighed. He was the only one not wearing white or gray, and with no reason to be there besides that it pleased the Khumar. Nazir, he realized, for all that talk about giving him choices, had never intended to take no for an answer.

The Hunt

The hunting ground was an hour's ride north from the main camp. An hour of flat-out continuous gallop on the toughest horses in the peninsula. It wouldn't have been possible without these mounts, not with such ground conditions and at the pace they were going. Having adapted to the desert for generations, these horses could endure a ride at bone-breaking speed without rest or water over a ridiculously long distance, with the best being those bred in the Vilarhiti mountain range in the north. Vilarians, being the fastest and toughest horses in the peninsula, used to be worth their weight in gold for outsiders to get their hands on them. Springer was one of them, and it was no surprise why they all found it so difficult to keep up with Nazir.

There used to be more of them around before the Salasar took the Vilarhiti, Djari had told him. *'The Rashais have our best horses now. Thousands of them,'* she'd said, rubbing down Springer one morning as if it had been her horses they'd taken. Then again, losing the Vilarhiti and those horses was a catastrophe for the Shakshis. The right horses could win you a war and shift the balance of power if one knew how to use them, and they had fallen into the hands of a man who knew exactly how.

The Salar had been breeding them quite successfully for more than a decade in the royal stable. A number of these horses had been given as gifts to the important figures in the Tower since the taking of the Vilarhiti. He wondered what Djari would say if she knew how common they had become among the elites of Rasharwi who never used them for anything more than accessories of status. Dee, too, had ten of these horses—the original ones taken from the valleys of Vilarhiti, no less. Hasheem could still remember him strolling through the stable, admiring them and saying out loud how clever it had been for the young prince who was now the Salar of Rasharwi to have won him over with these mounts. *"It's remarkable, isn't it?"* Dee had said. *"How just ten horses could change the fate of the entire peninsula given to the right person?"*

Ten Vilarian horses had, indeed, made sure the right people conveniently died in an untimely manner (or timely, depending on whose perspective it was) to open up a path to the throne.

He could use one of those horses right now, Hasheem thought. They were made for this, not to be holed up in some fancy stable in the city. In fact, he might have been riding one now had the Vilarhiti not fallen.

The hunting party led by the Khumar and his fifteen escorts merged with the rest of the hunters who'd been waiting along the route. The hunters consisted mostly of promising warriors in gray, with a few White Warriors in the mix, and in the end their number reached over a hundred riders. From what Hasheem had been told, only twenty hunters were painstakingly tried and selected from each of the five camps to attend, not including the ones that had been handpicked by the ruling family themselves to participate. According to Djari, it was a great honor to be at the hunt on Raviyani, and one's entire family status would be elevated in the Kha'gan when a son was selected. It had become clear to Hasheem, who rode among them this morning, why they considered it so.

The ride was brutal enough without having to keep up with Nazir, who happened to be a superb rider on the back of a Vilarian horse. They were running on hard ground with enough scattered rocks and obstacles along the path to trip any horse with a careless master. The sandy trail, treacherously narrow and flanked by steep cliffs on both sides, was covered by what looked like a sandstorm made by the passing of a hundred horses at full gallop. Around him, the sound of hoofbeats roared like a continuous, never-ending thunder, making the ride as deafening as it was blinding. Together, they drowned out most of the senses one might need to succeed in what could only be called an act of suicide.

It *was* an act of suicide, especially for those who didn't have enough skills or experience on horseback or the trust of one's horse. The thought came to him as he pulled up the scarf Djari had insisted he wear to cover his nose with both hands, and he was still adjusting it when a small rock appeared out of nowhere. Instinct made him squeeze his thighs to evade it without checking the surroundings. Summer jumped to the right and almost collided with another horse whose rider, having been forced to leap over another obstacle in his way, landed in front of him. Hasheem swore under his breath, leaned back on the saddle with all his weight and jerked the reins to back up. Startled by the unexpected interruption, Summer reared up on his hindquarters, neighing loudly as he tipped him backward. Hasheem grabbed onto the mane, caught himself just in time as he slid down Summer's back, and narrowly escaped being unhorsed.

The small pause had, however, caused a sizable distance between him and Nazir, and Hasheem found himself riding now in the worst part of the party. Space tightened threefold around the middle of the stampede, where a larger number of riders in the back tried to push forward, merging into those nearer to the front and forcing their way in. Hasheem scanned the surroundings and realized the safer place to be was either the far back or at the very front close to Nazir, where there was more room to ride. Hasheem considered falling all the way back to avoid being unhorsed and trampled to death on his first Raviyani. He didn't have time to finish that thought when the rider next to him fell and disappeared without a trace underneath the storm of sand and the thundering hooves coming from behind. The fall went on to disrupt a number of horses coming up at speed, causing havoc at the rear and resulting in two more riders falling off their horses.

The back wasn't an option, Hasheem decided; not unless he was content with being embarrassingly far behind, which would reflect badly on Djari. The safest place to be was around Nazir, where fewer horses were able to catch up with him and those who could were riding carefully around their Khumar. Djari knew this, had warned him of it before they rode out of the stable, and had even given him the horse to do just that.

Looking down at Summer and the riders in front of him, Hasheem made the one decision necessary to survive. He shortened the reins, leaned forward, and kicked Djari's best horse into a full gallop, despite the lack of room and the number of riders he would have to pass. Confident, sure-footed, and quick as a cat, Summer made his way through the crowd at mind-numbing speed, turning cleanly and swiftly left and right around the other riders at the slightest pressure from his knees.

He was one hell of a horse, Hasheem thought breathlessly, realizing for the first time the true extent of the privilege he'd been given. He'd ridden Dee's Valerians on occasion, but never at such speed, or under such a circumstance that would have brought out the best of their abilities, and yet he doubted they would be much better than this. Summer was brilliant in both responsiveness and skill, and Hasheem found himself admiring Djari endlessly in his mind for having shaped and trained such a magnificent horse. All the family mounts were trained by Djari, from what he knew, and she'd disciplined them to the point of obeying her vocal commands like impeccably loyal soldiers. It was for this, and the fact that Summer was her most frequently-trained horse, that Hasheem saw as the sole reason why he might survive the hunt that day.

In just moments, he found himself riding with Nazir and the rest of the leading party once more. A few paces in front of him were Zozi and Khali, following closely behind their Khumar to the right. They turned to look at him. Khali flashed him a grin; Zozi looked half-surprised, half-disappointed he hadn't died already; and Nazir only nodded. His own expression, Hasheem would have guessed, probably matched that of Zozi. He was equally surprised and disappointed to be alive considering he might have to do this all over again every Raviyani if it pleased the Khumar.

The thought made him understand something that hadn't occurred to him before.

They do this every Raviyani. He shivered. Every month, the new generation of Gray Warriors put their lives on the line for what was considered a ceremonial ride, a game, to test and sharpen their skills. There were riders as young as ten among them (six was how early some began training), and he counted at least eight riderless horses along the way. There would be more accidents before the hunt was over, and not all of them were going to make it, not in that kind of stampede. The riders hadn't slowed down or glanced at those who'd fallen. They were used to this, to dying and being killed, to riding out from families and lovers on a day they were supposed to be celebrating knowing they might not return.

It dawned on him that day, in the middle of the race to the hunting ground, that he was now living among the hardest people in the peninsula, and that he was being forged, willingly or not, into something equally hard. He might actually be seen as one of them from the eyes of an outsider.

No, he *was* one of them, Hasheem corrected himself. They *were* his people, had been from the beginning despite all the years he'd been away from the desert. He could feel it here, now, in the way his heart pounded in answer to these hoofbeats, in the excitement that filled his lungs to the point of bursting as they thundered through the valley, in how hard, how fast a rush of energy forced its way through his limbs, making him feel alive in the midst of danger, death, and madness. It was in his flesh and blood, built into his very instinct; this yearning to embrace the constant danger, of facing and conquering his worst fears as a part of everyday life. This was who he was, who he had always been, and where he was supposed to be all along.

It was also why he'd survived in Rasharwi, Hasheem realized. He was a Shakshi. Hardship and warfare were his people's occupation; the ability to endure and prevail had been passed down for generations to every Shakshi man, woman, and child. This was the reason the Salasar had never conquered the White Desert. You couldn't break people who lived to defy death every day while hiding behind the safety of a wall. Not without wounding yourself in the process.

He remembered asking Dee about that—how Salar Muradi had done it, how the Vilarhiti had been taken. "*With half the Salasar's army,*" Dee had said. "*Dead,*" he'd added. Half the Salasar's soldiers never returned from that valley. The loss had been so great that it had taken them a decade to rebuild and replenish the supplies that had been lost in an event both sides would call a massacre. The Rashais had taken the Vilarhiti, but lacked the resources to go on with the campaign. With a crippled army, the other acquired provinces had taken the opportunity to rise up and fight for independence, resulting in another decade-long internal conflict Salar Muradi had been forced to deal with. Despite his eventual success, the long simultaneous battle against three provinces had kept the Salasar's army from marching into the White Desert again for eighteen years.

To most people, conquering the Vilarhiti was seen as the biggest achievement in the history of the Salasar. Those who had been directly involved in it, however, were often caught saying behind closed doors and amongst their most trusted companions that it was the biggest mistake Salar Muradi had ever made, victoriously or not.

But he had long since learned from that mistake, and could be expected to not make it again. "*The next time he decides to strike, it would be a war to end all wars,*" Dee had said. And he would strike, eventually. Everyone knew this. The massacre at the Vilarhiti had left a scar too deep for a conqueror like Salar Muradi to not seek retribution. It was why he'd kept a Bharavi by his bed—for the same reason Za'in izr Husari kept his wife's setting at the dining table every night.

And there was pride in all this—in knowing that despite everything they'd taken from his people, they were still standing. No, not just standing, Hasheem corrected himself as he looked around him once more, but riding hard on a land that was still free, keeping tradition, holding pride, and smiling in the face of danger and the possibility of death. You could see it on all their faces, taste it in the air they breathed—the sweet, addictive flavor of true appreciation of life that could only be acquired from having defied death, or the possibility of it.

Djari was right. He *was* enjoying this. But he would have enjoyed it more had she been with them. He could imagine her smiling, those intense yellow eyes glowing in excitement, and that odd silver hair tangling in the wind as she raced across the valley. He smiled briefly at that image, then realized that he might never see it. She would be married in two years into another Kha'gan, where she would likely be kept safe inside only to breed more oracles. If there had been anger building in his chest for Djari's lack of freedom, there was twice more of it now.

A horn sounded from up ahead, and he shook himself from that thought. They must be close to the valley. This stampede was only a ride to the main event, after all. *The real hunt*, Hasheem thought, *is about to begin.*

An Impossible Task

A suffocating thickness filled the air as the hunting ground came into view. The riders picked up speed at the first sound of the horn and, like a starving, salivating pack of dogs seeing the promise of a meal, more than one hundred horses thundered up the hill, racing each other toward the bowl that lay up ahead. Hasheem drew a long breath to steady his nerves as the ground underneath him rumbled and was hit with the raw, overpowering scent produced by a mixture of sweat, saliva, and freshly-oiled leather riding high above the smell of horses. The stench of excitement woke him up, raised his pulse, snapped his mind into place. '*Men,*' Dee had once said, '*are creatures driven by the desire to prove themselves through danger, and more so in the presence of other males.*'

A stupidity, to be sure, but true nonetheless. There was an undeniable yearning in the pit of his stomach, a thrill so close to seeing a beautiful naked woman that made it near impossible to retreat in the face of danger. He could see fear in the riders around him that matched his—*fear*, of course, was what made it so exciting. It was written on their faces, in how tightly they held the reins, in the stiffness of their shoulders. They were all smiling and breathing as hard as their horses, as if they were riding a woman and were getting close to reaching the climax.

The horn continued, piercing through and rising above the deafening roar of the stampede and the hammering beat of his heart, carrying with it a promise of death that awaited them in the valley, and of the madness that was about to erupt.

They reached the top of the hill, and Hasheem realized with a punch of disappointment in his stomach that the plain below was empty. Not a single gazelle on the ground or around it. Not a soul.

Where are they?

Another horn sounded from the opposite direction, and the rider next to him smiled, showing a row of crooked teeth as he shortened the reins and secured them on the saddle.

From the eastern slope, the gazelles poured in, numbering in the hundreds. Behind them, a different group of riders was driving them hard, herding them into the valley. Hasheem looked to Nazir for a signal to slow down that would give the hunters time to ready their bows and didn't find it. The Khumar continued at full speed as they descended into the bowl, heading straight for the herd. One hundred galloping horses were about to crash head-on into as many gazelles on a stampede. On purpose.

This is suicide. Hasheem swore under his breath, staring in disbelief at the catastrophe that was about to unfold.

At the very front, about a hundred paces before they clashed with the panicking gazelles, Nazir unslung his bow and nocked an arrow. He did so on a galloping horse, standing high on the stirrups, back straight as a spear. The riders behind him followed, mimicking their Khumar to perfection. Without slowing down, they watched in anticipated silence, bow in hand, steering the horses with their knees as Nazir picked his first target. His arrow's fletching was painted blue and gold, Hasheem noticed, like the sash he was wearing. This was, after all, a ceremony as much as a game. The gazelles were to be offered to the goddess tonight. It was why they hunted only adult males.

Still galloping hard toward the herd, Hasheem held his breath as he watched, and realized that the other riders, too, were doing the same. This was their Khumar's first time leading the hunt, and the first ceremonial shot had to be done right. A defining moment for Nazir, a reputation that would stay with him for a long time, a test he had to pass in front of a hundred spectators. Hasheem's stomach churned at the thought. *Don't miss*, he caught himself praying—something he didn't do very often. *Don't fucking miss.*

Nazir's hands shook a little. He lowered his bow. Closed his eyes. Drew a breath. Exhaled. The hands steadied. Nazir opened his eyes, gripped tight and more surely this time on the curve of his bow, and trained the arrow once more on the target. A gust of wind rushed through the valley, tugging Nazir's long silver hair into a wild dance behind him as he rode high on Springer, his attention hooked on the gazelle whose life he was about to end, and made everything else disappear for an instant.

And in that short moment of suspended time, when one could almost sense the arrival of Death for its offerings, Nazir flicked his fingers and released the arrow.

It pierced through the air, flew straight into the herd, and buried itself in the throat of the chosen gazelle, killing it instantly. The hunters erupted into a high-pitched battle cry as they drove their mounts forward into the horde of animals. In half a breath, arrows were being loosed in all directions amidst horses running at full speed. Gazelles zig-zagged around the riders, causing havoc in the small, confined space of the valley. Men shouted and yelled at each other to get out of the way as Hasheem watched and realized he was supposed to shoot down an animal in the middle of all this and ride out with his life and his limbs intact. More importantly, he had to get Summer out of this madness without a scratch or risk being skinned alive by Djari. One could definitely die doing this (or afterward, in his case), and he wondered how many usually did every Raviyani.

The only way out of this mess, Hasheem decided with a groan, was to get out of it as soon as humanly possible.

Without wasting any more time, he unslung his bow, fitted an arrow, and shot at a gazelle. It didn't touch the creature—it wasn't supposed to—but it landed close to a horse nearby, causing it to jump to the side and nearly throw its rider off its back. The rider swore a string of words that had something to do with Hasheem's mother as he righted himself on the saddle. By the time the hunt was over, Hasheem figured he would be the most hated man on this side of the peninsula.

There were four shots left in his quiver. All hunters including the Khumar were allowed just five arrows, all fitted with blue and yellow feathers resembling those of Nazir's, each one painted with a specific number on the shaft to identify the rider who made the kill. It meant that he would have to shoot four more times in the middle of it without hitting a horse, a man, or a female gazelle before he could leave the field with some honor intact. Easier said than done, considering what had happened on the first shot.

He'd come expecting it to be a one-sided mass slaughter—a hundred riders taking his pick from just as many gazelles. The reality, as much as it pleased him, was far more complicated. The hunt required one to carefully pick out a male gazelle, identifiable only by the barely visible white blaze on their forehead, which required facing it head-on to be certain. These White Desert gazelles, being no bigger than the size of a small fox and quicker than their horses, made it painstakingly difficult to get close enough to identify a male target, and by the time that happened, it was almost always too late to take proper aim at the animal unless you were that good a rider and archer.

All the while, one could only pray that one's fellow archers were as good as they were meant to be and that their arrows didn't end up halfway in your thigh or in the flank of your horse. The latter would also result in a bad fall, followed by being trampled to death by the other horses or the gazelles they were meant to hunt.

It wasn't even hunting. This was a battle, where carelessness or a small mistake could kill.

And so Hasheem did the only thing he could do to save Djari's horse, which was to shoot his arrows ceremoniously to empty his quiver and ride out of the hunting ground as soon as it was done.

Sitting atop Summer on the slope, looking down at the scene below, Hasheem realized these warriors were engaging in the activity with unreasonable ease and inappropriate humor that was becoming more and more ridiculous the longer he watched. While very few managed to shoot down a gazelle, no one had died or seemed to be dying despite the chaos and the impossibility of it. All the hunters took great care before releasing their shots and would often allow the gazelles to get away rather than risk injuring other riders or their horses. Apparently, it was more embarrassing to accidentally shoot someone than to go home empty-handed. Some did miss, however, and while he found himself wincing every time a rider came limping out of the plain with an arrow wound, the men on the slope who'd already emptied their quivers were seen placing bets as to which loser's arrow it was they saw embedded in someone's thigh or other, more hilarious body parts.

Which was what Nazir was doing, leaning his weight on one side of the saddle while listening to Khali's suggestion regarding whose arrow they'd just seen sticking out of his cousin's butt.

"How many did you get?" Nazir asked when he noticed Hasheem joining them on the slope.

Hasheem raised a brow. "Grays or gazelles?"

Nazir chuckled. "Both."

"None and none," he replied. "I got myself out with my behind intact, does that count?"

It earned him a laugh from both the Khumar and the young Gray by his side. Hasheem glanced at the boy's quiver and wondered how many of those arrows had been shot ceremoniously and how quickly it had taken him to finish shooting the rest after knowing Nazir had emptied his. Between gazelles and Nazir, there was no question which one of the two was the better catch, if one were smart enough.

"How many did you two get?" he asked, guiding Summer to stand closer to Nazir.

"I got two. Khali shot one," Nazir replied lightly, then added with a touch of concern, "Looks like we're going to be short today."

So there was a certain number they were supposed to bring back. That was new information to him. "How many do we need?"

"Twenty-five to thirty gazelles is a good number," Nazir said, keeping his eyes on the valley down below. "Anything below twenty is...unfavorable."

Unfavorable wasn't good for a Khumar's first time leading the hunt, Hasheem thought, and began to regret having shot those arrows so ceremoniously. He looked down at the plain below and counted the gazelles and hunters. There were fifteen downed gazelles that he could see and about twenty of the latter left.

"How many can one bring down on average? Given more room?" he asked.

“About five to one, if we’re lucky.”

Hasheem swore under his breath. “Hunters to gazelles?” That would give them just four more. *If they’re lucky,*

Nazir nodded. “Unless we have really good archers down there still. The gazelles have more room to run.”

It was true, now that he looked again. With fewer riders, the field was wider now and a large number of gazelles had already fled the valley. The best chance was at the beginning of the hunt, and a truly competent archer would have already taken his shots. One could do that very effectively in such chaos if one could aim and release fast and accurately enough in quick succession.

“What’s the most someone has shot down in a day?”

Nazir drew a breath, made the face of someone who had something stuck between his teeth. “Four.”

Four gazelles with five arrows. That was one hell of an archer. “And you didn’t bring him?”

“I didn’t bring *her.*” Nazir sighed. “That was Djari’s number earlier this year.”

Of course. Djari was their best archer and someone who could ride like she had been born on horseback. This would have been the perfect playground for Djari, if only she could come. “Why didn’t you?”

Nazir shifted uncomfortably at the question. “It would have taken five Gray escorts,” he said. “Five of our best who would miss out on the hunt...”

Five Grays who would have preferred to hunt than to guard a girl. “And they weren’t willing,” Hasheem finished the sentence. It wasn’t hard to arrive at the conclusion. One complaint and he could see Djari taking it as her duty to opt out of the event. Djari was Djari. Responsibility came first, always.

Before he could voice his protest, another horn sounded from the western side of the valley. Nazir turned swiftly toward the sound. Khali swore, loudly.

“They’re early,” Nazir said. The lightness of that statement, however, didn’t match his expression.

Collision

A gust of wind rushed through the valley. Nazir's zikh snapped sharply behind him, his eyes fixed on an empty spot far away, giving the rest of them a sense that he was seeing something they couldn't. For a moment, he seemed to be here and not here at the same time, and Hasheem wondered if everyone else felt the way he did watching their Khumar. They were all watching him though, quietly and anxiously judging from the way their horses fidgeted. Horses were damningly quick at sensing when their riders were about to piss themselves.

"Who's early?" Hasheem asked.

"The Kamara," Khali replied. He'd gathered both reins in his hands and sat tight on the saddle. "They aren't supposed to be here until we're done."

The Kamara Kha'gan was their rival in the north. They shared a border made up of the Djamahari mountain range. Territory disputes happened from time to time between neighboring Kha'gans when it came to taxing travelers and caravans in the White Desert, but they were considered mild conflicts and hadn't happened as often in the past. With the Salar's raiding parties pushing in more aggressively from the east, the Kha'gans had less room to move. This in turn created more frequent conflicts regarding borders that weren't always clearly defined in the desert. There had been as many as two incidents in the short time Hasheem had been there between the Visarya and the Kamara, and eight men had been injured in the process. They were about to face another that day, from the looks of it.

"Why are they here at all?" Hasheem asked. They were never supposed to be in the same place. Entering another Kha'gan's territory required permission from the chiefs unless one came with the intention to invade.

"The hunting ground is always shared between Kha'gans," Nazir explained. There was unmistakable tension in his voice now, and those usually relaxed shoulders had become obviously stiff. "But there are agreements on its usage controlled by Citara. We have the priority this Raviyani."

Before he could ask more questions, a new batch of riders and gazelles poured into the valley, and Hasheem understood immediately why Khali had cursed just now. They were about to merge into one—the two hunting parties and gazelles—and Hasheem didn't need to be told how many things could go wrong if it were allowed to happen. Shooting someone's cousin by mistake could be considered funny; shooting a member of one's rival Kha'gan, even by accident, was not.

Nazir, for all his seemingly limitless ability to control his emotions, looked like he wanted to kill someone with his bare hands at that moment. Hasheem wondered if he would actually see the Khumar losing it over this. That would have been a thing to remember for life.

It might also mean battle. Hasheem swallowed at the thought. Nazir had the authority to initiate it here if his patience were to reach its limit. He only had to shoot an arrow into the new hunting party to kill one man and all hell would break loose. He looked like he wanted to do just that, and the men around him knew it. They all seemed to have stopped breathing as they waited, just as anxiously as Hasheem did, for their Khumar to decide their fate.

Or the entire desert's, given how one thing could always lead to another.

A suffocating, toxic moment pressed down upon them as they stared at the tall figure in white. The silver of his hair glinted like a newly-sharpened blade ready to bite into flesh. Nazir's breathing was slow, barely visible from the movements of his chest. It rose and fell. Once. Twice. And on the third time came to a pause, and the world seemed to have stopped with it.

Gripping the reins until his knuckles turned white, Nazir drew another long breath, closed his eyes, and then, releasing it with a heavy sigh, turned to issue a command. "Tell Bhotsa to sound the retreat. The hunt is over."

Hasheem released his own breath at that and noticed the same reaction from the men around him. Whatever it was that gave Nazir that rock solid self-control needed to have a statue made in its image for men to worship for the next three hundred years.

Khali turned his mount immediately, then paused before he took off, having noticed something on the plain. "Zozi is still down there, and so is Khodi," he said, more to offer information than to object. "They're not going to be happy."

Hasheem followed his gaze to the valley below, saw both men, and resisted the urge to curse the gods. Khali was right. They were both sons of their chiefs. One, a proud, ambitious gray-clad warrior who would be severely pissed to miss a chance to make his mark, and the other...

The other happened to be wearing white, and it was he whose younger, gray-clad brother had been hand-picked by the Khumar to join his leading party without him. Hasheem hadn't noticed Khodi there until then. Zikh-clad warriors didn't usually come to the hunt, unless by invitation from the Kha'a or the Khumar. It was the Grays' playground and was considered beneath them, from what he understood. That day, Nazir had indirectly forced him to attend by inviting the younger brother and not the older. Khodi was going to have to prove he could bring down more gazelles than Khali to assert his authority, and now he was about to be pulled out of the hunt before he could. It wasn't going to end well, no matter how he looked at it. Nazir had picked the wrong day to be playing a dangerous game.

"They just have to live with it," Nazir said. "I'm not going to risk an open war over gazelles. Sound the retreat."

An open war on his first watch no less, Hasheem thought, shortening his own reins. "Does this ever happen?" he asked once Khali was out of earshot.

"Every once in a while, when there's a new Kha'a or Khumar."

"They knew you were leading the hunt," Hasheem said. Things were becoming clearer to him now. It was why Nazir was wearing his most formal attire. There was a chance they might run into each other, and appearance was everything. "They're testing you."

Nazir nodded. "A test if it's the Khumar leading the party and not the Kha'a. I can't make out who it is yet, but be ready to ride back to deliver a message if it's the latter."

"Why the latter?"

Nazir stared at the plain, his face unreadable as he explained. "A Kha'a can get away with a son going rogue from time to time. If he comes himself—"

"He's declaring war," Hasheem realized, with an urge to swear. "That's why you didn't bring Djari."

"It was her choice this time," Nazir said regretfully, "but no, I wouldn't have let her come, not on my first watch. Neither would the Kha'a."

She probably knew it, Hasheem was certain. They all knew what might happen the first time Nazir was allowed to lead the hunt. Za'in izr Husari had sent his only son—their *only* oracle—out to be tried and tested, knowing what they stood to lose if things were to go wrong. It was why Djari had looked troubled that morning, seeing her brother in the stable. Luckily for them, Nazir's self-control had proven to be well beyond his age.

Their horn sounded soon after, and Hasheem could see the hunters bringing their horses to a sudden stop down below. They seemed confused at first, then turned to see the other hunting party heading down the slope and promptly pulled their mounts to the side, swearing viciously as they did. From the distance, he could see Zozi hesitate a little before deciding to loose his last arrow at a gazelle, killing it with the shot before riding back up the slope. It could be considered disrespectful, if Nazir had noticed the last arrow being shot *after* the retreat had been sounded. Luckily for Zozi, the Khumar had been staring at the other chief's son. The one wearing white.

The same one who had two more arrows in his quiver, having just shot the third, and was now turning to look in their direction. From the distance, Khodi's gaze swept over the men on the slope, and came to a pause on Khali, who'd just returned to Nazir's side. Time stood still in that moment, and everything around them seemed to have disappeared into the surroundings, leaving just the two figures, both wearing white, both with eyes fixed upon each other, judging, measuring, weighing the consequences of their decision, or the one they were about to make.

Then he saw Khodi turn his horse, not to the nearby slope, but toward the new herd of gazelles.

"Oh brother, no." Khali, who had remained quiet until then, mumbled under his breath as he watched his brother draw a new arrow out of the quiver. His gaze shifted back and forth between Nazir and Khodi, blood draining just as swiftly from his face.

An ordinary man might argue that there was only a minor difference between Zozi's last shot and the one Khodi was about to make. From the eyes of a leader of thousands, or even one hundred on the plain below, the difference was the size of his entire territory. One might have been able to turn a blind eye and call it unintentional if the arrow had already been nocked and loosed at the time the retreat had been sounded. Khodi, for the love of Ravi, had just drawn out a new one *after* hearing the retreat issued by the Khumar, and at the moment when the two herds had already collided.

And now loosed it.

The arrow, flying in a path as deliberate and determined as the man behind it, caught a gazelle easily in the throat, killing it instantly. Thrown forward by its own momentum as it collapsed, the dead gazelle slid across the ground to the right, and ended up under another rider's galloping horse. The horse reared up, throwing the rider off its back in the process and landed him on the path of another rider coming from the opposite direction. It left no time, no room for the second rider to pull back his mount or jump over the man on the ground. The horse ran over him, and somewhere in the middle of the swirling sand kicked up by its hooves, Hasheem could hear the sound of bone breaking from where he stood.

The sand settled. The first rider was on the ground, lying still on his back with his head turned to one side the way no head was supposed to. The dead rider's arrows, Hasheem noticed with a chill running down his spine, had been fitted with feathers of red and blue—the colors of the Kamara Kha'gan.

There was a gasp from Khali, whose face had turned as pale as a corpse's. Next to him, Nazir, who had been watching the whole thing in silence, was wearing an expression that Hasheem thought might have been what it looked like when he lost it.

It could freeze the blood in your veins, give you nightmares for weeks afterwards, just watching him that day, Hasheem thought. Nazir's yellow eyes weren't glowing as he thought they would. They were cooled, still, and almost white. White, like a thick layer of mist had just rolled over them. His expression was flat and unreadable—a picture of thin ice over a black, bottomless sea in winter. It felt to Hasheem that Nazir wasn't looking at the plain before him at all, but rather at something only he could see, something in a different place or at a different time.

The air around him had somehow turned colder, and Hasheem could see the trails of his breaths as he exhaled. He looked around and realized he wasn't the only one. Every rider nearby was breathing the same cold air as they watched their Khumar, fear clearly written on their faces, waiting for it to pass.

They say the air turns cold when the door between the spirit world and the living world opens. It occurred to Hasheem then that what he was witnessing might not have been Nazir losing it, but having one of his visions. After all, what were oracles if not someone with a link to somewhere no ordinary man could enter? Perhaps even more than a link. Nazir, at that moment, didn't look like something of this world.

After a short time, the cold subsided. Hasheem saw Nazir's eyes return to their normal color and those shoulders relax a little. The look on his face, however, hadn't changed.

"Take five men," he said to Khali without turning away from the plain, his voice thin and quiet enough to kill a man in his sleep. "Bring your brother in and meet me at that big rock by the tree."

Not Khali, Hasheem thought, squeezing his eyes shut at the way Nazir had chosen to strike. Anyone but Khali would have been kind. There was already enough conflict between the two brothers as it was without adding more salt to the wound that way.

He opened his mouth to speak, but Khali had already turned away. To his surprise, the command had been followed promptly, without so much as a breath in between. Hasheem would have thought him heartless had he not seen the look on Khali's face before he'd turned. You could mistake him as the one who'd been given a death sentence as opposed to the person sent to deliver it. Nazir hadn't looked at him once, or at anyone for that matter. He just stood there—a lone figure watching the scene below, holding the lives of two hundred people in that valley in his hands and trying to decide what to do with them.

Or perhaps it had already been decided, and he was just preparing himself for what was to come.

Down below, a Kamara rider shouted something back to the others as he dismounted to drag the dead man off to the side. Soon after, a small group withdrew from the field and rode back toward the slope they'd arrived from. He saw Khali escorting his brother off the ground, the other five warriors with him—all wearing a zikh. The hunt went on, of course, for the Kamara. They couldn't stop, or the gazelles would be gone.

"Come," Nazir said, turning his horse. The rest of his fourteen escorts turned theirs promptly to follow their Khumar. All but Nazir took out another quiver full of arrows from the saddle bag and replaced it with the empty ones. The arrows were unmarked this time. They weren't meant for the gazelles. There were no limits, no marks needed for identification, no need to count the dead if they were to be used on men.

"Hasheem, be ready to ride to the Kha'a at my signal," Nazir said to him. "If my father rides to meet us, you stay and protect Djari."

The man wearing the red and blue sash was young. His dark chestnut hair had been shaved two finger's width above his ears on either side. Over each of those lines was a single braid that had been twisted together with colored threads matching the sash he wore. Two painted stripes decorated his left cheek, a thicker one in red and a thinner one under it in blue. He was clean-shaven, like all young Shakshi men were, with a strong jawline that spoke of years of hard training in combat, matching the outlines of his harshly chiseled, rather massive figure. His deep-set eyes—a piercing shade of green—were intense, unyielding. The Khumar of Kamara, also wearing a zikh, looked like a seasoned warrior who spent most of his days wielding that massive axe on his back to hack off limbs.

And Nazir...

Nazir looked like some vengeful spirit you didn't fuck with who'd just been thoroughly and deliberately fucked. Which wasn't at all far from the truth, if one had seen the exchange of looks between him and the man who'd fucked up his first time leading the hunt

Retri

before shit started raining from the sky. Khodi might as well have thrown a spear at Nazir and it would have resulted in something a whole lot less complicated.

The more Hasheem thought about it, the more he wanted to shoot the arrogant prick who was standing, still straight-backed and proud, between the five zikh-clad warriors that had escorted him up the slope. Khali, however, had chosen a place by Nazir's side, away from his brother. Hasheem would have done that too if he were in the boy's position. It was better to be seen as far removed as possible from the idiot in white given the circumstance. For the first time since they'd met, he felt a little sorry for

bution

the boy.

The two parties faced each other twenty paces apart. Each formed a half-circle on opposite sides of the rocky slope with their Khumar at the center, flanked by a similar number of warriors in a mixture of white and gray robes. All were still mounted, except for Khodi and two of the white warriors who'd brought him out who now positioned themselves on either side of the chief's son.

Hasheem looked around, noted the number of bows drawn on both sides, each already fitted with an arrow, and realized that Nazir was about three bows short in comparison. It would have helped if he also carried an extra set of arrows, but Hasheem, being the only one not in white or gray and without any real skills in particular as far as everyone was concerned, had been considered both unimportant and unqualified to guard the Khumar and therefore left uninformed of these protocols. In other words, he was a useless figure on that plain, except if they needed a runner to deliver a message.

A message containing news no one wanted to hear, he thought with a frown. It wasn't an easy thing to swallow, and he found himself grinding his teeth once more at the lightness of his quiver. He'd been used, for cheap, and sometimes even offered for free in exchange for a favor or two, but had never been useless. There was a price to the comfort anonymity offered, and he might have to pay for it this day.

On the ground, next to the Khumar of Kamara, was the body of the gray who'd fallen. He'd been laid on his back, his limbs arranged neatly on a horse blanket that had been spread with obvious care. The young man couldn't have been much older than he was, and his hair—shaved in a similar fashion—was a shade or two lighter than that of the Khumar. There were also colored threads in his braids, Hasheem saw for the first time, swearing profusely in his mind. Only elite members of the Kha'gans wore their colors in their hair to the hunt.

"The boy was my father's favorite nephew," said the Khumar of Kamara, with a voice as harsh as his features and the confidence of a man used to issuing commands. "His death must be answered for appropriately as a member of the Kha'a's family. I await your proposal, Nazir Khumar."

Hasheem swallowed as he listened. There was to be no time wasted here. No subtlety needed. The negotiation was going to be short and quick and decided right where they were, as though it were a matter that could be easily settled. Only everyone on that slope knew how high the price would be if some kind of an agreement couldn't be reached that day.

Next to him, Nazir sat his horse as light as a feather, his expression a neat and terrible one in contrast to the other Khumar's loud and near-barbaric appearance. *A ghost and a demon,* Hasheem thought. It was difficult to tell which one of them would win if they ever fought, and he hoped it wouldn't come to that.

"His death," Nazir said, his usually silky-smooth voice now thin as a blade, "was an accident and no fault of ours, Baaku Khumar."

"An accident," Baaku replied, "that could have been prevented had your rider retreated as he should have."

"An *accident,*" Nazir repeated crisply, "that could have been prevented had you observed your time of arrival more carefully." He paused, raising his chin a little higher. "*As you should have.* For this, I, too, await your proposal for compensation."

It occurred to Hasheem then that Nazir had never had the intention to compensate for any death that occurred on the plain that day from the very beginning.

'Always negotiate from a position of strength, even if you have to make shit up,' Dee had said. The risk attached in this, however, was much too high in Hasheem's opinion to be using that tactic. On the other hand, Nazir was their future Kha'a with the entire Kha'gan's reputation to uphold. He couldn't afford to be seen as a leader who was afraid to go to war, at least not in front of his men.

"Unless, of course, it was intentional," Nazir added silkily, despite the directness of his words and what they implied.

Silence slammed upon them like a hammer. From below, the sound of death and slaughter grew louder as if to offer a taste of what lay just around the corner should they decide to go in that direction. Baaku Khumar sat still on his horse, his face unreadable as he stared at Nazir, contemplating his next course of action, measuring the other man as he did. The men on both sides shifted on their saddles, holding their breaths as they waited for a response. Hasheem realized, amidst the crippling tension that permeated the air, that this was where the road forked for the Kamara. To say it was a mistake was to show incompetence and to bend to the Visarya. Deny it, and Nazir would have no choice but to consider the act deliberate and a declaration of war.

As if to experiment, Baaku Khumar urged his horse forward a step, and in doing so triggered a simultaneous response that resulted in thirteen arrows being pointed directly at him at execution range. It was answered just as swiftly by sixteen more being trained at Nazir from the opposite side, every single one of them aiming for a swift kill.

Hasheem forced himself to remain still, knowing it would only take a twitch of a horse or the slightest movement of a hand to initiate what could only be called a mass slaughter by that rock. Neither Khumar would make it out of that place alive should a single arrow be let loose, and then both Kha'gans would have a perfectly good excuse to go to war.

Nazir sat calmly on his stallion, oblivious to the number of arrows that surrounded them. His eyes remained fixed on Baaku, who returned his gaze with no less conviction. After a suffocating moment, an understanding seemed to pass between them, and Nazir's lips curled up a little into what appeared to Hasheem to be a ghost of a smile.

"Stand down," said Nazir, to which the archers unenthusiastically lowered their bows. "I'm sure we can settle this in a more civilized manner, or can't we?"

Baaku Khumar stilled for a moment, and then signaled his archers to do the same. The arrows on both sides, Hasheem noted, were still nocked to their bows.

"Your explanation, Baaku Khumar," Nazir demanded.

Baaku shrugged. "Gazelles can be unpredictable."

Nazir considered the reply, or pretended to, and nodded. "So," he said, "can a man."

It was difficult to tell which *man* he was referring to, and the double meaning didn't escape the other Khumar's notice, judging from the grin that followed.

"Still, a mistake that offends must be answered for."

Nazir nodded. "Concerning both pride and *punctuality*, I'm sure."

"The moment we entered the valley, the ground was ours. It's considered an intrusion to remain in the field and theft to shoot and kill our gazelles. For these offenses, we have the right to kill on sight or at least capture to exact the punishments we see fit. For causing the death of a member of the Kha'a's family," Baaku said, pitching his voice to carry, "it's death to one generation of our choosing."

Hasheem looked at Nazir, whose expression remained unaltered. A generation would mean Khali or their parents on top of Khodi. Between a boy and a chief, there was no doubt which generation the Kamara would choose. Losing a chief would put the camp in a period of vulnerability and subject the Kha'gan to possible attacks. They could lose both men and territory from this single incident if Nazir couldn't negotiate them out of this.

"The way I see it, the valley was still ours at the time of your arrival," Nazir pointed out. "When you entered the field, you intruded on *our* ground and were deliberately preying on *our* gazelles. I could have shot your cousin and any of your warriors and it would be well within our rights. His death is your own doing, not ours."

Baaku sneered at that, his white teeth flashing as he did. "Perhaps," he replied, "but you forfeited your right to the ground when you sounded the retreat, and he shot our gazelle *after*, not before. Take the matter to Citara if you want. The White Tower will say the same."

It would all come down to this, of course. Khodi's action had been more than just a show of defiance toward his Khumar, but also a breach of protocol from the Visarya side that put the entire Kha'gan at risk.

Nazir's expression turned grim for a moment, but it was soon replaced by a smile thin enough to shave off a skin.

"Oh, I can take the matter to Citara," said the oracle, "but then you will also forfeit your right to the hunting ground for at least five years for breaching protocol. You know this." Nazir reached over to pat Springer on the neck. "Try me again, Baaku. What retribution do you seek?"

The sneer faded quickly from the other Khumar's face as he realized too late the consequences of his own threat. The prospect of losing the rights to the hunting ground altogether wasn't a risk worth taking, considering how important it appeared to be for the Shakshis.

"My cousin's life must be honorably compensated," Baaku replied after a moment of consideration. "A member of the Kha'a's family is worth at least five men of equal rank. I expect them to be delivered before Raviyani is over."

That would be five Grays, Hasheem thought. Five young men—or boys—from the Kha'gan put to death or subject to torture. It wasn't a big number, but no matter who Nazir chose, it was going to create some bitterness toward the ruling family, and conflict from within the Kha'gan would follow. The easiest way to bring down cities and empires was to rot them from the inside out. He'd learned that from his mentor a long time ago. A smart move by the Kamara, if a little too bold.

Nazir listened and nodded. "Or one White Warrior who is also the eldest son of our chief. It is reasonable compensation and should be acceptable." He paused and added firmly, "In the eyes of Citara."

Khali stirred a little at that. A small distance from him, his brother was standing with his back straight, showing no signs expected from a man who was about to be offered to the enemy to be dealt with as they pleased. Then again, Khodi was a White Warrior, someone who'd taken an oath to die for his land. A life for a life was the best Nazir could do to control the damage Khodi had caused, and they could only hope the Kamara would agree to it.

Baaku Khumar shifted his weight in agitation, and then raised a hand to beckon his men forward. "It is," he grumbled. They, too, had damage to control. "We'll take him."

"That will not be necessary," Nazir said, his eyes fixed straight ahead at Baaku as he signaled his own man. "Khali."

The Choice We Make

The address had been a command, spoken in a tone as firm and resolute as the crack of a whip. Hasheem whipped his head around just in time to see Khali loose his arrow. It zipped through the air and pierced cleanly through the socket of Khodi's right eye, killing him in an instant, leaving no time for a sound to escape his lips at the moment of death.

Atop his horse, Khali sat stiffly on the saddle, his expression betraying no remorse, no guilt as he lowered his bow. He turned to Nazir and bowed, as if to express gratitude, like he'd just killed a gazelle and was accepting a compliment. Nazir acknowledged the gesture, but kept his attention on the Khumar of Kamara.

"There was no need to waste your arrow or your time," Nazir said. "And if you do not require a body, I would like to bring him back to give him a burial befitting his rank and status. Will this be acceptable?"

A small pause from Baaku Khumar before he dipped his head slightly. "It will be."

"For your breach of protocol," Nazir said, wasting no time in between, "I will require ten gazelles tonight and two hundred silas for each unfired arrow as compensation for the offense done here today."

Murmurs rippled among the Kamara warriors, and their Khumar shook his head in disbelief.

"You might as well ask for my sister." Baaku Khumar snorted. "Five gazelles is all I can give you."

"Then we take the case to Citara," Nazir concluded, and turned his horse to leave.

The Khumar of Kamara stared quietly at Nazir's back as he rode away, considered it for a moment, and said, light as a tap on the shoulder, "*If* you survive to carry the news, of course."

The sound of twenty-nine bows being raised and stretched to their limits filled the meeting ground without the need for command. Hasheem gripped the sword at his waist as silence pressed down upon them with the weight of a mountain. Nazir's capacity for control—one that had been challenged since the Kamara entered the valley—had been rock-solid so far, but an open threat required a man of power to rise to the occasion to lead other men. He didn't see how Nazir could avoid bloodshed, not under the circumstances.

Keeping his back to the Khumar, Nazir turned slowly to look over his shoulder. The wind picked up speed and lifted his zikh in the air, its corners snapping like a snake lunging at its prey.

"Oh, I'll survive," he responded. His eyes flashed an unsettling shade of gold, as if to remind them all who and what he was. "Would you like to know if you will?"

Baaku Khumar swallowed, and realizing it, adjusted himself quickly to hide the vulnerability that slipped through his mask of confidence. Hasheem released the breath he'd been holding at the gesture. It was the end of the conversation. You didn't argue about your death with an oracle, not one as powerful as Nazir, and especially not in front of your men who were waiting to replace you as Khumar. Baaku knew this. He parted his mouth to speak and then closed it again, taking a little more time before coming to a decision.

"Five gazelles and two hundred silas for each man with unfired arrows. Take it or leave it."

Nazir nodded. "It will do. I will be expecting them before sunset."

The deal was settled, and the Kamara dispersed with a grumble soon after, returning to the hunting ground. Hasheem grimaced as he watched Khali climb off his mount and headed to where his brother's body had been left by the rock. The boy's usual relaxed and smooth features hardened as he stood above it, his shoulders stiff as a statue.

Not a boy, Hasheem corrected himself, cold anger rising and wrapping its tendrils around him. There was no trace of innocence, no hint of any youthful eagerness left on that face. The moment Khali shot that arrow to end his brother's life, it had ended a boy's life along with it and given birth to a man.

A man who would kill, from now on, in cold blood, in spite, seeking retribution or some form of justification from every corpse he created for what he'd done today. And he would never find it. No matter how long or how many men he would kill. Hasheem knew this. He'd been that boy, and now that man.

He turned to stare at the Visarya warriors that began to clear out from the ground, clenching his fists to hold back the rage that had been consuming him since the command was made. Sensing his hostility, Nazir paused to look over his shoulder, catching his gaze. Hasheem bored into those yellow eyes, seeking a hint, a trace of guilt or regret from the oracle, and didn't find it. Nazir's expression was flat, unreadable, and offered no emotions one might expect from a man who'd just ordered a boy to kill his own brother. For the first time since he'd been taken into the Kha'gan, Hasheem realized how little he knew of Nazir or what he was capable of.

A vision came back to him then—a memory he'd stashed in the dark corners of his mind long ago. Suddenly, he was back at Sabha, looking at the captain who was stepping around the bodies that littered the ground toward them.

'Him, or it's both of you.' The captain's voice had been quiet, but the words had echoed back and forth off the stone walls as if to make sure neither of them would miss them. He remembered the horror on Aziz's face, how quickly blood had drained from it at the thought of being put to torture if he didn't comply. He remembered the tears in Aziz's eyes when he had lunged forward with the dagger. He remembered the weight of the knife in his own hand too, the sound it made as he slipped it into Aziz's heart, could still feel the warmth of the boy's blood as it trickled down from his fingers to his elbow.

Aziz, his only friend in the dungeon, the only one who'd watched his back, cleaned his wounds, kept him fed when he'd been returned too late to the cell, dead by his own hands in the Trial of Sabha.

And he'd done it, as instructed. He'd killed Aziz. At Sabha, you did what you were told, especially if you hadn't been through life long enough to grow a spine. At ten years old, nothing scared you more than the prospect of being tortured and burned alive, even if you'd already been passed around to entertain more soldiers than you could count and thought you knew torture.

At ten years old, you also didn't forget the faces of those who'd done things to you.

And it was the same cold, unanimated face, the same look in the captain's eyes he was seeing in Nazir's.

It might have been more merciful to kill Khodi right on the spot. Hasheem knew enough to have figured that out and might have done the same had he been in Nazir's shoes. But it didn't have to be Khali. It didn't, no matter how disrespectful his brother had been, or what wrongs he'd done. And yet Nazir had issued the command as though it had been the most natural thing in the world, with no more hint of remorse than the captain who'd forced him to kill Aziz that day. And for what? For publicly defying him? To state his authority? To make a point?

Nazir turned Springer around and headed toward him. Hasheem kept his gaze fixed on those eyes, ignoring the other warriors who had also turned to watch their Khumar. Disgust coiled in his stomach like some creature that fed off rotting carcasses, eating him slowly as the distance between them narrowed.

"Hasheem." Nazir reached out his hand to clap his shoulder as he'd done several times before. "Come."

The creature in his stomach lurched at the touch. His vision blurred for a split second and in that blind rage, he lashed out with it, slapping away the hand with enough force to throw Nazir off balance. "*Don't. Touch. Me.*"

Those words, delivered through gritted teeth, finished at the same time as another searing, scraping sound of a sword being cleared from its scabbard. Hasheem wheeled, hand already on the hilt of his sword, to see Zozi on his horse a short distance to his right with a blade raised and ready.

"An assault on the Khumar will cost you a limb of your choosing," said Zozi, in a tone as sharp as the weapon in his hand. "Make your choice, ogui."

'It's never over until you're on your bed with a drink in one hand and a woman in the other, and even then she may still slit your throat.'

Where Real Torture Begins

The wind howled as it rushed over them, adding yet another blood-curdling note to the rumbling hoofbeats and the sounds of slaughter down below.

Ogui, Zozi had called him. A Rashai word they used to call raid survivors with no use in the slave quarters or the pleasure district. Those who became beggars or scavengers, wandering aimlessly in the desert with no real purpose in life. The scum. The garbage. The leeches of society.

Better a leech, Hasheem thought, *than one of them.*

"Take your pick, why don't you?" Hasheem hissed, his rage about to go through the roof. "I'll be sure to take one of yours when you come for it. What are you waiting for?"

Zozi swore and kicked his mount forward, closing the gap between them. Hasheem's hand gripped harder on the hilt of his sword and pulled, was about to finish yanking it out of the scabbard when Nazir's voice speared through the air and stopped him halfway.

"Clear that blade, and I *will* have that arm, right here, right now. You—" The Khumar whipped his head towards Zozi. "*—Stand down*!"

A stillness slammed down on the three of them. Zozi yanked back his horse like he'd run into a brick wall, blade frozen in midair at the command. Nazir sat like a statue of some vengeful god on his mount, waiting for a reason to strike. Hasheem held on to the hilt of his blade, watching his opponent quietly and waiting. The first reaction to that command, whatever it might be, wasn't going to come from him.

A few breaths later, Zozi sheathed his sword and pulled back a step, before inclining his head respectfully to the Khumar. Hasheem snapped his back into the scabbard but kept his hand around the hilt. *'It's never over until you're on your bed with a drink in one hand and a woman in the other,'* Dee's words circled in his mind as he continued to assess the situation, *'and even then she may still slit your throat.'* He'd learned that lesson a long time ago. Had survived heeding it. He wasn't going to quit now.

"I will have no more bloodshed on my watch today." Nazir turned his horse to face Hasheem. "You will have to pick a limb, or Djari will pick one. Do what you need to do to get your shit together. I expect you back at camp before Raviyani is over. Run, and Djari will pay for your treason. Do it, and I'll hunt you down like a dog and tie you to the gate of Sabha after I'm done working on you. Zozi." The man straightened abruptly at the tone, the small grin that had been drawn during the speech disappearing in an instant. "You will accompany me back to camp, where you will be on guard duty tonight for having fired that last arrow after the horn. Try me again, and we will be discussing which limb of yours to remove."

And with that, Nazir turned his horse and left with the rest of the White Warriors, followed not so far behind by Zozi, who looked like he'd been forced to swallow some horse dung.

Hasheem watched the party disappear from the slope, his stomach churning at the number of choices he had to make. Losing a limb wasn't a problem—missing body parts were a common enough sight where he'd lived or around here—but staying meant he would have to live with these men, who weren't any different from the Rashais they called their enemies. Everywhere he ran, he seemed to end up where he'd started.

'Run, and Djari will pay for your treason,' Nazir had said, as though it was even a choice.

The sun was low on the horizon, bleeding on the hunting ground below and painting the ivory rocks of the desert with hues of orange and yellow. The hunt had ended and the warriors had begun to clear the valley floor. Hasheem turned to the one figure left by the rock, at whose feet lay the body of his brother. Khali was standing there, staring at the arrow sticking out of Khodi's eye as if it were a strange object he'd never seen, his face a sheet of ice over a bottomless depth of some muddy water you didn't want to step in.

It might have been the need to justify the situation, or simply the way Hasheem had chosen to distract himself, that led him to climb off Summer's back and approach Khali. It wasn't something he would usually do, not with someone he'd just met or knew so little about.

He stopped a few steps behind the boy, giving him time to notice his presence. Khali tilted his head back just enough to identify him and turned back to his brother, or what was once his brother.

"You shouldn't be here," Khali said after some time, eyes still fixed on the corpse.

"You'll need help bringing him back." It was the least he could do seeing as no one else was around for that. They were all trying to keep their distance, it seemed.

"You need to leave," Khali replied, without turning around, "before Nazir finds it another offense."

"I don't give a damn how Nazir finds it." The words were out of his mouth before he realized it might, indeed, be considered another insult. It would probably cost him another limb. He'd lived with worse. Everyone who'd survived Sabha had lived with worse.

Khali shut his eyes and sighed, as if annoyed by the need to respond. "You don't get it, do you?" He shook his head and turned to look at Hasheem, a grimace on his face, eyes filled with too many emotions to name. "My brother defied the Khumar. That made him a traitor. That made *me* and *everyone* in my family a traitor. We all die tonight if the Kha'a doesn't find that arrow a sufficient show of loyalty." He pointed at the arrow in his brother's eye, grinding his teeth as he spoke. "Until that decision is made, my family is a threat to the Kha'gan, and so is anyone who associates with me. You are Djari's sworn sword and blood. She's held accountable for all your actions. You need to leave now, before someone sees you aiding me and makes the wrong assumptions."

It hit him like the wind that was tugging furiously on his hair, bringing with it the numbing cold that made it increasingly painful to stay exposed in the receding sunlight—these facts he should have known from the start, having spent so much time in the Tower. How had he not seen it? Khodi had been the eldest son of their chief, a man who ruled one-fifth of the Kha'gan's population. An act of defiance from him was treason that extended to the entire family. They could never be trusted now, not until they could prove, somehow, that the incident was an isolated case of a son going rogue and not a conspiracy against the ruling family.

If the Kha'a doesn't find that arrow a sufficient show of loyalty.

It *had* to be Khali. Nazir knew this, and had made sure of it to try and save the boy's life. The execution had to be done swiftly and without hesitation to prove his loyalty to Nazir. Khali had to loose that arrow without pause, without betraying the slightest hint of bitterness as he did or afterward, to show them how far he was willing to go to fulfill a Khumar's command. Still, his family remained at risk tonight, and him being here, offering a hand, could kill them all.

He was, after all, Djari's sworn sword and blood. His wrongdoings were also hers. She would be punished along with him if he were to be considered a traitor by the Kha'gan. Nazir or the Kha'a would surely end that possibility before it became a reality, even if it meant putting an entire family to the sword before word got out that Djari's new sworn sword was taking Khali's side in this.

"I didn't ... know," he said breathlessly, his skin crawling at the ignorance he'd shown. This was both dangerous and stupid. He had defied Nazir in public, put an entire family at risk, and Djari along with it.

Khali shook his head, his expression somewhere between pity and disgust. "No," he said. "How could you have known? You walk among us like a ghost, leeching on our food and water when Nazir stood up for you, made you Djari's sworn sword, and brought you into his family. *The Kha'a's family!* You've been here a month, and all you've done is lurk in the shadows, excluding yourself from everything as if we're not good enough for you. Make a decision, *ogui,* or your ignorance will bring down this Kha'gan and everyone in it. Are you one of us, or are you not?"

In front of him, Khali stood with his chest heaving, burning green eyes pinning him down. And all Hasheem could do was to stand there, looking back, searching for the right words to respond to what he knew, deep down, was the truth.

He *had* been living like a ghost in the Kha'gan, without use or purpose, passing each day watching everything from afar. He held no position because he didn't want one, and had even turned down the possibility when Nazir offered it to him. The emptiness of his quiver was the result of it, and so was the fact that he was standing here when he should have understood the risk and followed Nazir back to camp. His existence was a liability to Djari, to Nazir, to the Kha'a's family. It would ruin them, unless he committed himself to the Kha'gan and earned his place in it.

He never gave Khali that answer. He left him there and rode back alone to camp, lost in his own thoughts and exhausted by everything that had happened that day. The thrill of the hunt still lingered under his skin, the pounding of his heart that had made him feel so alive it could still be felt in his chest. He had found a part of himself that had been lost long ago in the desert. He'd found Djari, the shining beacon that was giving his life direction, purpose, and hope, things he hadn't known he was still capable of having. And he'd found Nazir, who wanted to give him a place, a position, and the power to change things. He could stay and embrace it all. Become a real part of the Kha'gan. Get his life back. Start over. Live, and love again.

But was it ever that simple?

Hasheem sneered at his own thoughts. Starting over had never been a problem. It was living and caring for something or someone else that scared him to death.

Everyone he'd ever loved died, everything he'd ever cared about, had been burned to the ground. He'd been through all that, only this time he wouldn't survive it. He didn't think he would.

Perhaps it was why he hadn't interfered when Mara was married, knowing what he knew. Why he hadn't gone to see her when she sent the letter. Being involved was to tie himself to yet another thing that could be lost, and he'd lost Mara anyway, for not allowing himself to love her, or to lift a finger when she had asked for help—all for the fear of losing someone. Guilt was always easier to live with than failure, just as it was always easier to turn a blind eye to things and blame someone else.

But there was no room for that pathetic, cowardly way of life now, was there?

'Your ignorance will bring down this Kha'gan and everyone in it. Are you one of us or are you not?'

Khali was right. He would have to make that choice now, with Djari. Stay and be a real part of the Kha'gan, or leave before Djari had to pay for his treason.

He looked down at the scars on his wrists, made by the shackles of Sabha, smiling grimly at the thought that suddenly came to his mind. Life was so much easier when choices were made for you, and he was beginning to miss that lack of options. Dee had said something about it the day he'd paid for his freedom from the House of Azalea, as he walked his new apprentice out of the pleasure district.

"Welcome to deepest level of hell, where real torture begins and doesn't end until you're dead."

He hadn't understood it then. He was beginning to now.

The sound of hoofbeats caught his attention. Hasheem looked up toward the horizon, saw a group of riders galloping toward him from the east, and pulled back on instinct. He was in the Visarya's territory, but there was no reason why Nazir would send another group riding at that speed to the hunting ground at this hour.

No. Hasheem swore under his breath, shortened the reins, and tied them to the saddle to keep his hands free. He would need both of them for this.

The riders were wearing black, and they were coming for him.

My Source Of Strength

Was there ever a more fucked up Raviyani? Nazir sighed as he kneaded the throb in his temple, his other hand already undoing the buckle of the sword belt as he rushed toward his tent. How was it, that for who and what he was, he hadn't seen all that coming? Being tested on his first day leading the hunt could be expected, but losing the firstborn son of a chief could not. As if that wasn't bad enough, now he was going to have to hack a limb off his sister's sworn sword and possibly toss away all his plans for the boy or be considered a weak Khumar. He didn't even want to think about what Djari would say about that. More importantly, what she would do to interfere.

The booming first beat of a Raviyani drum sounded from where the main bonfire had been lit, snapping Nazir out of his thoughts for a moment. The celebration had already begun. He would have only a few hours to freshen up and get ready for the big events later that evening while music and dance ensued. For all the shit that had managed to happen on a single afternoon, he needed days, not hours, to straighten things out and rearrange his thoughts.

Brushing aside the bad feeling in his stomach that told him bigger problems were yet to come, Nazir strode into his tent and reached for the goblet on the table, utterly thankful for the one hurricane lamp that had already been lit for his return and the wine that sat waiting on the table. *At least one person had enough sense to follow instructions.*

A hand landed on his shoulder, yanking him back and throwing him off balance. Catching himself just in time before crashing into a desk, Nazir spun around to face the attacker. Through the dimly-lit space, the intruder lunged forward to grab him. Nazir stepped to the side and dropped low to the ground to slip a dagger free from his boot. Rising to his feet just as the intruder's arm passed over his head, he took the man by the throat, pushed forward and slammed him down on the table nearby. Arm raised high over the figure much larger than he was, blade already flipped into position, he plunged the dagger into the wood, landing it next to the intruder's ear, carving a small wound on the man's earlobe.

"Give me one reason why I shouldn't gut you right now." Nazir growled at the newly-formed, searing heat of something closer to pain than anger rushing down his stomach.

The man underneath him stilled and tugged up the left corner of his mouth into a half-smile, his green eyes catching the light from the lantern. "Oh, I can name a few," said Baaku, his gaze traveling down from Nazir's heaving chest toward the gap between his thighs. "But the fact that you're hard as fuck right now should be sufficient, wouldn't you say?"

Nazir squeezed his eyes shut, registered the truth in Baaku's words for the first time, and sighed at yet another thing he couldn't control that day.

"We need to talk." He twisted the dagger in his hand, deepening the cut that was already bleeding. Outside, the drums seemed to have picked up speed, or perhaps it was just his pulse.

Baaku's half-smile stretched into a full grin as Nazir's steel bit deeper into his earlobe. The hard muscles of his chest rose and fell under Nazir in swift succession, as if in anticipation of what he knew would follow.

"Later," said the Khumar of Kamara, mouth splitting a little apart, inviting, suggesting, reminding him what it had done and could still do given opportunity and permission.

Permission didn't really need to be given, not when they were what they were and how their past private encounters in that tent had turned out in the past two years. Even without those memories, even with the bad feeling setting up camp in his stomach and the rage banging on the door for a way out, he was, Nazir admitted—his sense of responsibility slowly being replaced by something urgently else—,indeed hard as fuck from the confrontation at the hunting ground and the fight just now.

Oh well.

"Later," Nazir agreed, caving in to the growing pressure down below and the promise of release. Release was what he needed, and Ravi be damned, no one could ever offer it to him quite like this man he already had between his thighs.

⁜

ONE OF THESE DAYS, he was going to die fucking Nazir.

It wasn't the first time such a thought had occurred to Baaku. There was always danger in what they did, for who they were to each other, and what they'd kept hidden from the eyes of the world. There was also danger here, coiling around them like a slippery, slithering serpent, its hardened, unforgiving length squeezing in and out as they tore and ripped from each other everything that stood between them, feeding hungrily on the forbidden fruit they knew was going to kill them slowly.

And yet he would always come back to this. To surrendering himself completely in the maddening scent of spice and wine in Nazir's hair, to discovering himself and losing it all over again in the void they created. He was there and not there, alive and then burned alive, pleasured and mercilessly tortured as they collided and wrestled, clawing at one another like two hungry beasts fighting over a fresh kill. In the battle of sweat and muffled screams, of flesh against flesh stretched thin over corded muscles, their grip on reality loosened and tightened as they slid in and out of time and place, bringing him close and then closer to the edge, to a place where beginnings and endings collided and merged into one.

Even now, after all had been done, when all the shivering, shameless groans and dirty insults had faded, when hands and tangled limbs had finished making their mark on heated skin and torn garments, the taste of his own blood that lingered on Baaku's tongue—or just the mere scent of it—could still turn him on like an inexperienced boy seeing a naked girl for the first time. Nazir liked to bleed him in the middle of sex, sometimes just before his release, other times from the beginning. He did that every time, without fail, in different places and many different ways. To Baaku, the very sight of Nazir—his dangerous, scheming, blindingly beautiful and terrifying Nazir—eyes bright and gleaming with satisfaction, licking the blood off his fingers, could finish him off faster than any experienced whore ever could.

The bleeding had become one of their rituals. It was a part of the process, a fee exacted in exchange for pleasure. He wondered sometimes if it had been the sight of blood or the drawing of it that Nazir wanted, or if he simply needed some justification for what they'd done to offer himself release.

Probably both, Baaku thought, rolling his shoulders back to loosen the muscles tightened from the ride earlier that afternoon and the vigorous activity they'd just shared. You could either live with guilt, or you could seek some kind of retribution for the wrongs you'd done. He could understand it, or at least pretend to. To Baaku, there was no guilt in this, no regrets when it came to things one couldn't control. And truth be told, what had happened between him and Nazir the first time they met, or every time afterward when they were together, Ravi herself couldn't stop it if she came down from the sky and offered herself as the alternative.

Or perhaps it was just him, Baaku thought as he watched Nazir cross to the table and seat himself, already dressed and irritatingly composed compared to the state he was in. Brushing aside the thought that had been bothering him for some time, he pulled on his breeches and followed, taking a seat on the opposite side. Leaning back on one of the cushions embroidered in Samarran style, he realized they were new, as were many things in that tent. New, priceless items meant the Visarya was doing well. A good thing for Nazir, not so much for his father or his own Kha'gan. Which brought him to the other, more pressing situation.

"So," he began, pouring himself a serving of wine, eyeing Nazir as he did. "Who's the pretty boy?"

Nazir's goblet paused for a moment in midair before he quickly resumed the motion. "Djari's sworn sword."

Baaku snorted. "How the fuck did that happen?"

A small shrug. An effort to not meet his eyes. "Chance."

Baaku shook his head at Nazir's usual effort to hold back information.

Some things never change. "Chance is what happens when you find a goddamn horse running loose in the desert, not your sister's sworn sword." Lowering his cup, he stared openly at the Khumar. "*Who's the boy*, Nazir?"

"You wouldn't know him."

He had an itch to roll his eyes and deliver some spiteful response to that. Didn't. The image of Nazir on the hunting ground looking pissed enough to disembowel him and save his entrails for breakfast was still too fresh to risk another episode. Being tight-lipped about things was just Nazir being Nazir. He'd gotten used to it. Sometimes he backed down, other times he didn't.

This time, he couldn't.

"Oh, I know lots of things," he said. "Including the fact that a certain Shakshi slave has recently escaped Rasharwi and is being hunted down as we speak. A *very* high profile Shakshi slave."

A small pause, followed by a forced, ceremonial arch of that neat, elegant brow that usually appeared before Nazir changed the subject. "You have spies in Rasharwi now?"

"I don't have to have spies in Rasharwi." He did, but Nazir didn't need to know that, did he? "The reward for his head is fifty-thousand silas. Enough for every man in the peninsula and his grandmother to be looking for him. Enough for both Sarasef and Saracen to be actively searching. Cut the crap, Nazir. Are you or are you not in possession of the Silver Sparrow of Azalea?"

Silence hung between them for a moment. Nazir placed down his drink and caught his eyes, promising retribution and something longer-lasting than physical pain if the answer to his next question turned out to be the wrong one. "Is that why you're here? To see what I have under my sleeve?"

It would come to this, of course. Two years of actively sleeping together and the closest he could get to gaining that trust was still the distance between Nazir's tent and his own on the other side of the Djamahari. "Yeah, I came here to spy for my father. See what you're up to. Hoping you'll spill some secrets I can use to fuck you over. That sort of thing." It came out with more spite than he'd intended, but that anger had to go somewhere.

As always, it didn't work on Nazir. The bastard was just sitting there, calm and composed, possibly bored. Throwing those words at a corpse two days dead might have gotten him more reaction. Baaku knew this, but had felt the need to bitch about it anyway to at least make a point.

"Look," he said, leaning forward a little. "That boy is too well-known to be kept hidden, and you know it. He'll lead them right here, to Djari, to you. Do you know what they pay for a pretty oracle's head these days? A hundred thousand silas, easy. Do you *want* to know what they pay for a Bharavi? Enough to feed an entire Kha'gan for a year. What's the boy doing here, Nazir? What did you see?"

Nazir drew a breath, held it, and pulled back his shoulders. "I know the risks," he said, chin raised like an overindulged prince addressing a peasant. "Do you know yours, after pulling what you have today? Tell me." He paused, allowing a breath to pass before delivering the blow. "Why was the hunt early, Baaku?"

Baaku swallowed. He knew the timing of the hunt was going to come up sooner or later. Nazir was never going to let something like that go, even after having demanded an arm and a leg from him. Their Kha'gans had been in conflict for longer than they'd lived, but that afternoon was the first time the two of them had confronted each other in person. It hadn't been his choice, of course. Nazir should have known this, and the fact that it required an explanation raised his anger to another level. "I'm still under the command of my Kha'a. You would have done the same."

Nazir's eyes blazed golden at that. "I would have advised a different course of action to mine."

Assuming he hadn't, of course. Assuming, as would be typical of Nazir, that he hadn't fought with his own father over this and suffered the consequences, that he'd had no problem whatsoever barging into the hunt to threaten and humiliate Nazir in front of his men. "I'm a Khumar, not a fucking oracle," he rasped, words pouring out of his mouth before he could stop himself. "I don't happen to have prophecies to make people shit their pants and bend to my wishes, in case you forgot. Not everyone is as privileged as you are."

Nazir froze at that. His lips stretched into a thin line, pressed tight together as if to hold back a retort he would never, ever let slip. Baaku watched the Adam's apple in that throat bob, felt the distance between them widen to where he could no longer reach, and realized how precisely his words had hit the mark.

Fuck.

Somewhere in his mind, an image of Nazir resurfaced, one of him sprawling naked on the bed, head resting over crossed arms, staring up at the ceiling.

"*It's strange,*" he'd said, a foreign, delightful note to his tone that disappeared too swiftly, "*that my visions never seem to come when you're around.*"

There was a reason why Baaku had been allowed to sneak in here and walk out alive as many times as he had, and why he was here at all despite Nazir's unwillingness to consider him an ally.

Nazir hated what he was. Hated it enough to cringe every time he was called an oracle, enough to actively seek an escape from it, to have even risked coming to him on nights when he shouldn't. Tired, hollow-eyed and face feverishly pale like he'd just been dragged through hell and back, those nights he'd simply crashed on Baaku's bed, slept like a baby, and left by morning. There had been no explanations, of course, no spilling of secrets or his ferociously-guarded vulnerability, but one would have to be a fool to not see it or care very little to not notice how much he craved a sense of normalcy in his life.

A sense of normalcy only he could give, but one he'd also destroyed just now.

Sighing, he squeezed his eyes shut and kicked himself mentally over that slip of his tongue, knowing the damage it had caused. "Look," he said. "It doesn't have to be this way. Consider my last proposal. My father is ready to negotiate for Djari's dowry. He's already discussing it with the council. The offer will be made as soon as she turns sixteen. Give her to me and we end this now. We can fight together, unite the other Kha'gans to attack Sabha and the rest of the fortresses, and take back what's ours." It could be done, if enough Kha'gans were united, but it would have to start with two influential ones working together to bring the others into submission, and it had to be done quickly.

"Muradi is mobilizing his force," Baaku continued. "My sources tell me he's building two hundred ships to cross the sea to Makena. The cavalry is ready, with our own goddamn horses taken from the Vilarhiti. He's already training his men out there in the desert as we speak. They'll come prepared this time, by land and by sea to attack us and Makena and take whatever's left of this peninsula once and for all. We can't be sitting here fighting each other. Work with me here. We need to act and act *now,* and you know it."

From across the table, Nazir leaned back on the cushion and swirled the contents of his cup at leisure, as if he were listening to some background music that added flavor to the drink in hand. The burning amber of his eyes as he stared back at Baaku, however, told a different tale. He sipped his wine, took the time to savor it, and placed the cup down neatly on the table. "And who leads us?"

A hammer of words, spoken as lightly as a woman's touch, coming down to smash open the gate where a monster resided. Baaku curled his hands into fists under the table as a newly-formed, dreadful feeling settled in his gut, making him sick to his stomach.

"What happens when your father has my sister?" Nazir continued, words light as a feather, but sharp enough to sever a limb. "What do you think will happen then if you cannot influence him now? You don't think I know what's happening? Why he sent you to the hunt early? What did he want you to do, Baaku? Force me to make poor decisions? Create as much trouble as you possibly can to weaken us from the inside out so he can ride in with an offer we can't refuse? *Do it,*" he snapped at the first hint of Baaku opening his mouth to speak. "Lie your way out of this and I will make sure you don't leave this tent alive. You were right. I am an oracle, born with privilege and not afraid to use it to make people shit their pants. If you think your offer of small pleasures will turn me into an idiot you can coax into offering you my Kha'gan on a silver plate, you'd better think again before I realize how little I need you or your cock around here."

⁜

SOMEWHERE IN NAZIR'S MIND, sitting in his tent now vacant

of another man's presence, his mother's words came back to him like rain falling on an already wet and heavy garment.

'*For everything everyone will suffer, you, as the messenger, will suffer it tenfolds*,' she had said, her small, delicate fingers running gently through his hair. '*Find your source of strength, my son. Find as many as you can, keep them close, and whatever you do, don't let go.*'

Nazir sat on the bed, squeezing his eyes shut at those words and the painful truth that accompanied them. *Keep them close*, she'd said, as if it were a choice for him to make.

As if anything was ever a choice.

It certainly had never been *his* choice with Baaku, Nazir thought, wincing at the memory of their first meeting years ago. How certain he had been, staring at the green-eyed, brown-haired boy he'd met in that cave, that he would become the man in his visions whose face had been obscured until then.

There had been nothing he could do about it afterward, no way to stop the turn of events that followed. The visions had kept on coming, more frequent and clearer as time went by, until there had been little left of their future he hadn't seen.

Their future...or the lack of it.

The image of Baaku just before he'd left the tent replayed itself in his mind, his own words still raw on his tongue.

...before I realize how little I need you...

"*Have you, Nazir?*" Baaku had replied after a long pause, face pale and etched deep with too many emotions to name, a strained, painful smile on his lips. "*Ever needed me in your life? Even once? Besides to make the visions go away?*"

He hadn't answered that question. Couldn't. From the way those eyes had dropped a shade and the resignation of his nod, Baaku had understood it. Sometimes, a deliberately timed silence was more than enough.

Baaku had looked at him then, torn flesh and tattered pride all written on his face, his fists clenching tight to squeeze both their hearts. "*I thought so.*"

It was for the best, Nazir thought, trying once more to swallow the lump in his throat that had been refusing to dissipate. Some prophecies demanded actions, some sacrifices, and others simply acceptance. This one with him and Baaku was going to take all three, and even then he wasn't even sure that would be the end of it. Still, he had to try. He might not be able to change the future, but the sufferings could be lessened, turned into something else, made bearable to those involved.

Lies and more lies. He shook his head at his own folly. *When has that ever worked out for you?*

The sound of hurried footsteps pulled him from his thoughts. Someone called and asked for permission to enter. He gave the clearance, but didn't like the panic in that voice.

The guard in gray came in, gave him a slight bow, and adjusted himself. He swallowed, looked at his Khumar like he was biting on a bad tooth, and said, "We can't find Djari."

ConseQuences

Conceited half-blood son of a Shakshi whore, Azram cursed for the twentieth time that evening—inwardly, of course. Nobody voiced a bad opinion about that wretched mother and son in the Black Tower without getting themselves on his father's list of possible threats to his favorites. If it hadn't been for the public decree made known to every soul in the Tower that everyone on said list would be promptly executed should any harm come to them, Azram would have made sure that they died a death to remember a long time ago. He would have handled the killing himself, and kept the blade as a souvenir.

As things stood, all he could do was to watch them strut about in the Tower, untouchable by all but the Salar, who happened to enjoy doting on them beyond reason. Whatever he did, however hard he tried, it was always going to be Lasura who had the attention. But being overlooked and humiliated on the road the day before or never being chosen to accompany the Salar on a hunt was one thing. Having to sit through the banquet held in honor of his arrogant, entitled half-blood brother's triumphant return tonight was something else.

The bastard had brought back three eaglets. *Three.* Had strode in through the tall double door of the throne room with them wrapped in the Salar's very own bear pelt robe with nothing but scratches and scraped knees from the climb. The entire room of almost a hundred influential court officials, in their excitement over the birds, had erupted into cheers when their Shakshi prince sank on his knee before the throne and presented them to the Salar.

There had been pride in his father's eyes then, despite the cold, expressionless mask he always wore. Pride that had never extended to any son but Lasura in the past seventeen years. Just like those half-formed grins and glances of affection—however brief and discreet—that seemed to always pass over him and his brothers to rest upon the black-haired, yellow-eyed freak of a boy from the moment he'd been born. It was said that his father, the undefeated Salar Muradi of Rasharwi, the most feared man and ruler in the history of the Salasar, had picked up the baby and held it in his arms. Had even smiled holding it, if the tales from the midwives present could be believed.

Azram had never been touched by his father. Not once. Neither had the other princes.

The choice to keep his distance had been deliberate, everyone knew. Attachment complicated things when he had to order them executed. It was the secret to his success. His father trusted no one, allowed no weakness or sympathy to cloud his vision. He knew the world at its worst. Expected it. Expected all his sons to try to kill him for the throne.

Except for Lasura.

Azram slammed the door open and strode into his bedchamber, thankful for having reached it before he started voicing those thoughts out loud and get himself thrown off the Tower along with his mother.

But a scent halted his steps the moment he entered. *Gardenia and rose.* And a hint of something else he happened to know and remember.

He shut the door behind him, latching it carefully before turning back around to observe the surroundings. His ladies-in-waiting were nowhere to be found, he'd just noticed.

"Don't worry," came a sweet, melodic voice from behind the flowing white curtains that decorated the four-poster bed, "your mother has dismissed the girls. We are alone."

His memory of the scent wasn't wrong after all, Azram congratulated himself. Neither was his prediction about this visit, apparently. He knew exactly who it was. Had been counting down the hours to when she would appear again in his bedchamber since the return of his father.

He took his time to cross over to the bed, a smile playing about his lips. "What's the matter?" A breeze rushed in, parting the curtain to reveal the tall, voluptuous figure behind it. "My old man wasn't good enough for you?"

Amelia turned on her side, leaning her weight on her elbow to gaze at him with practiced laziness. The sheer Makena silk nightgown wrapped around her small waist and rounded hips with her new position, both begging to be touched. She kept her head tilted back, allowing an unobstructed view of the gown's plunging neckline that showcased the two firm, flawless breasts he had come to know by heart and enjoyed many times. The sight of them could always make him hard, knowing what their owner could deliver beyond the perfection of her figure and youth. Amelia knew this, of course, and also knew exactly how to put herself on display to bring about such an effect.

She fluttered her eyelids and smiled innocently at him, "I liked the son. Wanted to try the father. Can you blame me?"

Of course, you did, you spoiled, overprivileged, back-stabbing bitch.

Azram paused to stand by the bed, looking down at her with a mask of disinterest. "Of course not," he said, running his eyes up and down her form, and finding what he was searching for. "He's a handsome man, still very much in his prime." Placing his hand gently under her chin, he tilted her face up a little, exposing her long, elegant neck for a better view. "With all that power, you thought you could take the shortcut, get what you wanted without having to waste your time with the son plotting and scheming your way up, didn't you, Amelia?" He trailed his finger down her throat and paused just above the collarbone where the raw, red marks still lingered. "That didn't work out too well for you, did it?"

Amelia pursed her lips and slapped his hand away. In her eyes, he could see shame, disappointment, and anger being tossed together and rolled into something else that was going to benefit him greatly.

It wasn't really a surprise. He'd seen it coming the moment she'd laid eyes upon his father, had seen the shift in alliances as clear as the blush on her cheeks that ran down to her breasts. Amelia was supposed to be his eyes and ears, and hopefully an influence if she could somehow grip the Salar's attention with her youth and prowess in bed. Instead, the plan had backfired and his ticket to the throne had decided to jump ship for an easy way out and possibly the thrill of being with an older, more experienced man.

A foolish mistake. Azram grinned as he lowered himself down to the bed, drinking in the bruises on her neck and arm like a fine Samarran wine as he did.

"Oh, come now, Amelia," he said with exaggerated sympathy, registering the pout that was still there as he brought her arm to his lips and planted a kiss on the bruise. "Don't give me that look. Unlike my father, I happen to be a very, *very* forgiving man. Is that not why you're here?"

He wasn't, really, but their relationship had never been one that called for loyalty from the start. She knew what she was getting out of it and so did he. They also knew how fragile the alliance was, how easily it would break if a bigger fish ever came along.

Amelia shifted her weight, angled her body more toward him and raised her chin a little. "I'm not here for a forgiving man." She raised up her long leg, allowing the silk to slip back toward her hip and reveal a more than generous view of her thigh. "I'm here," she said, as she navigated her foot over his swelling cock, hovering a mere inch above it as if toying with the idea of contact, "for a man whose balls are big enough to take what he wants, when he wants it." The contact came, and Azram bit back a groan as her foot circled said balls with practiced precision. "Are you that man, Azram?"

He sucked in a breath, feeling lightheaded by the growing pain in his groin and the turn of his fortune. "I am." He trailed his hand up her leg, pausing on the inside of her thigh where the skin was most tender. "I'd be happy to demonstrate that for you."

Amelia tucked back the ebony strands of her hair and pushed herself up. Poised like a goddess on her knees, she slipped the gold chains that held the gown together off her shoulders, one after the other, revealing her full, jutting breasts that sprang free from the confining garment. He reached for them, fondling the stiff peaks of her nipples as she settled herself on his lap and wrapped her legs around him. Azram slipped his hand up her leg, under the silk, and felt himself growing twice as hard the moment he found the warm, slippery wetness between her thighs. She made a sound that fell somewhere between a whimper and a gasp when he made a circle with his thumb, arched her body back with the flexibility of a cat far enough for him to suck on a nipple, and cried out a moan he knew to be an exaggeration. It didn't bother him. The thought of a woman going out of her way to please him always added to the pleasure, even if he knew a price would be exacted at some point. It made him feel powerful, underlined the fact that he had something to provide. Must be what his father felt like every minute of his time sitting that throne.

He worked his hand in deeper and felt the small muscles under her soft, delicate skin tighten as she rocked her hips to give him better access, her breasts moving with the motion, one in his mouth, the other against his palm. She guided him up with her hands and slipped her tongue into his mouth. She tasted like wine, like a ripened fruit screaming to be peeled and bitten into. Her hand slipped back down and found a way to his cock, did something with his clothes to free it.

He pulled her toward him in urgency, guided her hip to where the throbbing between his legs was screaming, and pushed his way in. Amelia grabbed a handful of his hair, yanked it back the same time her legs fastened around his waist and locked them in the position, making it impossible for him to move. "I will need more from you, *Prince*," she said, with an edge to the address, sinking her fangs into the word. "Get me what I want, and I'll give you what you desire the most. I'll give you the Salasar."

A smart move, to force an agreement from him with her thighs around his waist and his cock already straining deep inside her. Because by then he was ready to give her the world, the throne, the crown if he had it, if only for the much-needed release. "Well, what do you have in mind, my lady?"

And there, in her steady, bottomless dark eyes he saw the true extent of his father's mistake, and the result of the irreversible, inconceivable, unforgivable damage he had made.

"I want him dead, Azram," she said. "Him and his Shakshi whore before the next summer is over."

Presu

An ugly beast,
tossed carelessly into the
middle of the room
for all to see,

mp-tions

Jarem stood with hands behind his back, watching the Salar go through a stack of reports in his study, and entertained himself with an image of Deo di Amarra being thrown off the balcony to pass the time. The Khandoor was late, yet again, to the summons.

Such insolence, displayed too many times to count, should have ended with Jarem's fantasy being realized, and yet it hadn't. The Salar had somehow developed an unprecedented amount of patience with the grotesquely wealthy merchant and royal advisor who seemed to be able to get away with anything in the Black Tower, including making Salar Muradi of Rasharwi wait.

The door creaked open, and in walked Deo di Amarra, bringing with him the same air of grandeur a highly sought-after performer might produce upon his initial entrance to the stage. A robe of priceless grey wolf pelt swept across the black marble floor as he approached in slow, lazy steps toward the desk behind which the Salar sat. Three large rings set with rare gems large enough to buy a small army adorned the fingers on both his hands. Underneath the robe, a deep blue tunic of finest Makena silk stitched with silver threads peeked out from the luxurious fur, completing the picture of a man wealthier than the Salar.

Which might very well be the case, Jarem thought bitterly. The Khandoor owned close to half the businesses in Rasharwi and probably had investments in more. The house of assassins he operated—

not so secretly—happened to be the most expensive in the Salasar, one only the elites and the powerful could afford. Now, as a royal advisor to the Salar, Jarem didn't want to imagine the amount of bribes and favors that must have been going into his pockets. Deo di Amarra was a figure that could shift the balance of the peninsula if he wanted. Had shifted it, actually, in exchange for a handful of Vilarian horses that made sure Prince Muradi ascended safely—and in a timely manner—to the throne. Jarem happened to know first-hand whose names had gone into that infamous Jar of Souls as a part of that transaction.

The Khandoor paused before the Salar and bowed, its execution making the whole thing feel more a display of gratitude than an offering of obeisance. As always, he seemed to take pleasure in appraising the furniture and the decorations in the room while waiting to be addressed. If there was any amount of sweat breaking, the kind commonly found in most men around the Salar, it didn't show.

"You're late," said Salar Muradi, without looking up from the report.

Di Amarra dipped his head—a gesture so slight it didn't move a strand of that eye-stinging red hair. The small, sardonic grin on his lips was also there, as usual, to irritate Jarem.

"Regrettably so, my lord," he replied. "I thought it wise to have a little chat with our heroic prince before I came. It took me a while to find a moment alone with him. The Prince Lasura is why I'm here, I presume?"

Jarem shot him a glare. "Have a care, di Amarra. Your presumption may contribute to your premature death if you keep this up."

Di Amarra turned, ran his gaze over him from head to toe, and frowned. "The only thing that's going to give me a premature death, Commander, is the sight of that dull, horse-dung green tunic you're wearing. It's sucking the life out of me as we speak."

Jarem raised his brow at another insult. He'd gotten used to them by now, having had to deal with it for the past two decades—nothing else but sheer necessity would ever get him to endure their encounters. "Does it now?" he said. "You should have told me. I would have worn it sooner if I knew."

The Salar looked up from the report then, a grin playing about his lips. "Horse-dung tunic aside," he said, leaning back on the velvet cushion, "let's hear the rest of your presumptions, shall we? Why do you think you're here, di Amarra?"

Jarem glanced at the Khandoor, searching for any sign of stress on that laid-back, half-sobered expression, and didn't find it. The question was a test of sorts. It was how the Salar measured the competence of his men, from which he would often draw the conclusion of who should exit the chamber through the door and who should use the balcony. Most grown men shit their pants during the process. Di Amarra had been placed on it every time he was summoned and somehow had never yet broken a sweat.

"The way I see it," Deo di Amarra mused, rubbing his thumb thoughtfully on his clean-shaven jawline, "you have three very large problems at present that require immediate attention; namely the prince, the birds, and the Rishis, my lord."

Tapping his fingers on the arm of the chair, the corner of Salar Muradi's lips lifted into a more visible grin. "What about the prince, then?"

"Well, you gave the prince an eagle tonight, my lord, in front of the whole Tower, more or less."

Jarem, having been the one who suggested the idea, stepped in at the criticism. "It's not unusual for the Salar to reward his men for their accomplishments, di Amarra."

"In diamonds and golds, Commander." The words rang like steel being drawn out of its sheath, despite the intentional drag of the syllables. "Spotted eagles are gifts for kings and high chiefs. They have always been a symbol of leadership, of power. As of today, the only man in the peninsula besides the Salar who owns a spotted eagle is Prince Lasura. If I were to elaborate on that, my lord—" He turned back to the Salar, catching his gaze as he did. "—the *only* prince in the Tower who happens to be of Shakshi blood."

Jarem swallowed, took a glance at the Salar, whose expression hadn't changed, and tried to set something straight before it did. "He is also a son of the Salar who's being given a gift by his father."

"A son born to a mother of Shakshi origin taken as one of the prisoners from the Vilarhiti, Commander Sa'id. *Prisoners* we have been putting on auction as slaves and whores in the Salasar for centuries. The only status they'd ever held in Rasharwi were at your feet or in your bed, not standing in the throne room with a spotted fucking eagle on his shoulder. You can make a whore of someone's wife and it will end with a duel, but put a slave above the master, Commander, and you'll have yourself a rebellion."

"You *will* watch your tongue in the presence of the Salar of Rasharwi, di Amarra!"

"I'll watch yours, Commander Sa'id." A harshness to the words, made worse by the rasp his wolf pelt made as it scraped against the stone floor when di Amarra turned to face Jarem. "He won't be for long if you keep feeding him advice as horrifying as your sense of fashion."

Jarem opened his mouth to respond, but snapped it shut at a raised finger from the Salar.

"You believe this translates to me favoring Shakshis over Rashais?" the Salar asked thoughtfully.

"In my words or Commander Sa'id's court-sweetened, milk-diluted tongue, my lord?"

Deceitful, manipulative, arrogant son of a—Jarem stopped himself just in time when he realized he was mumbling it, though not loud enough to be heard.

"In as few words as fucking possible, Deo."

Di Amarra nodded, smiling at the permission and the deliberate use of his first name—a signal that all formalities were to be dropped without being penalized. They talked like that sometimes, during practice duels. The Khandoor was, after all, a master assassin and one of the best swordsmen in Rasharwi. The Salar never passed on that kind of opportunity to sharpen his skills. That, and they went back a long way, almost as long as Jarem's own acquaintance with the Salar.

"Then yes, my lord, it does." Di Amarra nodded. "You do favor your Shakshi wife over your Rashai ones—that is not a secret—and where a man puts his cock usually reflects his character. It's been almost two decades and you haven't sent another army into the White Desert. To the public at large, you gave eight thousand Shakshi captives from her homeland a fenced off sanctuary and declared them untouchable. What they're saying on the street is, in as few words as possible and foregoing court-obligated fairy dust sprinkles, 'the Shakshi witch's got the Salar by the balls.'"

Jarem sucked in a breath at that, took a glance at the Salar, and didn't find the reaction he'd anticipated.

"And you've just confirmed the witchcraft by offering a spotted eagle to her son," di Amarra continued. "Tomorrow, they'll be betting on Prince Lasura being made heir to the throne, and if that idea were to spread—well, every Shakshi slave owner and whorehouse in the Salasar will have something to say about it, and *precautions* are going to be put into action. You'll be facing an internal war before you even march into the White Desert, my lord, or as soon as your army crosses the gate of Sabha."

"That is absurd!" Complete nonsense, in fact, in Jarem's opinion. "Prince Lasura is the son of a prisoner of war. Everyone knows he has no right to the throne. You're making a fuss out of nothing more than gossips and half-drunk conversations behind closed doors."

"Am I?" A sharp edge to di Amarra's tone now, despite the mocking lightness of that voice. "Empires are built on gossips and whispers behind closed doors, Commander. They have also been sacked for less." He turned back to the Salar, a jeweled hand sweeping out to address the surroundings. "Your very own empire has been built on nothing more than whispers and talks between the three people in this room and the fourth who now guards it, my lord. You, as a former prisoner of Sabha, the son of a mother charged with and executed for adultery, are a living example of how fragile laws and traditions can be with regard to who ascend the throne. This is a serious threat, my lord, make no mistake about it. The hay is already there, waiting for someone to strike a flint."

An ugly beast, tossed carelessly into the middle of the room for all to see, Jarem thought, holding his breath in anticipation as he observed the Salar, waiting for some kind of lightning to strike the Khandoor. Questioning him about Zahara and the prince was already pushing the limits, but the subject of his mother was something nobody in their right mind would ever bring up. He half expected the man to be thrown out of the balcony in the next few minutes, but there had been no change in the Salar's flat, unreadable expression as he listened, not even the twitch of an eye.

"I had no idea you care so much about my rule," the Salar said, with unreasonable calm and a chuckle to boot. "Have I really been away long enough for you to grow some loyalty, Deo?"

Di Amarra frowned. "Love, loyalty, and faith are products of the heart, my lord. They are dangerous, unpredictable, and mind-clouding tools successful rulers never rely on. Greed and ambition, however, are much more reliable. Feed a hungry dog like a pig, and you can count on him to serve and protect the hand that does so for life. I happen to be—" He bowed and pressed a palm to his heart. "—both greedy and ambitious, my lord. Your safety and the stability of your empire are making me rich, and I don't intend to be poor anytime soon."

Despite the absurdity of it all, the Salar smiled. He might even have been pleased by the answer. "Fair enough. Go on. What about the birds?"

Di Amarra adjusted his robe, brushing his thumb lazily along the luxurious fur. "What you choose to do with the remaining one has consequences of rather large proportions, my lord. You can either kill it or offer it to the right person, which cannot be someone in the Tower or you'll create another cold war in your court and a demand for murder that will make me a very, *very* wealthy man this season, which, I can imagine, Commander Sa'id would not be happy about."

He definitely wouldn't. Jarem thought and resisted the urge to rise to the occasion.

The Salar nodded. "And the Rishis?"

"The failed assassination of Sarasef needs to be addressed immediately. The Rishi is now split in two. They'll clash soon. Allow that to happen, and no matter who survives, the Rishi will lose half its men, meaning we lose half the warriors who know how to fight and take the White Desert. Should Sarasef die, your contract with the Rishi will have to be renegotiated, and last I heard, Saracen intends to ask for a piece of the Salasar. An area south of Suma all the way to the coast, to be precise."

"How," Jarem interrupted, "did you come by that information?"

The venom in Di Amarra's smile was unconcealed, almost honest in its revelation. "Because I sold him the poison myself, izr Sa'id," he replied. "We shared a few drinks. You'd be surprised what a few pinches of Yarra roots and a little of something else can do to loosen a man's tongue."

"You made a transaction that could affect the Salasar without consulting the members of this court?" It was outrageous. The man needed to be thrown off the balcony before the day was over, according to Jarem.

Di Amarra shrugged. "I'm a businessman, Commander Sa'id, first and foremost. If you want to stop a transaction, you will have to outbid my buyer. It has, however," he added, turning to the Salar with a small inclination of his head, "allowed me to offer you this piece of information, as a token of my gratitude toward my highest bidder at present. The question is, who would you rather deal with, my lord: Sarasef or Saracen?"

Salar Muradi, grinning widely now and appearing more curious than angry at the Khandoor, leaned a little forward in his chair. "And who would you rather deal with, di Amarra?"

It took di Amarra no time to reply. "Saracen is an arrogant, ignorant fool. He would never last more than six months leading the Rishi, my lord. Then again, an imbecile is easier to deal with than a proud, intelligent man, which is, of course, what Sarasef is."

The same, almost exact words from the Salar with regards to Saracen, Jarem recalled. In a way, he could see why Deo di Amarra was still alive. The two of them were strikingly similar in their thinking process and level of intelligence, as much as he hated to admit it.

"I'd say," he continued, "if the Rishi is to be destroyed, I'd go with Saracen. If I want to continue using them, I'd support Sarasef but keep a very close eye on him. Which brings me to the conclusion that the best course of action is to send Prince Lasura away from the Tower with the two birds, and offer the other one to Sarasef as a gesture of good faith, and to get rid of it. Let him keep both the prince and the bird for leverage as you move your army to take care of Saracen, and at the same time, keep Sarasef in check. The problem is getting a proud, careful man like Sarasef to take the offered hand, and that," he paused, bright emerald eyes sprinkled with a Bharavi's yellow locked with the Salar's lapis lazuli blue, "is where I come in. How are my presumptions so far, my lord?"

The Salar kept his grin, rising from behind the desk and walking around it to fill three golden goblets with wine. He handed one to di Amarra, and another to Jarem.

"Your presumptions are brilliant, as always. However," the Salar raised the cup in approval and took a slow sip from it, "that's not the reason why you're here."

Di Amarra stilled at that, the iconic grin on his face fading slowly into a thoughtful expression. *Here comes the lightning.* Jarem gave the Salar a mental applause.

At a gesture from the Salar, he stepped forward, reaching into the pocket of his robe to produce a letter, crisply folded and stamped with the royal seal. "You have been charged with treason for offering aid to a slave convicted for murder. Your trial will be a week from now. Until then, you are to remain here as a prisoner of the Tower to await your sentence. *That* is the reason you are here."

A Deadly Weapon

Deo di Amarra blinked, twice. "You're going to imprison me?"

"We are." Jarem nodded.

"Over the escape of a convict?"

"One charged with the murder of a general of the Salar's army, five city guards, and thirteen soldiers. *Your apprentice*, to be precise." The most favorite apprentice, actually. That pretty boy had been brought up all too quickly from the pleasure district into the Tower almost single-handedly by his new master. To Jarem, something just didn't seem right with that, and in many ways, he was glad to have gotten rid of the Silver Sparrow.

Di Amarra listened with comical curiosity on his face and raised his brow in surprise. "So, one general, five guards, and thirteen soldiers died failing to stop *one* man from escaping the city," he repeated, pride all over his face. "Are you charging me for the competence of my apprentice, Commander, or for the lack of it in your men? Because I'm definitely involved in the former, but not in the latter. I'm afraid you're going to have to arrest the men in charge of security for that one."

"They're dead, di Amarra." The Salar stepped in, catching the Khandoor's gaze as he did. "As of this morning. All of them. Including your stewards who died producing evidence of the Silver Sparrow having returned to your estate before he escaped."

It was something of a rush, this morning's operation. The five officers in charge had been pulled from their homes before dawn and forced to explain why such an escape had been possible with hundreds of men being on watch all over the city and along the border before they were executed. Three stewards from Di Amarra's estate had been taken in for questioning—a lengthier process that had taken the interrogators as long as two hours to get anything out of them. In the end, only one man had spilled the information before they all succumbed to their injuries. An impressive set of employees, he had to admit.

To his right, di Amarra stood with the stillness of a black lake on a windless night, breathing as lightly as a ghost. He tilted his head slowly toward Jarem, just enough for the razor-sharp gleam in those green eyes to show.

"You took my men in for interrogation without telling me, Commander?"

The words dragged like a knife on bare skin meant to expose a vein, giving Jarem the sudden need to reach for his sword. It wasn't there, of course; the only one allowed to carry a weapon in the presence of the Salar was Ghaul. But the fact that di Amarra also didn't carry a blade rarely offered one much of a relief. The man might have been standing there with nothing in his hands except the rings on his fingers, but he could kill just as calmly, and with less.

"Under my instructions, di Amarra." The Salar, watching his advisor intently now, spoke with enough clarity to rival the hostility being shown by the Khandoor.

Di Amarra turned back to the Salar, and Jarem shifted his weight uncomfortably as the image of two hungry beasts circling each other suddenly came to mind.

Time limped by like an injured animal, and somewhere in the middle of it, di Amarra slipped into the privacy of his thoughts. His eyes flickered to the floor where he seemed to be examining a crack in the black marble absentmindedly. But one would have to be a complete idiot to believe an absence of mind was a concept that would ever fit Deo di Amarra. This was, after all, the man who had been called "The Red Mamba" in his youth, back when he was still a self-employed assassin.

After a moment, he looked up at the Salar. "I see," he said brightly, like someone who'd just solved a puzzle. "I presume you have a proposal for me then, my lord?"

Salar Muradi responded with a raised brow. "In exchange for allowing an act of treason to go unpunished? Are you so convinced that I'm above the law, di Amarra?"

"As all kings are, my lord," di Amarra declared readily. "Is that not the whole point of being called a *ruler*? To hold the power to bend and change the rules of men and the society over which he governs?"

"If he wishes for change, perhaps."

A small shake of di Amarra's head, followed by a ghost of a smile. "A ruler who does not wish for change does not rule, my lord," he countered. "He merely sits on a very large chair waiting for the next man who wishes for change to take it. It was *your* wish for change that brought you out of Sabha to this very chamber, *your* wish for change that has convinced you to sign my arrest. You must have wished to gain something from that signature. What would that be, my lord? I am very open to see if I can accommodate it at the moment."

Jarem took a glance at the Salar, who seemed to be thinking about those words, hoping that he wasn't truly considering them. He'd expected some negotiation from di Amarra, of course, but they hadn't really discussed the possibility of it. Salar Muradi, however, didn't discuss *everything* with anyone.

"Very well," said the Salar. "Since your apprentice has deprived me of my men and caused damage to the city, the royal army, and the reputation of Rasharwi as one of the most secure states in the Salasar, Commander Sa'id will name a suitable compensation to be paid to our treasury in gold, to which you will oblige. You will also take part in filling those vacant positions, by training the men I assign to the best of your ability and making sure the incident never repeats itself. I will test them thoroughly before considering the task done."

A surprise, but not exactly a bad one in Jarem's opinion. Putting di Amarra on the job had always been something they wanted to accomplish, but the man had so far evaded that responsibility by many clever excuses. It would strengthen the army and their security measures to a whole other level given the man's expertise, and at the same time, any escape and loophole found could be blamed on him, giving Jarem more opportunities to get rid of the man. For that, he decided to hold his objections.

"Meanwhile, you will accompany my son to the Black Desert, make sure Sarasef agrees to my offered terms, and see to it that everything goes smoothly. I want an army to be trained alongside Sarasef's mercenaries, and when it's ready, it will march into the White Desert with Lasura at its helm to bring down the Kha'gan responsible for burning the villages west of Sabha."

The Kha'gan responsible...

Jarem winced at the part of the plan he hadn't been consulted on and had always advised against. That particular wound inflicted by Za'in izr Husari himself in answer to his wife being mutilated and murdered by Rashai soldiers was still unquestionably raw on the Salar, it would seem.

Three large villages had been destroyed, burned down to the last woman and child by the Visarya. It had been a direct challenge to the Salar's rule, a blatant declaration of war, and it had taken everything he could come up with to stop the Salar from sending another army into the desert to wipe them out. Without a large enough army that knew how to navigate and survive in that harsh environment, they would lose half the men from the march alone to get to the Visarya, not to mention they'd have to pass several other Kha'gans' territories before that. Sending in a small raiding party was something that could be done, given enough discretion. Sending in a whole army would put the entire desert on alert, not to mention that Za'in izr Husari ruled one of the largest Kha'gans in the west, whose number of warriors they hadn't been able to estimate with accuracy. The Massacre of the Vilarhiti would repeat itself, in Jarem's opinion, only in this case they might not be the ones to claim victory.

Still, he could understand the drive. It wasn't just about pride or ego. The fire had destroyed everything along that side of Sabha and a large amount of funds had to be taken from other projects to rebuild, putting them on hold for years as the result. The Salar had visited the site himself the morning after it had happened, had stood by the piles of bodies burnt beyond recognition, trembling violently enough for the gesture to be seen by anyone within a hundred paces. It would be some time before Jarem forgot the look on his face, if ever. It would be some time before he could forget the image of what had been done.

But this plan could work. If they could combine their forces with the Rishi, get a large enough army to be trained by Sarasef with the help of Deo di Amarra, it might just be enough. By wiping out the Visarya—or even just killing Za'in—the White Desert would be thrown into an internal war. The Kha'gans would fight each other to claim the territory that once belonged to the Visarya and create a golden opportunity for the main army the Salar had been mobilizing to move in. At the same time, the royal fleet could be sent to attack Makena by sea, cutting supplies from being sent into Citara, and they'd win this war once and for all.

He had to admit, he was beginning to like the Silver Sparrow for making all this possible.

"And suppose I refuse or fail at any of those tasks, my lord?" asked di Amarra.

The Salar grinned. "Then I will sit on this chair and wait for you to be sentenced to death for treason. All your establishments and assets will then be taken over by the Salasar. Unless, of course, the Silver Sparrow were to be brought back to face justice and confirm your innocence in all this."

The Red Mamba's lips stretched back into a smile, before a clear, mellifluous laugh filled the room, along with his applause.

"Oh, well done, my lord," he said. "How exceptionally done. But just to make sure I understand correctly." A small pause, followed by a slight change in expression that gave Jarem another urge to find his missing sword. "You believe I have the ability to strengthen your army, fill your treasury, negotiate to gain you a powerful ally, and win you the biggest war this peninsula has ever known, and you will make an enemy of me if I refuse. Is that correct, my lord Salar?"

There was more danger in that statement than anything di Amarra had ever said, and for a moment, Jarem questioned whether it had been the right move to attack the Khandoor this way. A deadly weapon could cut you just as deep as it would in the hands of your opponent if not handled correctly, and they'd just unsheathed one of the deadliest weapons that had won Salar Muradi the Salasar.

A small pause from the Salar showed he was acutely aware of that fact.

It didn't, however, seem to bother him much, judging from the calmness of his gestures. "Your answer, di Amarra."

The Khandoor smiled, manufactured a bow for the Salar that could be called an exaggeration. "With your permission, my lord," he said, "I'd like to sit on it for bit longer while I take my leisure in your prison, which, in light of the fact that any man of luxury such as myself tends to not function well in poor conditions, I hope will be comfortable enough for me to offer you a rational answer. Would you like to take me now, Commander? Or do I have time to freshen up a bit before I go?"

⁜

THE DOOR CLOSED softly behind Ghaul, who'd come to escort di Amarra out of the study, leaving Jarem and the Salar alone in the dark chamber with something foul and heavy in the air to breathe. Salar Muradi, eyes still fixed on the empty spot where the Khandoor had stood moments ago, raised the goblet to his lips and sipped the wine quietly for a time before he voiced his decision.

"Keep an eye on him," he said. "If anyone gives him a visit, I want to know who and what is said. Make sure he doesn't know someone is listening."

"You believe he might be conspiring with someone, my lord?"

The Salar shook his head, still deep in his thoughts. "You can't hold a man like Deo di Amarra in prison if he doesn't want to stay in it. If he chooses to stay, there must be a reason. If he is working with someone, I want the entire operation uprooted and eliminated before I send an army into the White Desert."

Treason

The Rishis appeared just before the sun dipped behind the mountains. There were fifteen of them—tall, dark figures dressed completely in black, like creatures of the night that arrived too early to feed. Khali had been riding back to camp, keeping a generous distance behind Hasheem, when they came into view. He had waited and watched more than a dozen Black Desert mercenaries, armed to the teeth as if they were about to join a battle, target one man carrying no more than a sword, a bow, and an empty quiver.

The ogui who had only the day before been defeated by Zozi and just now proven to be a poor shot during the hunt didn't make a run for it. Instead, he exchanged a few words with the Rishis, nodded, squared his shoulders, and with an unnatural calm, cleared the sword from its sheath.

What happened after that could be called treason, depending on how one chose to see it.

From the distance, Khali reined in his horse to watch from behind a nearby rock as the Rishis closed in on their target. In the middle of that circle of fifteen raid-hardened men, Hasheem—swift as a bird and smiling while at it—weaved his way through them like a dancer switching from one partner to the next. He rode high on the saddle, sword leaping from grip to grip like a living thing to strike and parry, and in fluid efficiency managed to slip through three men to come out untouched on the other side.

He turned back to the Rishis. A dagger materialized, disappeared, and somewhere, someone dropped from a horse. Lay dead. The big Rishi on his left swore and came back, axe high and snarling, swinging for the head. Hasheem raised his blade to block the blow, switched the grip in midair at the last minute, dipped low to clear the axe's path, and from his opponent's waist snatched himself a dagger. Plunged it into the man's back as they passed and killed him on the spot. The blade came off, took down another rider in the chest with an easy flick of the wrist.

Three down. Twelve to go.

Another rider came up from behind, a curved blade gleaming in the dying sun. The ogui, having somehow sensed the attack in the middle of that commotion, turned, kicked his horse into a gallop and headed straight for the man. The Rishi's blade swept low as they met. Djari's sworn sword grabbed the saddle horn, swung himself off the back of the horse to dodge the blow riding sideways. Reached under the colt's throat with his sword hand as they passed, taking the rider's rein with two fingers that came momentarily off the scabbard, and yanked hard from underneath. The Rishi's horse screeched as it lost balance, throwing the rider off its back and knocking him unconscious with its hooves.

Still dragging the riderless horse along as he climbed back up on the saddle, Hasheem reined in the mare, tethered it to his saddle horn, and used the horse to block attackers coming toward the right. A dagger thrown out of nowhere came at eye-level, and was dodged by a hair as the ogui arched back with the flexibility of a woman. Hasheem came back up to meet another sword swinging at head height, blocking it with his blade before it bit into his nose. The free hand stole a whip off his opponent's saddle as the blades came apart, and with serpentine precision it lurched at the Rishi, wrapping itself around the man's throat. A hard tug sent him flying off the horse.

An opportunity opened, was seized, and with a timely release of the tethered horse, Djari's sworn sword wreaked havoc and broke through a line of three more riders coming at him. A noose tied with one hand and the aid of his teeth with a rope he took off someone slipped cleanly over a Rishi's head and snapped his neck as the ogui dragged him behind his horse. The fight went on, and all the while Khali watched, glued to the scene as the man continued to use everything at hand—the sand, the sun, the empty scabbard, his bare hands sometimes—to wound and unhorse his opponents.

Warriors didn't fight like that. They fought with pride, with rules, with skills honed to perfection by years of practice. This was something else, something the ogui had been hiding, lying about to keep a secret. It wasn't even swordsmanship, not the kind he knew. Compared to the White Warriors, the man was clumsy at best in the way he wielded his blade, but as much as Khali didn't want to believe what he was seeing and how betrayed he felt, there was a chance—a real chance—the ogui might come out alive fighting fifteen Black Desert mercenaries. Alone.

And he would have done just that—Khali would have bet on it—if Djari hadn't appeared out of the blue.

He saw Hasheem turn abruptly in her direction, frozen in the middle of the fight like a stunned gazelle sensing a predator. The Rishis turned with him and saw, just as Khali did, Djari's long, iconic silver hair billowing behind her in a damning proclamation of what she was.

Everything went to hell after that. The Rishis might have come for Hasheem—for reasons Khali had yet to find out—but with a Bharavi up for grabs, one might have thrown a naked girl into an all-male prison and expected less interest. With that sudden change of target, whatever chances her sworn sword had gained against the rest of the men were suddenly gone.

He was fighting now with something important to lose, with panic nipping closely at his heels, and fear that followed him like vultures trailing a dying man. And since this involved Djari—the Visarya's only Bharavi and daughter to the Kha'a—Khali had no choice but to step in.

It wasn't enough, of course. With four dead and one unconscious, they were still two against ten with a Bharavi to protect. Fighting ten Rishis was possible, keeping ten warriors off a girl was something else. To her credit, Djari took down two riders with her arrows that didn't kill them, but the moment they surrounded her, it was over.

The three of them were bound hand and foot, gagged, and tossed into a wagon with all its openings carefully covered. The Rishis took great care in keeping the current location of their stronghold in the canyons of the Djamahari a tight secret, and kept them in the dark for most parts of the journey.

They traveled at speed, stopping only briefly for food and other necessities, which didn't leave them much hope to be caught up to or discovered by the search party that would have been dispatched as soon as they knew Djari was missing. These men knew what they were doing. They'd been raiding and taking prisoners to Rasharwi for as long as the Salasar had been at war with the White Desert. The chance of them escaping was slim, especially when they were holding both a Bharavi and someone they'd sent fifteen men into Za'in izr Husari's territory to catch.

Not a usual risk Sarasef would take, unless it was for someone truly important.

That important someone was sitting across from him, eyes wide open and red-rimmed from lack of sleep, shoulders painfully stiff like a cornered animal expecting an attack at any moment. Behind him and to the right, Djari curled up into a ball, pretending to be asleep. It didn't fool anyone, especially not her stressed-out, overwrought sworn sword who seemed about to go over the edge.

Khali didn't blame him. A helpless young girl among near a dozen mercenaries and head hunters already agitated from a fight they didn't get to finish wouldn't last long anywhere intact. Anyone with eyes could see the way they looked at her. Anyone could sense the hostility they had toward her sworn sword, who'd killed four of their comrades and injured half a dozen more. It had, in fact, taken the man in charge of their party—the one with a patch over his right eye—more than a fist to stop the men from beating Khali and Hasheem to death. The need for release was so high it produced a scent.

And it was bubbling, intensifying like a slow-cooked stew left on the fire for too long—the inescapable tension that permeated so thickly in the air you could almost taste it in your saliva. He could see it in their eyes, in the twitch of their muscles when they came to deliver food in the wagon and untied the gag, could hear it in the way they began to snap at each other and the fistfights that followed more and more often.

It was only a matter of time before they came for her. All of them knew it, even Djari.

And they did come: on the third night, when they stopped for shelter in the canyons of the Djamahari.

*

THE DIFFERENCE BETWEEN a dangerous assignment and a suicidal one lies in the competence of one's men.

Bashir couldn't remember who'd said it—his memory had always been on the short side when it came to these things—but those words had been what he'd lived by for the past thirty years. The last time he'd neglected them, he'd lost an eye and nearly his entire company.

The right side of his face where the eye had been still itched like having spent a night with the wrong bitch in a whorehouse, especially in the cold. He curled his fingers tighter around the cup to stop himself from scratching it in public, pretending to warm his hand with the hot tea. Showing weaknesses in front of your men was never a good idea, especially under the current circumstances.

Sixty-two years of life spent serving the last Grand Chief and then his son had taught him a few things on how to lead men. That skill was the reason Sarasef still entrusted him with important tasks at his age. Thirty years ago, his fist alone would have been enough. Now, he could hardly get off a horse without feeling something in his knees.

But one could sometimes get away with a few weaknesses and old age given enough reputation and stature, and in that department, Bashir's was a name that got men to give up their seats and pour him drinks at most fires. Respect, even amongst thieves and cold-blooded murderers, was still a thing if one knew how to nurture it.

Given the men one had to work with weren't complete idiots, of course.

And this lot—Bashir swept his left eye around the campfire once more and sighed—this new generation of imbeciles who seemed to try a lot harder to extend the length of their cocks rather than the reach of their swords, was going to be the death of him.

With Sarasef and Saracen at each other's throats, the news of the Silver Sparrow being on the run had required immediate action, one that didn't leave him enough time to put together his choice of men, most of whom had left with other raiding parties heading in other directions. To make sure they beat Saracen to it, he'd ended up taking whatever was left at hand to ride out into the White Desert as soon as they'd gotten word of the Sparrow's sighting.

Bashir had always counted himself among the more simple and short-sighted men (he was a fighter, not a strategist) and had asked why it was so important that they got a hold of this Shakshi slave before Saracen did. The answer was one that made him volunteer to be here, bad knee, shit crew, short notice, and all.

"The Silver Sparrow is Deo di Amarra's best apprentice," Sarasef had explained. *"One of the best assassins in Rasharwi, whose skills we can use on our side if he's willing."*

Makes sense, he'd thought. They always needed good new recruits. *"And if he's not?"*

"Then we'll have something Muradi wants," said Sarasef, grinning like the mischievous boy he'd helped raise back in the days when the old chief had been alive. *"That boy was a high-end escort before he was sold to di Amarra. Do you know what that means, Bashir?"*

He didn't, of course, and had admitted as much.

"That he knows the Tower like the back of his hand, and every dirty little secret of everyone in it. That's why Muradi needs him dead. Having the right information," Sarasef had added, *"is how you gain the upper hand in business and politics. Getting a hold of the man who has it, Bashir, is how you win a war."*

"Are we?" he'd asked. *"Going to war?"*

The smile he'd been given, Bashir thought, was the one that made Sarasef—the younger of the two brothers—the Grand Chief of the Rishis. "*We are mercenaries, old man,*" he'd replied. "*War comes to us, not the other way around, but you can always count on its arrival.*"

Put that way, he could understand how crucial it was to have the Silver Sparrow, Bashir thought as he sipped the tea in his cup, keeping his eye on the men around camp. They also needed him alive, not dead, which was the problem.

The Sparrow had killed four of their men—one of which had been the youngest of the three brothers he'd taken here with him. Since the reward offered by the Salar was for bringing him in dead or alive, the men—especially the two brothers left—obviously wanted him dead. Explaining to them why Sarasef needed him alive wasn't going to work with these idiots, and now he had to keep an eye on this lot to not break command.

Which would have been doable, had they not also caught a Bharavi in the net. Za'in izr Husari's Bharavi daughter to be exact. He didn't know yet if she was going to be their biggest catch or the worst disaster he would bring back to their den, and knowing his own shortcomings when it came to politics, he'd decided to let Sarasef figure out what to do with her. There had, in any case, been no way of containing the men the moment they saw her. Bharavis and oracles fetched the highest price from the Salar, and these men were mercenaries and headhunters, not soldiers.

They were also *men*.

Tired, hungry, angry men who had, by the Rishi's law and tradition, always been given first access to their catch before selling them to the Salasar. And he had strictly denied them their privilege—their rights even—three nights ago. The girl couldn't be touched until Sarasef said so, or else the conflict their Grand Chief had been trying to avoid for two generations would be inevitable. Messing with Za'in izr Husari was off-limits, had been for decades. There were other Kha'gans to raid with less risks, less tendency to start a full-scale battle they weren't sure they could win.

There was, however, an art to keeping men in line, to diverting their attention, to making them believe holding back was in their own self-interest and would produce a bigger reward. He'd promised women, gold, and a rise in status. It worked most of the time, only this time something had been off from the beginning. Years of leading men had given Bashir the ability to sniff out hostility in the air like an experienced cook identifying an ingredient in a dish he didn't make. This time, though, he wished that expertise was at fault.

But life didn't give you that kind of luck. It never did.

From across the fire, the bigger one of the two brothers rose first, rolling his right shoulder to loosen a muscle. The smaller one followed, and together they walked toward him. Bashir checked his sword and dagger, and assessed the situation as they came closer, counting his men.

Of the eleven men left alive, four were too badly injured to fight, thanks to the Sparrow and the girl's arrows. Take away the two brothers, and the remaining five were what he had left to count on. Two of those he trusted with his life. The other three were new recruits that seemed manageable, but had yet to be tried and tested.

Five against two was a good number, especially when Bashir counted himself as the sixth.

He placed his hand on his sword as they came nearer, gripped the hilt in what could be considered a panic when he registered another set of movements from across the fire. The blade in his hand rang sharp and clear out of the sheath as he jumped to his feet on reflex. By that time, the two men he trusted had already had their throats slit from behind by the new recruits.

"Can I help you pieces of shit with something?" he snarled. "Wanna tell me what the fuck you're doing before I gut you both?"

"Sit down, old man," said the big brother, drawing the sword out of his scabbard and spitting on the ground. "This party now belongs to Saracen. We'll take it from here."

An Unforgivable Sin

"*Some mistakes*," her mother had once said, "*are not forgiven by the gods.*"

But she was the Chosen One, wasn't she? The gods had plans for her, hadn't they?

Djari had never voiced those thoughts, even though they had been the reason behind her every disobedience, every mistake she'd made. But one could take privileges and blessings only so far before they ran dry, and sometimes pride had its consequences. Pride, Djari knew, was one of her sins among many, and she was about to pay for it tonight, here, in the isolated canyons of the Djamahari.

They're coming for me.

She clenched her teeth against that thought and swallowed it down before it reached her face. She had seen it coming for some time, had understood it from the tightness of Hasheem's jawline and the way he'd jumped every time someone made a noise near their wagon. She knew, from that suffocating tension and the pungent sense of dread from both Hasheem and Khali, what was about to become of her.

In a way, it shouldn't be any different. Eventually, she would have to share a bed with her husband, a man of her father's choosing; a stranger, just like these men, if one were to look at it from that angle. For the past fifteen years she'd prepared herself to live with such an arrangement, and had accepted it as her duty to the Kha'gan. Put that way, she should have been prepared.

She wasn't.

The nightmares of her mother being attacked had returned, repeatedly, for the past two nights. They felt more real now than when she had them back at camp. The surroundings had changed in these new dreams to resemble where she was, as if they'd been premonitions. She wondered sometimes if Nazir's gift also existed in some amount in her. A disturbing thought, that, considering the situation.

And it was her mistake that had put her there. Sheer impulse was what had gotten her running to the stable as soon as word had come about Hasheem defying Nazir. Her impatience, carelessness, and pride were to blame for trying to gain some time with him. What she'd wanted to accomplish with that time, she wasn't sure. It had never occurred to her to wait—impatience was another of her sins—but the moment she'd seen the band of men surrounding him, she knew this was one mistake that would not be forgiven by the gods.

The metal doors clanged open, yanking her back to reality. Hasheem jumped at the sound to shield her with his body, his knuckles bone-white and trembling as he gripped one of the bars on the wagon's window. He was trying not to show it—the fear that had been eating him alive and terrorizing him for the past few days—had made a point of hiding his face, turning his back to her as much as he could. It hadn't worked then. It definitely didn't work now.

"Stay behind me," Hasheem croaked, his voice broken from disuse, or from panic, she wasn't sure. Their gags had always been applied during the journey but had yet to be put back on since the last meal. She thought perhaps now they didn't need to do that anymore. At night, deep in the canyons of the Djamahari, nobody would hear them if they screamed.

Two men came in, unarmed as they'd been instructed. The leader had made it clear no weapon was to be taken anywhere near Hasheem, and contact was to be as brief and as far from arm's reach as possible. *The boy will kill you with a tied up hand if you're not careful. Give him a weapon, and he'll kill the whole fucking lot of us, still tied up.*

Whatever Hasheem had been before he became her sworn sword had put them on high alert. They called him the Silver Sparrow. She'd heard something about that name and the reputation that preceded it. She wasn't sure yet what to think about that. There hadn't been time.

The bigger one of the two grabbed the chain attached to Hasheem's ankle, the other took the one around his wrists. She remembered how he'd almost strangled one of them to death with those chains two nights ago for coming too close to her. It had taken three men to save him before they beat Hasheem unconscious. They'd starved him on purpose since to weaken him, and now, together with the damage they'd done, he didn't seem to have much fight left.

Still, Hasheem growled and thrashed like a rabid animal as they yanked him out of the wagon by the chains. Two more men joined in to beat the fight out of him. She didn't scream or cry as it happened. She mustn't.

'*Shakshi women wave and smile when their loved ones go to battle,*' her mother had said. *'They need our strength to fight, not our tears.'*

The biggest man, the one who seemed to be leading them now, crouched down over Hasheem and yanked his head up by the hair.

"So," he said, "how would you like this done, pretty boy? Would you like to die first or watch us fuck her before I take your head off?"

Hasheem turned in that grip, spat blood in the man's face.

A fist came down on his jaw, followed by a kick in the ribs. The attacker straightened, shook his fist to clear the sting, and smiled. "Well then," he said, "die later it is." He jerked his chin to the men in front of him. "Go. Get the girl and bring her here."

She watched the two men come without making a sound. She realized she couldn't, even if there had been someone to hear it. Her windpipe had collapsed, her voice lost somewhere between the pounding of her heart and the breaths she couldn't seem to catch as she pressed herself against the wall.

She prayed then, for her brother, her father, for anyone or anything to intervene.

But the gods don't always listen, and life will take what it wants from you, even if you plead and scream. There would be no one to help her, not here, not now, the same way there had been no one to help her mother then.

Her voice came back in a whimper when they grabbed her. It grew into a string of useless, broken cries of pleading, then a shriek she couldn't control as they dragged her out of the wagon. One of the men punched her in the stomach when she hung on to the door, and was about to beat her again before the other one stopped him.

He liked his women screaming and conscious, he said. The one who'd hit her smiled at that. They were all smiling, she saw, like the crowd at Raviyani watching the goats being sacrificed, looking forward to sampling the meat—only she would be alive when they did this, and it wasn't the meat they were after.

They threw her on the ground just ten steps away from Hasheem. The men argued for some time about their turns, until the biggest among them stepped forward and took charge. The old leader was nowhere to be found. There was fresh blood on the big man's hands, she saw, and understood what had happened.

The first man in line climbed on top of her, pinning her down with his weight. A hand closed around the back of her neck, pushing her face into the sand, filling her mouth with it, choking her as she tried to breathe.

They came to her then—the images from those nightmares of her mother in the desert as the Rashais took their turns—only this time she could feel their hands on her own skin, their weight on her own back, their heaving breaths on her earlobe. They seized her limbs as they came, froze her on the spot in a panic. She gasped for air, for breaths, for something to release the pressure in her chest.

The sound of a sword belt being unbuckled came, followed by the loud rustling of fabric being loosed, and out there, ten unattainable steps in front of her, lying on the ground surrounded by three men, Hasheem cried out the sound of a man being ripped apart, of someone going through his worst nightmare, of a mother watching her child burn in the fire her father had set.

She watched Hasheem crawl over the sand as he did, made it a few feet before they kicked him and dragged him back by the ankle. A booted foot pinned him to the ground, pressed tight in the middle of his back to keep him in place. The new leader yanked up his head to face her, bent over to whisper something in his ear, and Hasheem thrashed under that foot, screamed a sound so animal-like, so terrifying, like something was being ripped from his throat. It went on, amidst the smiles of men who stood there watching, the cries of a beast being tortured that escalated into a shriek as the man above her took a fistful of her clothes and tore them open.

We are Bharavis...

A distant memory drifted into her mind. A voice so gentle, so strong from which limitless, immeasurable strength had been derived, time and time again.

"We are Bharavis," her mother had said, gripping her hand so tight it had left a mark, *"born to carry the legacy of our race, to ensure the continuity of our blood. Whatever happens to us, no matter how hard, how vile, we must survive and endure."*

And at that moment, when the night suddenly turned silent in her head, when all lives seemed to have stopped breathing, she felt him enter her.

We are Bharavis...

A burning, searing pain shot through her core, took away her vision. She bit down on her lip, gripped the sand under her straining fingers to stay silent, and repeated those words in her mind, hammering them into her existence.

No matter how hard, how vile...

He drove into her again, and again, without pause, without hesitation. Each time tearing her further, deeper, grunting louder as his pleasure seemed to escalate with every thrust.

We are Bharavis...

She gritted her teeth as she recalled the words she had been taught, forced her mind to trace them as she hung on to the last thing no man nor beast could ever make her surrender.

We do not break or bend in the face of danger. We thrive, in hunger, in thirst, in every torture the gods throw at us. And when the oases run dry, when all other lives have perished in the sun, we, as people of the desert, will live and survive drinking our own blood.

It was the first thing they learned the moment they knew how to speak, the writing on every wall, in every heart of whomever sought to call themselves a Shakshi. And she was a Bharavi, her mother's daughter, a child of Za'in izr Husari, a Shakshi to the last drop of her blood.

Djari swore then, by all the gods that had ignored her pleas, and all the beasts that gathered there that night, that she would find a way to survive this, just as every Bharavi before her had survived, just as every Shakshi before her had done for thousands of years. And if there had ever been a doubt in what her destiny would be or what role she would take in this war, there was none of it now, not after this. That day she'd paid for it, sealed it with her blood, and the blood of her sworn sword.

And there Hasheem was, bruised and bloodied from the beatings, dying little by little as he watched the man slam into her, as careless fingers searched for her hair, gripping it tight while he took pleasure after merciless pleasure, just ten steps too far.

But he *was* watching, every moment of it. He watched, as if turning away was a crime he would never commit, as if doing so was to hold her hand through it, to remind her what he was, what he'd promised to be the night she'd killed her horse.

You are an extension of me, she'd said without thinking or having considered the consequences.

And he'd reached out his hand then. A hand so large, so steady, closing around hers so tight. A promise under a starry night sky, unshakable even by the gods.

We do this together, you and I.

Don't do this alone.

In the span of those ten impossible steps between them, under the weight of the crushing sky and the men that held them down, their eyes met, locked together in an unspoken understanding. And she knew, she *knew* then, that this was no longer her pain to carry, but also his, and unmistakably theirs.

Don't do this alone.

She could see it so clearly then, could feel the certainty of it like the beating of her heart, like sunrise in the desert, like breathing, that she would never have to go through life, through marriage, through any promise of death, of pain and sufferings to come, alone, for as long as they lived. He would be here, by her side, even if their paths would forever run parallel to each other and never meet. He would be here, even if it tore him apart.

The man above her came to a pause. A strange, strangled sound came from above her, like the gurgling of someone drowning or choking on water. She turned to look and saw him swaying a little to the side, eyes wide and bleeding from his mouth. The man collapsed on top of her a heartbeat later and lay still, trapping her again with his weight.

A war hammer was sticking out of his back, massive, pitch-black and covered in blood. Djari traced her eyes over the crow figure carved into the hammer's head, up the length of the long handle to the dark hand that held it, and then toward the man who had killed the Rishi.

Above her, a large figure in a black, fur-trimmed robe towered over her and the corpse he'd just made, blocking out the moon, the stars, and the mountain behind him. He took a step forward, grimaced as he yanked the war hammer out of the dead man's back, made another face of disdain that rendered the number 57 tattooed on his right cheek unreadable, and let out a deep, growling sound of displeasure when he caught the attention of the man above Hasheem.

"You pathetic, good-for-nothing swine," he swore, pointing the war hammer at the man, "take your dirty foot off my Sparrow before I smash that useless brain out of your skull."

An Old

Acquaintance

Hasheem woke to the sound of her scream.

Or was it his? His sisters'? His mother's? Or Mara's, as he'd imagined in his nightmares?

They all sounded the same. Humans, when broken, all screamed the same way.

But the first time...the first time was when you screamed the loudest, when the wounds stayed open the longest, and was what you remembered for life.

They were all coming back to him now: the pain, the disgust, the anger, and everything in between, all floating on the surface like a long-dead body just risen from the bottom of a swamp. The stench of it pooled in his stomach, came up in waves to the back of his throat as images of the night before flooded his mind. It overlapped and intertwined with his own memories, making it impossible to tell the two apart. He could recall the rawness of his throat as Djari screamed, could feel the hand that pushed her down on his own back, could still smell that stench of blood and tears mingled with the sweat produced by the man above her, *above him*—

Hasheem rolled off the bed, stumbled at the searing pain in his ribs that sent him collapsing to the ground, and crawled over to empty the contents of his stomach into the chamber pot nearby. Nothing came out but blood and bile. He remembered then that they'd stopped feeding him two days before. Maybe more. *How long has it been?*

"Easy, boy." A voice so deep, so severe, so familiar came from the back of the room. "Those ribs are going to need some time to heal before you can move around like normal."

Hasheem tilted his head to look at his surroundings for the first time. Unpolished, white-veined black marble covered the floor, walls, and ceiling of the dimly-lit bedroom. An enormous six-pointed star-patterned wool rug from Cakora stretched elaborately from wall to wall in a chamber large enough to fit fifty men. Dark mahogany furniture accented with leather and gold was scattered sparingly around the space. But it was the brown bear pelt laid neatly at the foot of the bed that made him dead certain of where he was. He knew this bed, had slept in it, and would likely remember it for life.

Another memory from the night before flashed through his mind. Someone had come to kill those men before he'd passed out. Hasheem couldn't remember how it had happened with clarity, but he knew that voice, that thick Samarran accent, and the weighted, intimidating presence that usually accompanied it.

There was a sense of relief attached to that knowledge, and Hasheem allowed his weight to sink to the floor in exhaustion. At the very least, he knew this man, knew he could reason and negotiate with him. To a certain point.

"What did you do with her?" Hasheem asked, kneading his temples as he did. The pain in his head was killing him by the minute, and that was putting it mildly.

"That's it?" said Sarasef of the Rishi as he crossed over and lifted him up on the bed with one hand, as though he weighed no more than a child. Not that it came as a surprise. Those hands could smash a man's skull, and Hasheem had seen it done. "No *hello*? Not even a *thank you?* The last time I saw you, your manner was impeccable."

He shook away the hand that lingered on his arm, glared at the man old enough to be his father with a clear warning. A bad idea, considering where he was and what he needed, but he was past caring at that point. "Last time you were my client," he replied sharply, pushing that memory away. "Your transaction was done a long time ago. I am under no obligation to please you or your men. What did you do with her?"

Sarasef took a step back, stroking his beard as he considered something. "You believe I sent my men out to get you for this reason?" he asked, his expression flat and unreadable. "For pleasure?"

"Where is Djari?" It came out in a growl he didn't anticipate. His patience was running thin, and with Sarasef here, the memories of that part of his life were stretching it thinner.

"Safe. Protected." Sarasef shifted his weight, crossed his arms over the bulk of his chest—a gesture that told Hasheem he should now approach things with caution. "Now, you will answer my question. Why do you think you are here? Why did I risk my men to get you?"

He drew a breath and exhaled in a small relief. Safe and protected was what he needed to hear, and if one knew anything about Sarasef of the Rishi, questioning his word when it was clearly given was a deadly mistake. "I don't know." Hasheem sighed as he buried his face in his palm. He might have been able to guess a few reasons why, but at that moment, he didn't have the energy to think or care.

Sarasef grimaced at that. "I thought my offer would have made that obvious."

That made him look up. "What offer?"

Silence, and then an understanding. "Di Amarra never told you, did he?"

"Told me what?"

"I made him an offer for you. A large offer. A tenth of all my transactions with the Salar to be exact."

It took an effort to keep his jaw from dropping at that figure. A tenth of all the Rishi's transactions with the Salar was a number much, much bigger than his fee, not to mention an offer of continuous pay. For Dee to have declined was highly out of character. For Sarasef to have offered was nothing short of outrageous. "For me? To do what?"

"To work for us." The reply came readily, naturally, as though it had been said or practiced for some time. "I wondered why you didn't come to me when you had to run. Now I understand."

Dee had never mentioned it, not a hint from before or when he'd left the city. But even so, even if he had… "Go to you? Are you *insane*?" Hasheem rasped, anger pulsing in his veins at the very thought. "You and your men live and feed on the blood of my people, take coins for killing and selling them as slaves to the Salasar. I may have been raised in Rasharwi, served and serviced half the people in the Tower, but don't, *ever*, make the mistake of thinking that I would do any of it at will." He drew a breath, stifled a groan from the pain in his sides made by the broken ribs, and straightened. "I am Shakshi, in flesh and blood. No matter what you may think of me, so long as I am one, it will never happen. Believe it."

There were, of course, many things one could have said he owed this man, but to Hasheem, all those things had been paid for in full, if not still being paid for on his part. An entire winter he'd spent here in his youth had opened many doors for him, and perhaps had even led him here and to what he'd become—but none of those gifts had been, Hasheem realized even more clearly now, without a price attached. A price that he thought had already been paid within the walls of this room. Apparently, he was wrong.

For a long time, Sarasef stood silent and still, looking down at him with those crimson-brown eyes, not too different from an adult waiting for a child to settle down from a tantrum. He remembered then that the Grand Chief of the Rishi was a man equipped with patience as indestructible as a rock and a presence that weighed like one. It didn't, however, mean that one should ever take his patience for granted. Sarasef, if anything, was a man of principle, who was known to kill—indiscriminately—for that principle.

"I thought you might take that stand." He nodded calmly, thoughtfully. "In truth, I have been thinking about how to persuade you once you got here." Something in his eyes changed at that moment, and the sharp sliver of sunlight that came into the room through the window caught it, singled it out for Hasheem to see. "Now it appears I have a solution."

It crawled up his spine, sank its fangs into his back—the cold, terrifying realization of what it was he was getting at. "Don't," he found himself pleading, once more, to this man whose decisions, once made in the open, had always been final, immovable, and permanent. "Please, don't do this. I beg you."

"You don't leave me much of a choice, Hasheem."

"She is the daughter of Za'in izr Husari! You can't do this. It will start a war." He was yelling now, as though it would change anything, as if the gods had ever listened to his prayers.

Sarasef took a step forward, reached over to cradle his face with one hand. There was something close to pity in his eyes, as there had always been when he was about to deliver a killing blow.

"War, my boy, has already begun," he said expressionlessly, easily. "Muradi's emissary is coming, along with an army for me to train and a prince to lead it. Za'in izr Husari, unfortunately, is the first one he wants to see dead."

A Life Worth Ending

There were times when Lasura had been certain his mother had considered killing him. He wondered if she'd ever tried when he was little, or had come close to trying in the past seventeen years. Eighteen, to be accurate—one would have to assume she wanted him dead even before he came into the world as his father's son.

He also wondered if she would have succeeded, had his father not threatened to kill all those slaves should she try.

'Would it have been easier, Mother? If there had been fifty or a hundred prisoners instead? Would you have killed me then?'

He'd been foolish enough to ask the other night, half-drunk from too much wine at his father's table, half-deaf from the rage that poured out of her the moment she knew he'd accepted the mission to negotiate with Sarasef, as if he ever had a choice in it. That memory, as much as he wanted to forget, was still unbearably fresh and raw in his mind.

She'd straightened then, raising her chin to look up at him in disgust the same way she'd always looked at her husband. She hated their resemblance—the same black hair, deep-set eyes, harsh, prominent jawline, and the way they were built that held enough similarities to be mistaken sometimes by silhouette. That was the only thing his mother ever saw when she looked at him; the shadow of the man she wanted to see dead. The evidence of her defeat.

'*I should have killed myself before you were born!*' she'd said, grinding her teeth as if to keep at bay an even worse insult, which, given his mother's exceptional creativity in delivering them, could be possible. *'If I'd known you'd willingly slaughter your own people—'*

'*My people?*' It had slipped out of him before he could stop himself, the words he'd been trying to hold back for her sake, words he might have still been able to swallow had he not been so drunk, so tired from the climb. '*There are four Shakshis I've known in my life,* four, *and half of them would rather see me dead.*' Yes, dead. His own mother and her handmaiden to be exact. '*The Black Tower is my home, Rasharwi is my city,* he *is my father as much as you are my mother and at the very least he wants me to live! As far as I'm concerned, it was* your *part of my blood that has dragged me through all kinds of shit in this Tow—*'

The sound of her knuckles crashing into his jaw had finished the sentence for him, as always. She was too small to deliver a punch that would throw him off his balance, but that side of his face was going to bruise for some time. It used to hurt a lot more when he was little, but he'd gotten used to it after a few years.

It had become clear to Lasura a long time ago that what his mother couldn't take out on her husband, she resorted to taking out on his son. And while he could sympathize with her how all that anger had to go somewhere, being given his own quarters five years ago and allowing him the possibility of avoiding her most of the time was the best gift his father had ever bestowed upon him. Still, every now and then, she would pay him a visit, usually right after his father's return to the Tower. It always ended with her raging over something her son had done or hadn't done, but it had been a while since he'd goaded her into throwing her fist at him.

'*Oh, that was a good one, Mother,*' he'd told her, spitting the small amount of blood onto the floor to make a point. '*Are you calm now, or would you like another go at it?*'

She'd stood there shaking her fist as she looked at him, breathing hard from the exertion. No remorse, no apologies in those eyes, of course. The Lady Zahara of the Black Tower was not someone who apologized for her actions, nor a person you could strike at without getting your hand stung by her thorns in the process.

Neither was he, for that matter. He might be worse, if one were to consider that he was also a son of Salar Muradi of Rasharwi and had also been raised rather close to him.

'*You can't go through with this,*' came the command, the expectation. '*You will run. Disappear. I will get someone to help you escape, plant some evidence that you're dead in the desert.*' She was pacing now, arms wrapped tight around her chest, trying to come up with a way out of this mess. Or to beat his father at his own game, to put it more precisely.

It never ceased to amaze Lasura how his father had managed to live with this woman for so long without throwing her off the Tower.

'*And do what exactly?*' He'd raised his voice on purpose, made sure it carried the right amount of sarcasm. '*Herd camels? Raise goats and sheep for the rest of my life? Run and hide like a branded slave? Are you even listening to yourself?*'

She'd wheeled on him, eyes burning a terrifying yellow as she slammed her fist on the nearby table, spilling the wine from the unfinished cup. '*You will do whatever needs to be done. I will* not *let my own son ride against my own people, Lasura!*'

'*Or what, Mother?*' He'd snapped without a second thought, stared her down for the first time with every intention to put a certain theory to the test. '*What will you do? Strike me again? Kill another girl I sleep with? Poison my wine? Don't,*' he'd rasped a warning as she parted her lips, an old wound tearing open as he did by his own words, '*even try. I know you did it. I know how. I even know why. And I have, for the past seventeen years, allowed you to do what you want, but don't assume that there isn't a limit to my capacity to take your shit. Because there is, Mother, and you've just crossed it.*"

And it had all been there on her face; not the guilt, no, but the pure inconvenience of having been caught, the anger that things weren't going to go the way she'd planned, had been written so clearly in those eyes, in the way her lips had pressed tight together in displeasure, in disapproval, and for the ten-thousandth time, in disappointment. It had also been clear that for a short moment, she had considered poisoning his wine, and had visibly shaken herself free of such an idea over a thought that had come up. A deliberate choice based on reason. A careful consideration of consequences that might have followed. To Lasura, that had been enough to confirm some things.

He'd made his way to her then, pausing just close enough to be able to look down from his father's height, to make a point. *'Understand this, Mother. Your problems are yours, not mine, nor do they take precedence over my own, no matter how much you wish it so. I am not going to risk my life and everything I have to defy my father, your husband, the fucking Salar of Rasharwi, for a land I've never set foot on. And before I'm gone, I suggest you start finding yourself a new goat, or you won't have anywhere to empty your shit.'*

He'd thrown it all in her face that night, had stormed out of the room without another word. They hadn't spoken since then and he was glad she hadn't tried to reason with him again. It still stung, and he hated that it still stung. But life was life. You could fight and learn to live with scars, or you could run and live with worse.

And so, to Lasura, it was a common sight—an expected one, truly—to see his father looking at him with expectations of victories to be achieved, and his mother's silent wish to see him dead as he rode away from the two of them, standing side by side like Life in black and Death in white at the gate of the Tower that morning. His Shakshi swordmaster, however, wasn't there as he should have been. He wondered if he should be watching his back for that.

She would never go so far as to have him killed, though. He was certain of it. Something had been holding her back, keeping her in check every time she'd had that murderous look in her eyes, and for seventeen years, she'd sacrificed much to keep him alive despite her conflicting need to end his life. There was a reason for that. She had her own plans for him, just as his father did.

'*Women,*' he'd been taught, '*hold the power to give life and the accompanying strength to take it. Never, ever, give them cause to do so or underestimate them if you want to live.*'

A caution not easily brushed aside for a son raised by a Bharavi. He wondered sometimes if all Bharavis were like this, and had shuddered once or twice at the thought of meeting another, no matter how unlikely that was.

"Remind me to get you a salve for that bruise," Deo di Amarra, the same man who'd taught him those words, said without turning around. "It's been a while, hasn't it?" he added, amused. "She must be getting old. That's a baby one considering the last."

Lasura snorted at that. It needed no explanation. His mentor noticed some things people might but didn't, and others no man alive should. It was difficult to tell if he had a small gift of foresight or if it was his keen observation of things that allowed him to make these predictions. In this particular case at least, Lasura guessed it was the latter. He had, after all, been partially raised around this man for more than a decade.

"I expected to be dead by morning, to be honest."

"Unfortunately, my prince," Deo said, chuckling a little, "you're not getting out of this anytime soon."

He considered that for a moment, and decided to voice his suspicion. "I take it you're not going to enlighten me on that subject, are you?"

"Assuming I possess such knowledge to enlighten you with?" Deo raised his brow, then gave him a shrug. "Not until it entertains me, no."

"Ah, but you do possess such knowledge."

He took a sidelong glance at Lasura this time, slowing down his splendid Vilarian mount a little. "Are you asking me why your mother won't kill you?"

"I'm asking you why she needs me alive."

Deo laughed. "Love, of course."

He cringed at the word. "After all this time you've spent teaching me, you still think I'm an idiot, don't you?"

"Well, you haven't exactly lived up to expectation, my lord prince."

"Perhaps the master is to blame for that, not the apprentice."

Deo's lip curled up a little. "If all apprentices were to fail, yes."

"Of course," he said, and feigned a thought. It didn't need thinking, not really. "Didn't your Sparrow put you in prison recently?" That must have been a wound, but he had been meaning to wound. He didn't like the Sparrow. The guy had beaten him once in a duel. No one liked people who'd beaten them.

"Oh, I enjoyed my prison time immensely," Deo replied, smiling widely now. "A protected solitude is hard to come by for a man in my position."

Lasura rolled his eyes. There had to be some limits to how much one could adore a certain apprentice. "Have you been fucking him all this time, Deo? Or have you been wanting to and haven't succeeded?"

Deo di Amarra's laugh carried over to a few soldiers behind them, all of whom promptly pretended not to look or listen. "As much as I find my Sparrow a rare, priceless, and devastatingly gorgeous apprentice—with an absence of your mouth to boot, mind you—I am not a man who pisses on an exquisite rug he's trying to weave out of convenience. Though I'm willing to admit to having a weakness for these things, my prince."

Rare, priceless, devastatingly gorgeous, and deadly on top of it. The Sparrow was a walking testament to everyone else's inadequacy. Not too different from his father, actually. He'd met the Shakshi only once when Deo, out of the blue, had pitched them together during a training session. It wasn't even a fair fight. One could die staring at that face for too long. He wondered how many had.

A Beautiful Death: that was what they called it when someone died at the hands of the Silver Sparrow. He usually carved a bird somewhere on the victim—a signature as much as a statement that it had been a death commissioned by Deo di Amarra. The officials turned a blind eye to that. Those who might have avenged them didn't try. You didn't go against a man who owned the largest network of assassins in the peninsula and hope to survive. And of all his apprentices and employees, Deo kept this one the closest.

"You really do love that boy, don't you?" There was a touch of something pathetic in the way Lasura said those words he hadn't anticipated. It wasn't without cause, but he didn't like laying his emotions bare for all to see, not even to his lifelong mentor.

It must have shown, because Deo's expression grew soft and serious then. "I do. Everyone does. Everyone will." He sighed those words, his yellow-green eyes fixed on something, somewhere far away. "But there is, Lasura—" A deliberate use of his name to make sure the point was taken to heart. "—such a thing as being loved to death."

He didn't respond to that. Being loved to death wasn't a concept someone like him could understand. They rode in silence for the rest of the morning towards the Black Desert, where Sarasef's men would be waiting. Some time later, when they stopped for lunch, Lasura asked, though without understanding why he did, "So, love, huh?"

Deo just smiled. It was then that Lasura came to realize that his mentor would never specify what kind of love he had been referring to.

Premonition

The dark, narrow corridor echoed the sounds of tortured ghosts and men as the two men walked down toward the main hall. Cut deep into the Djamahari mountain range that had taken Lasura and Deo three days of being led blindly through the maze of its canyons to get to, the interior of the Rishi's lair resembled much of the Black Tower itself; only here, the rooms were cut deep into the living rock with passages to underground chambers where prisoners and future slaves were kept. The evidence of it was rising up periodically from the dark staircases they passed; the smell of blood, of human waste, of something rotten or about to decay, intensified and underlined by the barely-audible sounds of someone weeping and the clanging of chains.

Lasura held his breath as he walked by those staircases, willing himself not to think deeper into whatever lay at the end of the steps. Next to him, Deo appeared oblivious to it all. He seemed comfortable and at ease, as if he'd frequented that accursed place a dozen times.

Or perhaps he had and also knew something Lasura didn't.

Given that they both might never come back out of the chamber they were walking toward, and that there were just the two of them now—having been forced to leave the army and all their guards at the entrance three days' ride away—Lasura found himself questioning the composure of his mentor. He knew how well Deo could keep his concerns and discomforts hidden, but the way he looked tonight wasn't about concealing his emotions.

No, this time it wasn't Deo's powers of observation at play. This time it was premonition.

Lasura knew, because he'd had his share of them. Not in any way, shape or form, close to the visions one might imagine an oracle might have. It was more like a pressure or a weight in the pit of his stomach, an instinct that guided him to head in different directions without a concrete explanation why. It was the invisible tap on the shoulder that had made him turn to the mountain where the eaglets were, and the overhead reach toward a ledge on the cliff he hadn't known was there, leading him safely—and directly—to the nest he had yet to locate. There was, as much as he wanted to deny it, a power in his mother's blood that had been passed down to him along with her yellow eyes, even if in small amounts. And it was due to his own experience with these gifts that he'd always suspected Deo of a similar gift he might have been keeping hidden. There had been times when his mentor's awareness of things held no possible explanations. Too many times, in fact.

This time Lasura was certain—the same way he'd been certain about the birds—that he was walking down the exact corridor he was supposed to walk that was leading him to the exact chamber he was supposed to be in. He might even say, being acutely aware of the quickening of his pulse and the vomit-inducing pressure in his stomach, that all the events that had happened in his life until now had been leading to this very moment, to what was there waiting for him behind the pair of gigantic, centuries-old metal doors.

The screeching of steel echoed down the hallway as two men pushed the doors open. Through the opening, a spacious, two-story high chamber greeted them with its rose-red polished walls and floors. Like the rooms in the Black Tower, the main hall had been cut out of the mountain, only back home the rocks were all black. In the Djamahari, the mountain range was made up of large varieties of rocks and stones, ranging from the jet-black obsidian, the intricately veined white, red, and green marbles, to the most brilliant turquoise in the peninsula. From a distance, parts of the Djamahari looked like they were painted with stripes of rainbow.

In this room in particular the marble walls swirled with layers of red, copper, purple, and what appeared to be fifty other shades in between, accented and made more stunning by the occasional streaks of white as elegant as a lady's fingers. Along the walls, several dozen burning torches illuminated the chamber, each taking turns in lighting up their parts of the stage with flames that danced to the breeze coming down from—

Lasura sucked in a breath, held it at the sudden swelling of his heart. At the far end of the chamber, through a natural, circular-shaped puncture in the ceiling, the star-studded night sky stared back at him like the scintillating eye of a god. Directly under that eye, an empty, gold-veined black marble throne sat atop a dais three steps above the main floor. Carved from a single rock to form a raven nearly twice the height of a fully-grown man, the throne's empty seat was placed in the embrace of the bird's half-closed enormous wings, as if offering protection to whoever might sit on it.

"The Red Hall of Marakai," Dee said, the yellow of his green eyes growing brighter in the light of the flames. "Also known as the Secret Chamber of the Sky Father. This, my prince—" He turned to Lasura, sweeping his arms out at the wonders around them. "—is the throne room where Eli the Conqueror received his crown as the King of Kings."

It sure looked like something that belonged to the King of Kings, Lasura thought, still breathless and overwhelmed by the sight and the history that came with it. Thousands of years ago, when the peninsula had been one united nation, this very chamber had seen the crowning of the most brilliant supreme ruler and battle strategist who ever lived. A man he sometimes felt his father had been trying to become.

No, to *succeed.*

"And where he died," a deep, resonating voice boomed from a doorway on the left of the throne. "Right where you're standing, in fact. Greetings, di Amarra."

Lasura followed the sound to its source, catching the new figure as he ascended the dais. Wrapped in a cloak of black and silver wolf pelt, the man who could only be the Grand Chief of the Rishi had the height and mass to rival Ghaul and the severity of his father's presence all in one. His thick black beard and brows framed a face one might call handsome, had it not been scarred enough to give you nightmares. He walked with the slow, measured steps of a warrior equipped with enough confidence to fight something twice his size and half his age with bare hands. Hands, he recalled from several rumors surrounding the chief, that could crack a man's skull with a mere squeeze, and had done so many times.

Seeing him in the flesh, Lasura didn't doubt it.

"You like the pelt, I see." Deo inclined his head a little as a gesture of respect. The most minimal form of obeisance and his first words of address said a lot about the existing relationship between them. Lasura was beginning to understand why his father had handpicked Deo di Amarra for this job.

"It is a fine gift," said Sarasef as he seated himself on the enormous throne, somehow making it small. He took one glance at Lasura, then turned his attention back to Deo. "What will it cost me?"

Right to the point. No time wasted. No standing on ceremony, not even to address a prince of the Black Tower. Lasura briefly wondered if he should be insulted by obligation and decided it wasn't useful, not right now in any case. In a way, it did give him time to measure a few things before putting himself forward.

The Chief's relationship with his mentor, for instance, needed to be taken into account. And while it wasn't out of the ordinary that Deo would have thought of sending Sarasef an exquisite gift before their arrival as a gesture of good faith, the fact that he managed to have it arrive before they did would have required him to have it sent during or before his time in prison. A lot of conclusions could be drawn from that, if one were to think on it hard enough.

'Always consider an ally your weakness and an enemy your strength,' Deo had taught him once. *'Trust neither, and use both.'*

Wise words that had gotten him through all kinds of shit in the Tower. Words he would have to heed now, more than ever, having been thrown into the same room with men that were much larger than him in most ways.

"Your hospitality, for a start," said Deo. "A comfortable room. Good food. Some service, if you can spare a maid or two."

"It will be given," said Sarasef, his emotions fiercely guarded by the deep, growling voice one might equate with that of a beast. The number 57 tattooed on his cheek caught the light as he nodded, as if to remind them all who he was—the fifty-seventh leader of beasts. "And the rest?"

"The rest," Deo repeated and paused, as if taking time to decide—time Lasura was sure he didn't need. "The rest will be disclosed as soon as I am introduced to the person listening to our conversation from behind that door to your left, if I may be specific."

"Two," Lasura spoke up for the first time, a little surprised at his own decision. "There are two people listening, if I may be even more—"

The pair of reddish-brown eyes suddenly focused on him, clipping his words short as they were meant to. Still, out of sheer necessity, his mother's wretched pride, and his father's stubbornness combined, Lasura decided to meet those eyes head on and finished the sentence, "—specific."

From across the room, Sarasef stared at him with a gaze that could set the marble under his feet on fire, and somewhere in the silence that stretched between them, feeling the air turning into something thick and almost toxic in his lungs, Lasura had a vision of himself being hacked to pieces by the man's legendary war hammer right where he stood.

Which gave him the urge to back down and offer some form of obeisance to this man who could easily make another man piss his pants—him included—if only he decided to rise from that throne. But unlike Deo, he was a prince of the Black Tower, a son of the Salar. His presence, once put forward, must be acknowledged with proper respect by a man lesser than his father, or he would lose his ground and power to negotiate forever, both of which he needed if he were to be fostered by this man for perhaps a long, long time.

And so he stood and waited for that acknowledgement, feigning indifference as he had done so for hundreds of times to not shit his pants every time he was being judged by his father.

"You are the son of the Bharavi." The address, given after a long pause, was more of a confirmation than a question.

Of course, Lasura thought with some bitterness. It was always his mother he would first be identified with. He had her eyes, after all.

"My name," he began, making sure the words carried loud and clear, "is Lasura izr Muradi, a son of Salar Muradi of Rasharwi, supreme ruler of the Salasar." He saw Deo wince a little at that and decided it was too late anyway. "I am here to deliver a gift and an offer that is to be discussed in private. If you don't mind, I would like to know why your mysterious guests are to be included in this conversation, Grand Chief."

Another silence ensued, only in a shorter interval this time. Sarasef turned to Deo, an amused smile appearing behind his thick beard. "An apprentice of yours, I presume?"

"Royally appointed," Deo replied defensively. His mentor liked to remind people of that lack of choice sometimes. It had been a cruel joke between them for over a decade.

"Well then," said Sarasef, "I believe a little reunion is in order. You can come out. Both of you."

The door to their right opened, and into the chamber entered a young girl in white—no, a young Bharavi, now that he could see her eyes and hair more clearly. At the same time, and while he was still trying to figure out what to think of that, another figure appeared on the opposite side of the throne. One that seemed, for once, to have surprised his all-knowing mentor.

"Ravi's tits," Deo swore out loud. Not a common thing to witness, especially considering where they were.

To their left, the Silver Sparrow of Azalea appeared in a tunic of royal blue made entirely of Makena silk, embroidered with enough gold threads to light up a small room. Tiny gemstones were sewn into the sleeves and collar, and larger ones decorated his fingers. On his right ear, the signature golden ring worn only by Deo di Amarra's first-class assassin glinted in the torchlight. That famous face, however, had enough bruises and cuts on it to offer Lasura a small measurement of delight. But even with the battered face and the hollowness of his eyes, the most sought-after escort of the Black Tower—the fucking star of Rasharwi at one point—still managed to make everyone else seem ugly and underdressed being in the same room.

Not that it was unusual. All high-end escorts got dressed up that way for the job. In fact, it was customary for the client to have an outfit sent several days before the appointment to offer time for preparation and to make sure all their fantasies would be met. After all, the fees were quite ridiculous, and this one who could make torn-up, dirt smeared prison garb look good had been the most expensive and coveted in the Tower.

"Prince Lasura." The Sparrow turned to him and offered a flawless, unpretentious bow that told him the hard feelings he'd always had against the man had never been shared, taken into account, or even noticed. Perhaps he should be glad the man remembered him at all. "Dee," he continued, not at all happy to see his former master, from the looks of it.

The master, however, was even more pissed to see him. "Explain to me," said Deo, a rare rage in his tone, "which part of '*go west*' did you fail so miserably to understand? The last time I checked, this part of the Djamahari is fucking south."

In the

Some time ago, Hasheem Shad had discovered a craving for blood—the unique, oddly sweet scent of it, the sharp metallic taste that lingered on his tongue, and even the way it dripped down his fingers made the killing easier, if not also pleasurable. He didn't always enjoy fighting, but a part of him enjoyed killing, sometimes even longed for it, other times needing it to keep the monster inside him fed and contained.

He had been craving blood for the past five days. Now, more than ever, standing in the crimson-hued Hall of Marakai, looking at the two men who had come with their tidings. Tidings that carried with them a promise of blood.

"I brought him from the west, di Amarra," Sarasef explained, making a gesture at Djari, who was

Hands of Fate

standing on the opposite side of the throne, "as the sworn sword and blood of Djari iza Zuri, the Bharavi of Visarya." He gave a small pause to check their expressions. "The only daughter of Za'in izr Husari. More precisely, the man your Salar wants to see dead."

Standing below the dais, Djari stiffened a little at those words. Still, she remembered, as she always had, to straighten her spine when addressed by her title. A part of him wanted to believe nothing had changed, that she was still the same girl he had come to love and care for, but one would have to be blind to not see it, or be completely ignorant to not notice that change.

There was a severity to her presence now; a stinging sharpness, a dangerous gleam that glinted off her like a newly broken piece of obsidian. It wrapped around her like armor fitted with spikes and concealed blades to make those around her think twice before approaching. It had been five days since he last saw her—Sarasef hadn't let them meet since they were brought there—and Djari seemed to have aged ten years during that time. She had, he noticed, been avoiding eye contact with him ever since they'd stepped into the hall. He knew something about that, knew the feeling like the shape of every scar on his body and how long they continued to sting.

He also knew that she'd been told about this meeting, just as he had. There was no surprise on her face about what Sarasef had just revealed. The surprise was about something else, something no one seemed to have expected—not even Dee.

He followed her gaze to the center of the hall just in time to see the prince turning his attention from him to Djari. Their eyes met, and suddenly something in the hall altered, slipped free of its cloak, stepped forward to stand naked before their eyes. Hasheem could feel the hair on his arms rise to the sudden drop of temperature, could see his breaths turning white as he exhaled the same way he'd felt at the hunting ground when Nazir had his vision. On the throne, Sarasef sat with his hands curled tight around the armrests, watching the two of them as intently as Dee, who looked like he'd just seen a ghost. Djari's eyes were glowing bright amber, like Nazir's on the hunting ground.

So were the prince's.

And then, as silence tightened its grip around the chamber, as time seemed to have come to a screeching stop, a loud rumble filled the hall. It shook the ground underneath their feet, sent a tremor through the marble tiles and up their spines, rising and rising in intensity as it threatened to bring down the walls. The hall flashed white for a second, and through the opening in the ceiling—the one they called the *Eye of Marakai*—a spear of light slammed down into the ground halfway between Djari and the prince.

It blinded the hall, knocked out their hearing like a fist to the head as it left its mark. The running crack in the marble formed a long diagonal line across the room, ending on either side at Djari's and the prince's feet, as if a god had split the earth open, linking the two figures for them all to see.

For the world to see.

And through it all, as though they had been someplace far away, locked together in a battle no one else participated, the prince and Djari never took their eyes off each other, hadn't so much as stirred at the thunder and the lightning that ripped apart the ground between them. Djari held the prince's gaze, jaw clenched indescribably tight, face pale as a corpse without uttering a sound. Her counterpart shared that expression, only he was breathing twice as fast as she was.

"It would seem," Dee said at length, addressing no one in particular but bringing everyone out of their stupor, "that there are more witnesses to this meeting than the five of us. My lady," he turned to Djari, inclining his head a little, "if I may. Apart from what we know of your titles—" He paused for a moment, allowing his next words to resonate, to grip the attention of those present. "What else are you?"

Hasheem swallowed, taking a step forward to address the question himself, hoping to steer it in another direction. Before he could utter his first word, and for the first time that evening, Djari turned, caught his eyes, and silenced him with a look. Clearing her throat, she pulled back her shoulders and pitched her voice to carry, addressing the entire hall, if not also the gods above. "I am a daughter of Ravi, born on the veiling of Rashar. My first breath has brought with it the darkening of the world and the circlet of fire. In the eyes of Ravi," she said, and, as precise and steady as the way she drew back her bowstring to shoot a target, loosed the flaming arrow that ignited the conflagration that would later spread through the peninsula, "I bring with me an ending of the war and the reign of Rashar."

It was a declaration of war, backed by the very hour of her birth and the hope she'd brought to the White Desert with her existence. Dangerous, considering where they were and the revelation she'd just given her enemies. With a stroke of a quill and a bird sent to the Black Tower, the Salar would never hesitate to send an army to get rid of her, even here, even if it would mean taking down the Rishi. Hope, or more importantly, an embodiment of hope backed by the gods, had to be extinguished as quickly as possible. That had always been the way by which Salar Muradi achieved victory and remained victorious. It was why he'd hunted down oracles before all else. Once word of this got out, he would hunt her down with everything he had.

Hasheem shuddered at the thought, and yet he knew it had been necessary under the circumstances for Djari to reveal her identity. War was coming with the arrival of the prince and Deo di Amarra. Whatever Sarasef decided could mean victory or defeat for the White Desert, and that decision, Hasheem knew, could be shaped by what she had been prophesied to be. Still, Marakai, the Sky Father, had made his mark tonight, and the line had touched two people in that hall. There was a meaning to that he had yet to decipher, a meaning only Dee seemed to understand, judging from the grin he was failing to contain.

"I see," said Deo di Amarra, turning to Sarasef, who seemed to have retreated into the privacy of his own thoughts at the revelation. "I take it you have shared with our guests the details of the Salar's proposal sent prior to our arrival?"

Sarasef nodded grimly. "I have."

"And in having done so, they have offered you an alternative? That is why they are here, I presume?"

For that, Hasheem stepped forward to reply. "I have." It had been him who requested that they be present, him who had offered Sarasef the alternative. Judging from the surprise on Djari's face, he figured Sarasef hadn't told her about that detail.

Dee's attention was on him now, studying his expression closely with a practiced calm. Only Hasheem had been with him long enough to recognize the signs that told him his mentor's mind was racing for answers at this very moment. For the very first time, Deo di Amarra had known nothing of what he'd walked into and had not been given time to deal with it. He wondered if it would make a difference. He also wondered if something else would.

Without removing his eyes from Hasheem, Dee said, "Might I inquire that it be shared with the rest of us, then? To be fair."

Hasheem turned to Sarasef for permission and was relieved to see it given. It wasn't easy for him, hadn't been from the moment he knew who had accompanied the prince. The last person he wanted to go against was this man, who had taught him everything he knew, the same man who had made him into what he was now. The least he could do was to try to be fair, even though fairness had never been a concept that existed in the world they lived in.

"The alternative is to not bring in an army to defeat Saracen," he said, searching his mind for the right word, and realized there were none, "but to have him killed."

It would solve all their problems. Sarasef wouldn't need any more men than he already had to deal with Saracen. Without a leader, the faction that had defected would be in disarray, giving Sarasef an opportunity to round them up and win a number of them back—if not most—over time. They were, after all, mercenaries not loyal to any nation or land, but to any man who could fill their pockets. Should he do so, Sarasef could reject the proposal, send the Salar's army back where they came from, and avoid conflict with the Visarya for the time being. Sarasef could be—*might be*—forgiven for the mistake of having captured Djari in exchange for stalling the war.

A good alternative, except for one problem. To Sarasef, it would mean killing his own brother when he could have been taken alive.

If that meant anything to the chief, Hasheem couldn't tell. Sarasef wasn't the kind of man who wore his emotions on his sleeve.

Neither was Dee, for that matter.

With a disturbing quietness only those closest to him understood, Deo di Amarra kept his eyes on Hasheem as he considered the stakes at hand, perhaps also trying to decide his next course of action, and maybe, just maybe, where he wanted to stand in all this.

For a time, no one spoke a word. Even Djari seemed to be drowning in her own thoughts, or waiting to see the next turn of events. She had, he realized, become uncharacteristically calm and far removed from the image of the young girl he'd come to know. A searing pain shot through his heart at the thought, pried open an existing wound that wasn't going to heal anytime soon.

The one who broke that silence, the only one who wasn't attached to anything in that hall, was the Prince. "You are just one man," he said matter-of-factly, that hint of mockery in his tone audible.

Hasheem turned to him and stated in the same manner, "It only takes one."

"To fight his way through a thousand men?" The disbelief was not concealed this time.

"He doesn't have to." Sarasef picked up the conversation. "My brother has gone to lengths to get his hands on the Sparrow on his way here. If he were to escape from my care and stumble into Saracen's men, he would be brought directly to him, alive."

My care. Hasheem winced at those words. There were too many things attached to that. Sarasef's intentions to keep him for one, the unwelcome affection the chief harbored toward him for another. If the clothes he'd been offered hadn't already given it away, those words would. He could only wish the meanings behind them wouldn't be caught and later turned into a weapon.

"Perhaps," the prince countered. "Only he would be tied up and relieved of all weapons when that happens."

Hasheem clenched his teeth and made a decision, one he had been reluctant to make for some time. What he had been wasn't news to the three men in that hall, but it was the one part of his life he hadn't wanted Djari to know. There was no avoiding it now, however—not with what was at stake. "Not in bed, no. He wouldn't tie me up there," he said, and forced himself to not look at Djari or what would be on her face then.

"Assuming he takes you to bed, of course."

At another time, in a different place, Hasheem might have been able to hold back some of his rage. But there and then, having been pushed to reveal that life in front of Djari, trying to deal with everything that had happened and was happening, together with his craving for blood that was growing by the minute, his control was slipping. *Had slipped.* "I *am* the Silver Sparrow of Azalea, do not forget, my lord prince," he reminded them. "That reputation has been earned, not given to me by birthright. It is a profession at which I happen to excel and have dominated for the past five years. For this, you will believe it when I say that if I want you in my bed, you *will* be. The same goes," he turned to Sarasef, "for Saracen."

The prince swallowed, shifted his weight uncomfortably at words he knew better than to put to the test. Hasheem had been trained for that. People like him had all been trained to lure, to catch, to release with strings attached. Strings he knew when and how to pull to get them to come back, to spend more coins—to find coins they didn't have—to pour it all on him. It was the whole point of being good at it, the only way he could seize some power and control back into his life, even if for a short time. Not too different at all from holding a knife to a person's throat, if one were to look at it from a certain angle. The desire for pleasure was a thing as powerful as the desire to live, and he had been the master of both, to men and women alike. With men, it was always easier. Men could be triggered, driven out of their senses and reasoning, made to salivate, to beg, to spill secrets at the mere thought of what he could do to them.

And what he could do, Sarasef himself knew it by experience, well enough to suck in a breath the moment he'd finished his sentence. There was a certain comfort to seeing it, even at the cost of having unpleasant memories resurface. At the very least, the one man he needed to convince needed no convincing.

"A fine plan," said Deo di Amarra lightly—too lightly for his liking. "Getting Saracen alone isn't the problem. I have, in fact, turned down his offer for the Sparrow three times in the past. Killing him is also a relatively easy task for all my best assassins. But how, may I ask—" He turned to address Sarasef and Djari both. "—do you intend to get my Sparrow out alive and back in your *care*?"

Hasheem bit his lip over that. Leave it to Dee to figure out so swiftly and clearly the stakes those who opposed him had to lose. He would remember Sarasef's offer for him, of course, however long ago that was, and it had been folly to have wished that his mentor wouldn't catch those words. His life did hold meaning to the chief and to Djari, and neglectfully, he hadn't really considered the possibility of walking out alive if he were to do this. It would be different from escaping the city he knew, with secret passages to avoid running into a whole brigade of guards. This was breaking out of a camp of a thousand or so mercenaries. He hadn't planned to die when he came up with the offer, but the fear of dying had never been a factor in whatever he decided to do. Dee knew this, of course, and also knew that he wouldn't have thought of a solution to that problem, old habits and all.

Before he could figure out an answer to that, Djari stepped forward and ascended the dais, pausing to stand side by side with Sarasef, like an equal despite their height difference. "We'll get him out," she said, her voice traveling around the room with its echoes, "with *our* warriors."

I will **kill** whomever she wants to **see dead**
and fight **wherever she wishes** me to fight.
If she wants the world **set on fire**,
I will **strike** that flint myself.

Against All Odds

Lasura had envisioned his mother just like this in his nightmares; with her silver hair shimmering like a newly-honed blade, her eyes burning an incinerating amber as she told his father he would never have the White Desert in this life or the next. An old story he'd been told by both his parents. A story filled with rage from one and intrigue from the other.

He wondered if this had been how it felt, if his father's heart had beaten just as fast, as heavy, and with so much need to engage. For the first time in his life, Lasura understood why his mother had been kept alive all these years, how powerful her presence had been to his father, looking at the young Bharavi standing in front of him in that hall.

There had been no vision in that moment before the lightning struck, no voice in his head that explained how or why it happened. His whole life had simply begun to make sense afterward. His existence became clearer, like stepping out of a fog or breaking the surface of some dark water he'd been drowning in. And then, rising from the ground, wrapping around them like a storm—a power so strong, so unstoppable that had filled the hall and altered their surroundings. In the middle of it all, he could sense some things being shifted into place, and others propelled into motion. He knew then that their meeting had been planned a long time ago by something—*someone*—much bigger than all of them.

And so had she, that much he was certain. She knew, and was using it to her advantage, standing there so tall despite her small frame, fearlessly and deliberately declaring war with the Salasar. With his father, to be exact.

Our warriors, she'd said, as if she had the authority to decide any of it.

No one had seen that coming; not even the Sparrow, who was staring wide-eyed at her. It occurred to Lasura then that she must have made the decision just now.

"The Salar is not the only one who can offer you an army." She turned to Sarasef, speaking as if the dais also belonged to her. "Promise a safe return for me and my men, and I will see that my father sends our warriors to deal with your brother. You can send these men back to the Salasar. There is no need here to start a war."

Words of pure arrogance, with no consideration given to consequences, Lasura thought. She looked and sounded like his mother, and that irritated him more than anything else.

"There *will* be war, my lady," he said, turning from her to address Sarasef. "If you side with Za'in izr Husari, Grand Chief, you break your alliance with the Salasar." He paused, feeling a tug from years of being taught discipline and diplomacy telling him not to finish that speech and decided to ignore it. "My father will crush you both, I assure you."

She shot him a glare, placed a foot forward as if to challenge him into a duel. "He can try."

"He *will* try," said Lasura, rising to the occasion, "and succeed as he did in the Vilarhiti."

"*Don't,*" hissed the Sparrow, "be so sure."

"And are you?" Lasura turned to face him. " Are you sure you want to do this? Have you given any thought to what could happen? Our mentor, your master, the man who bought you from the House of Azalea and set you free, *twice*, was held in the Tower's dungeon before we came. He is being charged with treason for aiding your escape, for *your* murders. He will be," he rasped, a raw, rumbling anger rising in his chest at the thought, "executed for *your* crime if we fail in this negotiation. Be sure, Sparrow. Be absolutely sure where you want to stand. Because as far as I can tell, he has been your family and your savior, and Rasharwi your home, for a lot longer than your Bharavi and her Kha'gan. Yet you would choose this path? To stand there and see them both burned?"

The hurt in those cold gray eyes could be seen from across the room. It disappeared the moment the Sparrow took a glance at Djari, his expression replaced by the look of a man who'd made his decision long ago and was harboring no room for alternatives. There was a bond between them just as clear and irreversible as the crack on the marble made by the lightning, and for all the pain he'd let slip, the Sparrow stood his ground.

"I have sworn only one oath in my life," he said, holding Deo di Amarra's eyes as he spoke. "It is to Djari Iza Zuri. You ask if I will see them both burned. My answer, Prince Lasura, is yes, and I will do more." He paused and turned from Deo to address the room, making sure the words could be heard and remembered for life. "My place is between Djari and whoever brings her harm. I will kill whomever she wants to see dead and fight wherever she wishes me to fight. If she wants the world set on fire, I will strike that flint myself. I know where I stand. It will not change for as long as I live. The question is," he said, turning his attention to Lasura, "do you?"

It shouldn't have mattered. Words from a man one barely knew shouldn't hold significance to him, to anyone. And yet Lasura found himself unable to reply to that; at least, not with the same conviction shown by the Sparrow.

"You are the son of a Bharavi," Hasheem continued. "Born to a mother who has been captured, abused, and enslaved by the man who wiped out her home. You don't belong in Rasharwi. Half the Black Tower sees you as an excess, an unworthy resident, and the other half wants you dead. Yet you are standing here, proposing to fight for a land that will never count you as one of its own—"

"No land will count me as its own." Lasura cut in mid-sentence, his control slipping at words he'd heard a hundred times from his own mother. "Including the White Desert, whose people will hunt you down like a dog if they knew what you were, just as they would hunt me down for sharing my father's blood. If Rasharwi falls, I will die with it. The Shakshis will have my head after they've hacked off my limbs and put it on a spike. *That* is the land you think I should be fighting for. What's the difference, Sparrow? Tell me. What is it that my father did that you or your people haven't done? How many villages has Za'in izr Husari burned? How many people—*innocent* people—has he killed?

He took a breath, to bring his anger down a notch. "This is warfare, make no mistake about it. We are all monsters here, fighting for the survival, the prosperity, the peace of our own people at the cost of others. I will fight for my right to live. That is where I stand, and you can talk to me of righteousness, of mercy, of a world better than the one I live in, when the Shakshis are ready and willing to accept us as their own and for who we are." He turned to Sarasef, realizing just then that he had raised his voice into a shout. Didn't care.

"There will be war, no matter which side you choose to fight on, Grand Chief. I have brought with me a gift for kings: a young spotted eagle from the same nest as the Salar's, as a gesture of good faith. An army is waiting for you to ride against your brother, should you choose to use it. In return, we ask that you train our army to fight and aid us in the campaign to take the White Desert, starting with the Visarya Kha'gan. And when all is done—when the peninsula is united under one rule—," He took the pause needed to offer what he had been given permission to, should the situation call for it. "—you may take your share of the land. An area from the south of Suma to the coastline, given to the Rishi to use and govern under the rule of the Salasar for as long as you remain our ally. That is our proposal."

It was a tremendous offer. Sarasef and the Rishi would control the entire southern coastline, including the ports of Samarra, the taxing of its wine production, and all trades done in the province. It should matter enough to shift a mountain, but if it did, Sarasef didn't let it show.

"And if I refuse?" asked the Grand Chief, calmly.

Lasura swallowed. They could die for this, Deo and he, in the very room where they stood. "Then we go to Saracen, and you will have to fight both your brother and the Salasar."

"But not the White Desert." Djari's voice filled the hall, drawing everyone's attention.

The girl couldn't be more than fifteen, Lasura thought, perhaps younger if one were to consider only her size and physique, but somehow she could always make herself feel like a threat. Her arrogance, most of all, made him want to prove her wrong. Constantly.

"The *White Desert*, my lady?" he asked. "How many Kha'gans are at war with each other right now, iza Zuri? Enlighten me, if you will."

"The Kha'gans will unite given a common enemy. It has been done before. When that happens—"

"*If* that happens." The retort came out of him like instinct, trained to perfection from having dealt with his mother for nearly two decades. "Who do you think will unite the Kha'gans? Who is fit to lead that army? Za'in izr Husari, whose legacy has brought the most bloodshed in the White Desert's history? Another Kha'a your father will bend to? *You*?"

"She is," said the Sparrow, "backed by the gods. Do not forget."

"So," Deo di Amarra said, turning every head toward him, "is Prince Lasura of Rasharwi."

The room fell into an abrupt silence. They were all staring at Deo now, quietly, thoughtfully. Lasura turned to his mentor, lost, confused, and feeling suddenly sick. "What?"

Deo ignored him and turned to Djari. "You are not the only child who has been born with a prophecy to end the war, my lady," he said, to all of them, "nor is the White Desert alone in possession of oracles."

A nauseating feeling pooled in his stomach, rising up Lasura's throat. "Deo..."

"We have been keeping this a secret for seventeen years, my lord prince," Deo said, with a touch of regret in his tone—one that disappeared all too quickly. "It's about time you and everyone else knew of the prophecy made by the High Priest of Rashar before you were born." Turning back to Djari, he continued in a flat, business-like tone. "You could feel it, couldn't you? Just now, before the lightning struck. The prince is your counterpart, your opposing force. You *know,* and have witnessed, as we all have, that there are two sources of power here, not one."

Djari clamped her mouth shut at that, her expression hardening, turning sharp enough to inflict a wound.

"In the eyes of Rashar and the Sky Father, who has made his mark here today, the fate of this peninsula is in the prince's hands as much as it is in yours, iza Zuri. Prince Lasura carries the same prophecy to end this war. He was, my lady, if we are to measure the significance of hour of birth here—" Deo gave a small pause to take aim with the truth before throwing it at them. "—born on the bleeding of Ravi."

There was a hush in the room, one that created a bone-chilling feeling Lasura would never forget. His being born on the night of a blood moon held as much significance as Djari's being born on the darkening of the sun. It would have mattered to his mother most, underlining his existence as a curse on those who worshipped Ravi, and marking him as a blessing for the ones who opposed them. To everyone in that hall, his existence was now the key to victory or defeat in the war to come.

To him, it revealed things he had been questioning all his life. "*We?*"

"Your father and I," Deo replied. "The High Priest was killed the night the prophecy was made, by the Salar's order. I carried out the command myself. No one else knows. "

It explained many things, proved a number of his theories, and brought forward some truths he'd long been trying to dig up. All that attention, those privileges, and countless opportunities that had been given to him above all other princes. Words that had pushed him to try and try, despite the disqualification of his blood, to become better, stronger, wiser, as if there had been a purpose or a role he needed to fill. Things he had so foolishly taken as something else, as something more—

It came up out of him like a flash flood, an annihilating torrent rushing out of a dam cracked open from being filled beyond its limit—the rage, the disappointment, the pain, all rolled up into one unstoppable decision that propelled him on a path he hadn't seen coming.

You have your plans for me too, haven't you, Father? Just as she has. That is all you see, isn't it? A key to your victory? A weapon to prove her wrong? A tool to get you what you want?

They were all the same, every last one of them. The same wretched, condescending, manipulating scum who thought they could spin him to their heart's desire, who thought they had the right to move him at will. For seventeen years he'd played all those roles, had bent over backward to live up to expectations. Well, here and now was where it stopped.

Fuck destiny. Fuck Fate. Fuck all of them. And if the sky would come tumbling down from the choices he made from now on. If the whole world would burn because of them, fuck that too.

"Forgive me." A quiet rumbling—a tenth of the much louder one in his head—slipped through the gap of his gritted teeth. "I am—" He drew a breath, curling his hands into fists to keep the roaring, rabid beast inside of him from breaking loose, "—done with this negotiation, and everything it entails. Go ahead and start your war. Burn down this peninsula and everything you see fit. Do whatever needs to be done, but leave me out of it." He turned and headed for the door. "This is not my fucking problem anymore."

Of Religion and Men

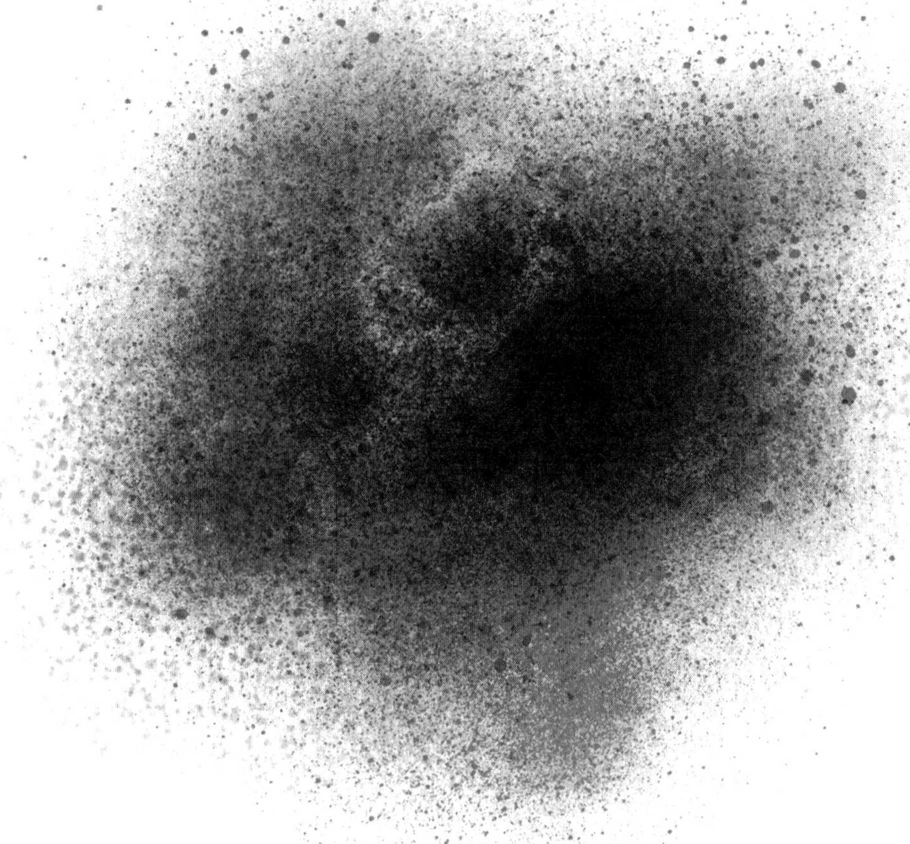

It began with the death of one man.

Azzam izr Yosef, an old priest of Sangi temple, a man highly respected by his peers and much beloved by the people of Rasharwi for his contributions to the poor, was found dead on his bed one morning. The cause had first been declared unknown, until someone suggested it might have been a heart failure from old age. The late priest's steward argued, however, that his master's health had been too excellent for such an ailment to have taken his life. Other speculations then spread through the temple, most agreeing with the steward's claim. It was murder, then, someone concluded.

The conclusion, by protocol, led to an investigation and an autopsy done by a physician sent from the Black Tower. The verdict had, indeed, been murder by way of poison. The administration of this poison was then traced to a special tonic Azzam had always taken before bed, one usually prepared for him by a Shakshi slave girl who had been working in the temple for the past two years.

It had to be her, one of the priests concluded. The accusation, having been promptly backed by other priests out of convenience, spread quickly through the streets of Rasharwi. By the next morning, the slave girl was brought to the city's main square in front of the public, and strapped to a post above a large pyre. Burning was the proper form of punishment for bringing death to a priest of Rashar. The approval of such sacrifice had been obtained some time during the night from the High Priest of Sangi, who, of course, had the authority to decide on religious ceremonies and rites in the area. It was to be done at sunrise, said Yakim the High Priest, under the eyes of the sun god himself.

But this was Azzam izr Yosef, someone in the crowd argued just before the burning. This was a priest who had given aid and homes to hundreds of Rashawi's orphans and unfortunate souls. A sacrifice of one Shakshi slave wasn't enough, by far, to justify the murder of Rashar's most esteemed servant.

More sacrifices then, an elderly woman suggested, followed by excited nods from the crowd that quickly grew into a discussion. One hundred Shakshi slaves was a good number, they all agreed afterward. It would send the right message, prevent such things from ever happening again. The Shakshis need to be taught a lesson and put in their place before they rose up against their masters, threw the entire city into chaos, and harming women and children in the process, shouted a young man on a pallet with a shaking fist, next to a proud mother who cried listening to her son.

The problem, of course, was whose slaves would be burned. Someone suggested a draw. Others argued that contributions were to be made by those who owned the most slaves. The clever man who had suggested more burning in the first place came up with an idea. "There are," he said, pitching his voice to carry, "unclaimed slaves in the thousands in the Salar's Shakshi quarter, are there not? Surely, as Rashar's anointed ruler, his lordship can spare some for justice!"

The citizens of Rasharwi in that square came to the conclusion that ninety-nine more slaves were to be taken from the Shakshi quarter. Two-hundred men and women then marched from the city square toward the gate of the Salar's closed-off area, home to the original eight thousand slaves taken from the Vilarhiti—now numbering close to ten thousand—to make demands for the needed sacrifices.

By the time the news reached the Tower, a riot had broken out in front of the gate. The original group was then joined by more men and women who had heard of the commotion. By mid-afternoon, the Shakshi quarter was on fire, set ablaze by a mob of more than five hundred Rashais.

The Salar, having watched the plume of smoke from his balcony in a quiet rage, wasted no time in dispatching a thousand royal guards to crush the mob. By sunset, one hundred and twelve citizens of Rasharwi had been killed, and hundreds more were injured in the process. The fire in the Shakshi quarter was contained a few hours later and soldiers were sent to guard the streets leading to its gate to protect the area from another attack.

At the top of the Tower, watching the rise and fall of strong, broad shoulders from behind, Jarem knew how close his Salar's control was to breaking. The unrest might have been contained and the fire put out, but the Salar knew as well as Jarem did that this would not be the end of it, not by far.

'You could kill a person for silence, but never people,' Deo di Amarra had said.

Something needed to be done—and done delicately—before all hell broke loose. It just so happened that the one man who might have known best how to deal with it was a week away and deep in the lair of the Rishi. It was during these hours that Jarem was willing to admit the usefulness of Deo di Amarra. Fighting a war was the Salar's specialty, but keeping the city and the provinces under control was di Amarra's talent.

A bad move, Jarem thought, biting his lip, to have sent him to Sarasef at this time. Too late now to do anything about it.

"The men who suggested the burning," said the Salar, without turning around. "Find them and bring them here. Alive. Discreetly."

"You wish to interrogate these men, my lord?"

The Salar sipped the wine in his cup and took his time before he responded. "Someone is trying to stir up unrest in the city. See if they have recently been paid. I want the man behind this, Jarem. Find him."

"It will be done." Jarem nodded. Riots, protests, revolutions, and all things alike were almost always fueled by someone with power. Until they cut off the hands that fed or started the fire, it would never stop.

"And the Shakshis, my lord? More than half the quarter has been burned down. Yakim and the others are still demanding a hundred sacrifices."

"You can tell that entitled, self-absorbed, sick son of a pig to burn his own priests before he comes to me with his fucking *demands.*"

Those shoulders, Jarem saw, were trembling now. Not a great sign, though not surprising, given past encounters between the Salar and Yakim izr Zahat, High Priest of Sangi. The only reason the old priest still lived was because Deo di Amarra had advised it so.

'*Religion, my lord, is the most powerful tool a ruler can use to make or break an empire,*' had been di Amarra's counsel. '*There's no easier way to bring people together than to create blind faith that tells them living for your cause guarantees their suffering will end when they die. Of course, by the time they know you've been lying, they're already dead. Heads of religions are useful when you have them in your pocket. Keep Yakim alive and well-fed and he will make your war a crusade. Kill him, and you will be dealing with much, much worse than idiotic religious practices and create ten more enemies in his place, if you're lucky.*'

Those words had been taken into consideration and deemed sensible. Salar Muradi of Rasharwi may have been a vicious, unforgiving man, but never one without sense.

"Perhaps an offering of *some* sacrifices, as opposed to a full hundred, could be negotiated to quiet the situation, my lord?" Jarem said carefully. "As with moving the Shakshi quarters outside the city?"

Overpopulation and poverty had been issues for years in Rasharwi, while the Shakshi prisoners taken from the Vilarhiti had been kept safe and adequately fed. They were put to work, of course, in exchange for their food and other necessities. Their services, however, were offered solely to the Salar, who then utilized them to improve the Salasar's infrastructure and to strengthen its army. It was a great arrangement and one that had been working splendidly—only this view was not shared by the citizens of Rasharwi.

It never will be, Jarem thought. You couldn't count on people who barely had enough to eat to sacrifice for the greater good. You managed them, filled their purses with coins, sacrificed a few goats—or people—to keep them happy. Cruel, yes, but then again, the survival of all living things had always relied on the ability to be cruel, had it not? You hunt to eat, fight to protect your territory, kill innocents to protect your children if you believe it necessary. Alternatives, like kindness and good fortune, were not always offered by the gods.

"There will be *no* burning of those prisoners," the Salar pronounced. "Why do you think I've kept them here, given them jobs, made sure their needs are met? When I take the White Desert, the Shakshis will be here, working for us, with us. We must integrate them into our society, learn to live among them, offer them rights, or there will be bigger problems than what we are facing now. That balance is not going to be achieved by burning a hundred of their people as a sacrifice to a god they don't worship. Yakim can burn the woman, but no more. The Shakshi quarter will be rebuilt. Give Azzam a funeral worthy of kings, offer the people free food, lower their taxes for a month or two, pay Yakim to shut his hole, or do whatever else needs to be done." He turned then from the balcony, eyes blazing with a murderous gleam. "But make it clear that if they touch my prisoners without permission, a priest will burn for every Shakshi they kill."

And he would burn them, Jarem knew, if it would set an example and make sure his decisions would not be challenged again. Such things were important for a ruler to rule. Salar Muradi of Rasharwi was a practical man, not a religious one. The kind of man who wouldn't think twice to send a thousand men to their deaths if it meant saving twice that number. He would burn priests, men, women, or children if need be, Shakshis or Rashais, but it would always be for a reason, never his own satisfaction.

Those reasons, however, would not always be understood by men and women without his vision. Despite all the raids and wars he'd initiated, the Salar didn't hate the Shakshis, and never had. His ambition was to unite the peninsula, to take their lands to open up a better route to Makena, establish better trade, create more efficient ways to distribute resources, improve lives under his rule—all lives, not just Rashais. Such a legacy sometimes required bloodshed and sacrifices, and he would rather sacrifice *some* Rashai lives now and save the Shakshis in preparation for the integration to come. It was his way of ending the centuries-long war, of creating peace and prosperity in the peninsula.

Jarem could understand it, and he had, all this time, followed that dream. But something about this incident didn't feel right. It hadn't felt right from the moment the Salar offered a prince of Shakshi blood a spotted eagle. Di Amarra had made a good point about that. There were limits to how much one could treat people as equals. The citizens of Rasharwi weren't going to be happy with the Shakshis' new status in the Salasar. The peninsula could be united, but priority must be given to Rashais.

They needed to let some Shakshis burn to bring peace to the community, Jarem felt. A hundred Rashais had died today during the dispersing of the mob. More would die if Yakim decided to ignite such unrest again. And this time it would be a bigger, angrier mob, not to mention that the anger would now be directed at the Salar for choosing Shakshi lives over his own people.

Jarem loved and admired his Salar enough to die for him, but he could disagree with some decisions. And sometimes, helping one's master back on track when he wanders off the right path was also a job of an advisor, was it not?

He believed it was. Which was why he had decided to not report on a visit someone had made to di Amarra's cell before the man was sent to the Black Desert. There was a simpler way out of this mess. The Salar would appreciate it later on, he was certain of it.

"So," said Amelia, leaning back on her chair, "the mob has been contained?" It was difficult to tell if she was frowning over the news or the lack of cushioning on her back. The secret chamber above the prison cells of the Black Tower was sparingly furnished. It housed a dozen chairs, one round table, a modest fireplace, and two doors that opened to a maze of passages leading to many other chambers in the Tower.

"For now," Azram pointed out as he paced back and forth across the room. The anxiety was draining the wine in his cup all too quickly, and the calmness of his mother and Amelia added to it. "I talked to Yakim earlier. He will continue to call for a hundred burnings if we pay him what he wants. If Father still says no, we should be looking at a bigger mob in a few days." *It has to work,* Azram told himself for the fifteenth time. He was as good as dead if it didn't. They all would be.

"*If we pay him what he wants,*" Amelia repeated sharply. "You mean if my father pays him what he wants. It is a large sum of money you are asking, Azram. You might at least give credit where it's due."

"If you want to be Salahari, expect to pay for it, young lady." His mother, the current Salahari, would know this, of course. She was lounging now on an identical, simple chair to the one Amelia was in, but somehow managed to make it appear larger, more fitting for a queen. "Without my son, your father's money means nothing. You might also give *that* credit where it's due."

Amelia pursed her lips and looked away, ignoring the remark. His mother, for all her prowess in putting people in their places, was going to have a hard time dealing with her son's future wife. Azram might have grinned at that, if only he wasn't so damn nervous. The truth was they were all neck deep in this: he and his mother for having accommodated all this with their connection and power, and Amelia who had money to fund the operation without being noticed by Tower officials monitoring the royal treasury. Given time, however, everything could all be traced back to one of them—if not all. They had to do this quickly, and the man who had come up with this plan, who could also advise how to speed things up, was a week away in the Black Desert.

It was a brilliant plan, one befitting Deo di Amarra's reputation, to stir up unrest in the city using his father's blatant offering of privileges to the Shakshis. The hay had already been there, waiting for someone to strike a flint, di Amarra had said. It wasn't difficult to accomplish—they only had to pay a handful of people to kill the priest and speak up at the right time. Things were going as planned, but still there were things that bothered him.

"What if he doesn't deal with the mob himself?" He began pacing again at the thought. "We need him there when the time comes." The plan was to draw the Salar out of the Tower into a chaos large enough for them to carry out an assassination—something they couldn't do in the Tower or during his journeys to other provinces due to the tight security around him.

"Oh, sit down, Azram," said his mother, waving her hand at him. "You're making me dizzy. Your father is a military man with a bad temper. He has crushed almost every uprising himself in the past."

"This is *not* an uprising of the provinces, Mother." Azram raised his voice. It helped to release some of the tension in his stomach. "It is merely a mob. He just had it contained within hours. *Hours.* Without even moving from his study!"

"You are underestimating the power of religion, my son." The Salahari leaned back on her chair, admiring a ring on her finger. "There is a reason why Yakim is still alive to this day. Even your father wouldn't tread carelessly over people's faith. If he doesn't offer them the sacrifices, you can be sure the entire city would be outraged."

"And if he does offer them the sacrifices?" challenged Azram. "What then?"

"He won't." Amelia, who had been listening just as calmly as his mother, insisted. It amazed him how these two women could be so composed, so sure about this.

"And how would you know that, exactly?" The entire Tower would be supporting the sacrifices, including every one of his father's advisors. Perhaps if di Amarra had been here, he might have been able to influence some decisions.

Amelia smiled then, like she knew something he didn't. "Because I know someone who would be able to stop him, among other things."

"No one has that kind of influence over my father." He snickered at the very idea. "But try me. Who might that be, my lady?"

"You can call it a woman's intuition." She rose from the table with her cup and proceeded to the door. "But a woman's intuition, Azram, is always right."

The door opened, revealing a figure that seemed to have been there for some time, listening to their conversation. Azram's jaw dropped at the realization of who it was. A small gasp came from his mother, who, by the look of it, had not been aware of this.

"I have a plan," said the Lady Zaharra, the Bharavi of the Black Tower, "and a deal to make with the new Salar of Rasharwi."

An Embodiment of Long Lost Things

"Khandoor." Sarasef sniffed the wine after a few swirls, took a sip, and paused for a moment. "South? No—the oak there is sweet. This is rougher. Smoky. Almost burnt."

"Southeast." Nodding in agreement, Deo di Amarra reached over to fill his own cup and followed the same ritual. "Serefina."

"I didn't know they made wine in Serefina."

"They don't," di Amarra replied, his grin layered with a hint of pride. "I do. This is the first batch from my own production. What do you think?"

Sarasef paused for a moment before taking another sniff at the wine, trying not to appear surprised. It was normal practice for Deo di Amarra to bring some cases of his own reserves as gifts, but they had always been acquired wines, not ones produced by him. This was something new—though not out of the ordinary, given the man's ambition. "You're moving into the wine business now?"

"It's good business. And it's about time." Di Amarra looked expectantly across the table. "So?"

He took another sip, considering both the wine and the Khandoor's seemingly endless quest to own everything in life he could get his hands on. Sarasef had known the man since long before he took over the Rishi. Long enough to expect some things while holding an awareness that there was always an underlying motive to everything di Amarra did, including bringing his own wine to be tasted. A business proposal would be made from this later, among other things. "It's complex. Rough around the edges. Surprising in the aftertaste with a hint of pepper. I like it."

Di Amarra smiled. "And the prince?"

An almost seamless transition from wine to politics. *Subtle, as always.* Sarasef thought for a moment, weighing his feelings for what had happened in the Hall of Marakai earlier that evening. Some surprises there. A lot, if he were to be honest. "Also complex, rough, and surprising," he said.

Di Amarra nodded. "You wouldn't mind fostering him, then?"

Not so subtle this time, and much, much too fast. "*If*," he pronounced, "I decide to foster him. My decision has not been made, di Amarra."

To that, Deo di Amarra chuckled. "Oh, come now. You and I both know you're not going to risk losing the Sparrow by sending him to Saracen. You like that boy too much."

He could congratulate the Khandoor for that power of observation, but then his feelings about the Sparrow had never been a secret. "I do," he said. "You stole him from me."

A frown, or a mask of one. "Stealing is too harsh a word, don't you think?"

The only right word, according to Sarasef. "I had already begun training him. You had no right."

"You were slow in your acquisition."

"It takes time."

"Time to win him over?" countered di Amarra. "Asking him nicely was never going to work. Not then, not now. He would never work for you willingly, and you know it."

He did know it, had even been told as much by the boy himself. Then again, that part of the Sparrow was what held his interest and made it difficult for him to move on. "Not willingly, no. I know that now."

Deo di Amarra looked at him, rubbing his thumb slowly on the arm of the chair. The hint dropped had been taken. Sarasef could almost see something turning in that red head from across the table, trying to figure things out. It didn't take long. "Ah. The girl?" Di Amarra concluded. "Clever. But you didn't take Za'in's only daughter for this though, did you? The last time we met, you had sense."

"I didn't." Sarasef stifled a groan. The mess was still giving him a headache, even if it had also given him an opportunity to use her as an incentive to keep the Sparrow. "I sent men to get him. They brought back two others. She was one of them."

"Stupidity. Such a deadly disease." Di Amarra swirled the cup in his hand with the same speed at which he'd said the words. "Let's see...you could threaten to kill her to keep him, but then that would mean going to war with Za'in, which would be in the Salar's interest, and therefore you would sign our contract to reap the benefits. Or you can force him to stay in exchange for sending her home and side with Za'in instead, breaking an alliance with the Salasar in the process. That's what you're trying to decide?"

"Perhaps."

"You do realize there's a problem with the latter."

He did. "Is there?" said Sarasef, feigning ignorance. "Enlighten me, then."

Deo di Amarra leaned back on his chair, crossing his legs as he did. "Say that even if she can convince Za'in to join forces with you—a difficult task considering the Rishi's history with the White Desert—and even if you have enough confidence our boy wouldn't die trying to assassinate your brother, her terms were *very* specific. The return of her and her men, if I remember correctly."

"They were." He nodded. "You do."

"He is her sworn sword and blood, Sarasef. By their code of conduct, Hasheem is her responsibility to look after as much as it is his to die protecting her. She won't agree to this."

"I haven't negotiated."

Di Amarra snorted. "Djari iza Zuri is a Bharavi. They are raised to kill their firstborn before breaking a code. Even if she hadn't been raised by Za'in izr Husari himself—which she has—there would be no negotiation over this. You can't reason with Bharavis. Ask Lasura."

Judging from how messed up that kid was, he didn't doubt it. Although that might have been the product of the mother and father both. "A code, huh?" He swirled the wine. Took another sip. *Interesting.* "So, you think to abide by the codes and laws of Citara, she would do anything to protect her sworn sword?"

A small pause from the Khandoor, followed by the narrowing of his eyes. "You knew," said di Amarra, the ghost of a smile appearing on his lips, not so different from the expression of a young boy on the brink of solving a riddle. "That's what you're trying to decide. How to get her to agree. Not whether to side with us. You want an alliance with Za'in."

He took another sip of the wine and stretched the time, rubbing his thumb along the side of the cup. "Do I now?"

Shaking his head slightly, di Amarra corrected himself. "No. Not Za'in. It's Hasheem. You're persuaded by the Sparrow."

"I like the boy too much. You said so yourself."

"You will choose your side of the war based on the decisions of one boy?" The tone was laced with curiosity. An accomplishment, in Sarasef's opinion, if one could get such a reaction from Deo di Amarra.

"I will choose my side of the war," he said, leaning forward to catch di Amarra's eyes, to read them better, "based on the fact that you've risked your relationship with me to snatch him from right under my nose, that you've paid five hundred thousand silas for a single slave, and gone as far as bringing him into the Black Tower with you. You always have a good reason for doing things, di Amarra. What is it this time? Why Hasheem?"

For a moment, and only because he had been watching, Sarasef thought he saw a glimpse of restrained surprise in those yellow-green eyes. It lasted only for a split second, shrouded immediately by a shrug. "I've always liked pretty things. You know this."

"Enough to put yourself in prison for it? Or to risk your position, your power, your entire fortune to help him escape?" He had his doubts before. He was certain now. "We go back a long way, di Amarra. I know who and what you are. I know how and why you have achieved what you have. You specifically told him to go west, and out of pure coincidence, he ran into a girl chosen by the gods to end the war. And here we are—you, me, a boy and a girl both chosen by the gods, brought together into the Hall of Marakai to decide the fate of the entire peninsula along with none other than the Silver Sparrow you have raised, trained, and released back into the desert. This isn't just coincidence, or chance, or destiny, is it? You had a vision, didn't you? What exactly did you see?"

To Sarasef's satisfaction, the characteristic playful grin that had been playing about di Amarra's lips were gone. It had, somewhere along the way, been replaced by something much heavier and colder. The gesture alone was enough for him to draw some conclusions.

"So," said Deo di Amarra, looking at him from above the rim of his cup as he sipped the wine, "it's me you're wagering on."

It was his turn to shrug. "I'm a mercenary, di Amarra," he said. "I bid on the winning side. The side you have always managed to put yourself on."

"I *have* been sent by the Salar," replied di Amarra. "It should be obvious whose side I am on."

"Have you?" Sarasef grinned. "Been sent by the Salar? The pelt did arrive quite timely, by the way."

"You know me so well."

"If I do, we wouldn't be having this conversation," said Sarasef. "What's your stake in this, di Amarra? What kind of game are you playing?"

Deo di Amarra leaned back on his chair and smiled, showing a row of straight, white teeth.

"Wouldn't you like to know?"

⁂

THE WINE WAS TRULY QUITE EXCELLENT, if a little too young, Sarasef thought as he poured himself another cup before heading to bed, bringing the bottle with him. He'd had a bit too much tonight, and yet he might still need more. Sleep was hard to come by these days when there was so much to think about.

Especially now that more things had been revealed—all at once, to make matters worse. He never thought he would live long enough to be a part of the final war between the Salasar and the White Desert. No Salar had ever come close to mobilizing an army large enough to initiate it. No one but Muradi had ever taken—and held—a chunk as large as the Vilarhiti in the history of the Salasar. With Deo di Amarra as his advisor, even without a son blessed by Rashar to win the war, the thought of uniting the peninsula under one rule wasn't exactly far-fetched for this man.

But Deo di Amarra was, by nature, unpredictable, and if the man were to switch sides, things could shift with his decision. He wondered if Muradi had known this when he sent the Khandoor to prison. Wise as he was, Deo di Amarra was not a forgetful man. He took retributions in many forms, on anyone and without fail. He just took them with an unprecedented amount of patience and an impossible calm.

By logic, he should bet on Muradi to win the war. But then there were the prince and the girl in play, both of whom had been marked by the gods tonight. He could still feel the presence of something bigger than he was—than they all were—before and after the lightning had struck. Only an ignorant man would not take such things into consideration. There were, he had no doubt of it, as many forces in play in this war above as there were below. It would need to be taken into account.

But what of his own intuition? A leader should also listen to that, shouldn't he? After all, it had been intuition that made him the Grand Chief of the Rishi instead of his older brother. And as far as intuition went, he was almost certain that it was the Silver Sparrow of Azalea that he should be betting on. Or siding with, whichever side that may be.

He did like the Sparrow, too much for him to help himself and more than he should. The boy had been skilled, yes, but no more than some other, more experienced partner he'd had. He had been beautiful—and even more so now—but not unparalleled if one were to include women into the competition. No, it had always been something else that captured people's attention and carved him into their memories, making them crave more. Something much, much more complicated.

To Sarasef, the boy was an embodiment of everything they had lost that should have been saved. The only thing that separated men from the beasts they had all chosen to become in the fight for survival. There had always been fight in the boy when you beat him, hope when there had been no room for hope, compassion even for those who had broken him to pieces. Hasheem had never been naive, no, not even as a young boy. He knew the world for what it was and men for the monsters they could become. He simply believed the alternatives were possible. That there was room yet for things to change.

You could see it in the way he talked or looked at things. Even in bed, when he was always fighting something to get through the night. It was difficult to take your eyes off someone who made you feel so alive, someone who reminded you of something long lost you once treasured. They paid him for that—for a moment of experiencing something so incorruptible, so impossible to bend in this world.

And then there was that pride. That precious, indestructible pride you couldn't pry off him that had driven men like Sarasef out of their wits trying to conquer it, time and time again. Pride was what was missing in the men and women of his era, except in the White Desert. Pride was a necessity to find peace in life, and a flaw only when exercised in excessive amounts.

He had thought many times that if the world could be changed, it deserved to be changed by someone like the Sparrow. Now he could see that possibility becoming a reality. Knowingly or not, the boy had been pulling everything and everyone who mattered together, setting things into motion with every little decision he had made. Deo di Amarra had foreseen this, he was certain of it. His intuition, therefore, had been telling him to bet on the Silver Sparrow and whatever the boy chose to do.

It was that last conclusion, and perhaps also something more personal, that made him decide to do what he did when he saw the boy waiting for him in his bedroom.

"What would it take," said the Sparrow, standing by the edge of his bed in an exquisite black Makena silk robe Sarasef had given him, "for you to choose Djari?"

Sarasef closed the door behind him, then proceeded to place the wine on the table—both the bottle and the cup. "I told you I didn't bring you here for this," he said, making his way toward the Sparrow. There was a scent in his room now, one he remembered from long ago, and a new rougher, more manly one he didn't recognize. That excited him.

"You did, yes," Hasheem replied levelly. His hair was untied, unbraided. It was longer than what Sarasef recalled. He remembered wishing it had been. Remembered how it felt, too, when he'd wound it around his fist. He could do that easily now. He wanted to.

"And yet you are here." He stepped closer to the Sparrow, felt the heat traveling down his stomach and further below the moment he realized there was nothing underneath that silk robe.

"Yet I am here." The boy—the young man now—shifted his weight as he spoke, and in doing so, allowed the front of the robe to part a little more. "To negotiate. If you're willing."

It was deliberate, of course—that slight change of posture. Sarasef had been with enough men and women like him to know when he was being played. It didn't, however, mean knowing would excite a man any less. "I thought you traded in different skills now."

"I do," Hasheem said. "I might kill you." He took a step nearer. "I can."

It *could,* easily, kill him—that string of words so strategically chosen to accelerate his pulse. It nearly did, if only he hadn't reminded himself to breathe. The danger was real enough, considering the situation. But the mere fact that Sarasef now knew very little of this young man who happened to remember exactly where and how to push him made what happened afterward...inevitable.

"Remember," said Sarasef as he seized the space between them, along with the promise of danger being offered. "You came to me."

The Remnants of Pain

Lovemaking was an art he had long perfected. When you were trained that young, had half a brain and enough opportunities for practice, you learned quickly how to make people suffocate by the simplest touch, and then, at your permission, thrash, tremble, and scream. The technique differed with every man or woman. People required different things to be brought that close to madness or to surrender control and place themselves at the mercy of your fingertips, sometimes for a word uttered a certain way. An expensive escort understood the difference. A cheap one did not.

Hasheem had always been quick to read people, and being able to do so allowed him to take charge. In his line of work, one was either the victim or the deliverer. He enjoyed being the latter. There was power in being able to make people beg and scream.

But there were always clients like Sarasef; men and women who were born to lead and conquer, whose surrender you couldn't hope for. Sarasef had never, not once, surrendered control. He would take what was offered, at his own pace and permission, and stop—yes, stop—the moment he was close to losing it. Unlike most men, the Grand Chief of the Rishi had never allowed himself to finish by someone else's doing. He also liked to put his control to the test, to see how much pain and restraint he could stand before allowing himself to climax. The battle could go on all night, sometimes several, before he would allow himself that release. It wasn't the only test Sarasef put himself through. He had walked to see how far he could walk, climbed to see how high he could climb, starved himself to see when he would collapse, and for no other reason but to constantly test and extend his limits.

Evidence of such a habit was there for all eyes to see, drawn permanently on almost every inch of his body's canvas. Especially now that he was lying in bed, stripped down to the skin, Hasheem could see once again the beauty of those remnants of self-inflicted pain. All five hundred of them.

They said Sarasef began scarring himself for every man he had killed since he was ten. *It's an old practice of his warlord predecessors he'd decided to pick up*, was the story told at taverns and campfires. The real story, explained to Hasheem by the man himself years ago, was different.

'*Warlords? My predecessors were a bunch of slaves on trading ships,*' he'd said, laughing and shaking his head. *'They wouldn't even know how to carve up a fucking deer if you gave it to them whole.'*

'Why then?' Hasheem had asked.

Sarasef's expression had turned uncharacteristically mild as he considered the question. '*My father brought back some captives from a tribe who had these scars when I was twelve. I got curious. Asked them how and why they did it. Thought it was a fun thing to try at the time,"* he'd admitted with a shrug. *'Just your average stupid boy looking for trouble to kill time. Wouldn't have known where to point if somebody asked where my brain was supposed to be.'*

Those captives had been women too, Sarasef had told him: women and girls who carved themselves because, where they came from, it was considered a thing of beauty. To the men, the more scars a woman had, the higher her threshold of pain and the higher her success rate at delivering and raising a child.

'I started with twenty. It hurt like a bitch and gave me a fever for a week. I didn't know how to clean them back then. Didn't learn it properly until the third time.'

The third time was when he'd turned fourteen, Sarasef had explained. He'd carved himself a hundred scars in total that year, then fifty more in one sitting the next, and another hundred in the following year. When he'd turned seventeen, he'd completed the rest of his five hundred over one night. *'I was trying to beat this legendary woman the tribe told me about who had four hundred of them and ten children. I could go for more, but then I might have to carve up my balls, and that didn't sound like a good idea,'* Sarasef had said, chuckling.

He probably would have to, Hasheem remembered thinking. The five hundred he had were now spread out across the front and back of his torso, both his arms, and halfway down his thighs. He hadn't carved his face because it might interfere with the chief number tattoo on his cheek (that one was truly of Rishi tradition), and Sarasef had planned to become chief since he was a lot younger than ten. It had happened. Some men could plan for something their whole life and achieve it.

'*You know what the craziest thing is?*' he'd added, a little drunk from the wine they were sharing. Wine could always get him to talk more than usual. '*One of the women of the tribe told me delivering a baby was still more painful. Makes you think twice before fucking with mothers, doesn't it?*'

Hasheem imagined it would, and thought that it might be why Sarasef had never gotten married. He'd slept with women sometimes, but had never kept one around for long. To Sarasef, making women give birth was an act of cruelty and the making of monsters, and he wasn't cruel or stupid enough to do that.

A perspective Hasheem could see himself sharing, and admiring the man who'd shaped it. He often found those scars beautiful and the man terrifying. One could do that—be in awe of someone who terrifies you. Such conflicting feelings, along with Sarasef's habit to torture himself in bed over an extended period, however, made spending a night with the chief a nightmare for Hasheem, or any escort Sarasef chose to challenge himself with for that matter.

At least a better nightmare than the ones you've been having, Hasheem thought. They came almost every night now, those dreams, especially the one with Djari he couldn't shake off. He was hoping being here with Sarasef would help Djari, who needed Sarasef on her side of the war. That and because, sometimes, the only way to live with nightmares was to replace them with less traumatizing, newer ones to focus on.

They still hadn't talked—him and Djari—not even after the meeting.

It had been her choice to avoid him, not Sarasef's decision, he knew that now. He also knew why, having been through the same ordeal long ago. You didn't want to talk about things you needed to forget. Holding a conversation meant having to explain, to relive the event. And then there was the sympathy one had to deal with. You could take more from those who had already lost with sympathy, drive the nail deeper, make sure the wound never healed.

It would take time, even with all the trust they had, even with him knowing what she needed, for things to go back to normal again, if ever. Until then, he had to control the damage, hold himself together.

Easier said than done when you hadn't slept for a week.

Hasheem sighed at that thought. He would have to find a way to get the rest he needed soon, or there would be no way he could kill Saracen as he'd proposed. His broken ribs were taking a longer time to heal than usual, and he could barely focus with this growing headache.

A breeze came through the window as he lay awake, looking at the patterns of Sarasef's scars, bringing with it the cold and the strange music of the night. The wolves were howling somewhere far away, breaking the silence with a perfectly timed, continuous chorus. The wind rushed through the canyons and their crevices somewhere in the distance, creating a tune that complimented the call of the wild. And then, rising above it like subtle percussions, a rustling of feathers from an owl hunting nearby, a soft crunch of small creatures running across the sand, and—

A whistling of metal as it cut through air.

Hasheem wheeled, caught sight of the fletching on the arrow as it flew, and felt it bite into his right arm before he could clear its path. He grunted, saw a figure at the window nocking another arrow to the bow as he pushed himself up, and this time, by reflex, lurched forward to shield Sarasef with his body. The second arrow took him on the back of his left shoulder, propelled him forward as he lost his balance and fell on the chief. Sarasef jerked awake at the contact, took a quick sweep of the surroundings, and within seconds was on his feet with the war hammer in his grip. The massive weapon zinged through the air over Hasheem's head toward the figure at the window, knocking the man off the ledge and together, man and hammer tumbled down the side of the mountain.

Hasheem pushed himself up as he heard more men coming into the chamber through the window. *Three*, he counted, and looked around for a weapon. Didn't find one before an assassin climbed onto the bed, blade high and ready.

No time for that now. Hasheem spun into position, snatched the bed-sheet from behind, and threw it at the intruder, kicking the assassin's legs out from under him as he did and pinning the man on the bed with his hand around his throat. The assassin thrashed under his weight, grabbed Hasheem's wrist, and tried to twist himself free. Tightening his hold, Hasheem gripped the arrow embedded in his arm with his free hand, jerked it out with a grunt, and plunged it back into the man's right eye, killing him on the spot.

Behind him, the other two assassins flanked Sarasef from the left and right, both armed with daggers. They went for him at the same time: one aiming for the throat, the other at his leg. Dropping low to dodge the blow coming from above, Sarasef caught the opposite blade as it came with a grip on the man's wrist. A quick twist of the arm cracked a bone somewhere and sent the man screaming as he dropped the dagger. Sarasef, still in a crouching position, spun back to the other assassin as he snatched the falling weapon in midair, flipped the blade around in his hand, and with the sharp end up forced it into the man's head from under his chin, burying it all the way to the hilt. The man dropped dead with a twitch still going as the other one on the ground scrambled to clear some distance. Sarasef, growling like a pissed-off beast being involuntarily kicked out of his slumber, walked toward the living man, snatched him up by the collar with one arm and threw him against the wall, cracking the marble in the process.

The assassin crumpled to the ground, looked about ready to piss himself as Sarasef took four heavy steps to stand in front of him. Didn't have time to cry for mercy when the chief grabbed a nearby chair and began to hit him with it. The chair broke piece by piece as the beating went on. When only a leg of it was left, Sarasef tossed it away, breathing heavily for what appeared to Hasheem to be the need to soothe himself rather than to catch his breath.

It took a lot of effort to kill a man with a chair. Hasheem knew from personal experience, and to have gone through with it when a knife was readily at hand meant something more than death was needed. Looking at Sarasef, who was standing there stark naked over the mutilated corpse, straining muscles cording in and out under his dark skin now glistening with blood-infused sweat dripping off five hundred self-inflicted scars, Hasheem wondered if he'd looked like that when he killed the general, and if Sarasef's affection for him had something to do with it. As if feeling his eyes on him, Sarasef turned to look, and swore when he saw the arrow still embedded in Hasheem's shoulder.

Too late, Hasheem thought as he slipped out of consciousness. "It's Zyren," he said. "The arrows…have been dipped in Zyren." He knew the scent of Dee's favorite poison, knew exactly how it worked to kill a man, and how fast it could.

In the Name of Rashar

"All four of them?" Jarem looked up from the parchment on his desk.

"Yes, Commander," confirmed the man before him in a nondescript black cloak. "They seemed to be working on a plan laid out by Deo di Amarra. The Lady Zahara, from what I heard, has just joined them tonight."

"I see." Jarem placed down the documents and leaned back on his chair. "Tell me what you've heard, every word, exactly as it was said."

The spy reported his findings, which revealed the details of the plan and those involved in the conspiracy. When he finished, Jarem paid him for a job well done, and then paid one of his officers to kill the man on his way out of the Tower. A pity, given how skilled the spy was, but loose ends couldn't be left untied, not now and not with what was at stake.

It was a problem—a huge one, in fact, and one Jarem hadn't seen coming. A conspiracy this large formed by none other than Deo di Amarra before he conveniently relocated himself out of reach was bad enough without all these influential figures in play. The Salahari alone, being a regular patron of most temples in Rasharwi, had enough priests on her payroll to start a crusade. Together with Amelia, whose ambitious merchant father could move large funds at will without having to pass the Tower's scrutiny, the conspiracy was rock solid in foundation. The fact that the Salar had yet to name an heir also made Azram the most reasonable successor, being both the eldest of the living sons and one by the Salahari. And now, with Zahara in the mix, things could easily get out of hand, even with Jarem already knowing all their plans.

Something had to be done before all hell broke loose. It would, however, mean dealing with all four of them at roughly the same time. *At the right time.*

The Salahari couldn't be killed—there was too much at stake for that given her father's political power and her involvement with the priests. Azram, however, could be exposed together with Amelia, and then both could be eliminated for treason. They might even be able to pin the same crime on Amelia's father and seize all his assets before executing him, or press the man into giving up his fortune to the Salasar in exchange for his life. It would benefit the Salar and his projects immensely. But before all others, Zahara, being the most immediate threat to the throne, must be the first to go. The question was how to do it without getting half the people in the Tower killed—himself included—for a death declared off-limits by the Salar.

He would need a scapegoat for this, Jarem thought, drumming his fingers on the desk. The murder would have to be committed by someone outside the Tower. Someone with his own motive that couldn't be traced back to him. Someone the Salar wouldn't think twice about killing.

"Imran," he called.

The door opened and in walked General Imran izr Imran, pausing to execute a crisp salute two steps into the room. The General had been with him since the massacre of the Vilarhiti—the only man, in Jarem's judgment, whose loyalty couldn't be bought. "Commander."

"Put together a unit of a hundred men. They are to be stationed here in the Tower waiting for my command night and day. Replace all the guards around the royal family, and make sure they do not leave the Tower until I say so for their own safety. I want a full report of everyone coming in and going out of the Tower on my desk every morning, starting tomorrow." Jarem rose to his feet and grabbed his robe. "Get me a horse. I will have a talk with Yakim, wherever he is right now."

⁜

THE GIRL WHIMPERED as Yakim wound his fingers around her hair, pushing himself deeper into her mouth. He usually preferred girls with more meat on their bones and more spirit to break. This one—just shy of eighteen and sent to him from the countryside by a pious couple—had been brought up almost too well where faith was concerned. It didn't take much to convince her to surrender completely to Rashar, to be blessed by the god's embodiments on earth, such as Yakim himself. Then again, such a plain, insignificant life should find it a blessing to be of service to a High Priest. She would live in comfort and luxury here, in the temple of Sangi, if she served Rashar well. Her parents, of course, would also reap the benefits. After all, rewards should be given to poor farmers who sent their daughters to serve in the house of Rashar.

"Good, my child," he told her, gripping her hair tighter as he guided her into a desired rhythm. Virgins needed to be taught, yes, but there was always something sacred about the first time they allowed themselves to open up to his divine power and to tremble before it. The girl, plain as a poor man's bread, was indeed trembling as she knelt before him—a perfect overture to the deflowering soon to come. After which time, she would follow the others' footsteps and become Rashar's blessed and humble priestess in the temple of Sangi. It was what all women should strive to be, as much as it was his lifelong goal to make sure as many as possible succeeded.

Her whimper grew louder as he sped up the pace, filling the private prayer room reserved for the High Priest of Sangi with sounds that opened up the path to heaven. Divine power was everywhere here. He could see it, most of all, in the mirror at the other end of the room that revealed an image of the greatest offering to the god himself. A daughter of Ravi—kneeling as she should—in front of Rashar's truest vessel.

It was in the middle of such thought when the door to the chamber was flung open, and through it strode in three men, two of whom were the priests he'd put in charge of guarding his privacy. The third man—the one in front—arrived in full uniform, armed, confident, and paying no attention to the pleas from the priests behind him.

Startled by the interruption, the girl jerked back in panic, hiding her face in shame. Under the circumstances, it was reasonable, expected even, for any man involved to feel the same. But there was, Yakim decided, a difference in how a man should act and how a High Priest of Rashar could.

So Yakim izr Zahat did what a High Priest should, which was to lean back on his chair and resume what he had been doing. Here, in the temple, even the Salar himself was expected to bend in respect to him.

"Continue, child," he said, guiding the girl back to where she was. "One mustn't allow mere mortals to interrupt one's service to Rashar." Turning back to the men, he gestured for the two priests to leave and spread his free hand toward the chair on the opposite side. "Commander Sa'id, please, have a seat. To what do I owe this pleasure?"

The commander, eyeing him with a distaste he didn't try to hide, went to pour himself a drink before settling down on the chair with an air of someone who owned the place. Yakim had never liked the man or his master. They were both savages, and neither had respect for the temple. They would pay for their sins, of course, in time.

"I bring a message from the Salar," said the commander.

Yakim held the man's gaze as the girl continued the interrupted service. "I see. Go on, izr Sa'id. I'm listening."

Jarem izr Sa'id looked at the girl, hesitated for a moment, then replied casually, "Your request for the burning of a hundred Shakshi slaves has been denied. The Salar also wants you to know that if you proceed without permission, a priest will burn for every Shakshi you put on a pyre. That is his answer to your request."

Yakim smiled, partly over the message he had been expecting, partly over the pleasing warmth between his legs. "So..." He paused to tug hard at the girl's hair earning himself another whimper from her. "...the Witch really has him by the balls, it would seem."

"Watch your tongue, Yakim," snapped the commander crisply, "or this may be the last time you are serviced in the name of Rashar."

"Sound advice." Yakim nodded. "And one you should also offer the Salar. Temples and their priests have served as the pillars of peace in every city for as long as religion has existed, my lord commander. Faith is what holds people together as one, not swords or rulers. It is the Salar who ought to be more careful with his tongue, or this may be the last time *he* is serviced in the name of Rashar."

A bold statement, Yakim knew, but a true one. Rulers of all nations have had to bend to religion and its leaders for centuries, even Salar Muradi. *Even Eli the conqueror.* It needed to be said, in his opinion, if only to demonstrate the power of Rashar himself.

Jarem izr Sa'id placed his cup down on the table neatly and leaned forward. "Is that a threat, Yakim?" His hand moved back to caress the hilt of his sword. "Are you threatening the Salar of Rasharwi? My superior? The man I would die for?"

Yakim swallowed. He had forgotten how loyal the commander was to the Salar, how far back they went. Salar Muradi might not risk a war with the temple, but one of his loyal subjects like Jarem izr Sa'id could kill him for personal reasons, take the blame, and the peace of the city would still be intact. Yakim might have held enough power over the people of Rasharwi to have clashed with the Salar many times and survived, but he was wise enough to know where the line was. He adjusted his expression and begged Rashar for forgiveness for his arrogance.

"I'm merely stating the importance of holding peace, Commander," he said, clearing his throat. "There must be some form of punishment for the Shakshis to settle this unrest. A ruler cannot be seen to put his mistress before the people. He is allowing himself to be put under the spell of a heretic, and we, as his loyal subjects, must free him from such witchcraft. Don't you agree?"

To Yakim's relief, the commander slipped back into his usual composure, letting go of the sword. He leaned back on his chair and picked up the drink again. "I am a soldier, Yakim. It is not my expertise to identify or deal with witchcraft," he said, his expression flat and unreadable. "You will have to enlighten me, if you believe he is bewitched by a certain Shakshi, as to how we might fix this situation."

Yakim thought for a moment, his eyes fixed on the symbol of Rashar at the far end of the room, hand still working on the girl's pace. "I believe, Commander Sa'id, that the people do need retribution," he said, thinking now of the last time he'd had a pureblood Shakshi girl kneeling before him and Rashar, and how appropriate, how empowering it had been to have served the god in putting a daughter of Ravi—and therefore the goddess herself—in her place. "Or some form of submission from the Shakshis—a sign, if you will, that they are willing to bend their knees to Rashar, if burning is not to be allowed."

It would be a peaceful way of settling this turmoil, yes. Yakim congratulated himself for such a brilliant solution. He could see it now, the sons and daughters of Ravi submitting to Rashar, turning to the right path. A redemption to go down in history, made possible by Yakim izr Zahat High Priest of Sangi. A legendary accomplishment on his part.

The thought gave him a surge of energy, and he urged the girl into a faster pace, imagining something else on top of the success of his career. "It doesn't take much, truly. In fact…" He paused to breathe. The possibility that the mouth around his cock could come from a certain Shakshi brought him close to his climax. "It might...only take one Shakhi to bend."

The girl, whimpering louder from the force of his grip on her hair, fell into a perfect rhythm with his guidance. He could already see it, could smell that corrupting, suffocating scent that had been taunting him for years. "There is one thing the Shakshis...treasure above all else, some… thing they would…die to protect." He pictured himself running his hands over that dark honey skin, through that silver hair, as he slammed the fire out of those yellow eyes with his god-given power. Yakim clutched the arm of the chair, straining for support.

"Give us...the Bharavi, Commander. Make her...bend to Rashar in front of the people. Give us...the Witch." The girl cried louder from the force of his hand, and he shivered with excitement at the sound. Yakim closed his eyes, saw a revelation of himself replacing the Salar of Rasharwi on his dais and the Bharavi between his legs, then forced himself into the girl's mouth one last time and shuddered as he came. "Then, and only then, will all sins be considered paid for."

⁜

IT WAS ALL TOO EASY, Jarem thought on his ride back to the Tower. Not that he had expected it to be hard, but he had gone prepared to offer a few speeches for Yakim to come to that conclusion. The man's arrogance and blind faith in the god could be counted upon for him to make the most stupid mistake no sensible person would ever arrive at, but what Jarem hadn't known about was his obsession with the Bharavi. It was clear as day what had been on Yakim's mind when he brought forward such a proposal. Jarem chastised himself for having missed it. There must have been a look, a gesture, something that could have given it away every time Yakim looked at her in the past that he should have caught. Jarem made a mental note to be more observant of his surroundings in the future.

It made sense, however. Yakim izr Zahat despised women and their goddess. He considered them corrupted, inferior beings that needed to be taught humility. Such a view had never been a secret, and who else would aggravate him more than a Bharavi—a woman believed to be a direct descendent of Ravi, proud enough to shame a peacock? A woman, as many believed, who had the Salar himself wound around her finger?

The problem was that Jarem couldn't tell how true such a statement was. The Salar definitely had other plans for Zahara, but there were times Jarem felt the presence of something else that clouded his master's vision. Women, Jarem reminded himself, had been the cause of countless leaders' falls in the past. It was his job to make sure that didn't happen to Salar Muradi.

Which meant that he would have to find a way to make the Salar agree with this proposal. It would take only three days of cleansing for a heretic to be converted. They could promise a large enough escort for Zahara to make sure she would be safe before her return to the Tower. The Salar could be made to see the benefits of ending the conflict with the temple and the people, and at the same time it would send a strong message that the Shakshis could be made to accept their rule and live peacefully among them. A winning solution for the Salasar and all those involved, as far as he was concerned.

Assuming that Zahara never returned to the Black Tower afterward, of course.

It had to be done, Jarem decided, for the love of this nation and the making of a ruler who would exceed Eli the Conqueror.

Don't Look

Djari watched the scene with hazed-over vision and the detachment of someone not present in the room but above it, looking down. A cold, coiling creature came alive and slithered in her chest as she did, wrapping its length around her heart and beginning to squeeze. She snatched it by the throat and crushed the life out of it, making sure it stayed dead with the same determination she had to not move from the spot or stir at the image before her.

On the bed, the healer was bleeding Hasheem into a bucket, trying to drain the poison from his blood. The blood of her sworn sword—hers, since they were considered one and the same—dribbled down his arm, thick and almost black, like Lady's when Djari had slit her throat. Lady had been like this too—lying still and barely breathing—during her last

moment of life.

She squeezed her eyes shut and shoved the memory back into a distant corner of her mind, behind the wall over which other things had been tossed. *Don't look back. Look forward. Look somewhere else. Anywhere.*

There had to be a large, rotting pile of dead things behind that wall now, and it was growing higher by the minute. She could smell the acrid, nauseating stench of it everywhere she went. It clung to her like body odor, like a dirty, ugly stain of past mistakes that would always show no

Back

matter how much effort she'd put into scrubbing it out. They would have to be dealt with soon. Just not now. Not yet.

Not yet, had been the words she repeated over and over since she arrived at the lair of the Rishi. She couldn't see Hasheem, couldn't talk to him—not yet, anyway. Some things you could only live with when you didn't give it meaning, or when you didn't see it on other people's faces. She had been avoiding him for that reason, waiting for the time when she felt she might be ready to deal with it.

Such a time may never come if he dies tonight.

Another creature wrapped itself around her heart and squeezed. She crushed that one too and tossed the carcass over the wall. *Don't think about that. Not now. Not yet. Not until it happens.*

"Is there no antidote?" Behind her, Sarasef spoke calmly. Only the frequency at which the Grand Chief was shifting his weight told her he was anything but calm.

Deo di Amarra sighed. The sound carried and filled the room with more toxicity, as if there hadn't already been enough of it for all of them to wince every time they breathed. "No, there is no antidote. You use it on people you want to see dead, to make sure they *stay* dead." The reply came with too many emotions to name, although *pissed* might have been the most prominent note. "That's the point of Zyren."

"So he will die?" asked Sarasef simply, and yet somehow she could hear him stumble halfway through the word.

Gathering the leftover bits and pieces of her strength, Djari made herself look at Deo di Amarra, asking the same question though in silence.

He shook his head in frustration, in anger, in uncertainty loud enough to tear through any hope one might be harboring. "My first-class assassins take poisons on a regular basis in case an accident happens. Under normal circumstances, he should be able to withstand its effects. But he wasn't exactly in perfect health before this, and being shot twice means there's a shitload of it in his body now. We can only try to bleed it out without weakening him too much. He's going to have to fight the rest, and I don't know if he can. Having pulled an arrow out that way," he said, and paused as if to swear in the privacy of his own mind, "allowed the poison to spread faster and more effectively."

It *was* stupid, even without the poison, to have pulled out the arrow. She had been trained in the art of healing and knew something about that. Another thought occurred to her then. "If we cut off the arm," Djari asked, remembering how her master healer had dealt with some snakebites and similar wounds in the past, "will it stop the poison from spreading further?"

Deo di Amarra blinked, twice. "He is your sworn sword, my lady. He will need that arm to fulfill his duty."

"He can still train with the other." A few missing limbs was common enough in the Kha'gans. It didn't make anyone useless. She didn't understand the reluctance. "If you must do it to save his life, you have my permission. Cut it off."

Sarasef, who had been listening quietly, turned to di Amarra. "Well?"

There was a frown on di Amarra's face, one he didn't try to hide. "With all due respect, my lady, this isn't the White Desert. Hacking off limbs is not the solution to every *fucking* problem." He was also close, she realized, to losing it, and Djari held her tongue from giving that insult a retort. Hasheem seemed to trust this man—perhaps even love him as a mentor—and so would she. He was their only hope now anyway, being the one who had sold the poison to Saracen and therefore knowing something about it. There were, Dajri remembered with a bad feeling in her stomach, so many things she didn't understand about the situation. She would have to talk to Hasheem about that when he recovered. *If he recovers.*

"It's too late for that now anyway," di Amarra added. "An amputation has to be done much sooner to have any effect. All we can do, I'm afraid, is to keep him strong, treat his symptoms as they come, and pray that he has enough fight in him to survive this." He looked at her, his lips quirking up a little. "He may still lose that arm if the wound doesn't heal properly. You may still get to show off a sworn sword with one arm after this if it pleases you, my lady."

Djari would have sneered at the mockery had the situation allowed it. A warrior with missing body parts was always honored and elevated in the Kha'gans. To the men, it was evidence of a seasoned fighter to be respected. To the women, it showed hardness—a sign that the man would father strong offspring who could survive the land. Life in the desert didn't make room for excuses. Relying on favorable conditions to survive was a degenerative disease for Rashais that didn't exist among her people. The truth was, where status was concerned, Hasheem might even be better off with a missing arm if he could still be just as deadly. It was the least of her worries.

What was important was that he lived, or that he wouldn't die for nothing. She had no time, no room for grief now, and definitely not before it happened. Hasheem's sacrifice would have to hold meaning, or his life wouldn't.

"Grand Chief." Djari turned to Sarasef, keeping her head held high the way she had been taught to do. "I would like to discuss something, if I may be direct with you." She waited for permission to speak, trying to ignore the fact that he stood at least two heads over her height and could crush her skull with his bare hands.

Sarasef nodded. "You may."

She planted her feet on the floor and braced herself before speaking the words. "My sworn sword has taken an arrow—two in fact—in your place tonight. You are also a man born of the desert, and by our similar code of honor, I believe you now owe him a life debt. Do you agree?"

A hush from Deo di Amarra, followed by a small rise of his lips that she took to be approval.

"I do," replied Sarasef readily, expressionlessly. "And?"

She took a step forward, forcing herself to come up with the courage she needed. "As his soul bearer, I hold the power to call upon that debt on his behalf. I ask that you join your forces with us, set me and my men free, and send Muradi's emissary home. Then, together, we will deal with Saracen." She caught his eyes, held them, and despite the generous amount of sweat seeping through her palms, continued with words that could get her killed. "But understand that if my sworn sword dies tonight, I will hold your brother responsible. You will give me his head, or you will stay out of it when we hunt him down. It will be my vengeance to take. Do you agree to my terms?"

From his towering height, the Grand Chief of the Rishi stared down at her like something that could eat her alive and was trying to decide if he should. There was still blood on his forearm, she noticed, along with parts of his neck and face from having beaten a man to death with a chair.

"I see," Sarasef said at length. "But tell me, iza Zuri, how do you intend to save him from your Kha'gan and Citara if I agree to his return?"

Her mouth went dry at those words. That was, she realized belatedly, another thing she had tossed over the wall and forgotten.

"Hasheem's identity is now in the open. Your people will ask questions, and there will be no hiding it. You are correct. I am indebted to your sworn sword, but you must know by now that there is much more to it. You understand my personal attachment to the boy, my affection for him?"

Those facts she had neglected were staring at her now in the face, and Djari suddenly felt the need to throw up. Sarasef was right. Hasheem's identity would no longer be a secret after this. They'd kill him once they knew he'd been living in Rasharwi. Even if her father were to turn a blind eye, Citara wouldn't. For the moment, she had no idea how she could save him if he were to return. Unless...

'You understand my personal attachment to the boy, my affection for him?'

"I do," Djari replied thoughtfully. There were still so many things she didn't know about Hasheem, but one thing that hadn't escaped her notice was how strong his relationship with the chief had been in the past. "I understand."

Sarasef took a step closer, making sure she heard every word, remembered every sentence. "Then write to your father, iza Zuri. I will offer the White Desert my alliance if you can make it happen. But understand that such an alliance rests on the Silver Sparrow—your sworn sword—being alive and unharmed. If anyone, anyone at all, so much as takes a finger from him for a reason I don't see fit, I will take him back, I will go to Muradi, and you will have me as your enemy. That is my condition. You will put it in writing, and I will have it sworn upon. Or he stays here, and you return without him."

The Perfect

Solution

Shadows danced along the walls like an anticipating audience of what seemed to Khali a hundred men—an illusion made by the many hurricane lamps that had been positioned hurriedly upon the news of his arrival. Under the scrutinizing gaze of ten White Warriors, two of whom were the Kha'a and Khumar, Khali sat, both out of breath and energy, trying to hold his nerves together in the middle of a half-formed circle of men bigger than him in every way.

Almost every way, he corrected himself, made an effort to sit taller than he wanted to. There was power in holding information, and at that very moment, having been sent to deliver a message of epic proportions by a man of the same magnitude, Khali knew the power he held over the fate of the White Desert, and therefore the men in this gathering.

To his right, his father, as chief of the northern camp and a member of the Kha'a's council, was watching him with an expression halfway between relief and worry. It appeared no punishment had been given to his family for what had happened on the hunting ground. If they were still waiting for a verdict on that incident, then this was his chance to redeem his family's virtue, gain himself some recognition, and maybe even elevate their status.

It would, however, take some guts to rise to the occasion in front of these men. The Kha'a's council of eight White Warriors consisted of the four chiefs of the northern, eastern, southern, and western camps, the head of treasury, the Kha'a's appointed representative in the White Tower of Citara, the master of rites who oversaw all the religious ceremonies in the Kha'gan, and the commander of the Kha'gan's combined army. Piss off any of these, and one should prepare for a life of struggle—however long that may be—not including, of course, the part where your limbs came off should the act of pissing off include a public display of disrespect. His words and opinions, if they were to be given, had to be chosen carefully here.

The Kha'a lowered the letter when he finished reading, handing it to Nazir, who, after going through its content, passed it on to the rest of the council.

"You have seen all this with your own eyes?" asked the Kha'a with an unearthly calm. "You were present during all these events?" Za'in izr Husari seemed fully alert and awake, as if he hadn't just been roused from sleep in the middle of the night. But this was, after all, a man who had personally led a battle for three consecutive nights without rest and won. *Several times, in fact,* Khali reminded himself.

"Not during the meeting, Kha'a, no," he said, keeping his tone as level as he could. "I was held at a different location from where Djari and Hasheem were. I have, however, seen the Salar's army on my way back, at the entrance to the canyon. From what I could see, I believe there were somewhere between two and three thousand of them waiting for a command from Deo di Amarra and the prince."

For a moment, the council members seemed to have stopped breathing all at once, and Khali couldn't help noticing how the mention of just one name could suffocate the entire population of men both wise and way past their prime in that tent. Then again, this was the man who had handed Muradi the throne, had been said to have come up with the plan that brought down the Vilarhiti and afterward helped the Salar put an end to the uprising of the provinces. A few thousand Rashais could be dealt with given their own number of White Warriors, but that number led by Deo di Amarra—or Muradi himself for that matter—was going to give a lot of people in that meeting something to have nightmares about for some time.

"The threat may be real," said Zahan izr Abari, chief of the southern camp and Zozi izr Zahan's father. "But how are we to believe that Sarasef, who has been doing business with the Salasar all this time, would suddenly want to ally himself with us?" He turned to the Kha'a, pursing his lips a little. "It sounds to me like a trap, Kha'a, if I may be bold."

Agreements could be heard around the half-circle. The Kha'a considered for a time and turned back to Khali. "You have an explanation for this, I hope?"

Khali nodded. "The proposal for an alliance, Za'in Kha'a," he said, recalling the explanation Djari had given him before he made the journey back, "had to do with a life debt owed by the chief to your daughter's sworn sword. A debt that Djari has taken the liberty, as Hasheem's soul bearer, to use in the form of an alliance with us to win this war. It is also the reason why Sarasef has called for Hasheem's safety to be guaranteed in writing. Apparently, he saved the chief's life from an assassination attempt by his brother, Saracen."

"And the reason for having taken our Bharavi in the first place?" Zaharran izr Shalyk, Commander of the Kha'gan's combined army and the Kha'a's appointed battle strategist, asked in a tone as composed as the Kha'a. Of all the council members, Khali noticed, izr Shalyk might have been the only one whose expression hadn't changed once after reading the letter or hearing his account. A man to be observed most carefully, in his opinion, and one who had asked the one question he wished he didn't have to answer.

"The attack," Khali paused to swallow, "wasn't meant for our Bharavi, izr Shalyk. The chief had given no such orders. I was there. I can assure you the target wasn't Djari."

"Then why were they here," asked the Kha'a, a trace of anger in his tone, "in *my* territory?"

Khali drew a breath and decided there was no possible way to go around this without revealing one crucial piece of information that was going to complicate everything to another level. "They came for Hasheem. That was their original plan."

Low murmurs rippled around him from the men present, but the man who asked the question was Zozi's father. "Why him?"

Khali looked at Nazir, who had been sitting next to the Kha'a with a pained expression. Permission to reveal the truth had to be asked, as the answer would concern Nazir's suggestion to take Hasheem into the Kha'gan in the first place.

Understanding that it was now his cue to speak, Nazir drew himself up despite the fatigue he had seemed to be suffering from. The Khumar looked like he hadn't slept for a week. Khali wondered why.

"Because there is a bounty on his head, being offered by the Salar. The boy was a branded slave from Rasharwi, currently a fugitive from having murdered a high-ranking official. You will know him, I believe," said Nazir, pausing momentarily as if to ready himself for what would follow, "as the Silver Sparrow of Azalea."

The murmurs, this time, grew louder and with enough hostility to poison the air they breathed.

"That traitorous, shameless male escort of the Black Tower?" izr Abari rasped, shifting his weight as if to rise to his feet and assault Nazir in the open, but managing to stop himself out of some last-minute restraint. "I believe you owe us an explanation, Nazir Khumar, as to why such a person has been allowed not only to live, but to become your sister's sworn sword and blood."

Nazir straightened, and even with that obvious exhaustion on display managed to look taller and bigger than everyone in the tent when he spoke. "*That traitorous male escort,* izr Abari, happens to be the most favored apprentice and first-class assassin of Deo di Amarra—who, as you have clearly stated, has spent years in the Black Tower, and before that the fortress of Sabha and the streets of Rasharwi. He knows the structure of all three, their strengths and weaknesses, the way in and out of the city, and as di Amarra's closest apprentice, one can safely assume he would also know the pillars upon which the Salar has built his strength."

He turned, then, to address each and every man present, his voice pitched to carry. "He is, at this moment, by the hands of Fate and through his acquaintance with the Grand Chief of the Rishi, the one who has brought us not only this warning of an imminent threat, but also a chance to form an alliance that may change the outcome of the war. The boy is Muradi's greatest weakness, our best weapon against him and has, I remind you, sworn an oath of loyalty to Djari iza Zuri, our Bharavi and the one chosen by the gods to end the war. *That* is the vision I have been given, and why he has been taken in as Djari's sworn sword. We need him to win this war."

An argument of impressive weight, Khali thought, and one that should hold. But then again, some men were never in tune with the bigger agenda. As with all gatherings, no matter how powerful or wise the men—or women—were, there would always be some who agreed, some who did not, and some who were waiting to ride with whoever came out victoriously rather than risk picking a side too soon. Khali knew where his side was, but he also knew when to voice it and when not to.

"This is absurd!" Zahan izr Abari hissed. He looked like he wanted to throw his fist in the air, but didn't. "A former branded slave of Rashawi cannot be allowed to live among us without breaking the code! Citara will never allow it."

A series of nods and agreements traveled from one end of the semi-circle to the other, with the exception of the Kha'a, Nazir, izr Shalyk, and his father who could, after the incident Khodi had created, be expected to not voice any opinion at this point.

"Then we make sure Citara doesn't know," Nazir countered.

"And risk losing our seats in the White Tower for defying them? Over one boy we don't even know we can trust?" said Joshi izr Bashir, the Kha'gan's head representative in the White Tower's high council. As spokesperson who carried out all negotiations and requests between the Kha'gan and Citara, izr Bashir's concerns were always focused on not pissing off the Devis who ruled the sacred city. A sound reason, given how much the Kha'gan's livelihood depended on being in their good graces.

"Za'in Kha'a, if I may," Zaharran izr Shalyk said thoughtfully. "Even if we were able to hide the Sparrow's identity and keep him alive as per Sarasef's request, the nature of this alliance may be a problem in itself. The Rishi may have avoided raiding our territory for decades, but they have never held back on the others, and they will not take this alliance lightly. If our plan is to unite the Kha'gans to fight the Salasar in the war to come, this alliance may become a problem. More than that, Citara might consider this an issue that requires their permission."

They might, Khali agreed—and the Devis would say no, he was sure of it. Those sheltered, over-privileged, self-elected bunch of Bharavis who ruled the White Tower had never set foot outside of Citara. They wouldn't know a damn thing about the real struggles out here in the desert. Their decision, as always, would be based on what they were told about the conflicts, on paper even, and it would pass easily, no matter the consequence. This offer of alliance, if it reached the ears of even a single Devi, could be a huge problem. Unless...

"The more immediate problem, izr Shalyk," said Nazir, with an unusual hardness in his tone that almost sounded desperate, "is that they have my sister; in other words, our Bharavi, who is the key to uniting the Kha'gans by both marriage and what she is prophesied to be. Getting her back is the priority at this moment. If we lose her, we lose our hope in joining our forces with another Kha'gan without going to war with them."

War was the only other choice, of course, Khali thought bitterly. A Kha'gan as large as theirs would only agree to form an alliance through an offering of a Bharavi who would, in turn, breed them oracles—or more Bharavis—to grow in strength and influence in Citara. Without Djari, the Kha'a would have to try to take over these Kha'gans by force, which would lead to more deaths and lessen the number of men who could fight against the Salasar. The best course of action, where the bigger agenda was concerned, was to get Djari back and marry her before the Salar moved his main army, and marry her to a Kha'gan as large as possible and as soon as possible. Still, he wondered if they even had time for that. Djari was barely sixteen. It would be two years before she could be married as per tradition. They could secure an alliance now with some contract, yes, but a lot could happen before she gave birth to a daughter or a son which would tie the Kha'gan to them for good. To Khali, an alliance with the Rishi was a form of security they could have now, immediately.

Khali glanced at his father, gave him a look he knew would be recognized.

His father nodded, then turned to the Kha'a. "I believe, Za'in Kha'a, that my son has more insights to share with the council, if he may have permission to speak."

All eyes were on him now, Khali could feel it like the cold, sharp edge of a knife on the back of his neck. He looked at the Kha'a and waited.

"Go on," said the Kha'a.

Khali cleared his throat, making sure his voice wouldn't fail him. "I believe, Za'in Kha'a, that there may be another solution to this," he began, taking a leap that could earn him recognition or ruin his chances to be in the future council entirely. "By now, I think we can all agree that the news of Djari having been taken is no longer a secret. Why not play it for what it is—a mistake made by Sarasef's men, one the chief is willing to correct by sending her back to us to avoid a conflict? Then it would only make sense for us to send a large group of White Warriors to escort her back safely from the Black Desert, would it not? And if our escort happens to run into Saracen's men—"

"It would not be seen as an extraordinary circumstance if a battle ensues," said Nazir, rising to the occasion to finish the sentence, giving it the needed weight.

Khali nodded, making an effort to hold back a smile. "That way, we can form an alliance with the Rishi by aiding Sarasef in dealing with his brother, without having it known by anyone on our side of the desert apart from those in this tent."

He paused, allowing time for the idea to come alive in the minds of those who chose to see it. Saw about half of them listening to him intently, considering the possibility in earnest, judging from the way they rubbed their chins or stroked their beards.

"As for the Sparrow," Khali continued, riding the opportunity before the moment was gone, "I doubt very much that we can hide him here successfully. But we can fulfill that part of the agreement by letting Sarasef keep the Sparrow. He need not be our responsibility to protect."

At that, Nazir grimaced. "We need him here if we are to utilize his knowledge."

True, Khali thought. He hadn't considered how to fix that particular problem. But if it solved other ones—

"Or we keep him away until this thing blows over," said izr Shalyk, turning all heads toward him. "And we bring him back with a new identity, integrate him into the Kha'gan with a new name Citara and the outsiders wouldn't recognize or relate to the Sparrow. His time here with us has been brief and largely unknown, has it not?"

Nazir shook his head, but one could see he was not completely disagreeing with the idea. "It would take many years before people forget this happened. We may need him before then."

And with that, an idea came to Khali, loud and clear as a horn signaling the beginning of a hunt. He waited for no permission this time. "We could send him to Al-Sana. If one of us can convince izr Imami to take him in."

There was a rush of drawn breaths in the tent. Khali could almost hear the key turning, the click of a lock being released before a door opened before him. "He would not only be out of sight while staying within our reach when we need his knowledge, but would also be trained under Akai izr Imami during that time. Your sister—" He turned then to Nazir, seeking a form of backup he knew would come. "—will have a sworn sword trained by a legendary master." A *legendary master who isolated himself on a mountain too remote and treacherous for people to climb without dire cause to ever find out the Sparrow was there.* "And if one of us were to adopt him—" He could see it clearly now, yes: that perfect solution to the problem concerning the Sparrow, "—he would also be a White Warrior worthy of being placed on the council, where his insights could be utilized without anyone raising a brow."

Along the semicircle, Khali could see a few heads nodding in agreement. On his father's face was a faint smile only those who knew him well would recognize. Izr Abari pressed his lips into a thin line, eyeing him with the jealousy of a father for his son's rival. An enemy he had made tonight, Khali noted, but one that was worth gaining considering the recognition from the Kha'a, who happened to be grinning at the moment.

Nazir, however, for all that this solution should have pleased him, wasn't smiling. That face, if anything, told Khali there was something they had all missed, something only an oracle could see and was unwilling to share.

Or was it simply fatigue? He wondered.

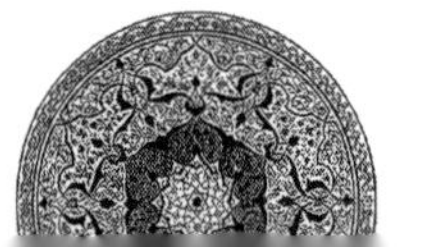

My One Unattainable Goal

Lightning flashed across the burning sky streaked with grey clouds above a dying, bleeding sun. It lit up the right side of his father's face, cast an almost black shadow on the other, giving his dark eyes a flash of gold as he slammed a fist into his mother's jaw. She flew across the room to land near the wall he had been curling up against, next to the fireplace that had gone out a while ago from the storm. In front of him, the blood of his mother's lover was still gushing out of his headless body. It made a small pool on the stone floor, creeping toward where he was, swallowing up slowly but steadily whatever was left of the distance between him and the embodiment of death that was his father.

A knife was flung in his direction. It landed by his foot, flailing like a living thing tossed alive into an open fire. Another lightning strike, and the small blade flashed white, its silvery sheen glided along the sharp edges from one end to the other as the light faded. The ground shook underneath him as the next thunder came, rendering all the other noises around him into a faint, muffled sound as he stared at the blade, pressing himself harder against the wall as if it would somehow offer protection.

'*Pick up the knife, my lord prince*,' someone told him. '*Prove your loyalty, if you don't want to die,*' said another. '*Examples have to be set, sacrifices must be made. Do you understand?*'

The sky flashed once more, and there, in front of him, his mother was smiling, weeping, and whispering something to him all at the same time—something incomprehensible, inaudible.

His vision turned black when the next thunder came.

⁂

RAIN POURED DOWN from the roof like a smooth screen of living crystal. Salar Muradi reached out with one hand to catch the falling water, turning it around to watch as the cold numbed his fingers the way it had back then. He remembered the rain being colder that night, colder than when he'd entered the gate of Sabha through its open courtyard.

Cold enough, he thought, that he didn't remember feeling a damn thing after having slit his mother's throat. Didn't remember how she died or what she had said before that, either. She had begged to die, and everyone in that room had wanted her to die, that was all he remembered.

It was the same two years ago when he'd ordered the execution of Kuyo and Keijin. The same numbness had been with him then, watching both his sons' heads rolling off the block and landing with a soft thump on the wood. '*Examples have to be set,*' a voice in his head had said then. '*Sacrifices must be made.*'

Examples and sacrifices.

And they had to be—set and made—as with all things. Some people had to die to build a bridge for other generations to cross. Someone had to be willing to carry that weight, to make that decision. Life, of any kind, survived on the death of another. You could only limit killing to the things you eat if your life was the only one that mattered. Saving an entire city—or an empire—was always going to take more. It was a matter of mathematics, of proportions.

'*A leader must be content with blood on his hands,*' Eli had written. '*His, the enemy's, and that of the men he leads.*'

It was the kind of truth no one wanted to hear. The kind of truth that was easy for lesser men to point fingers at, and in doing so make themselves acquire a sense of power without responsibilities attached. Being responsible for so many people's lives required killing just as many, sometimes more, depending on who one wanted to protect. Sometimes it had to be your mother, your father, your sons, to save the lives of thousands. Just because they were his blood, did it give them more right to live than someone else? Did it make him more of a monster to kill his own child than that of another man's? You would have to be a self-absorbed, entitled hypocrite to measure a life that way. Logic and simple mathematics were the only way to justify killing. *Kill them, if it makes sense*, di Amarra had agreed.

And he had lived with logic and sacrifices all his life, had been used to it to the point of being numb to these things.

But not for this.

Never, as a matter of fact, when it came to Zahara.

She was, though he had tried to deny it, his only weakness; his one illogical, erratic decision for the past eighteen years. A weakness that must be dealt with, something he had delayed and neglected for far too long.

And it was time to end it. It was time to make the same sacrifice he had made on that rainy night thirty years ago.

Now, watching the cold rain dripping off his hand, slipping through his fingers, he just wished he remembered what his mother had said.

⁜

SHE WAS DRESSED IN WHITE, like the first time they'd met, only tonight it was a nightgown he'd given her, clean, dry, and intact. Makena silk at its best, made and stitched in the Rashai fashion and done by the hands of a Rashai dressmaker.

It was as far as one could go to force her into a role she didn't want to play. You could put a tiger in sheep's clothing and it would still try to eat you if you were not careful. And Zahara was much, much more than that. She was his match, his undefeated rival, his twin even, if he were to be honest with himself.

She turned to greet him with surprise written on her face—an expression that was still there as she offered him her usual show of pretended obeisance. He hadn't come to her chamber often. In fact, one might be able to count the occasions in the past eighteen years on one hand.

"To what do I owe this pleasure, my lord?" she asked as the chambermaids scurried outside and closed the door behind them.

He smiled at those words. *Pleasure*, she'd said. Pleasure had never been a part of their encounters—not for her at least. It was a lie she knew he would catch—had always made sure he would catch, by the hundred different kinds of blades hidden in each syllable she chose to fling at him. The woman was never out of weapons, truly.

Even now, standing in front of a window through which a blistering wind rushed past her small frame, her long, tangled silver hair danced defiantly in it, coiling in and out like a band of unforgiving creatures made to sink their teeth into anyone who approached. The harsh lines of her face made harsher in the flashes of lightning multiplied the severity of her presence, complemented, all too appropriately, by the brutal sound of her silk dress snapping in the storm that raged and poured into the room.

The sky flashed once, followed by thunder trailing closely on its tail. It shook the ground between them, struck him like a punch in the gut, left behind something to prolong its delivery of more aches and pains in his torso, in his chest.

It always felt like this in her presence. In the storm, the calm sunny day, the cold quiet night, or here, in the flickering light of the lanterns. Despite all the warning signs and the undeniable danger tugging at his conscience, he was always helplessly drawn to it, like a craving of some potent drug he'd gotten used to and couldn't live without, like the quaint taste of blood and saliva following a jaw-crushing blow fighters learned to appreciate, or like that overpowering, orgasmic rush of energy that made you bounce back up after being beaten close to death during hand-to-hand combat. She could do that to him by just being there, taking up space in the same room, sharing the same air he breathed.

It was true now, just as it had been eighteen years ago. That part of their relationship had never changed.

He closed the distance between them, watching for—and seeing—the signs of her struggle to not flinch at his advance. She succeeded, as always, but it was never without an effort. It pleased him to see the effort.

"Is it so strange," he asked, studying her expression as he did, "that I might want to see my wife before she is delivered to god?"

She put on a smile, masking just in time whatever it was that had bothered her before it was brought too far forward. "You make it sound as if I'm about to be sent to slaughter."

"It is your slaughter, is it not, Zahara?" The name rolled off his tongue like honey, like wine. He liked the taste of it on his lips. Liked the way her breath caught every time he said it. There was power in this, as with every look, every touch that earned him a reaction she would always fight so relentlessly to crush out of existence. "For what you are, who you are, and what you represent? I am amazed, to tell you the truth, that you seem so willing."

And he would have been—truly amazed and bewildered—had he not known better.

She stiffened at that: a gesture so small he could only see from years and years of having studied every inch of her, every move she made, no matter how slight, and every snag in her breathing pattern. The command to have her bend the knee to Rashar and convert her faith had not brought forward the expected reaction, if one knew her character well enough. It had, however, brought forward the expected reaction when he'd confronted her with the lack thereof just now.

A confirmation of sorts of what had recently come to his attention. An open wound to accompany it—one that was sure to leave a scar if it ever healed. Not unexpected, no, but a cut was a cut and pain was always there whether or not you saw the blade coming. And he had seen the blade coming. He'd simply failed to put up his defenses, or hadn't wanted to.

Such discomfort lingered for just a moment before it was promptly replaced by a clear determination to stand her ground. If there had been any guilt in it, she hadn't let it show. He didn't think there would be anyway. Guilt was for people who didn't mean it, and Zahara had lived to do this as her sole purpose in life.

"To save the lives of thousands, my lord?" she said, her voice a note higher, crisp as a blade. "I have lived with worse."

A knife that, blunt and serrated along the edge, one inserted between his ribs with a twist as it went in. And he was bleeding in earnest, he admitted, only he had also bled worse and enough times to find the smell of blood pleasant. That night in particular, and for good reason, he found himself wondering if there were ways around it. If some things could have been done or unspoken words could have been said to not have it come to this. He would miss this smell of blood, surely.

"Is it really that hard to bend to me, Zahara?" He reached for her hair, winding the silvery strands around his fist, making sure he would remember the feel of it on his fingers. "To accept your role, your place by my side, even once?"

Deep down, he already knew the answer to that. Once had always been too much to ask. Once was something she would never offer. Then again, once would have never been enough for him to consider her conquered...or to ever call her *his*.

"Would you, my lord?" she asked, eyes blazing golden, holding him as if by knifepoint, putting his own theory to the test. "Accept such a role, in my position?"

Would I?

He smiled at that.

She smiled back. Triumphantly. "I didn't think so."

That might have been it: the thing, the trigger that could always start the fire in his belly, fueling the need to strip her to the skin and force her into submission—that taunting, arrogant smile so close to a daring challenge from an equally-skilled fighter that could always get him excited, get his blood racing.

"You enjoy it, don't you?" he said, cradling her head on his open palm, leaning close enough to feel her shivering on his hand, to feel the heat of her uneven breaths on his cheek. "Staying always out of reach? You like being this." He tilted her face up to meet his, to see her eyes. "This unattainable goal of mine."

The growing heat pooled in his stomach, spilled over, dripped down to meet the pulsing ache between his legs that had been there since he saw her. How was it possible, he often wondered, that he could never control himself around her after all this time?

And Zahara, despite knowing what it would do to look at him that way, despite the torture she knew she would have to put herself through for doing so, said, "Is it any different from what you do, my lord? You, of all people, should understand the sheer joy of letting me sleep next to a blade I can't kill you with." She pressed herself closer to him to make a point, her presence crowding at his chest, forcing the breaths out of his lungs as she spoke against his lips. "I *am* unattainable, no matter what you do to me. Is that not why it entertains you so to torture me this way? Because I am the one thing you want that you can't have? Go ahead and try, my lord. You won't have it, not for as long as I li—"

He didn't wait for her to finish the sentence. Couldn't. His control had been gone long before that.

The taste of her lips stung him like acid, set something alight in his throat that made its way down his stomach and then further down. The rigidity of her mouth, her tongue, was there to taunt him, as always. They were straining, tensing as hard as the hand on his arm to refrain from ever kissing him back. She had whimpered, had moaned, had sometimes cried at the pressure of his mouth, his hands, but she had never, not once in the past eighteen years, allowed him that much.

It took no time, no time at all for him to rip apart the silk of her gown and take in the scent of her, to taste that aching, agonizing sound of restraint from her lips. Restraint, because as much as her mind and her pride always denied him, her body never could. There was a part of Zahara that craved the same battle and bloodshed that he did, the part that responded to threats with an unstoppable drive to never retaliate, to stay on top of the game rather than to turn from a fight. He knew it from the first time he'd touched her, knew it like the crude, acrid stench of blood and sweat from an opponent refusing to die and admit defeat to his last breath. It hadn't even felt like rape—she'd even made sure of it the first time he took her, had taken off her own clothes and stared him down, told him to go for it if he thought he could break her. You couldn't take anything from a woman like Zahara if she wasn't willing to give, couldn't wound her without getting yourself cut in the process.

They hadn't made it to the bed the first time. There had been no time, no patience for that, none whatsoever of those things he could have mustered then, or now as he pulled her down to the floor right where they were. Through the window, the storm was still rushing in, its loud, reverberating rumbling falling in rhythm with the thundering beat in his chest, in his racing pulse, in the roaring unstoppable influx of need, of want, of maddening hunger until there was no telling the two apart. He laid her down on the cold marble, felt a stirring of her body trapped underneath his weight, and found himself shuddering at the response. Outside, the rain smashed hard against the window ledge, throwing droplets of water on their skin, on her hair, on the torn, tattered silk still clinging to her limbs. She clenched her fists on the fabric of his robe, clinging desperately to control as their bodies collided, as sweat and water, and their cries merged and blended into one.

He remembered it then, that first time when it had been just like this. When the blistering heat of the desert turned their skins slick with sweat, when he could taste it all on his palette—that salty, tangy, slightly bitter taste of body fluids and blood from unclosed wounds. She hadn't fought him openly then—she couldn't, not for the promise of death he'd declared for thousands. She'd carved him up in return, digging her nails into his flesh, tearing his skin open and had drawn blood—the blood he'd painted on her body and feasted on.

She was doing exactly that now, stretching her claws against his back, sinking them in as he devoured the taste of her, pressing his lips hungrily on her bare skin, here, there, and everywhere he could reach. Her breathing quickened as he made his way up her torso, her chest heaving for breath the closer and closer he came to her heart, and then, at the same moment he closed his mouth around her breast, a searing, burning pain tore through the skin of his back at the same time that her body arched clear off the floor, straining every muscle in her limbs to not make a single sound.

It didn't stop him. All it did was to drive him deeper into the maddening scent of her, to press himself harder against her skin, to dig and dig again for the roots of her limits until he could tear it all down.

Somehow, he never could. You could drive Zahara up against a wall, threaten to break every bone in her body, to sink your teeth into her flesh and drink her blood and she still wouldn't surrender. But it was exactly this that had kept him coming back for more, what had given him the constant need to stretch her thin, to push and torture her to the extent that there was nothing that could have been said or done to avoid what he had to do that night. She would never bend to him, to anyone. And neither would he.

But he would take this, this one last fight to his grave—the grave she would never see.

He looked at her then, taking in the sight of her as he lowered himself against her torso, watching her bite down on her lip, bracing herself for what she knew would come. She wouldn't look away, she never had. Zahara wasn't the kind of woman who ran from reality, no matter how painful. She would stare him down, as she was doing now, as he entered her, inch by remorseless inch, as if to remember every moment, to write down and add to her growling list of reasons why she wanted to see him dead.

And he had always enjoyed it, like staring death in the face, like being driven breathless and aching all over from a fight, like having that shiver running down your spine when you plunged a sword into someone you'd longed to see dead. She ground her teeth as she watched him, her small muscles corded and trembling at his thrusts. It drove him further and closer to the edge, forcing his body, his hands, his impossibly hardened shaft to dive harder, deeper into her, pushing them forward along the floor, cold marble scraping at his forearms, his knees. He could feel it all under his skin—the pulsing, relentless ache smashing itself against his limbs, rising and rising in intensity as she strained harder in his grip, her breathing falling in rhythm with his, her heart flinging itself against her ribcage and his answering to it, matching it in speed, in force powerful enough to kill them both, to rip them apart at the seams if it were allowed to go on much longer.

And then, when she let out a small whimper, as her teeth sank deep into the skin on his right shoulder, drawing blood, every muscle in his body went rigid, turned stiff as iron as they froze, and all the aching, agonizing pain that had accumulated in that brief battle between them shot down his torso, throwing him off, threatening to snap his spine as he bent back in his release. The growl she dragged out of his throat came with the thunder that shook the entire Tower underneath them, destroying them both as they lay spent and exhausted on the cold, wet floor.

Eighteen years, and she could still drive him so close to death, so close to breaking.

But it wasn't done yet. Not by far.

That realization came with a different kind of pain. He pushed himself up to face her, planting a soft kiss on her forehead, her cheek, breathing in her scent for one last time.

"Tell me something, Zahara," he asked, trailing his hands up her chest, brushing her collarbone, panting still. "What did my son promise you? What is it that you think Azram can offer you that I can't?"

Her breath came to a screeching stop at those words, and perhaps also her heart. "What—"

"Don't," he hissed, "even try. You know me too well for that."

She swallowed, pressing her lips together so tight he could see the blood draining from them.

"Did you think I wouldn't know?" He brushed his thumb along the smooth ridge of her jawline, coming to rest on her throat and felt the pulsing in her veins. "How much of a fool do you take me for? I know what you do. Everywhere you go, every turn you take. I know every man you so much as speak to. What did Azram promise you to get you to finally knife me in the back?"

She was trembling now, so hard there was no concealing it.

"Speak, Zahara," he rasped, his anger rising at the confession already on display. "The lives of thousands depend on it, and so does your son's."

She closed her eyes then, squeezing the one drop of tear down her cheek. When she opened them again, there were no more tears to fall. Her eyes were filled with hatred, with spite, with a hundred knives collected over the years coming out of hiding.

"Freedom," she said, stabbing him with the knife's point of each syllable she uttered, "of my people, of me, and of my son. But you should know—" She smiled then, more triumphantly than she had before and covered with enough poison to kill every living thing in that room. "—I would have done it in any case, if only to see you die."

It went through him like a spear, cast eighteen years ago only to arrive at its target now. He knew it, of course. Had known for a long time. He knew what she wanted, what he had done, how improbable, impossible it was for things to have turned out any other way. It was always going to come down to this. She would have to die, or he would.

He could feel her pulse in his hand as he squeezed, could feel something else in him dying every time she struggled to breathe. Her hands came up to grip his arms out of instinct, her legs thrashing next to his thighs as her body convulsed more and more violently under him. He waited for the same numbness to spread, the same voice to call for examples to be set, for sacrifices to be made.

It never came. All that was there, the only thing he could feel then, was the suffocation that matched that of the woman he was trying to strangle, and the pain, the excruciating, burning pain that kept on growing and growing until there was nothing else he could see but darkness. The only sound he could hear besides the rain pouring in through the window, the one that kept on ringing in neverending repetition, was that of his own scream the night he'd slit his mother's throat.

A Mistake Waiting to Happen

The sunset that evening reminded her of the massacre. The clouds had looked like this—torn to shreds and soaked through with blood. Only here and now, no houses were burning, no smoke was rising with the accompanying smell of charred human flesh to suffocate everyone who stood within a hundred paces from the fire. Out here, deep in the Djamahari, Djari imagined the screams of people being burned alive by the hands of Za'in izr Husari would have echoed everywhere if the same thing were to happen.

Her father had done that. A husband who had always been gentle to his wife, a Kha'a who lived to protect his Kha'gan, a parent who loved his children despite the harshness of his words, had done that. It was possible that the people you loved could do these things. It was also possible to continue loving them and hate the event, the same way she had hated sunsets for the memories of that evening, but not her father. Never her father.

Love, Djari realized, could make one so corrupt, so dishonest, so blind. Not too different—not at all—from hate, if one were to look at it from a certain angle. In a way, one could call it an act of love that had brought about so much hate in Za'in izr Husari. She wondered sometimes if she would have done the same in his position. She couldn't answer that, not with any certainty.

I have to start getting used to these things, Djari thought, fixing her eyes on the fading sun as it disappeared behind the mountain. War was coming, just around the corner. There would be blood where she was going. One day, in the near future, she might have to be the one doing the slaughter, the burning, the killing of babies and mothers. Those things came with war, no matter which side you were on—that much she had not been naive enough to believe otherwise. Sometimes life exacted such sacrifices for others to live.

Djari had decided long ago what sacrifices she would be willing to make, only the one man she would have liked to hold her hand through these things might die tonight.

In all fairness, it was simply another death she would have to endure in her lifetime as a Bharavi and the one chosen to end the war. A small snag only in a larger tapestry she would have to weave and sew.

Still, she had stood there by the bed last night, watching them bleed Hasheem with her heart in her throat, her strength draining from her limbs faster than his blood, realizing just at that moment that she was about to lose the first man she had come to love.

It had become clear to her then—fact by indisputable fact, memory after living memory—the reason behind every foolish thing she had done in the past few weeks. There was a *reason* she had pursued him the first night they met, a *reason* she had kept the arrowhead, had said the things she'd said, had ridden out of camp the moment she'd heard of the trouble at the hunting ground.

Had asked him to kiss her that night when she had no right to.

She had been certain then, as the thought of losing him sank its fangs into her heart, that love had been at the very center of it. He was her first kiss, her first breath taken away, her first skip of a heartbeat among many that followed and would continue to follow for a long, long time.

If he survives.

She squeezed her eyes shut at the other possibility, tried to force herself to not tremble at the thought, and failed at that too. She seemed to have failed at so many things lately.

"It's chilly out here, my lady." A voice she identified readily by its silky smooth Khandoor accent said from behind, pulling her abruptly out of her thoughts. "You might catch a cold."

She kept her eyes on the horizon as Deo di Amarra placed a cloak on her shoulders. The fox pelt was exquisite, warm, and priceless, as befitting a man who could afford a countless number of such things.

"Why should you care?" she asked, wondering if she should step back from the edge of the cliff. It would have taken just a push from behind to kill her on the spot. No, it would have taken less than that, considering who he was. "It would benefit you, would it not, should any harm come to me?" He was, after all, her enemy, perhaps the biggest one at present.

"Technically, yes." Di Amarra chuckled softly. "But I want my boy to live, and he would be pissed if any harm came to you."

It was said in the simplest manner, like reciting a fact in history everyone was expected to know, and yet it made her realize how profound that statement was. In many ways, she was still alive because of Hasheem, still safe because of Hasheem, still able to negotiate because of Hasheem.

He seems to have become my whole life, she thought.

"You really do care for him, don't you?" she asked, surprised at the vulnerability she heard in her own voice. "You and the Grand Chief?" It pained her to say it, despite the benefits of such knowledge. She didn't know what bothered her more—the fact that there seemed to be a mountain of his past she knew nothing about, or that he appeared to hold a special place in so many people's hearts, not just hers.

Deo di Amarra shrugged and fixed his eyes on a spot somewhere up ahead. He seemed to be in a strange mood. Calm, she thought, and yet troubled at the same time. "I can't speak for Sarasef—that part of his life I have not witnessed in person. I have, however—" He paused, drawing a long, difficult breath, as if to come to terms with something. "—spent the past five years shaping that boy into what I believed he could become. You could say I know him better than anyone alive. I've saved him, clothed him, cleaned up his messes. I know his worst nightmares and how he deals with them." The corner of his lips lifted into what she felt was a melancholic smile, perhaps also with a touch of regret. "It's hard to not care for something you took pains in raising."

She could understand it, she supposed. She had been through the same thing with horses all her life. "Five years is a long time." It felt like a whole other lifetime, in fact—a lifetime she hadn't been a part of, had actually been kept out of on purpose for that matter. She had mixed feelings about that, but anger might have been the most prominent one. She hated that she had to find out this way, that he had never had an intention to tell her.

"Long enough," Deo di Amarra said, turning to look at her now, "to know I can't kill you without destroying him."

"I barely know him." That came out more bitter than she would have liked.

"Perhaps," he said. "But he saw something in you in that short time, just as Sarasef saw in him, and just as I did. Whatever it was that made him swear such an oath to protect you told me he won't survive if I deprive him of it. Not this time."

"This time?" *Another mountain, another life*, she thought.

Di Amarra stilled, his brows knitting as if he were being forced to recall something unpleasant. "Do you know why he's on the run? Why he had to leave Rasharwi?"

She thought for a moment of what she'd heard of the Sparrow from listening to other people's conversations, pushing aside the anger that rose again in her chest, and shook her head. "Only that he'd killed someone important."

Di Amarra nodded. "The husband of a woman he knew. It was an arranged marriage by her family, a match for power and business opportunities. Turns out the general had a lifelong habit of abusing his partners in bed, one that had eventually driven her to commit suicide."

An ugliness settled in her stomach as Djari listened. *A woman*, he'd said. She didn't know what she was supposed to feel about that. The woman was dead, he'd also said, but death sometimes held more meaning than life. Her mother's definitely did. Her mother's had wiped out an entire village. "It was an act of vengeance then? The murder?"

"It was," said di Amarra. "The problem, iza Zuri, is that Hasheem had known all along what her husband was and had chosen to ignore it until it was too late. To top that off, Mara di Russo had decided to hang herself in his bedroom to make a statement."

The anger in his tone was not concealed. There was a meaning to that with regard to his affection for Hasheem. There was also another meaning to the story that brought to light the reason behind many of Hasheem's behaviors around her. Knowing him, she didn't even have to guess. "And he blames himself for it."

A nod from Deo di Amarra confirmed her thoughts. "Enough to throw his life away so he could carve up her husband. Enough for anyone to assume he would never make that same mistake again. And that, iza Zuri," he said, holding her gaze as if to make sure it would sink in, "is what you are—a mistake waiting to happen."

A mistake, he called her. And maybe that was what she was. What she felt for Hasheem, she admitted, could be called the biggest mistake she was ever to make as a Bharavi and his soul-bearer. But as much as she knew that was true, it need not end the same way. "I am not her," she said, grinding her teeth at the knife flung at her heart and the anger that came from somewhere she couldn't name.

"Are you not, iza Zuri?" He took no time to reply. No time at all. "You are a Bharavi, raised to marry the man of your father's choosing for power and the security of your Kha'gan. You will be made to breed, I'm sure, against your will, and as your sworn sword, Hasheem will be made to watch everything your husband puts you through. What you are is a repetition of a past he hasn't put behind him, a mirror image of a person he needed to save to close that wound. He isn't going to have it if your husband so much as looks at you the wrong way. If you break, for any reason—any reason at all—that he fails to prevent, it would be the last time we see him as the person we all know."

There was truth in what he said, tangible enough to make her see the shadow of the beast hiding around the corner. The fact that she had to marry wasn't new, and neither was the one that she would be used to breed. Many times. Perhaps as many as her body could endure. It brought back the memory of that night she had been shutting herself from, and Djari knew with every crawl of her skin and every wave of nausea that came with it why the woman called Mara di Russo might have done what she had. Having seen Hasheem that same night, she couldn't brush aside di Amarra's conclusion with any certainty.

"There is a monster in that boy, iza Zuri," he continued after a time.

"A monster the world has been feeding inside him since the raid that wiped out his Kha'gan. He lost his entire family overnight. His mother died holding him in her arms as they beat her to death. They kept him at Sabha for almost a year before he was sold at auction to the pleasure district, and anyone who has been at Sabha that long doesn't come out whole, especially a ten-year-old boy."

He broke off for a moment, his expression switching to a troubled one, though still calm and icily cold. "Hasheem has seen hell, my lady. He has lived in versions of hell most of us have never experienced, and while he's holding on to what's left of him that is human and good, you have become that one last torture needed for him to cross the line. And he *has* crossed that line many times—if unaware, mind you. They spent two days cleaning up the general's entrails from that room, and before that, I had to have the same mess cleaned up three times when he was on the job." He scowled at the memory, made a face of someone who had just swallowed something inedible. "As his mentor, I should have seen this last one coming. I could have dealt with it long before that. I am—" Deo di Amarra turned to look at her, his green eyes narrowed sharply as he spoke. "—trying to deal with it, this time."

The cloak felt heavy on her shoulders, and so were her limbs that seemed to have rooted her to the ground. She parted her lips to speak and realized she had nothing to say.

"Don't break, iza Zuri, no matter what happens," he said. His voice, she realized, had turned into a whisper so light, like a touch of a cold blade behind one's neck, that promised a quick and certain death should one make an undesirable move. "Because if you do, if you let loose that monster, I am going to have to kill him and you both. I do love that boy, iza Zuri," he said. "Don't make me."

The sun had disappeared somewhere behind the mountain. There was no light around them, none at all. No stars in the sky tonight.

"Keep the cloak," Deo di Amarra said, turning away as he did. "It will serve you well as a reminder."

The Brink of Chaos

"Where is the Salar?" Zahara asked her handmaiden, staring at herself in the mirror with a bad feeling in her stomach that something was about to go horribly wrong., The sight of her reflection only made it worse. The ceremonious, ankle-length crimson tunic had a v-shaped neck that did nothing to conceal the marks of his fingers around her neck. The bruise had become purple around the edges and would likely be visible to anyone standing within ten paces of her. She could really live without dragging that memory around at the moment.

"He hasn't come out of his chamber since last night," replied Kiara as she continued to braid Zahara's hair. Through the eyes of the other Rashai girls in the room, the tightness of her Shakshi handmaiden's jaw might offer a view that she was concentrating on the braiding, only Zahara knew it was more than that. There had been no words exchanged between them regarding what had happened (there had been no opportunities for them to be alone that morning), but Kiara had always been quick in observing and putting things together, and the damage had been enough to put her on edge.

Zahara shifted her gaze toward the nearby window. Outside, the sun was already halfway to its highest point, at which time the ceremony would begin. It was late morning, and the current Salar of Rasharwi was a notorious early riser, had been all his life. He rarely missed the morning bells that signaled prayer time even on nights when he'd gone to bed later than usual.

'Sleep is a complete waste of time,' he'd once said, bitterly. *'So many more things could be done if we didn't have to.'*

Such had been his belief for as long as she knew him. He worked tirelessly, Zahara hated to admit, on many things, from securing peace within the Salasar and strengthening its army to improving the infrastructure of its five provinces and their trading routes. There were times when he had awoken in the middle of the night to work on an idea that suddenly came to him, pacing back and forth until morning to try and test the new theory. The solution to build the Madira to bring water into the city had been among those. The canal was the first project he'd put into action as the Salar of Rasharwi, completed by the fifth year of his reign, and it was still being called the greatest accomplishment in the history of the Salasar today. He'd argued often that his most celebrated legacy had, evidently, come when he decided not to sleep.

Most accomplishments in his life had also been possible due to his habit of getting things done swiftly if not immediately, once decisions had been made. Knowing these facts, it meant that something was seriously wrong with how quiet things had been that morning.

He had, after all, caught her in an act of treason (she still didn't know who it was that had tipped him). Last night, she had expected to die, and since she wasn't dead, Zahara had been certain a mass slaughter of her people would follow first thing in the morning, and that arrests were going to be made as soon as the sun was up. So far he hadn't made a move or issued a single command. It wasn't like him.

Neither, she thought, was what he'd done last night.

She would remember it on her deathbed—the madness and chaos that had consumed the man who had spent nearly two decades torturing her, whose hands had, just hours ago, wrapped tight around her life with a genuine will to end it. There had been a fight within him then—Zahara could see it through the tears that had welled up from her shock and suffocation—one so violent it distorted his face, nearly disfigured it into something unrecognizable. He'd fought and fought then, his whole body trembling and straining to its limit, to finish a task that should have been so simple, so effortless for who and what he was. And then, when her world had begun to haze out of focus, her last breath used up and spent on her final moment of life, something tore through him, ripped him apart, and the man who had become her mortal enemy for the past eighteen years crumbled, collapsed, and cried out a sound that cracked open something inside of her.

The grip around her throat had released with a jolt, as if her skin had been on fire and it was burning through his hands, as if there had been some kind of acid or poison on her he'd forgotten about. But she knew—oh, she knew, from the devastating agony in his eyes, the pain, the anger, the disappointment, and the deep, deep hatred of his own weakness all rolled into one that had been written so clearly on his face with no way to hide—that there had been no amount of strength or will or reason he could have come up with that night or any time after to bring himself to kill her.

I have won this fight at long last, she had thought then, watching him from the wall she had crawled toward and pressed herself against some time later.

Silence had seized the room for what seemed like an eternity. He'd propped himself against the wall opposite to hers, the heels of his hands pressed over his eyes, his face completely shadowed by the arms that no longer looked as strong as she had come to know them.

'You want freedom?' he'd said at length and in almost a whisper, in a voice so drained of energy and conviction that made him sound so frail and fragile. His face, barely visible in the fading light of the lanterns, had gone as pale as a corpse's. *'I'll give you your freedom, Zahara.'*

Pushing himself off the floor, tying the belt of his robe absentmindedly, he'd turned to walk away, his shadow trailing after him like a long, dark stain on the carpet, like the one in her heart.

'I am done with you,' he'd said, keeping his back to her. His voice, she'd realized, sounded very tired. *'Take what you want and go. After the ceremony tomorrow, you do not come back here. You are free to leave, to do what you want to do with your life.'* He'd paused, drawn a breath, clenched his hands into fists. *'From here onward, I don't want to see or hear from you ever again. You will stay out of my life, out of my sight, and away from our son. Or they will all die. Every last one of them. That, I promise you.'*

And had walked away.

Zahara drew a long breath at the knifing pain in her chest as she recalled the event, wondering why there was a knife there at all. She should have considered it a kind of success, or at the very least a release from nearly two decades of pain and suffering, of having to bend the knee to an enemy she had longed to see dead. She hadn't felt any of it, not then, and not now that the initial shock had gone. There was nothing but emptiness inside her, as if her life had simply lost its purpose and she was now left alone in the dark, confused and not knowing where to go.

It made sense in a way, she supposed. She had, after all, been living every breath with a single determination to survive him. Somewhere along the way, his existence had become the only thing left she'd had to hold on to, the only incentive for her to draw whatever strength she had within her to remain standing. And now, even that had been taken away from her. Along with her son.

She might lose more than that if she couldn't get a message to Azram, Amelia, or the Salahari.

The plan had been to get her out of the Tower and into the streets, where a mob they'd paid for would be waiting. They had been counting on the Salar to lead the guards himself to deal with the situation as they held her hostage. Assassins had been placed along the way with poisoned arrows to shoot him from higher ground. When all was done, she would be allowed to escape from Rasharwi with a promise of Lasura's release once Azram was crowned. It all depended on the one gamble she had assured them would come through—that she held enough significance for the Salar to ride out of the Tower to save her.

A gamble that she had lost the moment he decided to come to her and end it all. Muradi, for all the monstrous things he'd done, had always placed the security of his reign, his ideals, his Salasar before all else. He was the kind of man who could do that—separate his heart from his head and could be counted upon to crush the former for the latter. Even now, when he'd failed to do just that, he had decided instead to eliminate her from his life completely, to remove the source of his weakness that everyone could see for good. It would be folly to believe now that he would come for her if the mob were to attack, and the mob *would* attack if she couldn't get word out to stop them. For all she knew, she could be burned on a pyre before she even reached the temple.

More than that, Muradi was aware now of their scheme (how much, she could only guess) and had up to that morning done nothing about it. From what she knew, all three of her accomplices had been advised to not leave their quarters by orders of Jarem izr Sa'id for security purposes. They were also closely watched by Jarem's new set of royal guards, which meant that it wasn't possible for Kiara to slip a message to them to call off the plan, or even if she could, that they wouldn't have been able to call it off without Jarem knowing.

For all she knew, the Salar might have been—should have been—ordering their arrests already, but so far he had yet to make a single move, hadn't even appeared from his room.

Something wasn't right. Zahara knew it in the pit of her stomach. She needed a moment alone with Kiara to discuss a way out of this mess, but Jarem had made sure the other handmaidens never let them out of sight.

Behind her, Kiara unfolded the red veil she was supposed to wear to the ceremony. It was customary for new converts and priestesses to cover their hair when entering the temple. For the ride there, however, Zahara had been instructed to leave her hair uncovered until she reached Sangi. The silver of a Bharavi's hair was a symbol to be displayed. That was the point of forcing her to change her faith in front of the crowd.

The veil was therefore draped over her shoulders instead, to be used later. As Kiara adjusted and smoothed it over her back, Zahara could feel something being slipped into her braid. She knew the weight of that object, the way it pulled on her hair. They'd done that countless times back in the Kha'gan. If you were born in the White Desert, you carried weapons on you at all times, including a backup one in case the rest were taken from you. It would come in handy if she ever needed one, but would it be enough?

⁜

JAREM IZR SA'ID stood by the balcony of his study with his hands behind his back, watching the procession down below with a grimace. The entourage that accompanied the Bharavi to the temple of Sangi consisted of thirty royal guards, four handmaidens—including the Shakshi girl closest to her—and a priest of Sangi sent to lead the procession. They had been instructed to take the longer route, passing through as many streets as possible and to make a full circle around the main square in front of the temple, where the biggest gathering would be waiting. The people of Rasharwi were to witness Zahara—the Bharavi and therefore an embodiment of Ravi herself—being carried on a sedan chair bearing the mark of the Salar for all to see. She was to be seen wearing the symbolic red tunic of their faith, surrounded by the royal guards in black and gold as she made her way to offer herself to the sun god.

It was a powerful message, a great way to smash the hopes of the Shakshis, a brilliant symbol and reminder of the Salar's victory at Vilarhiti. People would love this sacrifice. They would find their Salar just and willing to do what was right. It would solve all the problems at hand, strengthen the Salasar and Salar Muradi's rule.

Given that Jarem found out in time what in the nine hells was going on.

Imran, his trusted general, the man who was supposed to report to him this morning, was nowhere to be found. Up until last night, Jarem had spent every minute putting things into place, making sure everything was to go as planned while also making certain that none of it would reach the Salar's awareness. It was a huge risk for him to take—trying to deal with this treason on his own without informing the Salar in order to discreetly eliminate Zahara in the process. And the plan had been going well so far. He'd managed to confine all three accomplices, namely Amelia, prince Azram, and the Salahari, in the Tower under the pretense of tightening security, so when the time came they could all be exposed and arrested by the new guards he'd put in place days ago. He'd managed to get Yakim to be the one to suggest that Zahara be converted in this manner, had even managed to convince the Salar to agree by assuring him that she would be safely returned to the Tower afterward. It was a work of art, truly, to have done all this without getting any suspicion from the Salar that it had actually been Jarem who planted the idea in Yakim's head from the beginning.

He hated keeping secrets from his Salar, of course, and was expecting to be reprimanded for not informing his master immediately of the coup he'd discovered, but once all this was over and the three traitors had been arrested, Jarem was certain he would be forgiven, and perhaps even thanked for it. The Salar would probably be too mad with grief for a while anyway after the death of his Bharavi.

Said death was to occur after she reached the temple and once the ceremony was over. He had planned on killing her in the temple and placing the blame on Yakim for deciding to stick his cock where it didn't belong, and thus killing him, too, in the process. Two great things would be accomplished by this. They'd be rid of both Zahara and a priest the Salar had wanted dead for decades without angering the people. The priest's crimes would be exposed. The people of Rasharwi would thank him for it. A win-win situation for the sake of the Salasar.

It did, however, require that the mob those three snakes had paid for be stopped before it was put into action, for which he had prepared a troop in secret—to be led by General Imran—to deal with it this morning before Zahara left the Tower. It just so happened that he'd woken up to find Imran had somehow disappeared without a trace, and the troop was still waiting for someone to command it. He hadn't told Imran what the man was supposed to be doing, of course. It was important that as few people knew about the plan as possible until the last minute or else it might leak and ruin everything. The man had, however, been instructed with the utmost clarity to report to him at sunrise, which hadn't happened. Now he had to find a new substitute for the task or allow the mob to attack her.

It was a bold gamble on Zahara's part, Jarem had to admit, to have suggested using herself as bait. But it also meant that she was fully aware of her influence over the Salar, which, in turn, meant that she had to be eliminated as soon as possible, according to Jarem.

So from a perspective, he would at least manage to kill one bird if the mob were to be allowed to attack her on the way to the temple. She would likely die from it, or he could make sure she did (it wasn't difficult), and the traitors would still be exposed without any blame coming to Jarem for the death of Zahara.

The only problem was that he, too, believed the Salar would be down there to save her, which could kill him if everything were to go as Azram had planned.

The mob, therefore, had to be stopped. Or he would have to inform the Salar of all this as soon as possible, and also inform him of the assassins to make sure he didn't set foot outside the Tower. Jarem knew the Salar could kill him for this. There was a difference between a plan involving holding information from one's master that failed and one that succeeded, no matter how well-meant it was, and Salar Muradi had never been a forgiving man. He didn't take risks to give people a chance to mess things up the second time.

Jarem spent the next half hour pacing back and forth in his study to come up with a decision, and at last concluded that his life wasn't as important as the Salar's and his reign. If he had to die to save those two things, then Rashar had determined his life to hold such meaning. And with that, Jarem walked out the door to head to the Salar's chamber.

Only to find General Imran waiting outside in the corridor with what looked like the troop he was supposed to command.

He could have kissed the man at that moment, truly. "In the name of Rashar, Imran!" he said, half angry, half relieved to see the man. "Where the hell have you been all morning?"

Imran, clad in full armor and armed to the teeth, didn't reply. He stepped to the side and straightened, slamming his right fist against his chest as he did. The troop of a hundred men repeated the gesture in unison, splitting the ranks half way in the middle, the clanging of steel made by the abrupt, immaculately-trained action resonated down the corridor like a clap of thunder.

A man stepped out from somewhere around the back, walked up toward him through the neat, perfectly-formed path between the two formations. Behind him, a giant bodyguard followed just two steps behind.

"With me," said Salar Muradi of Rasharwi as he reached the front of the line. Rising above each of his shoulders, Jarem saw, were the gilded hilts of the two obsidian blades he only used for execution.

Lamb to the Slaughter

The girl screamed like a lamb in a slaughterhouse as his father fucked her, only lambs tended to stop screaming much sooner. The merchant's daughter couldn't have been much more than sixteen, obviously had never been touched by a man, and therefore hadn't lived long enough to understand that the point of rape was really because men loved to hear them scream.

Which was why the screaming didn't die down after a few minutes and would likely be repeated later tonight, Baaku imagined. It went on, one shriek after another, loud enough for anyone within a hundred paces to hear. Passers-by kept their mouths shut, of course. It might have been against the law to assault a Shakshi woman, but the emphasis was on *Shakshi*, not *woman*, and this one was from Harathi.

One of the many privileges of being Kha'a was the ability to choose the amount and nature of tax to be paid by caravans the way you liked. Every Kha'gan knew the size of the profits merchants made from trading with Makena—the richest and last free nation outside of the White Desert from where the finest silk and gemstones came. And since the only way to get to Makena by land was through the White Desert, the Kha'gans taxed whomever passed through their territories at whatever price they saw fit for the protection of the caravan and the use of their oases. It skyrocketed the price as well as profit of all goods from Makena, and when that happened, enough merchants could be expected to jump through hoops of fire to acquire these goods.

So when the Kha'a said the tax was to be paid by your wife or daughter in exchange for the entire caravan to make it in and out of the desert, the payment would be quickly delivered to his tent, screaming or not. These merchants always came prepared to lose something other than coins in any case. Most fathers understood the price to be paid for such high profits. The understanding, however, did not always extend to daughters or wives.

Baaku thought the practice might not have been received well at first by their own women either, but who was going to interrupt a Kha'a when said woman wasn't one of their own? You turned a blind eye to these things, and if you did that often enough, you adapted to it, learned to live with it, and eventually— conveniently—managed to forget it was wrong in the first place.

The same way Baaku had learned to live with his father's fist every time the old man was in need of something to beat up since he was six.

The same way his mother had learned to sit so still and unaffected while listening to her husband rape a girl as young as their daughter.

His two sisters, Akila and Naani, the first seventeen and the latter twelve, so far hadn't learned to live with it. The longer the girl screamed (which sounded like every fucking time his father slammed into her), they looked closer and closer to either vomiting or weeping, or both.

They couldn't do that, of course, not with the entire council in the tent and in the presence of a visitor.

Sitting opposite Baaku, Zardi izr Aziz, Khumar of Khalji Kha'gan, had been assessing both of his sisters since he arrived, seemingly oblivious to the screaming that had been going on the entire time. He was there to discuss his marriage with Akila—or Naani, should the first have already been promised to another Khumar. He was being made to wait, as per tradition, being only a Khumar and from a lesser Kha'gan. Things like that mattered when it came to negotiations.

Both of Baaku's sisters and his mother were also there, as per tradition. The law required everyone's consent when it came to marriage, including the girl being asked to marry. Such privilege was something Shakshi women had enjoyed for centuries, but if you were born daughter to the Kha'a or Khumar, you would be raised to show nothing but consent to marry any man your father chose for the good of the Kha'gan. It meant more food, more water, an ally, and therefore more protection during raids and internal conflicts. They didn't like it, of course, but such responsibility came with privilege, and only barbarians threw tantrums over responsibilities they had been born with. Denying or running away from a marriage might happen with daughters of a camel herder or a blacksmith, where a few goats were at stake. With daughters of Kha'as and Khumars, you could shame both your father and the man you were supposed to marry, and then spend the rest of your life cleaning the blood of thousands from your hands after the war you initiated. It simply didn't happen in the White Desert. Their women were raised independent, but never naive, spoiled, or self-centered. Out here, you couldn't survive outside the settlement, and if you wanted to survive in it, you learned to put the good of the community before personal interest.

It didn't, however, mean that Baaku enjoyed the screaming or the thought of this Khumar making one of his sisters scream, which was likely given the way he reacted—or didn't react—to the screaming from his father's tent.

*When I am Kha'a...*Baaku thought to himself, and then ended such a dangerous thought before one thing led to another. They couldn't afford more conflicts within the Kha'gan right now, not when the Salar was knocking at their door with an army big enough to paint the White Desert red.

And so he sat, fists clenching on the fabric of his zikh through the shrieks from the other tent, and then later through the negotiations when his father finally arrived. Baaku sat and listened (because that was all he was allowed to do) as they measured the value of his two siblings against coins, the number of warriors, horses, camels, and other livestock the Kha'gan could gain—in exchange, of course, for a powerful alliance and the delightful screaming of one of his sisters should the Khumar require it.

A small price to pay for the stability of the Kha'gan, one might say. An immense value to be attached to the life of one ordinary girl, if one were to look at it from a certain angle.

A torture bad enough, in any case, to send Baaku rushing out of the tent when it was done, shaking uncontrollably with the need for a drink, a drug, or an opportunity to kill something or someone as he headed toward his own.

To find Nazir in it.

The world seemed to come to a screeching stop around Baaku, or maybe it was just his heart. It happened. A surprise visit from Nazir could do that to him, had done so many times in the past.

It was nighttime and the tent was dimly lit, showing only the silhouette of a man sitting by his table with a book in his hand. Judging from the chunk that had been read, he must have been there for some time. Nazir looked up from the pages when Baaku entered, his yellow eyes glowing in the shadows that concealed the rest of his face.

"I thought you didn't need me," Baaku heard himself say, surprised at the spite in his own voice. He thought he had put it all behind him a week ago, when he had decided to walk out of whatever this was. He didn't realize how raw his wound still was until Nazir showed up. It pissed him off enough to do some real damage.

Nazir, being Nazir, didn't stir at that. He closed the book and placed it down softly on the table, unaffected by the words Baaku had thrown at him. "I can't sleep," he said.

That was all the explanation Nazir gave for being there; all the explanation he had ever given for coming to his tent, in fact. Even now, after what had been said the last time they met, there was to be no apology, not even a willingness to discuss it. He was supposed to forget and carry on as usual.

"Have you ever, Nazir?" Baaku remembered asking that night. *"Needed me in your life? Even once?"*

Nazir hadn't answered. His mouth had been clamped shut. Keeping something in, or keeping him out. Same difference. *You couldn't answer that question, could you? Couldn't even bother to lie to keep me in your life. And now you're here.*

He moved toward the desk halfway between them, took off the things he had been carrying, and dumped them on the table. Took his time doing that. He needed time. "Is that supposed to be my problem?"

"It isn't," Nazir replied without a pause, without a hint of emotion in that tone as he rose from the table. It didn't matter what Baaku said. Nothing ever got under that skin. "Would you like me to leave?"

The irony of it was that he didn't, and Nazir, knowing it with the accuracy of his goddamn vision, would always give him that ultimatum. *This is all I'm offering. Take it or leave it.*

And he had always taken it, had never managed to walk away. Even now, but for a different reason. At least, he believed it was.

"You can't leave right now," he said, sighing. "There are guards around. We have a visitor." Security would be tightened until the Khumar went to sleep. Nazir would have to wait it out. In here. His tent, Baaku realized, suddenly seemed crowded and small.

"I see," Nazir said. He was standing two steps away. Close enough for his breaths to be heard. For their breaths to be heard. "I'll wait, then."

He kept his back to Nazir, unnecessarily arranging things on the desk. An excuse, he knew, to not turn around. There were risks attached to that. "There's wine on the table."

"I know there is," Nazir said. Didn't move from the spot. Baaku wished he would. He wished he hadn't heard the question in that voice, or the vulnerability in it, either. He also wished those things hadn't settled in his heart and made such a big mess.

He wished for a lot of things when it came to Nazir. None of them had ever been granted.

After a moment, Nazir said, "Will you drink with me?"

The wind blew against the wall of the goat-hair tent, shaking everything in it. The question hung in the air between them, suspended there for what seemed like an eternity. Baaku drew a breath, and realized he hadn't done that for some time.

"I don't think so, no." He knew what would happen if he shared that drink, knew it like the ache in his own heart where that would lead to. It would bring them back to the beginning, back in the same circle, with Nazir using him to run from his visions, and him letting himself be used, eagerly, unconditionally, endlessly.

There was a pause from Nazir, followed by a drawn breath. A long one.

"This is it, then?" Nazir asked, the same way someone might have asked if you wanted food or wine. "Are we done?"

Those words, spoken in the way they had been spoken—as if it had been Baaku's decision, his call, his sin to carry—set something alight in his chest. The boiling, uncorked rage came up out of him like a flood, made him spin around to face the embodiment of his most persistent suffering in the past three years. "*What do you want from—*"

Words after words he'd meant to say crammed up at the back of his throat, held by the sight of Nazir's face that he could see clearly for the first time. There was a paleness to it that seemed to have aged him ten years, made more severe by the dark shadows under his eyes. His lips were pressed tight together, the muscles of his face painfully rigid and tense, like a man trying not to scream from a bad wound.

Nazir's robe made a soft sound as he stepped forward, pausing just a hand away from him. He pressed his forehead on Baaku's shoulder. His hands rose to grab a fistful of Baaku's sleeve, gripping it until his knuckles turned white.

It took Nazir a while to say it, and when it happened, the explanation came in a series of clumsy, almost incomprehensible strings of words, broken and interrupted by the excessive need for air. "They...took...Djari," Nazir stuttered, struggling at every syllable as if they had been bits and pieces of broken glass he was trying to spit out. "I saw...them. I see her... Those men...I can hear it. I...heard...I hear her screaming." Nazir's hands clung to his zikh, gripping it tight, hanging on as if it were the only thing left in life to hang on to. "...It doesn't...stop."

Baaku knew then, through the warmth and weight on his shoulder, his own rage draining away from him with every passing second, that there were things in life you didn't turn away from, things you treasured over your own heart, your own pain, to not let them break. To Baaku, Nazir was one of those things. Perhaps the only thing.

And so the circle would begin again, just like all those times before, and all the times that would follow. He knew it even as he reached out to wrap his arms around Nazir, as he held the trembling figure in his embrace, as he planted a soft kiss on his head and kissed again, that there was no way out of this for him, nowhere he could run without ending up right where they'd started.

Use me, then. Use me until you've spent your last breath. Let me be your source of strength until we tear each other to pieces.

"I've got you," he told Nazir. "I'll make it stop."

⁜

THERE WAS A SENSE OF CALM in the air when Nazir was here, curled up in his embrace, his head resting on Baaku's arm as he slept. He pushed back the strands of unruly hair away from Nazir's face, planted a soft kiss on his temple, and realized he could do this every day and still it wouldn't be enough.

"One day," he murmured softly, his fingers playing with a lock of Nazir's hair, "you'll be the death of me."

"Don't say that," Nazir said with his eyes closed. He must have been awake for some time and had simply lingered there, pretending to be asleep. He loved it when Nazir did that.

"I'd call it a good death," said Baaku, still playing with the lock of hair that kept falling back on Nazir's face. They were still clothed, both of them. On nights like these Nazir needed a rest, a good sleep. He'd slept like a baby last night. "Wouldn't mind that in the least."

"Maybe I would," Nazir said with a frown. His eyes were opened now. They were looking at him, reprimanding him. "Ever thought of that?"

Baaku pushed himself up on his elbow, studied that face as something occurred to him all of a sudden. "Is that what you've been afraid of?"

Nazir froze, clamped his mouth shut, and then abruptly rose from the bed. "I have to go. My father will leave soon. I should be at camp."

The convoy to bring Djari back from the Rishi was leaving that morning, Baaku knew—everyone knew. A gathering of five hundred White Warriors wasn't something one could hide in the White Desert, and they hadn't been hiding it. By then it was one of the most talked-about events and most likely known by Citara.

Nazir should be at camp—it was a sensible thing to do—but some questions were going to have to be answered that morning.

He caught Nazir by the wrist, pulling him back. "You saw something." It began as a wild guess, perhaps only half a suspicion, but from the way Nazir stiffened suddenly, Baaku knew it was more than that. "You had a vision, didn't you?" There was a reason why Nazir had tried and tried to put a wall between them, why he'd always held back despite the evidence that had proven the opposite. It dawned on him and brought everything up to the surface all at once. "What happens to us?"

It was all there on Nazir's face, in his eyes—the pain, the agony, the loss that confirmed Baaku's suspicion. "Nazir. What did you see?"

A sound from the outside drew both their attention to the door. Footsteps of men numbering in the dozens were heading toward his tent and came to a stop just in front of it. Nazir snatched the sword he'd placed by the bed, one hand already on the hilt, ready to clear the blade when the door opened.

Baaku jumped off the bed when the first man came in and realized, when he finally saw who it was, that there was no point to anything he might have or could have done to stop what was about to happen. None at all.

"I've always wondered if my pathetic, good-for-nothing son would ever produce anything useful," said the Kha'a of Kamara. "Seems you're not such a total loss, after all. Put the sword down, Nazir Khumar." He turned to Nazir. "There are eight hundred White Warriors waiting outside at my command. You can die here—"

Baaku stepped forward before he finished the sentence, placing himself directly between his father and Nazir. He wasn't carrying a sword, but the message should have been clear.

One of us is going to die here before that happens.

His father paused for a moment, stared him down in silence, and brushed it aside as quickly as swatting away a fly. "—or you can come with us willingly. It's not a problem for me either way."

"Go where?" He heard Nazir say from behind.

"To your father, of course," said the Kha'a. "To tell you the truth, I *have* been skeptical about dealing with a pureblood oracle after killing Za'in and his five hundred White Warriors in an ambush out there today.

It appears my failure of a son has just solved that problem." He made a gesture, and the two warriors behind him stepped forward, weapons in hand. "And since you seem to be getting along so well with my son, perhaps you will consider joining us instead, so I won't have to kill you and waste a perfectly good oracle. We'll talk about that when I'm done with Za'in. It's about time your father and I settle our unfinished business. Take him," he commanded the two zikh-clad warriors, "and make sure our own Khumar doesn't leave the tent until I return."

... never love
something so much
that you can't live
without ...
A World

Without You

The crowded room screamed of her absence. The voices around him were the wrong voice. Everything, from the one empty chair, the unclaimed spaces in the corners, the edge of the bed where he had hoped to find her, seemed to underline the fact that Djari wasn't there. She hadn't been since yesterday afternoon when he'd awakened, or later that night, or now.

It felt like waking up to a world without her in it, and somehow, he had a feeling that world was going to last.

Hasheem looked around the room as they changed his bandage and realized how familiar everything was. Sarasef and Dee were discussing something in the far corner with Bashir standing close by, waiting for a command. The healer and his helper were talking about his wounds, checking his pulse. The bedroom was the one he'd stayed in during his time here, before he had been bought by Dee. Everyone and everything, from the carpet to the chandelier on the ceiling and the mahogany bedside table had been a part of the memories of the Silver Sparrow.

I am back where I've started, Hasheem thought, feeling his time in the White Desert fading like a dream that had ended too soon. He realized then how much he missed it: those aching sunrises and sunsets over the smooth, powdery dunes; the silence and stillness outside his tent during the cold, cold nights; the smell of dried branches and sage in the wind that caressed his skin in the morning. That peaceful feeling in the stable, watching Djari with her horses. All of it was gone, lost as it slipped through his fingers like sand, like water you could only hold for so long before it all disappeared.

Since when has the White Desert become so much a part of me?

The wound throbbed as the healer wrapped the new bandage. His throat burned from the taste of the medicine and the fever he was still battling. On top of it all, the pain in his head felt like someone had taken a hammer to it. He was hungry, thirsty, tired, and now cranky from the presence of everyone in the room. Or from the one that was missing.

Where is Djari? He had wanted to ask several times from the moment he opened his eyes, had given himself explanations instead as to why she might not have been able to come—explanations he was running out of as time passed and Djari remained absent. Now, there seemed to be only one explanation left, one he didn't want to face just yet. Couldn't.

"So?" Sarasef said after the wrapping was done, looking down at him from the edge of the bed with a small frown. "Can he keep that arm?"

"I believe so, yes." The healer nodded. "Both wounds are healing nicely. He should be able to lift his arm freely in a week or two, but it would be a long while before he can fight."

Sarasef nodded, excused the healer and his help, and as soon as they were out the door, turned to Hasheem. "How are you feeling?"

He pushed back the hair that fell around his face, squeezed the bridge of his nose to counter the headache, and grimaced when it didn't help. "Like shit."

"You should be glad you're feeling something at all," Dee said, dragging a chair over to sit by the bed. He looked better now than yesterday when Hasheem had seen him. In the past five years they'd spent together, he couldn't remember if he'd ever seen his mentor so drained of energy. If it had been the possibility of his death that taxed Dee to that point, he'd never expected it.

But Dee was right. He should be glad. People didn't survive Zyren. The only reason he was still breathing was because he'd been force-fed the poison for five years straight, like all of Dee's assassins. Hasheem wasn't sure if he was supposed to be thankful for that. For all he knew, it could have been Dee who'd sold Saracen the poison.

Now that he thought about it, it probably *was* him. He wondered if Sarasef knew. Then again, it probably wouldn't make a difference. They went back a long way—Sarasef and Dee—but theirs was a relationship of such mutual understanding that killing each other was not off-limits if profits or sense demanded it so. *'It's the safest kind of relationship you can have, really,'* Dee had said once. *'One with no emotions attached. Just logic and reason.'*

"You, of all people, should know I'd survive," Hasheem said. It came out more bitter than he'd wanted it to. "I can't seem to die, no matter what I do." How he'd managed to survive this long when everyone else in his life was dead was a mystery. From the raid, the time spent at Sabha, the jobs he'd done for Dee, the escape from Rasharwi, being spared when caught by the Visarya, and now, even the deadliest poison in existence couldn't kill him. It felt sometimes that there was some divine being sitting up there having one hell of a time watching him suffer and keeping him alive for the sake of it.

As if Dee could read his thoughts, the corner of his lips lifted into an amused grin. "Sorry, kid. Just got to suffer like the rest of us for a while longer. Your role here isn't yet done."

"My role?" He could almost laugh at that. Almost. "What role do you suppose I have now? I can't do shit with these wounds." The plan had been for him to kill Saracen. It was the only card they had to convince Sarasef to side with the White Desert. With these wounds and the state he was in, that possibility was gone. Sarasef couldn't wait for him to heal. He couldn't afford to, especially with this latest assassination attempt.

He turned to Sarasef then, thought about it for a time, and decided to just deal with the issue. "What will you do now?"

"What will I do?" Sarasef traced the question like trying to describe the taste of something he'd been forced to eat. "Your Bharavi didn't really give me much of a choice. She muscled me into forming an alliance with the Visarya using your sacrifice to call on my honor. The other boy was released and sent back to negotiate that alliance four days ago. Za'in has accepted the offer. It's done."

Hasheem blinked. "She did that?"

Sarasef nodded. "While you were still sleeping. The reply arrived this morning."

Relief went through him like being doused with cold water in the midday sun. Hasheem sank into the pillow that had been propped against his lower back and allowed himself to breathe freely for the first time since he'd awakened. In a way, he should have seen it coming. Djari was Djari. She had her wits about her even in the most hopeless situation, and the guts to back it up. He wished he'd seen it though—that image of her trying to force Sarasef into agreeing to this.

"There is," said Sarasef, "just one problem to be discussed. They know who you are now."

The revelation hit him like walking into a barn to discover a corpse ten days late, and suddenly everything seemed to crumble. Of course—there had been no way to hide his identity after everything that had happened. That ugliness was out in the open, and there was no way to put it back.

He was the *Silver Sparrow*. That name would follow him everywhere, dictate everything in his life, no matter how long and how far he'd left it behind.

You thought you could run, didn't you? You were stupid enough to believe you could leave it all behind, start over, and the past wouldn't catch up and drag you down the same pit you crawled out of.

They would want him dead now if he were to set foot back into the Kha'gan. Even Djari couldn't fix that. If she still wanted him back.

'You traitorous whore,' the Bharavi of the Black Tower had called him once. He remembered her face then, the look in her eyes, the disgust in them that wanted to incinerate him on the spot. He'd wondered many times if Djari would have felt the same way had she known who he was. Now she knew, and she was avoiding him.

"I see," Hasheem said, pushing that thought aside. *She might still come. Tonight. Tomorrow. And everything would be as it was.* "So what happens now?"

Sarasef moved closer to the bed. Behind him, Dee leaned back on his chair, rubbing his thumb over the leather of the armrest. He did that when he was paying close attention to something, which told Hasheem this was also to be news to him.

"They want you escorted to Al-Sana, to stay there until this blows over. Then, you will be reintroduced into the Kha'gan with a new identity. That is the only way you can go back to the White Desert."

That surprised him. Gave him a glimmer of hope he hadn't anticipated. "For how long?"

"A few years." Sarasef shrugged. He had thrown a wild guess, from the looks of it. "Long enough for people to forget. Three. Maybe five."

Three to five years was a long time, but at the very least he could still go back. "Where is Al-Sana?"

"It's a mountain in the north of the White Desert," Dee replied instead, still rubbing his thumb on the chair's arm. "Treacherous to climb, so no one lives there except one zikh-clad warrior and the apprentices he chooses to train. Akai izr Imami is a legend. Everyone he's trained became Dyal champions at some point and ended up a Kha'a or on the council. If they want to send you there, it means they want you to train with him and return to hold a position." A grin appeared on Dee's lips at what seemed to have occurred to him just then. "Someone there understands your value as much as the two of us, it seems. Someone very, *very* smart."

Or had been given a vision, Hasheem thought. It had to be Nazir. No one else would have fought as hard for him to return, or had the power to influence that decision. "I see."

Dee tilted his head to one side, the same way he always had when trying to read his apprentice's mind. "You hate the idea."

"I don't want to hold a position in the Kha'gan." That came out easily. He had forgotten how honest and carefree he could be with Dee, how many times he'd confessed something to his mentor without holding back.

"Once, you wanted nothing more than to have control. You've worked and killed for it. Now you want anonymity?"

"Things were different then."

"How so?" Dee asked. "What is it that you have now that you didn't?"

He thought about that for a time. What was it that was different? His struggles in the Kha'gan were the same as in Rasharwi. He was an outcast, an excess no one wanted except for Nazir and Djari. He wasn't living any better, perhaps even worse than the life he'd left behind in the city. But there was, undeniably and persistently, a calling in his blood that had lingered since the hunt. A sense of peace even in the middle of chaos. A clear awareness of his own existence every time Djari was present. "A home," he said, and surprised himself as he did. A home he didn't want to lose.

There was an ache in Dee's smile, one that disappeared too soon. It suddenly occurred to Hasheem that his mentor might have considered himself a home to him after all this time. For a moment, he thought he should say something to rectify that, and then realized it wasn't needed.

Dee wasn't family. He wasn't home. He was a mentor who'd taught him everything he knew, a companion he could trust and be honest with, a helping hand that was always there when he needed it. Theirs was the kind of bond that didn't need to be nurtured, could be taken for granted even, and what he saw in those yellow-green eyes confirmed it so.

"I've warned you once," Dee said, "to never love something so much that you can't live without it. Do you remember?"

"I do."

"A home is one of them."

"I know."

"Then it isn't about what you want, is it?" Dee said, smiling like the first time he'd asked if Hasheem wanted to join his house of assassins. That memory was still so fresh in his mind. "There's only what you need to do, and what you must do to protect that which you can't live without. Fate will exact a heavy price for everything you treasure in life, and less so for those who treasure none. Only fools believe they can have something of value without sacrifice." He paused, leaned a little forward to look Hasheem in the eyes. "Go to Al-Sana and come back a man who can protect your home, if that is what you want. Or walk away from it, now, while you still can." He turned to Sarasef then, remembering something. "Does he have that choice?"

"Al-Sana is a part of the agreement," replied the Grand Chief. "But if he doesn't want to return, it can be accommodated."

"How?" Dee asked.

"The agreement rests on the fact that he is Djari iza Zuri's sworn sword.

They are willing to gamble on this because of his oath to her. If there were no such tie, they wouldn't risk it."

Dee frowned. "It would require getting her to release him from his oath, then. That could be a problem."

"It isn't," said Sarasef, turning to Hasheem now. "As of this morning, she has agreed to let you go."

Someone to Burn

The crowd wanted to see her burned.

Zahara knew this with the same certainty as she knew her own faith in Ravi. The heavy, distinguishable stench of pent-up, barely-contained need for violence was in the air as they paraded her down the streets of Rasharwi where men, women, and children had gathered to watch in large numbers. Retribution was needed—you could see it in their eyes, in the tightness of their jaws, the sneers on their faces. The riot had killed many citizens. All that loss and rage had to go somewhere. People anywhere needed someone to punish for their pain, someone convenient, someone not of their own if it could be accommodated. It wasn't even hate. It was simply the need to see someone else's suffering so they could live with their own.

Sangi temple and fortress were to the east of the city. The planned procession was to begin at the base of the Black Tower from its northern gate, then proceed via a longer, circular route around the Tower, passing through the western and then southern districts before taking the East Bridge across the Madira. They would make another round there, from north to west to south, passing through the poorer districts of the city before reaching the ceremonial square of Sangi temple in the east.

The mob they'd planned and paid for was to attack them on the last street before they reached the square as they left the southern districts. It would require the Salar to pass through the most number of streets and alleys should he ride out to get to her. She had no idea where the assassins had been placed along the way. There were said to be many, to make sure he didn't survive once out of the Tower. They had been instructed to shoot him from the rooftops with Zyren on their arrowheads. He would die, for certain, and quickly if he were to come out of the Tower. The mob would then keep her safe, waiting for things to quiet down before she was released, and Lasura would be freed once Azram was made Salar.

That plan, however, had been thrown out the window since the night before. He wouldn't come for her now that he'd decided to let her go. Prince Azram, his mother, and Amelia might have already been arrested. For all she knew, the mob might not have been called off, unless Muradi had known about that, too. It was a possibility, given who he was, but one so small only fools would count on it to survive, and she was not among them.

In the event that the mob had been dispersed, her next problem would be at the temple. Zahara didn't know which of the two leaders she was more afraid of. She had seen and heard of Yakim izr Zahat, the High Priest of Sangi, had noticed the way he looked at her in the past. A woman's intuition wasn't always right, but it was rarely wrong, and Zahara's intuition told her that Yakim would have her on his bed before the night was over if she ever reached the temple. As of that day, she was no longer protected by the Salar of Rasharwi. What would happen before or after the ceremony was something she had to survive on her own. Muradi had left no instructions that she knew of to any of his men. He'd simply said she was never to return.

Something hit her on the shoulder. Zahara looked down and saw an onion at her foot. The guards turned with her toward the direction it had come from. The small boy who'd thrown it ducked quickly behind his mother, who then placed her arm protectively in front of him. The mother and son were waved off by the guards with a small warning before they proceeded forward. Zahara turned to look and saw the woman smiling at her son as she congratulated the boy. He beamed back the smile of a celebrated hero. The crowd smiled, too at the boy and the mother, in approval. *Good job*, they said with their eyes. *Brave boy,* someone whispered.

Whispers, of course, could travel faster than any procession as long as there were no gaps in the crowd to break them, and if Muradi had been there he would have had both mother and son whipped in front of the crowd until no one was smiling, right where they were. '*You have to be ready to get rid of the flint, not to put out the fire*,' had been Muradi's reasoning when he ordered someone executed for defying an officer, '*or you'd be killing thousands when you only needed to kill one.*'

He had a point, Zahara had to admit. It wouldn't be long before *good job* became *good idea*, and *brave boy* became *brave people*. By then she had crossed the Madira into the poorer districts. The rich and the middle-class inside the ring formed by the canal might hold back their anger for fear of losing something valuable. The poor, with nothing valuable to lose and only satisfaction to be gained, wouldn't hold back if they wanted to stone someone to death.

'*An empty stomach makes people stupid and suicidal*,' she remembered Muradi's words, spoken one night when he'd been in the mood to talk. '*Poverty is the greatest threat a nation can face.*' He knew the problem existed in Rasharwi, of course. Had known since he was only a prince, and had been fighting it long before she was captured. She also remembered how the poor had loved him when she first came to Rasharwi. It had made sense then, as it still did now. After all, the prince had been one of their own—the only member of the royal household, in fact, who had mingled with the poor, shared their tables in bars and taverns, gambled, raced, wrestled, even engaged in fistfights here and there without bringing soldiers into it. The fact that they'd wanted him on the throne and had celebrated for the whole month when he ascended was no surprise to anyone.

But for all that he'd tried to solve the problem of poverty in Rasharwi, the steady rise in population ever since the Madira had been built to bring life to the former desert city had slowed the progress to a crawl. People from everywhere flocked to the city for its comforts and opportunities, and when they didn't make it past the competition, they ended up here, on the other side of the Madira, contributing to the population problem and looking for someone to blame for their incompetence, or for the wrong choices they'd made, or both.

It fell, of course, upon her people and their land to solve the problem. An expansion was needed, and conquering the White Desert—and Makena—could fix it. The Rashais believed it. They believed if the Salar took the White Desert, all problems would be solved. They believed if a Bharavi bowed to their god, they'd win the war. They believed she'd bewitched the Salar and kept him from achieving that goal, and that if they shamed her and stoned her to death their suffering would be gone. People would believe anything convenient to them, and they'd hate anyone most convenient to hate with the least consequences.

The people of Rasharwi called her the Witch of the Black Tower. She remembered Muradi laughing then, telling her it had to be the understatement of the long history of the Salasar, and had simply waved it off. In many ways, she had been a threat to his reign ever since he'd taken her here. And yet for eighteen years, Muradi had kept her alive and protected with all his power, despite the increasing number of people who'd wanted to see her dead. That protection, Zahara realized with a bad feeling in her stomach, was no longer there now.

She looked up at the Black Tower looming behind them, imagined a figure dressed in black standing at its peak, and a sudden, unwelcoming sense of nostalgia flooded through her. Somehow, a part of her felt missing, left behind in the chamber at the top of that mountain of obsidian, and in its place was a void she had yet to find a way to fill.

Someone threw an object at her. Another vegetable flung by an angry-looking middle-aged woman. The guards didn't see it. Only Kiara, who looked at her with a half-worried, half-furious expression did. Zahara shook her head and gave a small signal for her handmaiden to stand down. In that kind of situation, it was better not to anger the people further. They were near the southern district now. If she could get past that without a major incident, it meant that Muradi had dealt with the mob and Yakim would be her only problem. This mob, if formed, would be real. They would see the Witch of the Black Tower burned if it could be done.

It could, of course, be done.

And Fate, as always, had her own plans in these things.

What happened after that was a series of events that toppled atop one another, too fast and too chaotic for anyone to grasp or say for sure what exactly had started it.

She was still in the western district when the next object was thrown at her, this time accompanied by a curse that did alert the guards. Sensing a more serious threat than before, two guards were dispatched from the procession to deal with the man at fault. At the same time, another vegetable landed on her exposed collarbone, making a loud popping sound that drew the attention of the guards on the other side. She looked down, saw a smear of red liquid on her chest, and before she could tell Kiara it had only been a tomato, her handmaiden leaped in front of the sedan chair, a dagger produced out of nowhere in her hand and ready to end the next attack before it began. The guards rushed in to surround Kiara, believing it to be an escape attempt, stopping the procession as they did. Somewhere nearby, someone was yelling something. It was repeated by more people down the streets in front of and behind them, and before anyone realized what was happening, the noise escalated into a roar that could be heard two streets down.

Zahara, seeing a new group of people running out of the nearby alley to join the current crowd, wheeled and saw that the path behind her had already been blocked by hundreds of people who had gathered to see the commotion. As the roar grew louder and louder, more things were being thrown at her from every direction. Some of them hit the guards and the sedan bearer, and before she could hold on to something, the chair tilted to the side, throwing her off the seat and onto the ground.

Behind her, Kiara shouted something amid the now deafening roar of the mob as she fought her way through both the guards and the crowd toward Zahara. A man snatched Kiara's arm and dragged her out of the way before she could get close to the sedan. Zahara, rising to her feet, looked around for where the largest number of guards had congregated and decided to run toward them. They had orders to protect her, and therefore were her best chance to survive.

The Salar's men had formed a somewhat broken circle around the back of the procession, trying to keep the crowd away with their shields. To her relief, they seemed to be managing it to a point, and were beginning to gain back some ground between the sedan and the crowd.

And then she saw it—how everything went wrong in a blink of an eye.

One man near the front line took something out of his pocket. Before anyone saw what it was, a guard stepped in and, out of sheer instinct or panic, slashed the man with his sword in a single stroke from shoulder to hip. The man went down, crashing into the ground face-first, twitched a few times, and died within seconds.

There was a moment of stunned silence around the dead man—silence Zahara knew was going to be the calm before a storm. The first blood had been spilled, the flint had been struck, and now a raging fire was going to claim the city.

The mob closed in on them with a roar that could drown out thunder, filling up the streets from every corner like swarms of bees from ten different fallen hives coming together and aiming for one single target: her. She paused in the middle of her planned direction, realized the number of guards was nowhere near sufficient to control this crowd, and decided to turn to the nearest building to get out of the street, taking her chances at hiding in it.

She might have made it there in the middle of that chaos, might have even been able to slip through the crowd as they fought each other by simply covering up her silver hair, if only she hadn't been the only one wearing the red robe of a priestess in a three-block radius.

It didn't take long for them to grab her. It took even less time for them to bind her hands and feet and put her back on the sedan chair. The procession, one could say, resumed on the same path to the same destination it had been heading to, only now she was being carried and escorted by the people of Rasharwi instead of Muradi's men toward the altar in front of Sangi.

To be burned.

For Pride and Honor

Jarem had a vision of his head rolling across the floor to stop just short of the Salar's feet, and his master looking down at it with disappointment on his face—perhaps also a hint of regret for having trusted him this far.

It was the worst nightmare for a soldier—to die knowing his life hadn't made a difference, that his loyalty had been doubted.

He thought of saying something to fix the situation—an excuse, a good reason perhaps—and realized it could be considered an insult to his master's intelligence. The only thing to be done to justify his actions, Jarem decided, was to come clean and accept whatever judgment the Salar deemed appropriate. Traditionally, however, or at least under the rule of Salar Muradi, what he had done incurred the death penalty.

Jarem adjusted himself and straightened as he saluted the Salar. He was ready for that, too, and had been from the beginning.

"How much has Imran told you, my lord?" He asked what he needed to know, what he *had* to know, before he was to be executed. The truth was Imran should have had no knowledge of anything at all. The general had never been a part of any conversation. He had been kept outside of the loop and had only been ordered to tighten up security and to report here this morning, no more.

The Salar, dressed in his most formal attire as though he were about to attend an important ceremony, seemed a little pale and worn down that morning, as if he hadn't slept for the whole night. His expression was flat, unreadable, like that of a statue whose sculptor had failed to bring it to life. "I know everything, Jarem," he said. Words so softly spoken, yet made shockingly loud in what they implied. "Imran was ordered to follow, observe, and report to me on everything you did."

Jarem looked at the general then, trying to read the man he'd trusted and fought alongside since the battle at the Vilarhiti, and found no trace of guilt on that face. On it was only pride—the pride of a man who had done his duty to perfection. It only occurred to Jarem at that moment how much of a fool he had been to have believed Imran was loyal to him. He may have been the commander of Imran's division for two decades, but the men at the Vilarhiti had fought and died only for one man—the one standing in front of him now, just like then, with those obsidian blades on his back.

"I see," said Jarem. "Since when, may I ask?" *How long since you stopped trusting me?*

"I've never trusted anyone, Jarem," replied the Salar, to the real question that hadn't needed to be spoken. "You, of all people, should know this."

It was an answer in itself, really, for the Salar to have refused to go into specifics. *From the very beginning, of course.* "I suppose I do," said Jarem. *Except Ghaul,* he wanted to say. He didn't say it. It wasn't the time to express that kind of bitterness. Besides, he knew the explanation for that well enough. Ghaul had been someone who survived Sabha with the Salar—the prince at that time. If there was one person in this world the Salar would trust, it was always going to be Ghaul.

But a man could wish he might one day gain such trust if he stayed loyal long enough. A man could wish he might also one day become an exception, couldn't he?

As it happened, he wasn't going to live long enough for that.

"May I presume that you have dealt with the traitors, my lord? And the mob?" There were more important things that must be done and corrected before his execution.

The Salar nodded. "The mob has been called off. Azram, his mother, and Amelia are being detained, and so are the assassins you've sent into the temple."

Jarem sighed in relief. At least those problems had been solved. He could die without worrying about these things, even if the Witch would still be alive.

"I have," said the Salar, in a slightly altered tone, "also released Zahara from the Tower, as of today."

Jarem's jaw dropped open at that. "You have, my lord?"

"I know she's a threat, Jarem," said the Salar. "I've always known. You might have had more faith in my judgment. I have expected that much from you."

There was a trace of disappointment in the Salar's tone, if no more than a hint. It had been enough to tell Jarem, however, that somewhere along the way the opportunity to gain that trust had been given, but at the very first true test of loyalty, he had gone and done this thing. "I might have." He understood that now, and much too late. "I *should* have, my lord. I have failed you."

There was a pause from the Salar, a trace of hesitation Jarem hadn't seen often. He was in a different mood that morning. "You will not ask for forgiveness, then?"

Jarem smiled, painfully. "Now you have failed me," he said. "You know better than to ask that question, my lord. You cannot afford to forgive me, not for this. As your advisor, I would never ask you to do so. I may be a fool to have misjudged your strength to rule, but you might have had more faith in my loyalty and my pride. I have, my lord, expected that much from you."

And he had expected that much from the Salar, if trust was never to be given to the likes of him. People who begged for forgiveness didn't deserve to be forgiven. You accepted the consequences of your actions if your guilt was genuine. He had prepared to die the moment he set these plans into action, had known it might come to this, and made his peace with it. "You need to kill me for this to set an example, my lord. All I ask is that you let me die honorably, and without my loyalty being questioned." An honorable death, at least, was what Jarem knew he would be given. There was a reason, after all, for the Salar's formal attire that day. He had almost forgotten how thoughtful this man he had served for more than twenty years could be.

"To set an example," the Salar said, more to himself than to Jarem. He smiled then, bitterly, sardonically, as if he suddenly remembered a bad joke from the past. There was an ache to the way he'd spoken those words, one that bled into the room, and twisted something in Jarem's heart.

And then, like a veil being lifted from his eyes, like a clearing of a fog that had been clouding his vision, Jarem realized he knew the true meaning of those words and the expression on that face—the same one he had witnessed years before. The Salar—the crown prince at the time—had looked exactly like this one afternoon almost two decades ago, the day he had gone to the throne room to kill his father, the former Salar of Rasharwi.

'*What was it that you told me, father?*' The prince had said, pressing the knife on the Salar's throat, taking his time to drag it across. '*Examples must be set? Sacrifices must be made?*' His whole body had trembled then, his jaw clenched as tight as the hand that held the blade. '*You should have killed me then and set your example. Then I wouldn't have to kill you both.*'

The boy who was said to have never shed a single tear in Sabha, the same one who had grown into a man and later become the conqueror of Vilarhiti had stood then, above the corpse of the father he'd just slain, his whole body covered in blood from having fought his way in, and cried, once and only once. The day he became the Salar of Rasharwi.

He had ruled, since then, with countless examples set and sacrifices made, and every time, the face of that young man above his father's corpse had returned, if only for a split second. Jarem had never put it together until now. Had been ignorant enough to not see how much it had been taxing him to do these things.

And now he was asking the same of the Salar—to set an example, for his own honor and pride, for the safety of the throne.

You wanted *me to ask for forgiveness. And I have failed that too, haven't I?*

"My lord..."

The sound of the two obsidian swords being drawn cut him off mid-sentence, made a hundred men in that corridor jolt like they had been struck by lightning. The identical, indescribably sharp blades that had been handed down to every Salar of Rasharwi from his predecessor gleamed brilliantly in the beam of sunlight that came in the window. Somehow, a measure of peace settled in the silence that occupied the hallway.

It was time.

"You have been with me from the start," said the Salar. "This, I do not forget."

Jarem drew a breath and lowered himself to the floor, balancing his weight on both knees. His joints screamed at him for that. *I'm getting too old for this anyway.* "Nor will I, my lord."

"You will die with honor. Your loyalty has not been questioned. This, you have my word."

It was enough for him to know. Enough for a soldier to die without regrets, for his life to hold meaning. "Your kindness will not be forgotten, my lord."

The Salar nodded. If there had been hesitation, it didn't show. It was what he admired about this man; once a boy he had helped raise to become the next Eli the Conqueror, and perhaps, even, to succeed him.

"Your last words, Jarem."

Jarem izr Sa'id prostrated himself on the floor, stretching out his hand toward the hem of the Salar's black robe, and brought it slowly but steadily to his lips. There were no regrets in his heart then; none whatsoever to have lived and served this man.

"May all your dreams be realized, my lord Salar."

The two blades crossed in front of him, the open end of the X they formed trapping Jarem's neck in the middle. He could feel the weight of them on his shoulders then, and could feel also a tremble so small no eyes would have noticed as they slid against each other. Then everything turned black, and he could feel no more.

⁜

THERE WERE FEW THINGS in life that could shake Imran as a grown man, and it wasn't the sight of Commander Jarem izr Sa'id's head rolling off his shoulders, but that of the man who'd taken it that did so. The man who, as he stood watching the blood of his trusted subordinate dripping down the length of his blades, appeared to be carrying the weight of the world and that of everyone in it, alone. Wrapped around him then was a void so large and desolate the presence of more than a hundred men could do nothing to fill it—a cocoon of isolation guarded behind a wall no one could penetrate. He was still a figure so large, so grand among men, but one that Imran could feel had come dangerously close to breaking. It would take just one more blow, one last strike directed at his heart, for that control to come tumbling down.

Change was in the air after the death of the Commander. A good man had fallen that day, but something else that had been holding important things together had crumbled along with him. Imran wondered then, if the Commander could sense it, somewhere in the hallway where his soul might still linger, how his death was going to change the entire peninsula. If he could see, even now, the way Salar Muradi was standing above his corpse, both arms hanging loose, holding the swords as if they weighed a ton, as if that one single strike had drained the last of his strength. Jarem izr Sa'id had been the right hand man of the Salar, but that day, one could say he'd cut off both his arms in the process, not just the one.

And he would lose even more than that, if one considered how Commander Sa'id's wasn't the only execution the Salar would have to carry out that day.

There was his son—the *third* son now—his Salahari, and his newly-wedded wife Amelia. To set an example. For the security of the throne, the Salasar, and every life in it. It was for those things, and those things only, Imran knew. For the past two decades he had served this man both as a prince and the Salar of Rasharwi, there had never been a day he could say that the Salar had ever enjoyed his position. It was simply something he had to do, the only way he could make sense of his existence, a punishment even—one he seemed to have chosen to bestow upon himself to pay for some crime he had committed.

And he had, as of that day, driven away the only woman who might have come the closest to giving his life another meaning. One would have to be blind to not see it, the way his mood shifted when she entered the room, how much strength had been drawn from her presence in the past eighteen years. Commander Sa'id had seen it. It was why he'd thought she had to die, but he had forgotten why she also had to live.

The roar that came in through the window of the commander's study tore him from his thoughts. The Salar turned at the same time he did to the direction of the sound. Imran ran over to look out the window. Outside, a mass of people large enough to be seen from the Tower was pouring from every direction into the streets leading toward Sangi. It didn't take long for him to realize what was happening.

It took even less time for the Salar to realize it.

"Ghaul!!" Imran yelled at the top of his lungs as he ran back toward the door, knowing in his heart that this would be that last strike needed—

—and was proven right the moment he saw the black robe of the Salar from behind, its owner already halfway down the corridor.

"Guards!" Imran was screaming now, running as he did. "Block that exit. Don't let him leave the Tower! Ghaul, stop him!"

Ghaul, who had been following just two steps behind the Salar as he always did, turned to look at Imran, indecision written all over his face.

"There are assassins in the streets waiting to kill him! He can't go down there!"

The explanation sent Ghaul running ahead of the Salar to cut him off. "My lord," he said, "forgive me."

The Salar stopped in his tracks, turned swiftly to check his surroundings, and upon realizing all exits had been blocked, reached behind him for the blades he'd sheathed just before he set off and cleared them without a second of hesitation.

Ghaul, to his credit, didn't even flinch at the threat. He took a firm step forward, made sure his intention to not move from the spot was crystal clear. "I can't let you go, my lord. It's not safe down there."

From behind, Imran could see the rise and fall of the Salar's shoulders as he breathed. The last time Imran had seen him that mad was during the massacre at the Vilarhiti. *This isn't going to end easily, or well,* he thought. "My lord, let me take the men to get the lady Zahara. You don't have to go. We can get her back. Your people need y—"

"I will say this once and only once," said the Salar as he looked over his shoulder, his voice lifted to carry a command that could cut through steel. "You will come with me, down there, with a thousand men at my back, or you will get out of my way. Challenge me, and there will be blood in this corridor." He stepped into position, raised both blades in his hands, ready to strike. "It's going to take more than a hundred men to kill me. The first man among you who wants to die trying to kill Salar Muradi of Rasharwi will come forward and clear your sword now, on the count of three, or I will take my pick. *One.*" His voice filled every inch of the corridor, rang louder than thunder, clearer than the wrath of a god should one ever come down to strike.

"My lord," said Imran.

"*Two.*" The whole Tower seemed to shake at the sound. *It might even come down*, Imran thought, *if this continued.*

Ghaul stepped forward then, pain written on his face as he faced his master, his axe lowered in submission. "I have sworn to protect you with my life, and I will die protecting you. I am the first you will have to kill, my lord. My *Prince.*"

It froze the Salar on the spot, that last word Ghaul had chosen to address him with, and from behind, Imran could see the hands that held the swords tremble from where he was, and was certain the rest of the men had seen it too.

The Salar, a figure only half the size of his giant bodyguard, stood looking up at him, his breathing becoming lighter, shallower now, judging from the movements of his shoulders from behind.

It was spoken in almost a whisper, meant only for Ghaul to hear, but proximity had also allowed Imran to make out a few words from the Salar to the last man alive who held his trust.

When he was done, when those words had been said, Imran knew with a certainty he couldn't deny that they had lost this fight. There was to be no running from the path Fate had drawn for them—the path that had begun one evening after the battle of the Vilarhiti, when a woman was sent, dripping wet from her head to her toes, into the tent of the crown prince who later became the most powerful man in the Salasar. A woman who now held the fate of the entire peninsula in her hands.

"*Then you might as well kill me, Ghaul,*" the Salar said. "*That is my life they are trying to burn.*"

One thousand men left the gate of the Black Tower that morning, riding not so far behind Salar Muradi of Rasharwi, his bodyguard, and Imran izr Imran, now Commander of the Royal Army—the general who had been promoted right after the death of Jarem izr Sa'id and whose name would later be written by historians throughout the Salasar as the man responsible for ending Salar Muradi's reign.

A Declara

'Our people are free because we're free to fight, free to decide if we want to live or die. If we can't go where we want to go, love who we want to love, then tell me, what the hell are we fighting for?'

tion of War

The death of his father had come when he was thirteen. That vision, among many, had been one in which the gods decided to not reveal to him the time and place it was to happen. All Nazir had seen was that Za'in izr Husari would die from a blade, stabbed from behind his left shoulder, the tip coming out on the other side to pierce through his heart. He wore white, which was something he did regularly as Kha'a. It would happen in the middle of the desert, where he traveled frequently to hunt or in answer to a summons made by Citara. The landscape had never been clear to Nazir in his vision, and through the glimpse of what he had seen, no recognizable landmark had been there. The killer, too, had never been shown to him. These visions that had come to Nazir more than once gave him nothing to prevent any of it. The only sense of time they had ever offered him was the fact that his father looked to be the same age he was now when he died, and he had looked that way for more or less ten years now.

It would happen in broad daylight, on a day like this, where the sky was a deep shade of blue and mostly clear, save for the small clusters of clouds that looked like someone had left clumps of wool on it after shearing a sheep. But a day like that came often in the desert, and no matter how many things seemed to be going wrong that day, or how prominent that bad feeling in the pit of his stomach was, it didn't mean the death of his father would happen today. Wars and conflicts had always been and would continue to be a large part of Za'in izr Husari's life. It was likely—honorably even—for him to die that way, and not necessarily this day.

Or so Nazir told himself as he rode with the Kamara Kha'gan toward where his father and his warriors would be. They had brought him along on the ride in case leverage was needed. His hands had been tied in front of him, secured to the saddle of a horse that had also been tethered to a White Warrior's mare. Baaku had been held somewhere back at camp. They had him tied up, too, beaten into submission by order of the Kha'a. He had, after all, put up such a fight that it took four armed men to hold him down.

Aza'ir izr Zakai, the Kha'a of Kamara, had brought with him eight hundred White Warriors to fight his father. Among them, Nazir had overheard, was the Khumar of Khalji, Zardi izr Aziz, who had contributed to that number with his own two hundred zikh-clad warriors. It meant that this alliance and attack had been planned for some time, which didn't surprise Nazir. His father and Aza'ir Kha'a had been rivals for longer than anyone could remember. Nazir had never been told the story in detail. He only knew that it had begun over something inconsequential that happened one Dyal in Citara. Things had somehow escalated, accumulated, and intensified since then. Deaths upon deaths had piled up from their conflicts over the years until a truce became simply out of the question. It was why he'd never considered Baaku's proposal as anything but folly. Their fathers would try to kill each other if they were put into the same room for too long. They had, after all, wanted to kill each other for decades.

But Baaku was Baaku. He never thought anything was impossible. The fact that their Kha'gans were rivals had never, not once, stopped Baaku from pursuing him, hadn't even made him hesitate.

'I don't give a fuck if your father wants to kill mine,' he'd said the first time Nazir found him in his tent one night. *'Our people are free because we're free to fight, free to decide if we want to live or die. If we can't go where we want to go, love who we want to love, then tell me, what the hell are we fighting for?'*

What, indeed, were they to fight for if not for those things? Small pleasures that made life worth living. The freedom to make choices even if it might lead to an undesirable outcome. Is life not measured by how it was lived rather than how it ended or how long it lasted? Was it so wrong for him to seek some meaning to his life besides what it meant to others?

'*We may die tomorrow for all I know,*' Baaku had said, his face softened in the dim light of the tent. '*I don't want to die not having done this.*'

He remembered his own words then, also the beating of his own heart. '*You could also die doing this, Baaku.*'

Baaku had shrugged and smiled. '*Can't think of a better way to die, if you ask me.*'

Nazir had known then, as he made those five steps toward their first time together, how powerless he was against the hands of Fate or whatever gods had drawn a line for them to meet, only to have things end up the way they were now or were going to end in the future. The vision of Baaku's death had also come at that precise moment, when a space so large, so permanent in his heart had been seized and occupied by this man without his consent.

Baaku had worn a sash bearing the rank of Kha'a in that vision. When he was made into one, that future would be one step nearer.

It could happen today with what was about to go down. A fight between Kha'as was always to the death. Before the day was over, either he or Baaku would be made Kha'a.

Either way, I will lose one of them. Perhaps more than that, if one considered what would happen to Djari and Hasheem should his father lose this fight.

One of those possible futures was there now, staring him in the face as his father's company came into view.

The two armies met on a wide, empty plain a little under an hour's ride out of the Kamara's main camp. His father had paused and turned the group around the moment he realized he'd been followed. They took positions now, facing each other about a hundred paces away.

The battle didn't happen the moment they ran into each other; it would never occur that way in the White Desert. There were codes, honor, and traditions to consider in these things. A formal declaration of war was to be given before any fight to hold merit in the eyes of Citara. Witnesses from both sides to the agreed-upon terms had to be spared to report to the White Tower. A breach of these rules and traditions could cost a Kha'a his position, and sometimes also his Kha'gan if Citara demanded it.

His father urged his mount forward, followed by two of his chosen witnesses. Aza'ir Kha'a met him halfway with two of his own, one of which was leading Nazir's horse along to the meeting. He had anticipated this. Aza'ir could be expected to stop at nothing to damage his father's reputation, including using his son.

But if there was one thing Za'in izr Husari was known for, it was how calm he could be during the worst situations and how impossible it was to break that calm. The fact that the Kamara were there with eight hundred warriors didn't seem to trouble him, nor did seeing his son captured by the enemy. He simply took one glance at Nazir and shifted his attention back to the other Kha'a.

"Do I terrify you that much now, Aza'ir," said his father, "that you would go so far as to kidnap my son for leverage?"

A chuckle rose from Aza'ir's throat. Nazir braced himself at the sound, knowing the reply that would come. "Why don't you ask him what he was doing at my camp in the middle of the night? Or maybe you were the one who sent him to spy on us by way of seducing mine?" He then turned to Nazir. "Did it work, Nazir Khumar? Has my idiotic son spilled more than his seeds when you sucked him off?"

Refusing to rise to the occasion, Nazir kept his eyes on his father, didn't say a word. There were more important things than his reputation at that moment. His father knew it too, and brushed the insult aside just as quickly.

"I see," said Za'in izr Husari. "If my son has breached your territory, then you have the right to hold him hostage and demand a form of punishment. Only," he paused, the corner of his lips lifting into a sneer, "that is not why you are here, is it, Aza'ir?"

"No," said the Kha'a of Kamara. "It isn't."

Za'in nodded. "State your business, then, and be done with it."

"Very well," said Aza'ir izr Zakai. "I am here to lay claim to your life, your Kha'gan, and all its territories. You will fight us, here, until the battle is decided, or you can surrender both your life and your Kha'gan and no one else has to die. What will it be?"

Za'in izr Husari stilled as he made his decision, the fabric of his zikh billowed and snapped in the wind sweeping past them from the east. The men from both companies sat on their mounts in complete silence, waiting for the reply that would dictate the fate of thousands in the next hour. Everything was quiet, except for the signs of nervousness from the horses that could be clearly heard across the plain from both sides.

His father drew a breath, pitched his voice to carry. "Your quarrel is with me, and it will end with me. This is my proposal. I will fight you, here, in single combat, until one of us is dead by the other's blade. If I fall, you will have my Kha'gan, and no more blood is to be shed. If I live, I demand the return of my son and we will lay claim to the Kamara and all its territories. These are my terms, should you accept the challenge. You are, of course, free to have eight hundred men fight in your place against me and my five hundred." A small grin tugged on his father's lips, made him look like a boy for a moment. "It adds to my legend either way."

It would add to his legend, no matter how one looked at it. He would go down as the brave Kha'a who fought to defend his Kha'gan to an honorable death, or the one who defeated an army nearly twice his own's size by himself. The latter had been done—twice, actually. There was a reason people didn't mess with Za'in izr Husari, and a possibility Aza'ir izr Zakai had just made the biggest mistake of his life.

It also didn't leave much room for Aza'ir, not put that way—and if he wanted to keep his honor intact. Once challenged to single combat, no Kha'a could decline and not be called a coward. His father knew this, and also knew it was the only fair chance he was going to get given the number of warriors they were up against. A smart move, but not a surprising one, if you grew up watching him.

"Well then." Aza'ir peeled back a smile. "Choose your weapon, and let's get this over with."

A Fight

'A man who fights without fear is blind, careless, and clumsy. Fear for your life, never your enemy. That is how you win a fight against one.'

# of Giants

'*Fear can be your best weapon, if you know how to use it,*' his master Akai izr Imami had said. '*A man who fights without fear is blind, careless, and clumsy. Fear for your life, never your enemy. That is how you win a fight against one.*'

All his life, Za'in izr Husari had fought with fear, had done so enough times to get high from it. Nothing could excite him more than the feel of those icy talons climbing up his spine. Only fear could light up his senses all at once, like being thrown into a pit of vipers. Only fear could get his heart to pump that hard, that fast, as it delivered those sparks of lightning through his veins, making him feel twice as large and thrice the motherfucker to bring down and kill.

It had been this fear that stitched a smile on his face when Aza'ir's blade came down. The impact sent a sharp vibration up his arm as their steels met; the loud, tooth-aching clang of it woke him up like seeing a naked woman after a good long year of celibacy. His body reacted to it like instinct, his muscles screaming and tightening to the point of bursting as he drove the blade back, surprising himself with his own strength. He couldn't remember the last time he'd felt it. Peace was the price of having won too many battles, too many duels. At some point, nobody wanted to fight you anymore.

The next blow came high, aiming for his right shoulder. Za'in turned to meet it just in time with his blade, digging into the ground with his right foot as he pushed back. He took two steps forward and turned again, sinking low to deliver a thrust at the midriff. Missed by a hair when Aza'ir caught on and jumped back. A returning blow coming from the top sent a jolt up his arm as he blocked the attack, numbed the entire limb the same moment Aza'ir's fist landed on the right side of his face. Za'in staggered back, caught himself before losing his balance, took a moment to breathe as he kept himself at a distance.

That blow would have knocked the sword right out of his grip had the man been what he was twenty years ago. That punch, too, would have thrown him on his back by now. Aza'ir had gotten old; he was weaker, slower now than what Za'in remembered.

So, unfortunately, am I, thought Za'in izr Husari as he stood, chest heaving as if he'd just run a mile, trying religiously to pump air into his lungs. Twenty years ago, he would have dodged that punch cleanly, would probably have spun out of range before the sword came down. Like Aza'ir, he had become slower, weaker now with age, but perhaps also with peace.

I'm getting too old for this shit, he thought, shaking his head.

Not so old yet, however, to not get a kick out of it, he also thought, licking the blood from the cut on his lip, and rediscovering then, that long-forgotten addiction to the scent and taste that used to keep him up at night long after the fight.

Used to keep Zuri up too, all night, over a different need.

He smiled at that memory, spat the blood back out onto the sand and drove himself forward for more.

⁜

THE FUCKING BEAST should have been knocked unconscious with a punch that close. Aza'ir swore inwardly as he shook out the pain in his knuckles. He knew he would have been—in Za'in's place—especially at the age he was now. Had, actually, been knocked out before just like that by the prick one Dyal fifteen years ago during hand-to-hand combat. Back then, he could never get close enough to do this—the man had been too fast, too alert for that. And now that he could, he no longer had the strength to do it justice. It stung even more, standing there, panting in earnest from having delivered those simple blows and knowing they hadn't even made a dent.

The bitter price of getting old, that.

The next attack came before he'd managed to get his heart to slow. Za'in, fast as a fucking cat even at his age, closed in with a blur and a blade raised high. A flash of memory from the old days struck him then, plastered itself to the man at present as he rushed forward. The distant image of Za'in coming at him with a frontal attack, two-hundred pounds of pure, rock-solid muscles behind a four-foot length of heavy steel slamming down on his sword, breaking his wrist when it had landed. The same blow would cripple him now, he concluded, and decided to slip out of the way instead, realizing—much too late—that he had misjudged the situation. Za'in, grinning like an ugly Devil at the success of his distraction, switched his stance at the last minute, dropping low to the ground with an anchored hand, and used the momentum to kick Aza'ir's legs out from behind, landing him on his back.

A breath taken. A blink. An opening for Za'in to move into position, sword flashing silver as it caught the glare of the sun—now already high in the sky and perfectly positioned behind him. His dark silhouette loomed over Aza'ir, one foot nailing his blade to the ground, the other pressing down on his chest, crushing his already depleted lungs. A two-handed grip on the hilt plunged the pointed tip down at his right eye—

—and buried itself in the sand where Aza'ir's head had been. Took off a portion of his ear instead as he turned his head in time to dodge the attack. He twisted, took the slim opening as Za'in worked at repositioning himself to pull the sword back out, hoisted up his leg and kicked the man in the torso, rolling away out of range the moment he felt the weight on his chest lift.

It felt like slamming your foot into a fucking rock, and all it did was push Za'in back half a step, now with his sword pulled free from the sand. A quick toss of the blade turned the hilt back into position in Za'in's right grip as Aza'ir peeled himself off the ground. It came smashing down before he could block it with his own, took a good bite into his left shoulder when he failed to completely clear the path.

Rage spilled out of him with the blood that dripped onto the sand, painting half his torso red on its way down. He took three steps back to regain his breaths and footing, grinding his teeth at the pain in his shoulder and the pride Za'in izr Husari had, once more, and after so many times, sunk his blade into.

For three decades now they'd been at it. Duels after duels at Dyal events, taking turns to be tattooed champion. Every year the fight had grown closer, more personal, more intense. Then, when simple games had turned into Kha'gan warfare, Za'in still managed to stay one small step ahead of him. *Small matters*, some would say. *Petty feuds,* others had commented. Perhaps, he'd thought, but they were both predators and leaders of men, and a score uneven for men like them had to be settled one way or another and before they died.

It would now be settled with death, on this day, in front of witnesses in the thousands. *Feels like the Dyal all over again,* Aza'ir thought, snarling as he dove back into the fight.

⁜

HIS FATHER WAS SMILING. He was smiling in the middle of taking a blow, as he delivered one, when he was made to retreat. It matched the expression on the face of his opponent, Nazir realized, watching the two circle each other, reading and anticipating the other's next move with the carefulness and expertise of an apex predator on a hunt. The pacing of their footwork falling as one in near-perfect rhythm, like two dancers moving to the same tune, each taking turns to lead and follow, sometimes both. It was difficult to tell.

It must have been like this back when they were still competing at the Dyal. The annual festival held in Citara for the very best of White Warriors from every Kha'gan to compete in had been where they first met. Contestants were chosen from the most frequent winners on Raviyani, eleven months before the festival, to compete in the games. The warrior who won the most points from all events would receive a tattoo on their arm marking them Dyal champion. The most wins by a single man on record had been six. His father had been marked four times. Aza'ir had five, but only four of those had been acquired while his father still entered the games. It was said, at gatherings and around campfires, that unless Za'in izr Husari was among the contestants, winning didn't count much toward being the best warrior in the White Desert.

So when Za'in izr Husari had decided to retire from the events at the request of his wife, Aza'ir izr Zakai had also retired one year later, after his fifth victory. He had made it clear that there was only one man he wanted to defeat, only one score he wanted to settle.

It was about to be decided now: the fifth Dyal for the two of them, fought here, outside of Citara, with both their lives on the line and their entire Kha'gans as the trophy. Nazir had never had a chance to see his father compete in the Dyal. But watching them now, he could understand why those who had would swear the energy and anticipation at the festival had never been quite the same after the two of them had retired. The men present on that plain would be talking about this forever, he realized, over how they had been there to witness the deciding match between Za'in izr Husari and Aza'ir izr Zakai.

They engaged again. Two giants, moving against each other in almost a blur, too fast, too closely matched in skills, both wearing white, both of similar height, build and age. It was almost impossible to tell them apart if one were to stand a little further from the action. One could forget to breathe, watching them that day.

The footwork had been effortless, timed to perfection to bring them together and take them apart. Precise, powerful thrusts and strikes of their swords meeting one another in a flawless show of efficiency. Blow after decisive blow blocked just in time, as though every move had been choreographed and practiced beforehand. Nazir remembered then that they had been fighting each other all their lives. They knew each other's habits, strengths, and weaknesses, and knew them like the back of their hands, like their own.

But they weren't really perfect, those blocks that had seemed so effortless and efficient. Both were bleeding now, the white of their zikhs stained almost every inch with blood. Aza'ir's shoulder had a deep cut that made it increasingly difficult for him to move, while his father had only a few minor ones but in more places. Both men were panting heavily now, had been for some time from the exertion. It would be decided soon, not by the level of their swordsmanship, but by the strength and stamina left in them.

And then he saw it, just as everyone else did: the first sign of strength failing one of them. Under the scorching sun of the mid-morning, Aza'ir's legs gave out from under him, sending the man stumbling back a step as he stood waiting for his opponent's next move. Nazir knew, at that precise moment, that his father had won the day.

All eyes were on Za'in izr Husari then, watching him tighten the grip on his sword, raising it high in the air as he charged toward the Kha'a of Kamara. None of them were paying attention to what one man was doing at that moment, but all of them would later swear that they would never forget how an arrow, shot out of nowhere, had pierced Za'in izr Husari on his right thigh, throwing him off his feet mid-stride like a downed gazelle on a Raviyani hunt.

The Four Assassins

It was only one week ago that Omar izr Fadzeik had sworn that he would be the one to kill the Salar of Rasharwi. He'd had no hard feelings, no problem with Salar Muradi for all the years he'd spent living in the city, perhaps even liked him as a ruler at some point. But Omar had also been an orphan left in a dark alley in the pleasure district, and the man who had saved him, raised him, and made him who he was had just been named a traitor and could be executed by the Salar before the month was over.

He checked his bow and arrow again, up on the roof where he had been waiting, taking care not to touch the Zyren on the arrowhead. There were six arrows in his quiver, but only three had been dipped in the poison. Zyren was expensive, and any first-class assassin of Deo di Amarra was expected to hit the target, moving or not, with fewer than three. Omar had earned his gold ring at twenty-three, and had become the head of Deo di Amarra's assassins six years later. It meant that if he shot at something, that something would die.

But you couldn't shoot to kill with one shot when the target was on a horse with the front of his torso automatically protected. Not in motion and not at that range, unless you were good enough to get his throat or his head—a possibility, yes, but in their line of business and for the reputation of Deo di Amarra's house of assassins, a mere possibility wasn't something they acted upon. The goal, that day, was to shoot to penetrate the skin and in doing so allow the Zyren to work its magic. That much would have already been a challenge, given how many men would be surrounding the

Salar when he rode. One missed shot, and they would be able to locate him on the roof and the opportunity would be gone. Salar Muradi, one had to remember, had also been trained and advised by Deo di Amarra himself. The men he surrounded himself with were also expected to be able to kill with fewer than three arrows.

Omar had prayed that morning before he left his room, that the other three assassins would miss, and that he wouldn't. He would show his master what he could do, that he was still the best apprentice, the most reliable—not the Silver Sparrow.

The boy had been a pebble in his shoe the moment he arrived at di Amarra's residence. For almost two decades, Omar had been Deo di Amarra's closest apprentice. It had, however, taken him a decade to get from brass to silver to the golden ring he had now, years to be included in the master's inner circle and important meetings, and years more to be relocated to Deo's personal quarters. The boy had moved into a room next to the master on the first day he arrived, had received his golden ring in just two years, and became the only one Deo di Amarra took with him to the Tower. He was, Omar thought with a bitterness akin to the taste of the poison they were made to drink daily, also the only one who had been allowed to call their master *Dee.*

And now, that same boy was the one who'd gotten his master into prison and made him a traitor. That fact, most of all, made Omar swear, many times, that he would also be the one to kill the Silver Sparrow of Azalea one day.

For now, he had to kill the Salar. Omar tightened the grip on his bow, looking back toward the Tower for a signal from the other assassins who would alert each other the moment they saw him ride out.

⁘

EVERY YEAR IN RASHARWI, on the longest day of the year, a city-wide sacrifice was performed in front of Sangi temple to honor the sun god. Depending on the year's economy, three to five hundred animals would be slaughtered at the temple square, each offered by the citizens of Rasharwi and taken one by one to the altar to have its throat cut. The blood would be directed by a small man-made ravine to a large pool adjacent to the temple, where citizens could come to drink and paint their faces, believing it would bring good fortune and grant protection against evil spirits. The meat from the sacrifice would then be portioned and distributed to all the temples, to be cooked and shared during a feast on the following night. Drisuli, the week-long religious event also known as the Celebration of Blood by those who observed the centuries-old practice, was just two weeks away from now.

Zahara wondered then, watching the crowd cheer and roar as they gathered to watch her being tied to the same beam where they slaughtered the animals, whether they were going to cut her throat and drink her blood or burn her that day, or both. She was, in earnest, hoping for the first if Ravi would be merciful. It would give her a quick death, if nothing more.

The black-marbled floor at her feet, however, had been equally stained with blood and burn marks. She remembered then that they also burned people here when someone committed a grave crime against Rashar. She'd witnessed both during her time in Rasharwi, though not very often. Muradi, even with his decision to not ban these practices, had always expressed an aversion to these things and made a point of not attending them unless it was necessary. He hated excess of any kind. It was why he utilized the balcony when he wanted someone dead. '*It's quick, efficient, certain, leaves no mess to clean up here, and requires no labor to deliver the body down the Tower,*' he had explained to his sons once, after throwing a corrupt official off to demonstrate his point. She found herself agreeing with him sometimes, especially when she also wanted to demonstrate her point with him as the subject. She wished, though, having had that thought just now, that the citizens of Rasharwi would possess some of the efficiency of their Salar.

They didn't, unfortunately. The people had opted to burn her. The burning, however, hadn't been prepared on that day, which was why she had time to develop these thoughts while they were busy gathering firewood and hay for the pyre to burn her on.

Somewhere in the middle of it, the priests of Sangi came out to the sound of the commotion. Some of them tried to stop the crowd, fearing the wrath of the Salar. Others kept their mouths shut in the face of the escalating hostility of the mob. Soon, all of them retreated back into the temple. She hadn't seen Yakim the High Priest once that day. She wondered where he was.

Up there on the altar, a strange sense of calm settled upon her. She didn't understand why it did, or how she was still able to think and see everything that happened so clearly. She did pray, however, to Ravi and Marakai the Sky Father, that her people would be looked after, that the White Desert would win the war, that Lasura would not betray his own land. It didn't matter if she were to die here. Her death, in truth, had been long overdue—for eighteen years, to be precise. She had been ready then, had wished every day that it would be granted, and she was ready now.

The pyre was nearly finished. It was done in a hurry, but with enough hands to create something large enough to burn for a long time. Long enough for there to be nothing left of her in the end. She wished then that her ash would somehow find its way back to the desert, to the valley of Vilarhiti, bringing her home at last.

⁘

'PROMISE ME ONE THING. Swear on your life and the oath you've given me when I spared it,' the Salar had said, holding Ghaul by the collar, pulling him close enough so no one else could hear. *'If something happens to me, you save her and take her out of the city. You keep her safe. You protect her with your life. Do you understand?'*

And Ghaul had sworn, despite everything, despite knowing what it would do to him if it ever came to that. By then, he'd hated the woman with a passion that could make him do the unforgivable, the unthinkable. But this was the will of a man at whose feet Ghaul had laid his life so long ago, and she was, no matter how much the Salar wanted to deny it, the only woman he had ever loved.

He had known it from the first day in that tent, from the way his master had looked at her, from all the time thereafter when his eyes lit up the moment they saw her in the crowd. Ghaul also knew, from his time spent in the dungeons of Sabha with the prince, that once he'd set his mind to do something, you couldn't stop him if the whole world came crashing down in his path. That day, his only two options were to give him those promises or be on the other side of the line that separated his friends from foes, and Ghaul would die before he saw himself among the latter.

You could see it even then, as he rode out of the Tower that morning at killing speed, how he'd never looked back or around for where the assassins might have been, not once. Salar Muradi looked forward, here, at any battle, in the Vilarhiti even as arrow after deadly arrow from Shakshi archers rained down on him. The men who had survived that battle swore to this day, in the tales told over drinks at taverns or amongst friends, that the prince hadn't blinked once when an arrow made it through the guards and took him in the arm. That he had kept on riding into the swarm of White Warriors in the thousands, an arrow shaft still sticking out of his limb, to cut down everyone who came within ten paces of his path to victory.

'They are men, not beasts,' the prince had shouted before the battle, standing over a runaway soldier of their own whose head he'd just split in two with an axe, *'and if they happen to be beasts, you will die cutting them down or you will deal with me. Take your pick,'* he'd added, hefting the axe from the dead man's scalp, slamming it down again to hack the head off the corpse. *'My axe or their swords?'*

There had been no more deserters after that, and the men, seeing and following him in that battle, had all discovered something they never knew they had. The guards surrounding him now were mostly survivors of the massacre, with just a few younger ones thrown in. Imran had handpicked them himself as the Salar's personal bodyguards. Soldiers who had fought at the Vilarhiti alongside him usually stayed loyal for life, or they feared him enough to fight and die by any sword as long as it wasn't the Salar's.

And he had trusted them then, just as he was trusting them now with his life, riding and looking only forward in the direction of Sangi. The Salar, even as a prince, had always been a soldier first and foremost. He knew trust was important in combat even when he didn't trust anyone at court. It instilled a sense of pride and purpose in the men, made them want to follow you to their deaths. He could do that, had been born with such qualities, had gained himself a following even as a prisoner of Sabha when he was just a boy. These men would die for him, Ghaul knew, watching their faces that day. Every one of them would take an arrow for the Salar. That gave him some of the peace he needed.

The first arrow came before they crossed the Madira, shot from the roof of a two-story house. It hit one of the younger guards, took him off his horse in an instant. Imran yelled a command, and another man moved up to take his place. Before he could reach the gap, another arrow, shot right after the first, took out the guard behind the fallen one, creating an opening on the left flank large enough to take aim at the Salar. Ghaul whipped his head around to find the source of the attack and spotted the assassin running alongside the procession on the roof, already nocking another arrow. He calculated the distance, reached for the axe on his back, and before he could throw it, an arrow took the man in the chest and killed him.

The archer behind Imran who'd made the shot gave him a nod before falling back into rank. Imran congratulated the man and kept on riding behind the Salar, who didn't stop, hadn't slowed down even once during the attack.

One down, Ghaul thought, releasing the grip on the axe and keeping his eyes on the roof. He didn't know how many there would be, but knowing Deo di Amarra, there should be at least three or four if he had to guess.

Imran appeared to know that too, judging from how rigid he was as he snapped more commands.

The second assassin appeared just before they crossed the bridge, this time targeting the right flank. Two arrows, fired simultaneously from the front, flew in precision to hit two guards in the chests, creating an opening long enough to also bring down another one in swift succession. Ghaul, who had been on the right side of the Salar, kicked his horse into position to fill the gap, shielding his master as they continued to ride. The second assassin, much faster than the one before, sped up ahead of them, hopping from one roof to the next, keeping out of range of Imran's archers. Upon reaching the higher roof, the assassin turned and locked his gaze on the Salar.

The arrow would clear the guards from that height.

Ghaul broke into a gallop to get ahead, hand already on the handle of his axe, didn't make it in time to stop the arrow from being fired. It went over him, heading directly to the Salar, who, facing the shaft head-on, reached over his shoulder, cleared his blade in a blur to strike at the arrow in midair, cutting it in half before it reached him. The assassin went down at the same moment with an arrow to the throat, released by another of Imran's men.

Ghaul exhaled and found himself praying in gratitude. He'd forgotten sometimes that with or without the guards, Salar Muradi of Rasharwi was still one of the toughest men he'd ever met. He had, after all, survived worse, and too many times to count.

"I want four men with shields in front of the Salar," yelled Imran, coming up from behind to ride alongside Ghaul. "We're about to cross the Madira," he said, privately. "Stay close to him. The roofs are high there. The streets narrower."

Ghaul nodded. He had been anticipating that. The other side of the Madira was the poorer districts, where the buildings had been built in several stories to save space and in blocks of many interconnected structures, making the roofs both higher and easier to make a run ahead. The narrower streets also allowed attackers to shoot from a higher angle, creating a path that would clear the heads of the guards surrounding the Salar.

The third assassin was on the other side of the canal, waiting for them shortly after they'd crossed the bridge. Imran saw this one coming from afar, grabbed a bow from another guard before he broke off to gallop ahead and shot the man down before he could even nock an arrow.

Three down, Ghaul thought. *How many more?* They were close now to the square where the Bharavi was supposed to be. Once they had her, the Salar could take cover at Sangi and be fully protected. A few more blocks, and his worst nightmare should be over.

The problem, Ghaul realized at the same time he heard Imran swear profusely behind him, was how to get past this crowd.

They'd run into the back of the mob. The streets were packed to the last inch with civilians trying to push their way into the square. The thousand men they had could clear them, but it would take time—time in which the Salar would no longer be a moving target for the remaining assassins to shoot at. With the mob alone, a hundred things could already go wrong. But now this...

"Is there a different way to the temple?" He turned to ask Imran, whose face showed more concern than he would have liked to see.

"They're all blocked," he said, shaking his head. "This is the shortest way."

He looked at the Salar then and knew as soon as he saw that face that something had to be done quickly, before he took things into his own hands.

"Go on, clear the way," he told Imran. "Leave me a hundred men. I'll stay with him."

Imran was getting his men into position when someone in the crowd yelled something to the others, pointing at a spot between the buildings.

Up ahead, reaching high into the sky, a band of smoke was rising.

Of Lies and Excuses

The moment he saw Aza'ir's stumbling step, Zardi izr Aziz knew he would never make it out alive. Za'in izr Husari wasn't a forgiving man, had never been for as long as anyone remembered. He might offer you a chance to surrender if he were the one staging the attack, but he wouldn't let you live if you chose to attack him. In the case that Aza'ir lost this duel, Za'in would see to it that Zardi died on that plain along with his two hundred White Warriors.

And then he would head over to destroy his Kha'gan.

It was a mistake coming here, Zardi thought, swearing in his mind for the fifteenth time. They were supposed to attack the Visarya with their combined forces—that was the point of bringing their White Warriors—not to allow this single combat to happen. He had known of the rivalry between the two men, everyone had, but he hadn't thought Aza'ir would be this reckless or stupid.

He was about to be dead too, from the looks of it.

It required action—immediate action—before it was too late. His mind was racing for solutions as he watched the two of them circling each other. He couldn't run, not when he represented his Kha'gan as their Khumar, not as a White Warrior. He couldn't initiate the attack on the Visarya either, not after the terms had been stated.

He could, however, consider himself an outsider regarding this whole thing. The agreement, he remembered, was strictly between the Visarya and the Kamara Kha'gans. By law, there should be nothing wrong if he were to loose an arrow at one of them and declare his own war as the third Kha'gan present. That happened often enough in the White Desert. Conflicts between Kha'gans were not always limited to two parties. He might have been only twenty-two and only received his zikh just a year ago, but he knew these things.

And he did just that. He fitted an arrow to his bow and shot Za'in izr Husari.

The arrow hit the mark. Zardi congratulated himself privately for a good shot, watching Za'in tumble to the ground. The plain fell into shocked silence. All eyes were staring at Za'in izr Husari as he struggled to get back to his feet. The Visarya warriors had their hands on their weapons, but seemed to be waiting for their Kha'a to issue a command. It would have been ideal—for the Khalji and the Kamara both—if real battle were to break out at that moment. They had the advantage here, after all. Zardi was hoping the Visarya would initiate such a fight as soon as he'd shot at their Kha'a, but they seemed to be too disciplined for that.

The command never came. Za'in was either too proud, or he had other agendas. The man just pushed himself back up, getting himself ready to resume the fight. Zardi sighed in disappointment and decided that it was still a smart thing to do. At the very least this should now offer Aza'ir the chance to finish him. He might be congratulated by his father for this victory. He *should* be congratulated—

Zardi izr Aziz never finished that thought.

⁘

NAZIR FLINCHED as something slammed into the Khumar of Khalji, throwing him backward off his horse. The hatchet, he now saw, had buried itself in the dead center of his forehead, killing the young Khumar instantly. In the middle of the plain, from where the hatchet had been thrown, Aza'ir Kha'a stood with his hand in the air, breathing hard and looking like someone whose mother had just been insulted in front of his men.

It must have been a response born out of reflex, of madness and rage bursting at the seams from having been provoked in the middle of an intense, nerve-racking fight. You could see it on his face, in the snarl that still lingered, in the rage etched deep into each and every line chiseled by years of hardships. And then, in the regret that replaced it when he realized he'd just killed a Khumar of another Kha'gan without warning.

You didn't do that unless you wanted to start a war.

The sound of two hundred steels being drawn all at once by the Khaljis rang like a shriek of some divine creature about to release its wrath upon men. The same action was then mimicked in unison by five hundred more Visarya warriors in less time than it took one to swear, and then Aza'ir's own six hundred picked it up, bringing the tension to new heights with their own blades. Nazir didn't know who had been the first to set it off—with that many people it was difficult to see everything that was happening—but once the first move had been made, there was nothing either Kha'a could have done to stop the chaos that followed.

The plain seemed to roll over on itself as thirteen hundred horses broke into gallops, their thundering hoofbeats kicking up a sandstorm five hundred paces wide and twice as long, filling the air with blinding clouds of white sand to match the real clouds overhead. Riding above it, with it, a roaring of men and horses loud enough to bring down the sky had it been some kind of roof. The three companies clashed upon each other like bodies of running water coming to meet in the middle where the two Kha'a's stood, both of whom found themselves suddenly caught in the epicenter of something they could no longer control.

And then the killing began. White against White, Shakshi warriors against more Shakshis, drawing blood, severing limbs, cutting down brothers, fathers, sons, and husbands. Their very own blood, shed by men wearing the exact same garment, belonging to the same race, the same land, worshipping the same goddess, distinguishable only by the colors of the threads in their hair. Threads so small you couldn't see the difference from twenty paces. *Threads* that dictated whether one deserved to live or die.

A simmering, growing rage roared in Nazir's chest for a way out as he watched, biting back the disgust that pushed itself up the back of his throat. It didn't take the Rashais or an enemy from faraway lands, nor any race whose shades of skin or hair differed from them to bring down the

White Desert. There would be no common enemy, no evil on earth or in hell big enough to truly bring them together. What was an enemy, in any case, if not someone on the other side of the fence who refused to bend to you? What was the difference between fighting the Salar's army and this? What then, would winning the war against the Salasar achieve if this was what they did to each other? *Who are my enemies? What exactly am I fighting for?*

The battle went by him in a blur of red, silver, and white. For a moment, Nazir was lost in his numbness, in thoughts he no longer understood. He could hear nothing but the muffled cry of men fighting to kill each other, couldn't tell which side was winning, where his father was, where anyone was, and couldn't bring himself to care.

Maybe, there was no point to this, to any of this, after all. Maybe Djari didn't have to end the war and carry that weight. Maybe they could simply live and get on with their lives, waiting for their time to come. *What difference does it make? Why does it matter if we die by their hands or ours?*

Something crashed into him and threw Nazir off his horse, bringing the animal down with him by the rope that secured his wrists to the saddle. A hand yanked him out of the way before the horse landed on top of him. Nazir, trying to figure out what had happened, turned left and right to survey his surroundings, realizing he'd just narrowly escaped a spear thrown at him with the help of someone.

A warrior came rushing in, sword high and swinging. Nazir yanked on the rope to dodge the blow, but didn't have enough length on it to clear the blade. The figure next to him leaped into position, balancing himself on one knee to block the descending blow. Grunted when the blade came down on the steel handle of his axe. A small shift in weight, a leg digging into the sand propelled him forward, throwing the attacker back. Sinking low again as he charged forward, the axe head slammed into the man's torso, killing him in an instant.

It happened in a blink of an eye, so fast he would have missed it had Nazir not been looking. Baaku said nothing as he strode over to the corpse, stood over it for an unconventionally long time to look at something before anchoring his foot on the dead warrior and yanking his axe free. Bending over, he picked up the dead man's sword and his dagger then walked back toward Nazir. He tossed the sword and the axe on the ground, leaving just the dagger in his hand to cut Nazir's bond.

There was a heaviness on Baaku's face, a tightness to his jaw that made the task of cutting him loose seemed like a much bigger struggle than it should have been. He parted his lips and pressed them back together with a frown before deciding to ask, "Where are they?"

It needed no explanation; there were only two men on that plain that mattered. Baaku didn't look up as he waited for a reply. He kept his eyes on the dagger, the rope, the ground, anything but him. Nazir wondered what was bothering him more; hearing the bad news, or having to look at him when it was given.

Luckily enough, bad news hadn't yet happened.

"They're still in there," Nazir nodded toward the center of the fight, shaking his wrist loose from the bond. He thought he heard a sigh from the other man, only it sounded halfway between relief and worry. "How did you—"

A flash of silver came from behind Baaku. Nazir grabbed him by the zikh and yanked him off to the side, clearing the blade just in time. His other hand reached for the sword, brought it up to catch the blow in mid-air. The impact was still running down his arm when he shoved the man back, kicking the attacker's legs out from under him after a lunge forward. The warrior fell. Nazir raised his sword, moved in for the kill—

—and paused in midair as the man's braids caught his eye.

Blue and gold.

"Nazir Khumar," the young man said from under him, confusion all over his face.

It was one of their own—someone from their southern camp, the third son of a blacksmith he knew. Yusuf was the name, if he remembered correctly.

Nazir lowered the blade, gave the man a hand to rise. "Go," he said. "I have this under control."

Yusuf got up on his feet, looked at him, and then at Baaku, questions in his eyes. Nazir straightened and gave the man a look that made him take an involuntary step back. "Go." A command this time. *Before I'm forced to kill you.*

The message was promptly taken. Yusuf gave him a nod and went reluctantly back to where he came from. *To killing Baaku's men, of course. That was their enemy, wasn't it? The Kamara?*

An awareness came to him then, a thought nagging at his conscience about the dead man lying a few steps from them. Something about the colors in his braids, how Baaku had taken time staring at him.

He shook his head, crushed that awareness out of existence. *I'll deal with it later. Not yet. Not now.*

Next to him, standing with his hand wrapped tight around the handle of his axe, Baaku flipped the dagger belonging to the man he'd killed and offered it to him by the handle.

It was wrapped in red and blue—the colors of the Kamara.

No dealing with it later, then. Nazir drew a breath, felt like he was going to be sick, and looked up. The confirmation was there in Baaku's eyes, in the pained yet unwavering gaze he always had whenever Nazir's words or actions struck him hard. He knew without having to hear it spoken what it meant, what Baaku had just done to save him, without pause, without hesitation, what he himself had refused to do just now to his own man.

"Take it," said Baaku. His hand, Nazir saw, was steady.

He stared at the knife, saw it for what it represented, felt the questions like a dozen sharp talons digging into his heart all at once. He had to make a decision, here, now, who and what he would be fighting for.

But who was his enemy? *Who am I supposed to kill? Your men for my Kha'gan? My men for you? Who dies here, Baaku? Your father? Mine?*

As if he could somehow hear those questions without needing them spoken, Baaku said, no hesitation in his voice, "Go help your father. Kill who you have to kill. Stay alive, Nazir. We need you to win this war. I need you to live."

I need you to live. A simple phrase, two different meanings. He had a feeling he knew which one, had known for some time.

Nazir took the blade, nodded once, and went back to war.

⁜

IT WAS ALWAYS going to happen one day, one morning, one afternoon. He'd known it from the first time he decided to sneak into Nazir's tent. *You knew it was always going to happen*, Baaku thought as he swung his axe at the warrior in front of him, cutting him down and moving on to the next, cutting that one down too. *Someone has to make the sacrifices to bring them together. Somebody has to be the monster to set things in motion.*

Another man charged in from behind. Baaku sensed it coming with trained perception, caught the blow as he turned his horse to face the opponent, killed the man with the dagger in the other hand. Didn't look back to see which Kha'gan he belonged to. It didn't matter which. It couldn't matter. *One of us has to be the traitor. One of us has to take the blame.*

A Khalji was riding toward him, snarling as he raised his blade. Baaku grinned. *An easy decision to make, for once.* He threw the axe at the man, killing him in an instant. Rode toward the corpse to retrieve his weapon before turning back to follow Nazir.

They were heading toward the center of the commotion, to where the two Kha'as would be. Nazir was riding to protect his father. *To kill mine, probably.* One of the Kha'as had to die to bring this to an end. One Kha'gan had to lose. He knew what Nazir was riding toward just as well as he knew why he was there, following no more than a few paces behind. That decision had been made a long time ago.

Someone trained an arrow at Nazir from behind. Up ahead, Nazir was concentrating on driving back an older, bigger man with a spear. Baaku flipped the dagger in his hand, guiding the horse into position. *Don't look at the braids.* He raised the dagger, aimed. *Just kill the man.*

He made the throw.

The dagger caught the archer in the eye, right next to his braids woven in red and blue.

Baaku thought he recognized the man as he fell, and remembered suddenly those few drinks they'd shared one Raviyani with a few jokes in between. He remembered liking that man. It didn't matter. *It couldn't matter.* He strangled the life out of that thought, reached for another dagger in his boot, and kept on riding. *One of us has to be the traitor. One of us has to take the blame.*

Nazir turned to look over his shoulder then, the old man with the spear lying dead next to his horse. Baaku caught those eyes, gave him a firm nod. *It's all right. I've got your back. At whatever cost.*

At whatever cost. That's right. Drill that into your head, Baaku, make sure it stays.

Because it all came down to this: to the bigger picture, the bigger agenda. Nazir had to live, as an oracle, as the brother to the one who could bring them victory, and as the Khumar of the Kha'gan with the highest possibility of defeating the Salasar. As someone who shared the same vision of freedom, as the only one who was worthy of the task. Nazir had to live, even if everyone else had to die. *At whatever cost.*

He smiled at that thought, at the folly of it all.

So many excuses and justifications. So many lies. Who are you trying to fool?

Up ahead, the two Kha'as came into view. A ring was formed around them by White Warriors who were fighting to give them space, to protect their own Kha'as from interference. They appeared dangerously close to their limits, with Za'in limping badly from the arrow wound in his leg, and his father bleeding all over the place, chest heaving like a man close to collapsing. The fight was going to end any minute now. One of them was about to die on that plain.

Along with his son.

He looked at Nazir, saw the same comprehension in his eyes. It was common practice when one Kha'gan took over another. You didn't leave the son and heir of the man you'd just killed alive to take his vengeance. His father had said he would take that risk if Nazir were to cooperate as an oracle. It was as likely to happen as Za'in sparing his life if his father were to lose.

There were going to be two deaths, not one, on this day.

Time was no longer there for him to stretch, to linger in its short existence, to seek comfort from in ignorance or denial, to pretend what they had was going to last. It was always going to come to this, and it was here, now, caught up and taken him by the throat.

Someone has to make the sacrifices to bring them together. Somebody has to be the monster...

Baaku put away his axe and unslung his bow, remembering then the question he'd asked earlier that morning, when everything was still quiet, when there was still time.

What happens to us?

My Sin

to Carry

She remembered the smell of burnt human flesh, how different it was from goat or lamb. Or perhaps it was all in her imagination—a poor conclusion derived from seeing dead bodies that could be yours or that of someone you knew. Why would it be any different from animals? Were they not made from flesh and blood and bones just the same?

Zahara had seen those bodies before, in one of the villages on the outskirts of Sabha Za'in izr Husari had burned. Muradi had brought her along to witness the damage—he would never have missed such an opportunity to prove his point. The memory she'd managed to tuck away for years came back to her that day while they were lighting the pyre.

She remembered thinking then that he had taken her there to demonstrate how right he had been, that he would find satisfaction in proving her people to be as monstrous as he was. She also remembered how Muradi had stood in the middle of the rubble, in a field burnt to ashes littered with corpses you could no longer recognize, staring down at a charred figure of a mother holding her child as though it had been someone he knew, and had seemed to forget she was there entirely. He had issued the necessary commands, retreated into the privacy of his own room at Sabha, and stayed in complete solitude for two days. When he'd reappeared, the room had been destroyed to the last piece of furniture, and he had wanted war. It had taken his advisors half a day to convince him to delay that war, but since then no expense had been spared to prepare for it.

One could say that Za'in izr Husari had created an

even bigger monster with how he'd chosen to respond to his wife's passing. One could also say that it was a woman who had changed the fate of the White Desert forever if Za'in were to win this war.

History and future had always been made and changed by one life, one decision, hadn't they? Some people had the power to alter the lives of generations, while others were born to follow, to live with the consequences. Zahara couldn't help but wonder then if she also had such a power, if her death would mean anything, do anything to him?

'You could have been an exception. You and Lasura.' His words resurfaced in her mind, as if in answer to her question. *'I would have given you the world, the freedom you wanted, even put your son on the throne and given him control of the Salasar.'* An opportunity had been given then, one so large she had decided to crush it without hesitation.

Was I a fool? she asked herself then. Should she have taken that hand? Should she have bent to him, given him what he wanted and in doing so achieve what she couldn't do as his enemy? Could things have ended differently had she not dedicated her entire life to vengeance?

Would you have really done those things, for my heart in return?

She would never know that now. There was no point in thinking about what could have or should have been. In the end, she had to accept the fact that she had achieved nothing for her people, besides being made into an example of what might happen if the White Desert were to fall.

Let it not come to that, Zahara thought as she watched the smoke rise from her feet and up toward the sky, creating a curtain of white clouds around her, filling up her lungs and beginning to blind her vision. *Let me be the last, not the first, to burn at Sangi.*

It must have been the smoke that gave her the wrong impression, Zahara told herself, but she thought she saw him in the crowd, fighting his way toward her.

She wondered then if Zuri iza Sa'an also had a vision of her husband coming to save her before she died.

-!-

SHE HAD A BRASS ring on her finger, plain with a few carvings and no stones set in it. Her hand had wrapped across the child's face—boy or girl, he could no longer tell—as if to shield him or her from having to see what was happening. His mother had done that once or twice when he was young and terrified of thunder. *Mothers*, Muradi remembered thinking then, feeling safe all wrapped up and protected in her arms, *could be so fearless, so strong.*

They could also die being strong.

And it had been all he saw then, standing in the village Za'in izr Husari had burned, over the blackened body of a mother who'd failed to protect her child, how useless strength could be if you weren't the strongest or the toughest. He knew then that it had been his weakness that allowed it to happen. Their deaths had been his failure, his sin to carry. He could have seen it coming, *should* have seen it coming had he paid more attention, taken more precautions. Had he been a wiser, more capable man, a more competent ruler with enough power to prevent such things.

It never changed, no matter how much time had passed. He had felt just as powerless then as he had been at ten, when he couldn't save anyone.

And he was about to fail again that day.

The sight of that smoke rising to the sky had pulled him back to the village, brought back the image of the mother and child, this time with the silver of Zahara's hair among the ashes. The cold, cold rage that had been with him then returned with it, bursting like an overfilled damn cracked apart in the middle to feed his body from limb to limb with a craving for blood and violence, tearing his control to shreds all at once.

He didn't know how many people he'd killed to get through to the square, didn't count how many times he'd brought those blades down on somebody. The crowd rushed by him in a blur as he rode through the screams of men and women, the sound of their suffering muffled into near silence by the persistent pounding of his heart that grew louder by the minute. Somewhere in the numbness of his senses, even the awareness of death he had come to know so well seemed foreign to him.

The swords felt slick in his hands; from what, he couldn't tell. Perhaps blood. Perhaps sweat. Maybe both—he didn't have time to look. Behind him, his men were shouting words he couldn't comprehend, couldn't even tell if it had been Imran or Ghaul or someone else making that noise. He was too busy trying to clear the way, driven to near madness by something worse than rage that had taken root in his core, worse than the impulse to kill at the Vilarhiti.

It grew in intensity the closer he was to her. With every step came a fist clenching around his chest, squeezing it tighter, faster. The pulsing pressure that had been building in his stomach was rising and rising toward his lungs, his throat, choking him harder every time he breathed. In the back of his mind, an awareness of an outcome too terrifying, too painful to fully acknowledge was stalking him somewhere, creeping up on him like a beast hiding in the dark, waiting for the right time to pounce. His own heart, at that moment, felt like something foreign and treacherous that had been put there to kill him.

The soldier next to him fell off his horse, struck by something he later realized to have been an arrow. A whicker of air graced his throat as he turned toward the sound of someone calling him from behind, saw an arrow shaft from the corner of his eye as it went over him to take out another guard on the other side. Someone grabbed him by the arm and yanked him off his horse, took them both to the ground before he realized what was happening. The next thing he knew, he was staring at Ghaul crouching protectively above him, an arrow embedded in the shield he had strapped to his left arm.

*

LUCK, OMAR THOUGHT, grinding his teeth as he ran along the roof toward the square. *Sheer luck, at least for the second arrow.* The aim had been right, the arrow had flown true, and the Salar would have been dead instantaneously had he not turned at that precise moment. The first felled guard had taken that arrow for him, which couldn't be helped, and the third—he had to admire the Salar's giant bodyguard's sharp eye and quick reflexes for having pulled him off his horse in time.

Not an easy man to take down, Omar thought, grimacing at the situation. The soldiers were loyal to a fault, and the gods seemed to be on the Salar's side today. Still, he had three arrows left in his quiver.

Imran's guards were firing at him—four of their very best archers running alongside on the ground to hunt him down. Omar, however, had been among the best apprentices of Deo di Amarra, and being on higher ground with a clear view of the archers had allowed him to anticipate, time, and dodge those shots without breaking a sweat. He went from roof to roof and left them behind with the mob in minutes, clearing arrow range as he continued to follow the Salar.

Having to deal with the guards had taken his attention off Muradi for a few minutes, and for a moment he thought he had lost his target in the crowd. The problem fixed itself in no time, however. After all, this was Salar Muradi of Rasharwi—if the gold-trimmed, luxurious black tunic and those twin obsidian blades didn't make him stand out among the commoners of the city, his giant bodyguard did.

They were moving fast through the crowd, Omar saw, with Muradi snarling like something spat out of hell and cutting down everything and everyone in his path. The giant Samarran was running protectively by his side (the *left* side, where Omar had been aiming from), his axe high and ready to hack anyone who came within three paces of the Salar into pieces. Omar swore inwardly as he considered the situation. Even without the shield, the man was too big for him to find an opening to shoot. With it, the task had become impossible.

And so he kept on running, following them to the square. There, it would be open ground. There, he could get off the roof, disappear, take his pick on the new angle.

He happened to know exactly where that angle would be.

⁜

MURADI WAS CROSSING the square without an army, not one that Zahara could see. It was just him and Ghaul, pushing through the gathering, cutting down those in their way and clearing a path through to her. The crowd started screaming and running as they made their way to the platform like two dangerous beasts let loose in the city, only the square had been too packed for them to move very far. It became a stampede of sorts, and as she choked on the thick smoke that was filling her lungs, Zahara could hear the sounds of children crying, of women screaming, of people falling down and being crushed under someone else's feet.

By then she could no longer see—the soot had gotten into her eyes, stung them until she had to squeeze them shut. Down below, the flames licked at her feet, catching on the hem of her dress. And then—with a gush of wind, the weight of something large and soft falling and wrapping around her legs—the fire directly in front of her was put out and the heat subsided.

Someone put arms around her, reaching behind her back to cut her loose, and caught her as she fell. She knew who it was, knew it in her bones, under her skin, without having to pry her eyes open to see.

Why are you here? Why save me? Why do this here, now?

And he was holding her, touching her, searching for wounds, for cuts, for any damage done. "Zahara!" He pressed his thumbs on either side of her face, wiping the tears away, shaking her for a response. "Look at me! Can you see?"

"My lord!" Ghaul was yelling from somewhere nearby, panting, rushing. "We have to go!"

"Zahara!"

She squeezed her eyes shut, blinked twice, three times, before she opened them to look. She had to be able to see to run.

Through the billowing smoke, through tears that were still running from the soot, through the sound of people screaming and dying around them, he was there—her mortal enemy, her nightmare from long ago, the demon that had haunted her for eighteen years, the one man who shouldn't be here was there, covered entirely in blood like the first time they'd met, looking at her from a familiar height, through those blue eyes now filled with vulnerability, with relief—

—with terror as he grabbed her arm and yanked her off to the side, throwing her to the ground.

At noon, on the event that would later be called the Great Riot of Rasharwi, during the seventeenth year of his reign, Salar Muradi, Conqueror of the Vilarhiti, Founding Father of the Madira, Supreme Ruler of the Salasar and its five provinces, took two arrows in the chest and one in his left arm, falling on the sacrificial platform of Sangi.

A Small Price to Pay

'*Why aren't you afraid of me?*' Nazir remembered asking one night some time ago.

Baaku's brows narrowed. He seemed genuinely surprised at the question. '*Why should I be?*

Why? '*My power. My visions,*' Nazir said, not sure how to word it. People didn't need reasons to be afraid of him. '*I know things you don't want to know. Death, for example. How it happens. People are afraid of that. Often.*'

Baaku shrugged. '*We all die at some point. Why does it matter how?*'

'*Knowing makes it harder.*'

'*Not if you're prepared.*'

Is it? Nazir wondered. *Have I not been prepared all these times? For mother, for Djari, for us?* He asked, '*How do you prepare for death? For loss?*'

Baaku smiled, his features softened in the candlelight. '*By living every day like you're about to lose it all,*' he said, like it was the most natural thing in the world, as if it were easy. '*Nothing ever lasts, Nazir. I never think for a second that I might not lose you tomorrow, today, in the next hour. I don't need you to remind me of that with your vision. You have to be ready for life to end, or the only thing you'll die holding is regret.*'

Nazir wondered why that memory came back to him. Perhaps because of the way Baaku looked now as he fitted the arrow to his bow, how it matched how he'd looked when he'd said those words. There was no regret on that face, none whatsoever, then or before when he'd killed the first man, or the one after, or the one after. Baaku was Baaku. He didn't look back, only forward. He made hard decisions quickly, and acted on them without hesitation.

This day was no different. Nazir knew at whom that arrow would be aimed, knew what would happen if it hit the mark. He didn't try to stop it from happening. He couldn't. There was no stopping Baaku once his decisions had been made—you'd know that if you knew him well enough.

And so he watched, unable to remove his eyes from the figure he'd come to recognize in any light, from any angle, trying to remember everything that would soon be lost. He watched and did nothing as Baaku drew back the bowstring, aiming at Aza'ir izr Zakai, at his own father and Kha'a, to lay victory at Nazir's feet. To save his life, and in doing so put an end to his own.

It came back to him then, the vision he had been given when they first met long ago, one that had been repeated in his nightmares so many times thereafter. An image of himself in a ceremonial garment, standing over the knelt figure of Baaku under the night sky and the full moon overhead. Around them, a large Raviyani crowd was watching in silence, in anticipation. The chanting of a priest rose high over the beating drums that began slowly, steadily, before picking up speed.

He could hear that drum in his head as Baaku released the bowstring. Two separate times, two events overlapping; one happening, the other being shaped and defined by the first. The arrow flew. The image of him holding a sword sprang to life. The drums that weren't being beaten grew louder, faster, as if to accelerate the shot fired. Nazir held his breath, watching both reality and what was soon to be clashed upon one another, saw the blade in his mind coming down at the same time the arrowhead sank into Aza'ir's flesh.

The shot took Aza'ir in his right thigh as he attempted to dodge a blow from his father's blade, and in doing so caused the movement to falter. His father's sword came down on Aza'ir's left shoulder, hard and fast enough to split any man in half. Nazir closed his eyes as he turned away from the scene, heard the sound that matched his own sword coming down on Baaku's neck in his vision, heard another one slightly louder than the thud of Baaku's head as it hit the ground when Aza'ir fell.

Some things had been set on course, placed into position long ago. Some events were always going to happen whether or not you knew it would. Baaku was right. One had to be prepared for life, or die with regrets.

Nazir realized then that he regretted many things—one of which was never telling Baaku he would be the man who killed him.

⁂

IT WAS ALL RIGHT, Baaku thought then, watching his father's half-severed body collapse to the ground. Patricide happened in the world of power, in ruling families, in the courts of kings. The killing of one's Kha'a happened, on a regular basis. It made sense even. Nazir had to live. The Visarya had to win. The White Desert had to survive this war. For land, for freedom, for traditions.

A small price to pay for a bigger agenda, to be sure. The man was never a good father or a good husband anyway, perhaps not even a good Kha'a. Had he not grown up beaten, insulted, used, cast aside at convenience? Had he ever done anything right in the eyes of that man, or been considered even once as the son Aza'ir always wanted? Had he not, too many times both consciously and unconsciously, imagined this in all those hours of anger, of being knocked down again and again through the years? Had he not wondered what he could change or accomplish if he became Kha'a? He had a hundred reasons, all noble, logical, and honorable, even to shoot and in the process kill his father that day.

Not one of them had been enough in the end. Not nearly enough to keep the pain away in any case.

But it was all right. It had to be. A man did what he had to, what needed to be done. It didn't even matter under the circumstances—the pain, the disgust, this guilt he was feeling would be gone soon. As things stood, he wouldn't live past the next Raviyani, maybe not even tonight, or a few minutes from now. *A small price to pay. No need to be dramatic about it. Just make sure you don't piss your pants when that sword comes down.*

The battle went on around them. It always took time before the fighting stopped after the death of a Kha'a. News needed time to travel in the midst of chaos. Some men were going to die needlessly in this war because of it. Sometimes all of them died needlessly. The irony of it was the moment the fighting stopped and the killing ended, his death would then be decided. He could be killed instantly—it wasn't against the law—or he could be killed ceremoniously on Raviyani if Za'in would allow him the honor. He turned to Nazir, saw the man already looking at him, and realized all of a sudden why Nazir had refused to answer his question that morning.

It was all there, laid bare on Nazir's face—the vision he had been holding back. He could see it in the tightness of that jawline, the dread in his eyes, the single drop of a tear that rolled down Nazir's cheek. It wasn't just his death, of course. It was a lot more than that. He had completely forgotten one important tradition that applied to them.

The execution of Khumars and Kha'as were always conducted with honor, by the hands of someone of equal rank.

"Nazir..."

There was a sound—a strange noise coming from where the two Kha'as had been. Baaku turned at the same time Nazir did and saw everything that happened, how Fate had decided to interfere and change everything that day.

Divine InterVention

No one had seen where the sword came from. Speculation still abounds today as to how and why such a thing might have happened. Some offer a view that the blade had been knocked out of someone's grip during combat, and that the man had died immediately, leaving the sword unclaimed. Others were of the opinion that the owner of the sword may have lived, but had been too much of a coward to come forward. No one, however, would deny that it had been an accident, or something more; an act, many would swear, of a divine being who had their own agenda in mind. To make matters more complicated, the sword itself had not been marked by any thread or carving that would allow anyone to determine from which Kha'gan it had come from, and therefore neither side could be held responsible for the death it had caused that day.

The mysterious sword, spinning fast and high in the air as it came seemingly out of nowhere had, by sheer coincidence or a touch of some divine force, righted itself into the perfect position to pierce Za'in izr Husari in the back of his left shoulder, its tip penetrating through flesh and between bones to emerge on the other side, through his heart, killing him on the spot. Twenty-three witnesses had seen the sword as it struck, including his son and that of his enemy. None of them had seen where it originated.

In the case of such an event, where single combat resulted in the death of both parties, two things could happen. The two Kha'gans in question could consider the terms null and void and decide by another round of single combat or a full battle, or they could consider it a stalemate and take the matter to Citara.

In this particular case, the new Kha'as of Visarya and Kamara, both present in the field, had agreed to end the fight and leave it to Citara to make the call.

After two weeks, the White Tower released its verdict. The issue of arrows being shot at both Kha'as during single combat had been brought up, discussed, then disregarded. It was considered fair, as both Kha'as had been shot in the same place. And while it had been Za'in izr Husari who killed the Kha'a of Kamara, the unidentified sword that had ended his life immediately afterward had been considered, by a unified vote of all the Devis in the White Tower, a message that could not be overlooked. It was to be seen, Citara had declared, as an interference from a divine being, and therefore holding enough weight to override the terms set by the two Kha'as on that day.

There were to be no tributes offered between the Visarya and the Kamara, no absorption of any Kha'gan into another, including the Khalji. The event that had brought the deaths of almost five hundred White Warriors from all three Kha'gans resulted in no advantages being given to any side, no power changing hands except the change of two Kha'as and one Khumar.

All because of one unidentified sword that slipped out of someone's hand, many would say afterward over drinks and around bonfires.

The Visarya and the Kamara Kha'gans would remain rivals for many years, until another event took place that ended the legacy of one.

Za'in izr Husari's death on that day would be talked about for generations to come, mostly over how a legend had been killed by the hands of a god or a goddess, that it had taken a divine being to defeat him when mortals could not. Some versions of the story told to children before bedtime would add that this was how the gods might have chosen to punish him for his sins. Za'in izr Husari, after all, had committed treason when he'd killed his Kha'a to take over the Kha'gan—a common point to stress in the White Desert, among Shakshis. The same tale, told by a Rashai mother, would accentuate that Rashar had punished him for the burning of women and children in the villages outside of Sabha.

There were, of course, other tales of his life being told throughout the White Desert and beyond. The story of how a man born into a common-blood family of camel herders became a four-time Dyal champion, and later made himself the Kha'a of the largest Kha'gan in the west. How the same man had sired and raised an oracle and a Bharavi who would later change the fate of the entire peninsula.

Another story—the one involving a husband who had loved his wife at first sight and continued to set a table for her at every meal long after her death—the one that might have been the closest to defining who Za'in izr Husari truly was, and how that love had become the driving force behind everything Za'in izr Husari had ever done, was lost, gone with all the memories of her he'd taken with him as he died.

Life began, was lived, and ended. Some things were remembered, others forgotten. Some people left their mark on the world, others altered it. Some moved and shaped things for generations to come in ways they could never know.

Common

There were more than a thousand skulls in the Prayer Room of a Thousand Skulls. If Lasura had to guess, it would be closer to three thousand. No one truly knew how many remains Eli the Conqueror had brought to the crypt he'd commissioned during the last two decades of his life. The chamber had never been completely excavated, and some skulls had been placed on top of one another for lack of room. The crypt—the only name Lasura would call the place by—had been dug right underneath the Red Hall of Marakai. More than three thousand skulls, buried right under his throne.

No, not buried. Arranged, thought Lasura as he looked at the wall behind the black sarcophagus. Hundreds of human skulls lined up, filling every inch from one end to the other and from floor to ceiling, all facing forward. All four walls of the chamber had been decorated the exact same way, with more skulls lining the arch of the entrance.

Decorated also wasn't the appropriate word. It wasn't meant to be a work of art. All these skulls had simply been gathered, collected like books

Enemy

on the shelves, kept, and displayed with efficiency in mind to accommodate as many as possible. These were men, soldiers who had died fighting with him on and off the battlefield to bring peace to the peninsula. Eli had always written in his journal that his throne had been built on the lives of thousands. No one would have thought he'd meant it literally until they could see this place.

He was said to have prayed here often; it was why he'd chosen to call it the Prayer Room. Eli the Conqueror was a religious man, a firm believer in Marakai the Sky Father like most of his subjects. Those of the faith practiced sky burials, where bodies were placed outside, in the open, for birds and other prey to pick them clean. The remaining bones were then collected and kept in the family's home. For those who'd died fighting alongside Eli, the Prayer Room was where they kept the skulls to honor the dead.

They'd laid Eli to rest here when he died, in the sarcophagus placed at the center of the chamber, for people to come and pay their respects. The rectangular stone tomb had inscriptions of his life story, worn out almost entirely now by how many hands had touched it when people came to pray. After the rebellion following his death, this part of the Black Desert had been deserted, its secret entrance lost for almost eight hundred years, only to be discovered and occupied by the Rishis a mere century ago. They never found the mummified body of Eli, but the room had been where they found his journal, and the skulls had been enough to make the crypt a legend.

You would have loved to see this, wouldn't you, Father? thought Lasura. *This is who you want to be, to succeed, isn't it? The man who united the peninsula, who brought peace to these lands. You were prepared to sacrifice this many lives, to fight this many battles…*

But you couldn't sacrifice one.

He stepped up to the raised platform where the sarcophagus had been laid. The clack of his boots echoed softly against the countless dust-covered skulls. It came back toward him in whispers from all directions, like the sound of a thousand soldiers marching somewhere in the distance, caught by the wind and brought to his ears as it wandered ahead. The room was completely dark save for the light made by the one torch he'd lit by the entrance when he came in. The flame danced to the gentle draft coming through the ventilation shafts, casting thousands of shadows left and right of the protruding skulls, giving the impression that all three thousand of them were moving, looking at him.

Or judging me.

He wondered if this had been what Eli wanted when he came here to pray. To be judged by the dead and maybe, hopefully, make peace with them for what he'd done—or hadn't done.

It brought him back to the thought of both his parents. *Could you have*, Lasura wondered, *made peace with either of them if there had ever been an opportunity?*

A silly thought, that, and one too late in any case. In his anger, he'd decided to walk away from it all, and now he'd lost them both, on the same day. Many days before, actually. By the time the news had come from Rasharwi, it was all in the past, done, finished, over before anyone could have done anything to reverse it. *Not by me. Not from here, anyway.*

'*Life doesn't always offer a way out*,' Deo had once said. '*To survive, you must strike before Fate throws a punch. That's the difference between you and the Sparrow,*' he'd added. It had been after the duel, the one he'd lost and would always remember. *"He never thinks twice where he places his next step. He knows what he wants at any given time, in any situation. And you, my lord prince, you fought clumsily because you don't even know who you are. That's why you lost, and you are not going to win until you do.'*

Another memory came back to him then, of that day in the throne room: the image of the Sparrow stepping forward, planting both feet on the ground as firm and unshakable as a hundred-year-old oak.

'My place is between Djari and whoever brings her harm. I will kill whoever she wants to see dead and fight wherever she wishes me to fight. If she wants the world set on fire, I will strike that flint myself. I know where I stand. It will not change for as long as I live. The question is, do you?'

There had been a pang of jealousy running through his core as he watched, wondering what it would feel like to have something that mattered so much that one would go so far to protect it. What could have driven a man to make such a decision so unwaveringly? He remembered thinking that he had none of those things. That there wasn't, and hadn't been, a single purpose to his life besides what others were willing to use it for. He had walked out of the room over that thought, and still, he hadn't gotten one step closer to knowing who he was or what he wanted.

Now, with both of them gone, the path ahead was darker than ever.

This crypt suits me so well it isn't even funny, he thought, and laughed anyway. It bounced off the skulls and what sounded like a thousand snickering ghosts came back at him.

"My mother used to say—" A voice from the entrance finished off the echoes and started off new ones. "—that only a lonely person laughs when he's supposed to cry."

Lasura drew a breath, swallowed the taste of irritation down his throat out of manners, but made sure the sound of his sigh was loud enough to be heard across the room. "I would like to be alone, if you don't mind."

It didn't matter what he wanted, of course. It never did. Bharavis were all the same. She stepped into the room and walked right up to stand next to the platform, like she hadn't heard what he said or she never had any intention of considering it.

"I would like a word," said Djari iza Zuri, in the tone of someone used to issuing commands—and having them followed.

"Not now," he replied bluntly, making sure the tone was final.

It wasn't, not for her. "Now is a good time."

He turned to her then, harsh words and curses hanging off his lips, ready to be let loose. She just stood there, a head shorter than him and two steps below the platform, staring up at him with the same yellow eyes as his mother's, the same glow to her silver hair that could fill any space she occupied with a sense of vicious coldness that made one want to escape. They must have been at least twenty years apart, with facial structures that didn't remotely resemble each other, and yet she reminded him so much of his mother it was making his skin crawl. Especially that unfailing ability to look up at someone and still make it seem like she was looking down from a throne hovering high in heaven somewhere.

"Unless someone has made you the master of this place while I wasn't paying attention, that decision is mine, iza Zuri."

She frowned. "I don't like your tone."

"Good," he said. "I managed to succeed at something, then."

She took it with a flat expression that told him he hadn't succeeded in making a dent with that statement. "The right to be here is also mine," she replied calmly, like someone reading a book out loud, listing the laws of some order. "I did check with the master of this place. You can stay or you can go. That is also your right."

Fucking Bharavis.

"I understand you're used to getting whatever you want, my lady, but I am not your sworn sword or your subject. You might want to keep that in mind," he told her, turning back to the sarcophagus and fixing his eyes on the small crack on the lid, though not really looking at it. "Talk, then. Say what you need to say and then go, if you have no more business being here." What else was he going to do? Allow himself to be chased out of the room by a girl? He had too much of his mother in him for that.

She stepped up onto the platform and took her place next to him, as equals. He had reasons to believe, however, that she would have ascended higher if it didn't require climbing onto the damn sarcophagus.

He wondered if she had considered climbing.

"I heard about the Salar and your mother," she said, though not in a tone someone might have used to offer condolences. At the very least she didn't beat around the bush. Another resemblance to the way his mother did things, that.

"*The Salar* and my mother." He traced the words venomously, couldn't stop himself, not with the mood he was in. "He is also my father, in case you didn't know." It was incredible how both Bharavis seemed to think they could just omit that fact at their convenience and it would somehow stop being true.

"Your father, then," she said easily, though unapologetically, not that he could imagine this girl—or his mother—apologizing over anything. But there was the difference. You couldn't get his mother to call the Salar his *father* if you put a sword to her throat. A small difference, not even one that could be justified, but substantial enough to make him a bit more willing to listen. "Do you think they're alive?"

He laughed halfheartedly at that question. "Considering the circumstances? Maybe," he said, hating the uncertainty in his own voice. "Considering who they are? I'd make sure you see their bodies with your own eyes, if not try to be there to bury them yourself, before believing they're dead." *And even then, you may have to stick around to make sure they* stay *dead.* He stopped himself short of saying that.

The truth was, he wasn't sure. No one was. The news had mentioned his father being shot and his mother having escaped the burning, but they never found their bodies, nor Ghaul's. The hunt was still on. *A hunt,* of course. With no named heir, Azram had both the birthright according to the old law and the power of the Salahari to take the throne. If they were ever found, Azram would make sure they wouldn't be found alive. Their father could retake the throne at any time if he lived; he had both the right by law and the loyalty of enough men—and citizens—to do it. Azram or the Salahari would never risk that now that they'd achieved what they had. Not to mention Azram also couldn't call himself Salar until they produced a dead body, or until a period of two years had passed without their father returning for the throne. He was willing to bet both Azram and the Salahari were also not nearly convinced that his father was dead. *And if Mother is with him, well, she's not going to die before he does.*

But whether his parents were dead or alive, one fact remained true for Lasura: he couldn't return to Rasharwi with Azram on the throne.

The Black Tower was the only home he'd known; that was the problem. Deo was being called back to the capital with the army his father had sent here. The situation had changed, turned his world upside-down, and Lasura had yet to figure out what he was going to do about it.

He could feel her watching him from the corner of his eye, studying his expression with the openness of someone trying to size up a camel at auction. He turned from the crack he'd been pretending to look at to meet her eyes, and saw genuine curiosity in her frown.

"What?"

"I can't tell if you love them or hate them," she said.

He snorted. *Neither can I.* "Tell me when you figure it out." That much was true. Guess he would never know now. Dead or alive, it was unlikely he would see either of them again.

"What will you do?" she asked.

"Why do you care?" he countered, before coming to the realization that he knew the answer to that question, and the look on her face confirmed it. "I see. This is why you are here."

Her eyes widened for a second, then went back to their normal size. She adjusted herself, drew her back into a straight line, pulled back her shoulders, and lifted her chin higher, if that was possible. His mother, in the form of a young, tiny girl.

"The way I see it, this changes nothing. We still need to fight the Salasar—"

"*We?*"

"The White Desert," she corrected herself, a frown coming, in the distance but not quite there. "Your knowledge is useful, valuable. Perhaps enough to—"

"To do what?" He sneered openly at the idea. The very thought of it was laughable. "To allow me into a Kha'gan? To become one of you? I am the son of Salar Muradi of Rasharwi, your mortal enemy, the man who has been raiding your land for the past two decades. Your people will have me killed on sight, or at the mere mention of my name. Are you even aware of what you're suggesting? There are other ways to kill me, iza Zuri. You don't have to drag me into the White Desert to have me beheaded."

"If there is a way—"

"Your sworn sword is a pureblood Shakshi, my lady. He is one of your own, born and raised in the White Desert, raided, enslaved, tortured, and now being hunted by the Salasar, and yet your people will not take him back if they knew what he was. So long as the Shakshis make no distinction between what a man does and what he is or has been subjected to, there will be no sanctuary, no offering of peace for him or for me in the White Desert."

Something in his chest was rumbling now, and he heard his own voice grow louder. "Your path to victory will be no different from what my father intends to do or has done. It will be built on the blood of innocents, of orphans, of people you see fit to call your own or cast aside based on nothing more than your prejudice and some laws set hundreds of years ago. Even if there is a way, iza Zuri, even if you can hide me under a rock somewhere, tell me why I should fight on your side, for your land? Is it because my mother is a Bharavi? Because the same blood runs in my veins? My father's runs in half of them! Do not forget that for a second!"

He realized then that he had been yelling at her; that he had, somehow, rolled all his anger and anxiety and grief from what had happened into one weapon and flung it at a person he barely knew. His fists clenched by his sides, nails digging deep into his palms. He was panting, trying to catch his breath from the rage that had just poured out of him.

And through it all she'd listened with her lips pressed tight together, her eyes blazing a bright amber, still not backing down. "We share the same enemy," she said, desperate, but unwavering in her commitment. "He took your father's throne, drove them both into exile, if not to death. You know this. Everyone knows it. At the very least I would expect you to seek some retribution!"

"The way your father did, iza Zuri?" It came out of him before he could stop himself. He had been there too, at those villages on the outskirts of Sabha, had seen what was left of it with his own eyes. "You will have me set fire to my own city and see my people burn?"

She wheeled, her small frame seizing the distance between them as if to force him to back up a step. "*I'm not my father!*"

He took a pace forward, closing in, grinding his teeth as he stared her down. "*I don't know that.*"

"Then stop me," she said, her chest a mere inch away from his, and heaving for the same reason. "Stay and stop me when I cross the line. I need someone from the other side if I am going to try to win this war without becoming the monster I am trying to defeat. If it means something to you then be a part of it. I am offering you that chance, here, now. Pick a side. Don't run. Do something with your life. Or are you too afraid to choose one?"

It slammed the back of his throat shut, made his heart beat twice as hard and as fast as he tried to grip his control by the scruff of its neck. Because there it was, thrashing and screaming like a nocturnal creature being dragged out of its hole into sunlight; the ugliness, the truth behind his every action—or lack of one—for the past seventeen years. The one he'd locked up behind a door and thrown away the key so he didn't have to face it. This girl, young and small enough to be called a child, had barged in uninvited, kicked down that door, and dragged it out into the open.

'Pick a side…or are you too afraid to choose one?'

Silence closed in on them as they stood, tightening its grip around them until something felt ready to burst. There seemed to be something about this girl's presence that caught him somewhere between wanting to embrace her and strangle her to death. Standing there, in that crypt, he was having a hard time deciding between the two.

There was a sound from the entrance. It pulled them out of that fight, made them turn at the same time.

"The last time I checked," said the Silver Sparrow, the gold ring on his right ear flashing as if to remind them of what he was, "that is my job, not his, Djari."

Stay

'I need you to be what I am not. To be my eyes and ears when I can't see, to fight my enemies, and to stop me when I cross the line.'

With Me

'I need you to be what I am not. To be my eyes and ears when I can't see, to fight my enemies, and to stop me when I cross the line.'

Those words, said on a quiet night a lifetime ago, when they had been in a different place, at a different time, and two different people, came back to Djari as her sworn sword stepped into the Prayer Room.

Hasheem was wearing a crisp white tunic stitched with gold, a robe of black velvet lined with silver wolf pelt hanging loosely over his shoulders. His hair, unbraided and neatly combed back, had been gathered into a half-bun, revealing the gold ring on his right ear he had never removed and a clear outline of a face that seemed harsher than before from the weight he'd lost. Even then, even with those dark shadows around his eyes and the fading bruises on his face, there was a presence to him that was foreign to her. A presence of command, of coldness, of something sharp and bitter she hadn't witnessed back at camp. The man she knew had always been gentle, careful, and warm. The Silver Sparrow of Azalea, the young assassin standing in front of her now wearing silk and velvet and fur like someone who had worn them all his life, was not.

A lifetime ago. Two different people.

And it had felt that way in the throne room, when he'd appeared with Sarasef, wearing similar clothes, holding himself with a presence more regal than the prince himself as he talked to these people. Everything seemed to have changed the moment these people had walked into his life.

Walked back *into his life,* Djari corrected herself. Hasheem, after all, had a whole other life before they met, another story, another circle of people she never knew. *Another woman, there, somewhere, who knew him in ways I don't.*

Where was her sworn sword? She looked at him now and all she saw was the Silver Sparrow: an assassin, a stranger.

He stepped onto the platform, holding her gaze with a severity to his grey eyes she hadn't seen before. Next to her, Prince Lasura stiffened a little, putting himself in a defensive stance, even if discreetly. People here seemed to move around Hasheem with caution, she had come to notice. Then again, this was, after all, the Silver Sparrow of Azalea, Deo di Amarra's gold-ring assassin.

And he was angry. At her.

"We need to talk," he said softly, but in the way a pillow on your face was soft before it sought to suffocate. "Here, if the prince would be willing to leave, or we can take this outside. Your choice, Djari."

The command in that tone was unmistakable. This man, her sworn sword and blood, the one who had so far obeyed her every wish and been nothing but gentle with her, was not taking no for an answer. She didn't like it, but it would have to happen. They had to talk and get this over with.

She drew a breath, turned to look at the prince to ask him to leave, but there must have been something in her eyes that gave him a different message—one that made him step up to Hasheem and stand his ground instead of excusing himself.

"Your preferences aside, Sparrow," said the prince, with a heaviness to his tone that matched the way he'd planted those feet on the ground. "Djari iza Zuri came to me. Our business is not done. The way I see it, you can either join the conversation, or you can wait for her to finish. That is the proper respect for a lady I would expect you to know, coming from court and all."

There was a hush in the room, as if the ghosts of Eli's conquests had sucked in their breath listening, followed by a piercing silence that could crack the sarcophagus had it been allowed to last. Hasheem turned to the prince with an agonizing slowness, grey eyes lit up at least three shades lighter. His calculating, unprecedented calm gave off the same atmosphere as a physician carefully considering the idea of dissecting a man for the sole purpose of studying his organs. Alive.

"Have a care," said Hasheem. "This is not your place, Prince Lasura."

"Nor," said the prince, "is it yours, Sparrow."

"My presence here is welcomed."

"At what price, I wonder?"

"One you can no longer afford," said Hasheem, a man she didn't know, "given the whereabouts of your father."

The prince picked up his right foot and placed it in front of him, gaining ground. Hasheem stood firmly in his, staring back into those yellow eyes with his sharp silver. Death seemed to hover just above them, flapping its wings impatiently as Eli's dead soldiers stared at the guests in anticipation. No one was carrying a weapon in that chamber, but she remembered that Hasheem had killed before without one.

'There is a monster in that boy, iza Zuri,' Deo di Amarra had said. She could see a glimpse of that in the man standing next to her, could sense something clawing at the door for an exit. He had every right to be angry for what she had said and done, but that was the point di Amarra had come to her to mention—that she was someone who could bring it out of him.

"We can talk, here, now," she told him, stepping in. "The prince can stay if he wishes to." It wasn't personal. It shouldn't be. He was her sworn sword and blood, nothing more, and about to cease to be that if they could agree on it.

Hasheem turned to her, hurt, anger, and a dozen more emotions she couldn't name all there in his eyes. She had, after all, not taken his side in this. *There are,* she thought as she looked at him then, *two men now who want to strangle me to death in this room.*

"I woke up," Hasheem said, the crispness of that tone resonating in the chamber, "to the message that you are releasing me from my oath, I am here, Djari—" He paused, drew a breath as if to rope something within, and failed in the attempt. "—for an explanation *why*."

Why? There were reasons, of course, but which ones would she tell him? That this was dangerous—this thing they had, this situation they were in? That she didn't want to be the one who broke him? That there was a crack between them she could feel, that they were two different people now ever since she had been attacked and he had slipped into his previous role?

Or that despite it all, she still found it difficult to breathe in his presence, that there was still a knife left in her chest when she'd been told of another woman, that she was standing here, wishing that she wasn't who she was. A most dangerous, traitorous, and unworthy wish, a desire so unacceptable she couldn't afford to nurse it. It had to end, now, somehow.

"I wanted to give you a choice," she said, only that much. A lie, but a necessary one.

"A choice, Djari?" His voice grew slightly lower, softer. He seemed to be the kind of man who spoke more quietly when he was close to the limit. The kind that was most dangerous when he didn't say a word. "This is you making mine for me," he said, and added, *"While I slept."*

She didn't miss the sting of those last words. No one could have. What he had done for her wasn't small. "You've done enough."

A smile so thin it could peel off her skin. "And so I am no longer of use to you? Especially now that you have someone else whose knowledge you can utilize?"

"I've never—"

"Of course not." Hasheem cut her off mid-sentence, his chest heaving now, despite how calm he appeared. "You didn't take me in for that. You were the only one who didn't take me in for what I was. What changed, Djari? What happened while I was asleep? What have I done? What is my sin?" He paused, drew a breath, said through gritted teeth, "Tell me. Which part of my life, of what I am, disgusts you enough to make you want to run? You owe me that much explanation before you replace me. Is it how many people I've slept with, why, or who?"

-:-

THE SOUND OF HER FIST landing on his cheek sent a shock full of echoes across the room. Lasura jolted at the unexpected sight that somehow felt familiar to him. So familiar, in fact, that he suddenly felt a twitch in his cheek where his mother had punched him before he left. He had to wonder if women in the White Desert had been taught to throw a punch as a part of growing up, or if slapping was something too low and common for Bharavis.

Whichever it was, Djari iza Zuri had thrown that punch hard enough to knock her sworn sword back a few steps, forcing him to grab onto the sarcophagus for balance. The shock on his face was a sight Lasura would never forget, mostly for how much satisfaction it gave him. This must have been their first actual fight, from the looks of it.

"If I had known," she said, shaking her fist from the pain and trembling with enough rage to rival his mother's, "that you would think so little of me, I would have shot you twice and made sure you died on my brother's horse!"

Now that was a story he wanted to hear.

"I am a Bharavi, born to marry for the benefits of my Kha'gan. I have been raised *every day* to willingly open my legs for any man my father would choose for me, and I would have to let him do it, *every day*, for the rest of my life." Her voice rose and carried around the room in its echoes. "There are things the world asks from us. Things we all must do to survive, to fulfill our destiny. What kind of person do you take me for, to believe that I would judge you for this? *How could you*?"

The Sparrow, to his surprise, was still not having it. "What then, Djari? What bothers you now? The way I see it, you can't even stand the sight of me."

Lasura could probably admire such a tenacity to seek the truth, if only he hadn't been raised by another Bharavi and knew better. Oh, what his mother wouldn't give to get a chance to explain that to her husband.

The difference between them, however, was clear.

There was guilt on her face, dressed with some pain around the edges as she forced her breathing to slow. She went silent for a time, her yellow eyes softening by the minute as she looked at him, and in response, his rage, too, was subsiding.

You would have to be blind to not see the bond between them. There were people who fought to win, and then there were those who fought to break down walls, to grow closer, to know better, to not let go. She was incapable of hurting him at an emotional level, and neither was he. The Sparrow was standing there with understanding in his eyes, but without a hint of intention to retreat from this. In a way, Djari iza Zuri should have known, just as everyone else did, that there had been no possible way she could get rid of her sworn sword. He'd even said it out loud, or did she think it had been attached to his oath?

I know where I stand. It will not change for as long as I live.

And he had come here to fix whatever there was to fix. If Lasura knew anything about the Silver Sparrow, it was the fact that this was not a man who settled for any situation he didn't want to be in or agreed easily to back down from something he wanted. It had, however, never occurred to Lasura until then to fully appreciate the kind of man it would take to rise from Sabha and the pleasure district to become the wealthiest, most influential Shakshi slave the Salasar had ever known. *She has*, he realized with some amusement watching them that day, *no idea who she's dealing with, and no chance at winning this argument.*

"The truth, Djari," said the Sparrow, "or you will not have my consent. You need it to get rid of me. I know the rules."

She pressed her lips together, made a decision, and turned to face him. "I know about Mara."

There was, Lasura thought then, so much pain in that single breath taken by the Sparrow at the mention of a name. One could almost see the knife she had plunged into his heart, the blood dripping from it. For the first time that night, he looked away. For the very first time, there was vulnerability, hesitation, a stumble in the way he held himself. Lasura knew that story. Everyone in Rasharwi talked endlessly of what could be the most moving story of all time: how the Silver Sparrow had thrown everything away for love, and the pure tragedy of it. *Women could move mountains sometimes without doing much at all*, he thought. Mara di Russo, Za'in izr Husari's wife, his own mother, and now, if the prophecy was to be believed, Djari iza Zuri. All of them, somehow, had a finger, if not a hand, in shaping the future of the peninsula.

"What does she have to do with this?" It came out in almost a whisper, with dread so strong one could almost smell it in the air.

"When you swore that oath," she said, clenching her hands into fists, staring down her sworn sword from below, "was it for me, or for another woman whose image you confused mine with?"

A spear to the throat, that, Lasura thought.

"She is gone, Djari," he said, not as apologetically as he would have expected, if at all.

"Because you failed to protect her."

"Because I loved her." The reply came without a moment of pause or hesitation, as if he had decided the cause of her death a long time ago and been repeating it daily in his head.

"And you still do," she said. A confirmation, not a question she needed answered.

"I still do," he said, proudly, religiously. Something he intended to keep.

It had to hurt, of course, and he could see it on her face. Knowing something didn't mean it wouldn't sting, carve you open, leave a scar when you had to hear it spoken. Anyone who ever loved the Sparrow was going to have to live with Mara di Russo one way or another. And Djari iza Zuri was, whether her sworn sword was aware of it, in love with him when she should not be.

Two Bharavis and men they couldn't love, for different reasons.

"I am not her replacement or your second chance to right a wrong," she said, a trace of vulnerability in an otherwise rock-solid statement. "I cannot be that for you."

"You are not. You never have been," he told her, firmly, decisively. "There is no confusion here, Djari. She cannot be replaced. I know what I'm doing. I know where I stand. I know what you're afraid of. I won't cross the line. I promise you with my life. You can't get rid of me. Not for this. I won't let you."

There was, Lasura thought, more conviction in that statement than anything he'd ever done in his lifetime. This was personal, more intimate than he had the right to witness. There was, of course, a line to be crossed that was off-limits to them. Their lives would run forever parallel to each other but never meet, and he would do it in any case. He would lay his life, his loyalty, perhaps also the part of his heart she had obviously occupied at her feet, knowing exactly what was to come.

'I won't cross the line. I promise you with my life.'

A promise not so unlike his mothers' to see his father dead, despite what Lasura knew—and had always known—was going on between them. The truth the entire Tower knew except the two of them, who decided to deny it. A history that repeated itself with Bharavis and what they were raised to become. This wasn't even his pain, but it made him angry nonetheless.

"You can't get rid of him." Another voice came from the entrance, a voice he knew by heart.

Deo was standing by the door, carrying with him that atmosphere he always emanated before he struck you with bad news.

"Your father is dead, iza Zuri," he said. "He was killed on his way here. The alliance stands, but the attack on Saracen has been delayed. Your brother is now Kha'a and demands your return immediately with Hasheem. You need the Sparrow, my Lady, and your brother needs him to win this war without your father's influence over the Kha'gans."

She froze. Froze like the world had come to a complete stop and she was the only one left in it, lost and left behind in somewhere foreign. He knew the feeling too well. Two pieces of news, two tragedies, two losses; one that had arrived in the morning, the other at night. '*Your father is dead.*' Four simple words that could change your entire life, no matter how close you were to him, or how distantly you had been raised.

She clenched her hands into fists, clenched them until her knuckles turned white, her small frame trembling from trying to hold back the flood of emotions going through her. And yet she was holding it, her face hardening into a rock, her feet rooted firmly to the ground behind an invisible wall she seemed to have put up around the ruin and the devastation she harbored. Lasura wondered then if his mother had been like this from the beginning—a girl born and raised to carry so much pain, so much weight on her shoulders without ever asking for help. Someone who had been taught to fence herself off from ever receiving it. He had an urge to step up to comfort her, but one could die trying to climb or bring down such a wall.

Or maybe it was just his lack of conviction speaking.

The Sparrow had her in his arms before Lasura could finish that thought, holding her so tight in his embrace it felt as if he would lose her if he didn't. There had been no hesitation, no thinking required, no such thing as another alternative to what he had decided to do. This man would walk on fire to give her what she needed, and what she needed hadn't required a single word spoken.

She went stiff as a log at first, fought it with all she had to not let her walls crumble. He pressed his lips to her temple, said something in a mere whisper, and with those words shattered all that had been standing between them.

Lasura thought then that he'd never seen a woman cry like that before. It felt like the bursting of a dam, held at its limit for years and years, breaking apart all at once. It felt like a storm, late in its arrival, but one that tore through the desert, clearing everything in its path as it came.

Have you ever cried like that, Mother, thought Lasura, *at least once in your life? Do you still have a chance to cry, out there, somewhere?*

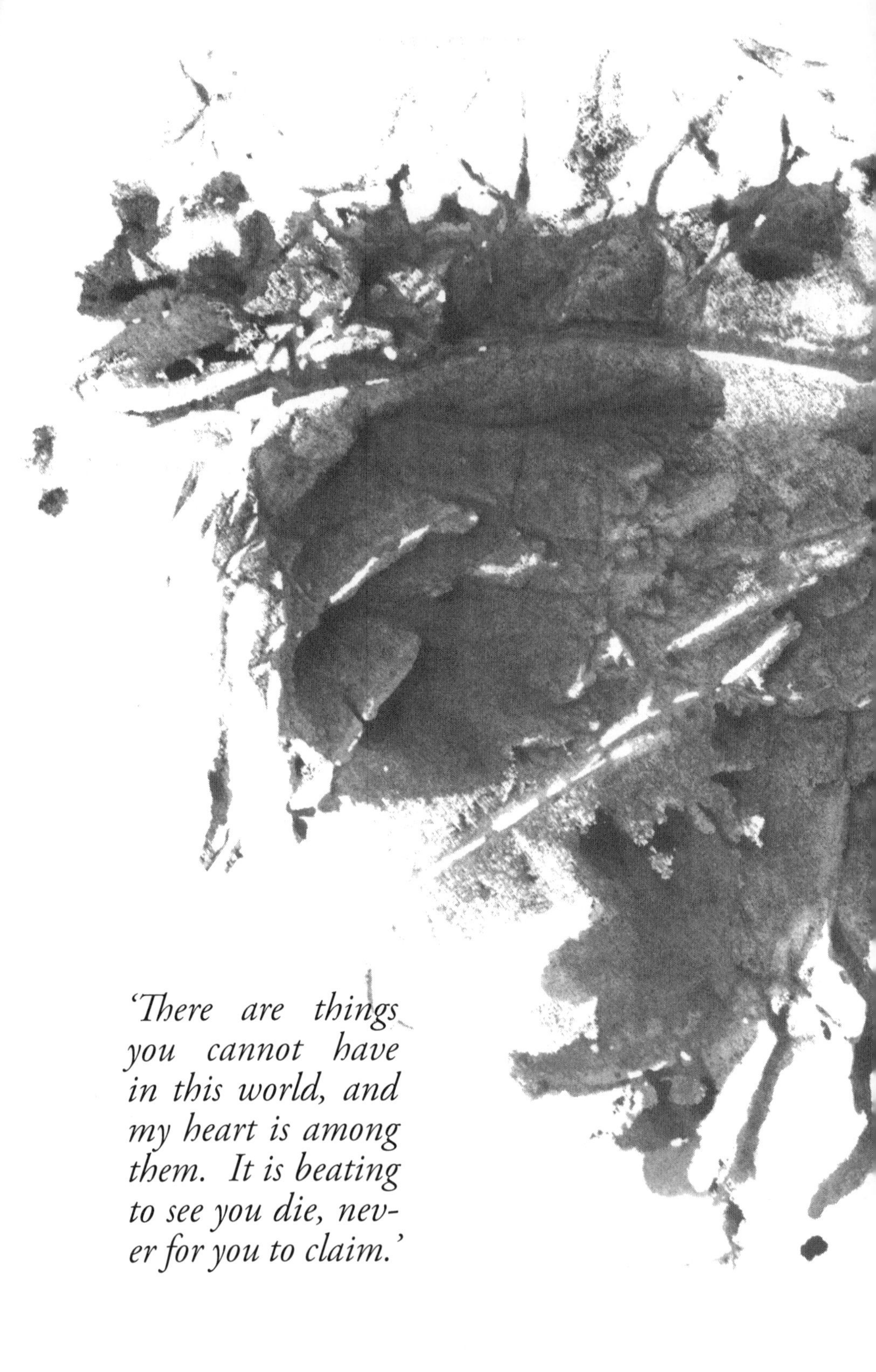

'There are things you cannot have in this world, and my heart is among them. It is beating to see you die, never for you to claim.'

No Other Way

'There are things you cannot have in this world, and my heart is among them,' she had said to him once. *'It is beating to see you die, never for you to claim.'*

And it was beating now, heavily, violently, as he lay dying in that cave. Standing a few steps away, Zahara watched, as she had promised herself she would, the process of his death leaving her with too many questions she hadn't been prepared to answer. There was a finality to that promise that went both ways, and that she couldn't deny. *What happens to my heart, my life, then, when he is dead? Will it still beat, or will it end with him? What do I live for, after this? Will there ever be a reason as powerful for me to draw my strength from again?*

He was breathing more faintly now, the three arrows still embedded in his body rising and falling more and more slowly the longer the day stretched on. The arrows that should have been dipped in Zyren, which would have killed him in less than an hour, somehow hadn't been. By sheer luck or fate or divine intervention, they also hadn't penetrated the organs that would have caused him to die quickly. But he was losing blood. A lot of blood. People died from that, slowly, unless someone were to interfere. Someone who knew how.

She did know how. Had been trained for it long before her capture. It was how she knew the arrows hadn't penetrated important organs, how she knew they hadn't been dipped in poison, how she also knew that he would die eventually if she were to do nothing.

To prevent someone from doing something about it was why she was still here, with him and Ghaul, who had taken them out of the city and hid the Salar in this cave near the border of Samarra. Being a Samarran himself, Ghaul knew the terrain, where to hide them, where to get water, and likely where to find help. There had been opportunities for her to run—plenty of them, in fact, given how Ghaul had been more focused on saving the Salar than keeping her in sight as per his master's instructions. He could be expected to do that to make sure she was safe. Muradi didn't like to fail, and he had come to save her, after all.

But she, too, didn't like to fail. He might live, and she had to be here to make sure he died. To see it, as she had promised herself long ago.

The reason why he'd come to save her at all was irrelevant. It didn't matter. It shouldn't.

Muradi was resting against a wall, breathing slowly but steadily and wincing every time his chest moved. The pain must have been great; she could feel it in her own chest watching him, in the satisfaction she gained from it. Somehow, the air around her felt rigid, barely breathable. It must have been something in the cave, or maybe the anticipation of seeing him dead was getting to her. Eighteen years of suffering was about to come to an end. This pain, this anger, this wound that seemed to be tearing open now in her heart would be gone when he died. If only she had one moment alone with him, it would end sooner rather than later.

"Ghaul," he said in almost a whisper, and even that much was an effort. "Go find water…food… some firewood."

Ghaul looked at her, all forms of hatred and distrust on his face. She didn't blame him. All this had happened because of her. He might kill her after this. She knew he wanted to. "Yes, my lord," he said, taking her wrist and beginning to pull her along with him. "You're coming with me."

"Leave her," said Muradi, command seeping back into his voice despite the state he was in.

"My lord." The giant Samarran grimaced. "It isn't safe."

"*Ghaul.*" The tone was final, leaving no room for objections, and implied no further explanations were to be given. When Muradi did that, you obeyed without question or you suffered grave consequences. He might not be in a shape to offer that consequence, but someone who'd known him as long as Ghaul had would know there was no point in arguing with him when he used that tone.

There was a tearing of flesh, a sense of a wound being cut open and left to bleed on Ghaul's face as he looked at his Salar. An understanding passed between them in the silence of the cave, an awareness so real and concrete one could almost reach out to touch it. Ghaul knew, as well as she did, what was truly being asked of him, what his Salar wanted. You couldn't serve a man every day for more than two decades and not know the content of his heart.

Or refuse his last wish.

It took all the strength he had to offer that nod, but he nodded and obeyed. Ghaul walked toward him, knelt down by his side, his hand picking up the hem of Muradi's robe, and he kissed it as he placed his forehead on the floor. He stayed like that for a time, his whole body trembling and fists clenched painfully tight, from hopelessness, from the loss to come, from the struggle to draw air into collapsing lungs resulting from what was being asked of him. A very large man, fighting desperately to hold on to a small end of a larger fabric, wishing he didn't have to let go.

Muradi placed his hand on his guard's shoulder, resting his weight on it gently, yet firmly, as if to make sure it would be felt through the armor. "You have served me well," he said. His face, Zahara thought, had never been milder. A face he'd never had for anyone, not for as long as she had known him. A face reserved for the one man he'd trusted the most, who had yet to fail him. The one man who was still not failing him at this very moment, even when what he was asking would leave too great a wound to ever heal. "Now go."

And despite how he appeared to be carrying the weight of the whole world on his shoulders, despite the feeling that he was dragging along a hundred corpses behind him for every step he took, Ghaul stepped outside of that cave and did what he was told.

Muradi looked at him as he walked out the entrance. He looked until the figure of his bodyguard disappeared from view and lingered long after. His breathing altered a little as he closed his eyes afterward, and silence settled upon the two of them for a moment.

"Do you have a knife, or do you need mine?" he asked, as he opened his eyes to look at her.

Short. Right to the point. As always. The man who had become her husband wasted no time, even with his own death.

She nodded, untying the ribbon around her hair and loosening the knot. The small knife fell into her hand. She gripped the handle and unsheathed the blade.

He smiled with pride, with the satisfaction of being right, of always being one step ahead of her. *Even now, on your last breaths, you insist on winning, on trying to conquer me.*

"Best do it quickly," he said, letting slip a small groan as he forced out the words. "Ghaul will be back soon. Have you decided how?"

"I've had eighteen years to think about it," she said, stepping toward him with the knife in her hand. "I still can't decide which would satisfy me more."

The smile widened. Whatever she did seemed to please him, to her irritation. "I could have given you a perfect solution if you had discussed it with me."

She was standing above him now, looking down at the weakened form of the man who had locked her in his cage for almost two decades, on top of having slaughtered her entire family, and yet she still didn't possess any power to make him suffer. "Only you," she said bitterly, "will go so far as to dictate how I take your life. You insufferable, arrogant, entitled prick."

He laughed, and coughed blood as soon as he did, his face crumpling for a moment as another wave of pain hit him. The grin did return soon enough, however. "I've waited eighteen years to hear you swear at me again. I should have made that an exception."

It made her feel like a child, like something small and harmless he'd never considered a threat. Even now, this close to dying, he was still considering her a plaything, an entertainment. Only Muradi would go so far as to take this opportunity to kill him and make it a gift, a favor, a bone tossed carelessly at her feet. She was the one holding the knife, and he would not allow it to give her power over him. It should have fed more fire to her rage, but she felt too exhausted, too used to it to care. “Must you try to make me hate you until the very end?”

His breath stumbled at that question. This time it seemed to have gotten under his skin. He parted his lips to speak, pressed them back together, and hesitated. Then, with an effort, he gave her a half-hearted smile, like someone trying to compliment a food he found inedible. “How else, Zahara,” he said, with short, painful breaths in between, “could I get you to look at me? How could I get your attention otherwise?”

It tore open a wound, forcing her to acknowledge a tumor that had been growing in her chest; an ugliness she had tried and tried to cure and cut out of her. “*Don't you dare,*” she said through gritted teeth, gripping the knife in her hand harder, needing to feel its presence. “*Don't you even dare go that far.*” There were dangers in those words, weapons hiding in each syllable. *Even now, you will take more.*

But he was not done. He wasn't even close to being done.

“Do you really not know what I've always wanted, Zahara? After all this time?” he said easily, carelessly, as if the implication held no such thing as consequences. “There is no other way I can have you, not for what I've done. I know this, and so do you.”

And there it was: the cold realization crawling up her spine that he had been right. That she had known what he wanted, all this time, and knew that there had been no alternatives, no possible way for her to forgive him for what he had done. That she would not have lived or stayed for a second longer if he had not bound her to him in this way. “It is not,” she said, through heaving breaths, through the searing pain in her heart, pain from a source she didn't understand, “for you to choose.”

“I never did, Zahara,” he said, grinding her name on his teeth like something he had been fed without consent. “I've spent my life trying to build an empire, to unite these lands. I've had to kill thousands of my men, thousands of yours. Do you think I wanted to? That I don't have to live with what I've done every day of my life? Do you think that I would sacrifice so much to have it end this way? To even risk it?" He paused and groaned at the pain, his chest heaving from the rage, the disappointment he had been holding back.

"I've never chosen this, to have you as my one mistake, my only obstacle, my most vulnerable flaw. I've tried a hundred times to let you go, and a hundred times more, and *every single time* I've failed. I've failed today. I will fail again tomorrow and likely for the rest of my life." Another cough. More blood. Shallower breaths. More pain in his chest. In hers. "Kill me, Zahara. That is the only way out of this mess, for the both of us."

And it was the only way. She knew it as well as he did, knew it with every unspoken word, with every look in his eyes, with every smile he had held back or forced out of existence in the past eighteen years. She knew that for all the relentless push and pull between them they'd spent a lifetime trying to deny, for all the lies they'd told themselves and each other, it all came down to this. He couldn't afford to have her, and she could never forgive him.

There had been no other way.

She lowered herself to the ground, the unsheathed knife held tightly in her grip. This was to be the ending of her pain, the start of a new life, the key to her freedom. He would die today, along with everything he'd brought into her life, into her heart that she'd never welcomed. "For the both of us," she said, nodding, and positioned the tip of the blade on his heart as she felt a taloned hand wrapping over her own.

"Tell me one thing, Zahara," he said, reaching for her hair, wrapping it around his fingers. "Would it have been different—" He paused for a breath, to swallow blood. "—had we met sooner, or some other way? If we had been someone else? Two farmers or camel herders, maybe?"

In another place, or another time...

She felt his hand on her cheek, felt the caress of his thumb, callused and covered in blood, in soot from when he'd pulled her out of the fire.

"Would you have loved me then?"

Love, he said. The audacity of it. The cruelty of those words. Such careless thoughts flung in her direction regardless of what he would leave behind. "Do you hate me for what I've done, or for the man I am?"

In another place, at another time, and given different circumstances. Her own thoughts, that night in the lights of the lanterns. She had thought then that she might have been able to admire him, that she might have even found a man she would willingly marry, if only they hadn't been on different sides of the desert.

What did it matter now?

The knife felt heavy in her hand as she pushed it into his chest, pausing just as it punctured his skin. A voice nagged at her conscience, telling her she'd forgotten something important, yelling at her to figure it out. She forced it out of her mind, shut it behind a door as she twisted the knife, pushing it in further. "What makes you think," she said, driving those words into his heart while those sharp claws dug now into hers, "that I would let you have such satisfaction? That I would tell you the answer to that question before you die?"

And then, as the hand on her face moved behind her head, as she felt the warm pressure of his fingers pulling her down, the hand around her heart sank its talons into her flesh, ripping it apart as his lips parted and closed over her own. She forced in the knife, made it only a finger's width further when the voice in her head began to scream once more, screeching loud enough to split it open. His breaths were hot against her skin, his heart hammering against her chest. He tasted like blood, like salt, like ashes from a still-burning fire. It filled her chest with poison, with something rotten that she knew was going to kill her.

She pushed in the blade, and he kissed her harder, deeper, groaning from the pain as he did, not giving up ground, seizing more.

Another fight. Another battle. Even here, now, with her knife halfway into his chest, aiming at his heart, he would not yield to her. And he would win it. He would die taking something of hers along with him. He was going to die content, after all that he'd done, after putting her through hell, after leaving her here to suffer the consequences. Alone.

Not a chance in hell.

She pulled out the knife, pushed herself away from his embrace. "No," she said, flinging the blade at his feet. "I'm not going to kill you. Not yet.

Not now. You are going to live, as a fugitive, a peasant, a man stripped of everything but the life I've spared today. You will live to watch your failure as a ruler, a conqueror, a man whose dream will never be realized. And I'm going to watch you pay for it, *every day,* until I'm satisfied with your pain. I have gained my freedom here, today. From here onward, I am no longer your prisoner, no longer under your command. You are going to live with that until I'm done with you. Your turn to suffer," she said, turning to leave, "begins *now.*"

The journey continues...

SIENNA FROST

OBSIDIAN

REVELATION

COMING SOON.

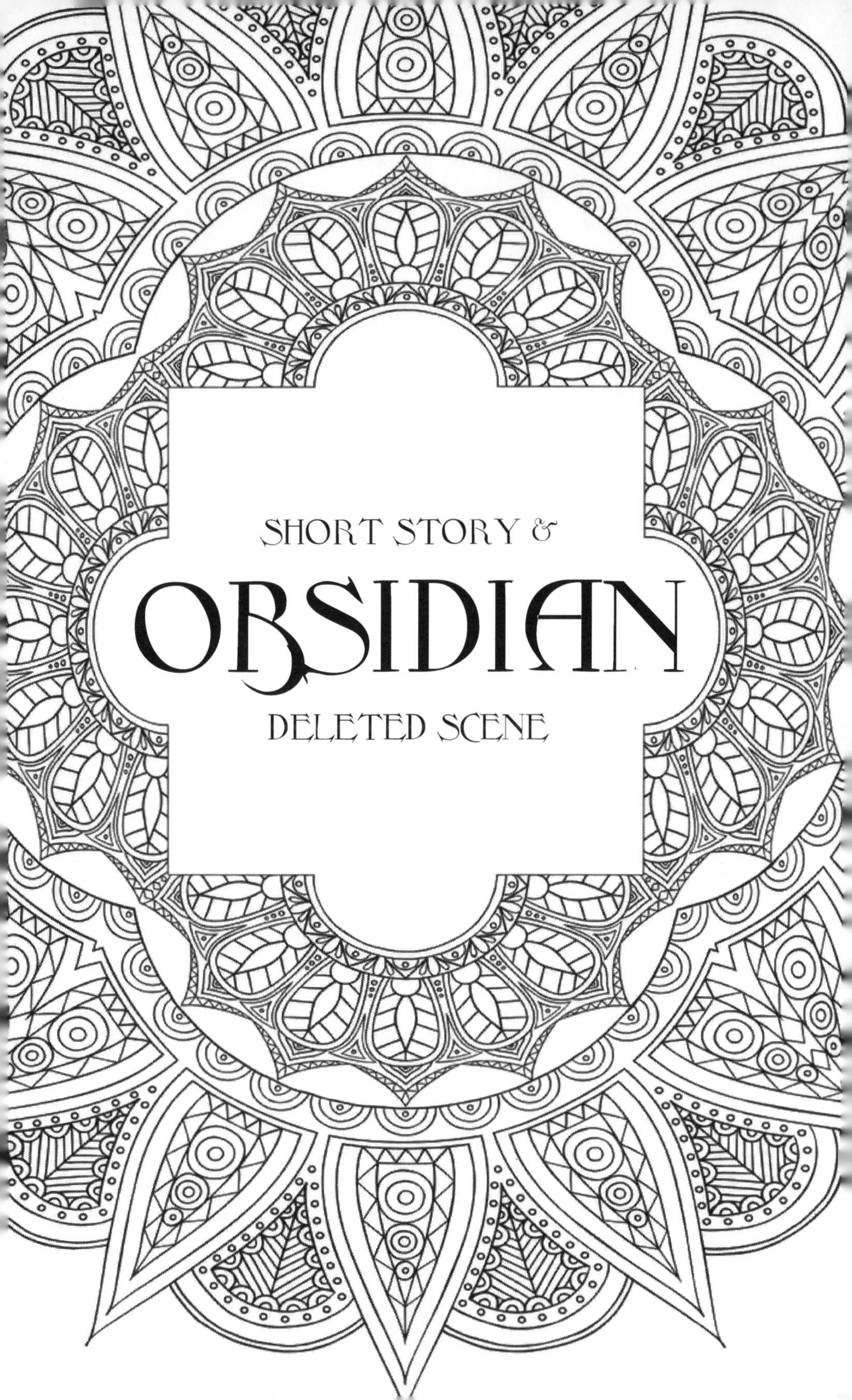

SHORT STORY &

OBSIDIAN

DELETED SCENE

No
Happy

A STORY OF NAZIR & BAAKU

Ending

The first vision he had was of his mother leaving. In it, she wore a blue gown; blue like the sky that stretched beyond the furthest dune he'd ever visited, beyond the faint outline of that white rock shaped like a woman's back, beyond places he couldn't see or imagine or follow. Behind her, the desert stood still and quiet, save for the occasional wind that whistled as it tugged on the hem of her dress and messed up the braids in her hair. It was early morning, and the horizon was dancing on its toes in a dress of pink, purple, and blue—a complex blending of gentle shades that revealed much, and concealed more of what lay beyond where the sky touched the sand.It wasn't too different from the way she'd smiled that morning. Not different at all from the way she'd always smiled at him, or Djari. There were things the kha'ari of Visarya would never say to her children—burdens she'd always kept as her own beneath the mildness of her tone and the mask she always wore.

Goodbye had been one of them. She'd never said that word, not once, no matter how many times she had to go away.

She hadn't said it that morning, either. She'd left him words he didn't understand, instructions he didn't know how to follow.

"Hold on to this for me." She took off an earring, one half of her favorite pair made of yellow sunstones with glitters in them—the same yellow as her eyes when she'd looked at that foal she couldn't save, or that time when she'd found him in her tent crying over something father had said.

He looked at the earring in her hand, and a strange chill he didn't understand climbed up his back–made him hesitate. "But you will have only one."

"If I ever lose this one..." She gestured at the one left hanging from her ear. "...then you will still have it, and we will remember it once existed."

"But what if I lose it?"

She paused for a moment to look at him—sensing, as she always did, the worry he'd failed to hide. "Then we will find something new. Something just as beautiful, just as precious."

"And if I lose that, too?"

"Then you must find another, and another, and another." Smiling, she reached out her hand to touch his face, her fingers cool against his skin. They were trembling, too, like her voice as she spoke, like the light in her eyes, like him as he sensed something wasn't right. "Never be afraid to lose things, Nazir. Life is only precious when you learn to love something enough to cry when you lose it." She leaned over and planted a kiss above his brow—not the kind she used to give after bedtime stories, or when he or Djari did something right. It felt more like a sword gripped before a fight, reassuring and unnerving at the same time. She said, "We must find the courage to love things and the strength to survive losing them, or else life holds very little meaning, and the world holds no joy."

Nazir didn't understand it; not truly, not at the time. He remembered taking the earring anyway. He remembered her smile before she turned away. He remembered the silhouette her gown made as it blended and disappeared into the blue sky when she left.

He remembered wondering why it felt like it was the last time he would ever see her.

The earring had gone missing when they brought her back–her favorite sunstone lost somewhere in the desert, buried in the sand. *Blue gown, swallowed whole by blue sky.*

He had seen that, too—how it happened, what they did to her, for how long, and how many times. He knew where those marks on her corpse had come from. He had seen it in his visions—first when he was twelve, several times more before their last conversation, on the day she was buried, and on nights like this: sitting here alone, far away from camp, running from responsibilities. Running from grief, from rage, and the hurt and disappointment in his father's eyes when he asked why his son hadn't seen it coming. He'd lied about that, of course. He *had* seen it coming. He just didn't know when it would happen.

Lies and excuses. Nazir caught himself at that thought. *You could have told someone. Something could have been done. You could have said something if you weren't such a coward.*

Too much of a coward, even now.

A gust of wind found its way into the cave and made the small fire in front of him leap and crackle. His eyesight flashed out of focus, returning with something foreign that revealed itself in the flame. A rock he'd seen too many times began to take shape. The screams that always came with it escalated. Nazir shut his eyes before the figure behind that rock came into view and scrambled back in panic, covering his ears as his back slammed into the wall. It didn't stop. Never. Not once. Anything he tried never stopped these things from coming true. They followed him like shadows, like the blood from his first kill that never seemed to wash off his hands. In his head, the voice continued to shriek, and the images that should have gone away transferred themselves onto the blank canvas behind his eyes, revealing more and more of things he hadn't seen but needed to forget, bringing them all closer, clearer, sharper—

—and then they were gone, snuffed out like a candle, like waking up from a nightmare into sunlight.

"Bad day, huh?"

The sword leapt into his hand by reflex, and with it Nazir jumped to his feet, spinning around to face the intruder.

A figure stepped into view from the back end of the cave—a young man in gray, braided in the Kamara's fashion. His hands held no weapon, both of them raised high in the air to make a point. There must have been another entrance somewhere. He should have checked before deciding to spend the night here.

"Stay where you are." Nazir raised the sword higher, keeping it pointed at the man who seemed to harbor no intention whatsoever of doing what he'd demanded.

Slow, steady steps brought the stranger into the light, close enough for more features to be revealed—features he shouldn't recognize, but did. A strong, sharp nose he'd never seen that felt as familiar as his own. A jawline that reminded him of a cat, accommodating the high cheekbone his hands knew without having touched. Blue-green eyes that accelerated his pulse, a wide, upturned mouth that had spoken his name on so many occasions, in memories that never happened. *Hadn't happened.*

"I'm not here to pick a fight," said the man from his visions—the ones that kept on coming, showing different things from different places. "You're a trueblood oracle." Another step closer brought him right up against Nazir's blade, its tip digging into the soft skin at his throat. "You know you're not going to die tonight, not..."

It must have shown on his face—the shock of recollection, the recognition he hadn't the thought to conceal as he stared at the man on the other end of his blade. The Kamara's eyes widened as his words trailed off, replaced by an understanding that settled upon him like feathers falling from the sky. "You recognize me..." He paused, green eyes narrowing as if to read further into it. "You know who I am."

Nazir shook his head and kept the blade in place, making sure the message was clear. Whether he knew that face or not, the man was still a Kamara, and he was a Visarya. "I recognize you from my visions. That doesn't mean I know who you are." Which brought him to the important question. "So, who *are* you? And why are you here?"

He had meant it as a threat, but there was only relief on the other man's face, in his shoulders that relaxed despite the sword at his throat. "It's Nazir, isn't it? You're Za'in izr Husari's son?"

How... Nazir stopped himself before he voiced a stupid question. *Of course he knows who you are. There is only one trueblood oracle around here.* "Your name and rank, Kamara."

He wasn't going to get it, judging from how tightly those lips pressed together. The young Kamara in gray who looked to be roughly his own age took a step back and gestured at the blade he carried. "I'm going to put my sword down, and then you can do the same. This is *my* cave. I come here often. That blanket you're using is mine. There is a burn mark on one corner. Do you see it?"

"Don't move," Nazir warned as the man's hand moved out of place, pressing the blade closer against the exposed throat.

The man stopped, putting his hand back up. "Look." He let out a heavy sigh as he shut his eyes for a moment. When they opened again, there was only calm. "I'm going to sleep here tonight. We can share, or we can fight. If you know you won't die here, and we do fight, it means I will be dead. This is *our* territory. You cannot afford to kill or attack me here without consequences. I *am*, however, offering you an alternative. Will you let me put my sword down?"

He did know it—the territory issue, the consequences of their fight should it happen, and the fact that he wasn't going to die here and now. His own death would come later, and not by this Kamara. This man, too, would live for a long time after this, and his visions had yet to be wrong. "Your blades. All of them."

The blades came off one by one—all four of them—laid out carefully on the ground and out of arm's reach. The axe he'd often seen in his visions wasn't there for some reason. The scar under the man's right eye, too, was missing.

Nazir put down his sword, but kept the dagger hidden in his boot. The dark-haired Kamara didn't seem to notice—or if he had, he didn't seem to mind. He sat down next to Nazir by the fire, made himself a cushion with the fur-lined robe he'd taken off, and lay down on his side, supporting his head with an anchored elbow.

"So," said the man when he had settled comfortably, looking up at him, "how long have you had visions about me?"

Nazir's breath hitched at the question. Three years, maybe five? But he didn't have to know that, or what had been in them. He twisted the cap off his wineskin, took a sip, and handed it over. He didn't really need a drink; he needed something to do, to keep his hands busy–something to distract him from memories too intimate to be holding onto while looking at the man responsible for them. "You said you come here often." He changed the subject, doing his best to conceal how much the question was unnerving him. "Why?"

A playful smile—one slightly off to the left side, the same one he recognized from his visions. "Why are *you* here?"

Nazir took the drink back and turned away toward the fire, ignoring the question. If the man minded his refusal to reply, it didn't show. He simply left it hanging, leaving room, allowing space for Nazir to pick his distance.

Silence tiptoed around the fire as they each pretended to ignore the other's presence. Between them, unanswered questions hovered overhead like a bunch of fruits dangling from a tree, waiting for someone to pluck them off the branch. The air felt warmer and thicker now in the cave, making it more and more difficult to breathe. It might have been the wine, the extra company, or maybe the sense of time and space closing in around them as they stretched their patience closer to the limit. In the end, it was Nazir who reached for the moment, having gone through pages after pages of his visions, turning them over in his mind until curiosity filled itself to the brim and spilled over for having nowhere else to go. He turned to the young man from his vision, picked something out of a distant memory that hadn't happened, and voiced it. "Do you always trust people so easily?"

The young Kamara turned, gave him the same shrug, the same grin on his lips, and the same answer he'd heard in his vision, word by familiar word. "People, no. I trust my instinct. Only that."

It took his breath away every time, made the hair on the back of his neck stand on end, sent flashes of lightning down his spine whenever his premonitions turned into reality.

The young man, having paid close enough attention, grasped it immediately. "Did I say that?" He tilted his head to the side, a child brimming with excited curiosity. "In your vision?"

"I don't remember," Nazir lied. He remembered them all, right down to the last line of their conversations. But they came to him in flashes, in chaotic jumbles of disjointed images that required him to put together like puzzles. Puzzles that were about to come together now, after so many years of waiting for the man to appear.

"What do you remember, then?" the Kamara asked. "What did you see?"

Us. Things. Your hands in my hair. Mine... in yours. "I saw those bruises. I wondered where they came from." He'd touched one, too, at some point. *Tonight? Or would that happen some other time?*

"This?" A hand flew to his face, rubbed the newly formed bruise near his right eye, as if he'd just remembered it was there. "Fathers can be pricks sometimes." A shrug, masking a pitiful smile. "Most of the time, in my case."

Fathers. Sons. Expectations. Same old stories that never seem to change, or end. "That's who you run from." He nodded, took another pull on the wineskin, and handed it over. "Your father."

The man took the offered wine and looked away for a moment as he drank. "It takes a night in a cave to not knock his teeth out most days, believe me."

A bitterness there, wrapped clumsily around a fresh wound, concealing it without great success. Nazir could understand it, he supposed. There were bound to be wounds for sons of powerful fathers. Only his own wounds ran much deeper than that, and from something else entirely. "At least it works."

The Kamara paused to study his expression. He did that often, as a young man in his vision and a grown one when they made love, sometimes before, sometimes after. "It doesn't work for you, though, does it?" he said. "You were running from your visions, weren't you?"

It doesn't, he almost said. Something stopped him just in time, a gentle tap on the shoulder, a whisper telling him to look. Nazir swept his eyes around the cave, at the surroundings that had become silent and peacefully still. No sound of her shrieking now—no rock of any shape or size behind which his mother had died screaming in the fire before him. Here and now, only the warm yellow light that danced delicately around the cave remained, revealing to him something he had failed to notice before. "It... did. Just now." *When you came in.*

The other man's curious eyebrow flew up almost on cue, as if he'd said it out loud. "Just now? When I came in?"

Nazir drew a sharp breath at the unexpected echo of his own thoughts. *Is it even possible? Or was it just a coincidence?* "Just now." He nodded, light-headed and overwhelmed by the new discovery and the future it might bring.

A chuckle, followed by a mischievous smile. "I have that effect on people sometimes. Didn't know I could chase away even visions."

Nazir wanted to laugh or smile in response, only both had become something foreign to him for some time. He wasn't sure for how long or why. Perhaps since his mother had died, or maybe long before that.

"What else did you see?" asked the young man, casually, abruptly. "About me. What did you see in your vision?"

He is trying to distract me.

Nazir thought for a time, turning an idea over in his head, playing with new possibilities he could initiate, or not. The cave grew quieter as they looked at each other in silence, its walls holding their breaths, waiting for his decision. In his head, an image of himself standing behind a thick red line materialized, and his mother's words hovered somewhere in the back of his mind, urging him to take the plunge.

'You must always find the courage to love things and the strength to survive losing them,' she had said.

"I saw a scar on the back of your hand. The right one," Nazir said, "and another one on your back."

The man listened attentively. A sliver of light quivered in the pair of blue-green eyes that pinned him in place, not wanting to miss a single twitch of his brow.

"There was also one right here." He reached out to touch the man's right cheek, under his eye where a line would one day mar that skin—expecting, even before he did, for the other's hand to brush it aside, or to raise a protest of some kind.

It didn't happen.

The line in front of him pulsed, once, twice, like the persistent pressure that kept tapping at his back, pushing him to take another step forward.

Nazir traced along the line of the soon-to-be scar and felt a stirring underneath his fingertips where they touched. The man from his vision shifted his weight as he watched and waited, his breathing quickening to match that of Nazir's. Next to them, the fire crackled, adding heat, rising toward the ceiling as if in anticipation.

"A long one," he said, and felt himself take that necessary step, crossing over the line to the other side, "on the inside of your left thigh, running down toward your knee."

A broken, ragged breath came from the man's lips as he exhaled, accentuated and made ten times louder by the silence that pinned them in place and locked them together in an understanding that needed no explanation. Nazir waited for the shock, the disgust, the awkward display of embarrassment or some kind of reaction one might expect from intimacy attempted too early, too fast, without permission.

It, too, never came.

The familiar stranger stared at him, chest heaving up and down from breaths taken too desperately, too swiftly in succession. "What did I do?" he asked. "In your vision? What did I say?"

Nazir swallowed the lump in his throat, willing his voice to steady and his heart to slow. *It would be all right, wouldn't it, mother? I mustn't be afraid to lose things. That was what you wanted, wasn't it?* He said, "You took my hand..."

The hand came up, wrapping tight around his fingers. "What else?"

It has to be alright. I am allowed to love, to trust, to have someone. "You turned it over—"

A kiss, planted on his upturned palm before he finished the sentence. "What else?" The man from his visions looked up, eyes bright in the light of the dancing fire.

There were a hundred things he could have said, a hundred more lies he could have told—only by then he knew he didn't want to lie anymore; not tonight, not to this person. "I don't know," he said, and it was the truth. "That's where it stopped."

"But could there be more?"

Nazir bit his lip, holding himself in check before taking yet another step forward. "Do you *want* there to be more?"

The man looked up at him, blue-green eyes tracing his face, seeking answers. "Do I?" he asked. "Do you?"

"I don't even know who you are."

"You do know who I am. You've seen me in your visions," he said. "Is that not enough?"

It ought to have been enough—all those things he had done, the things he had said, and still... "There is no happy ending to this." *No place for us.*

The man shook his head, brushing it off like loose sand on dried fingers. "I don't back out from a fight I don't think I can win. That is not what we do or who we are, is it?"

Is that who I am? Someone who would back out from a fight he thinks he can't win?

'Never be afraid to lose things, Nazir,' his mother had said. Her last words, her last instruction for him.

"No, I suppose it's not," he replied. It was about time he stopped being a coward, or that scared little boy too afraid to lose things. "What do we do about it, then?"

Another crooked smile appeared as the man let go of his hand. "Sleep, for now," he said, lying down on his arm, facing him. "You look like you could use some. I'll chase them away, those damn visions."

I'll chase them away. Just like that. "Even those of us?"

The man whose name he still didn't know yawned and closed his eyes. "Well, we don't need them anymore now, do we?"

Nazir did sleep that night, and for the first time in a long time, he didn't dream, and no visions came. And though the stranger who'd kissed his hand was already gone when he woke up, he did learn how to smile again that morning, and would remember it for a long time to come.

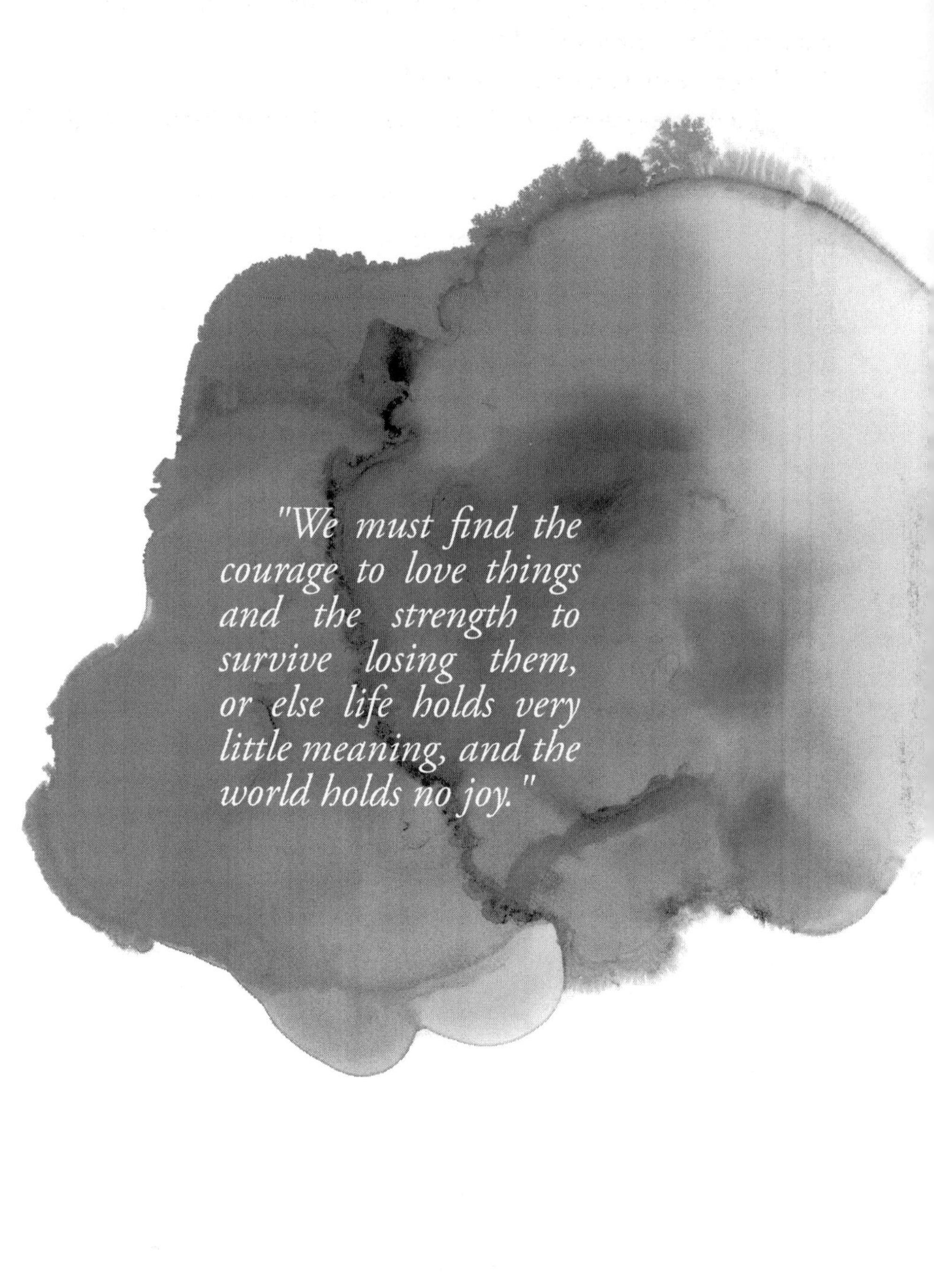
"We must find the courage to love things and the strength to survive losing them, or else life holds very little meaning, and the world holds no joy."

The Other Side of the Madira

The world made large rooms for monsters...

...and less so for those half-eaten by them.

The streets smelled like vomit, and the pleasure district's dark alleys always smelled like death, or something about to be dead, glazed with the scent of dried semen. It was where the city dumped the used and useless. Garbage disposal was a necessity in any human settlement, and in a city as populated as Rasharwi, an overflow of human garbage was always a problem.

The Rashais tried to keep their garbage on the other side of the Madira—a man-made canal that formed a ring around the central district of the capital. Water from three large oases were drawn into it, bringing the former desert settlement to life and at the same time efficiently separating the privileged from the poor.

Having lived on both sides of the Madira, Hasheem knew exactly how well that worked. The truth was garbage could be found anywhere, in many forms, sometimes more so among the rich than the poor. You could smell it if you stayed long enough for the priceless perfume to fade, and sometimes the stench was stronger than on the garbage side of the Madira.

Someone grabbed his ankle as he walked down the alley—an old man, thin and generously covered with what looked like his own piss mixed with something long dead in the sewer. The reek of undigested spirits stung his nose as the man spoke, begging, as they all did, for food and mercy. Hasheem dug into his pocket, took out a coin and dropped it into the man's cup. It clinked brightly as it landed on top of the already existing three. One would be enough for a small meal, and the other three could buy him a bottle of some backstreet liquor. They would be spent exactly that way, of course. Everyone who'd ever given coins in these alleys knew that.

You could call it stupidity, or a waste of kindness, to justify walking by without making contributions. You could also realize what happiness in life meant to those who had been born into less, where education and freedom didn't exist as options, and pride was a thing to be crushed out of existence by the overprivileged, who would make sure you never climbed out of that pit to ruin their precious landscape. The world made large rooms for monsters and less so for those half-eaten by them. It was why there were always going to be more monsters than men, no matter where and when you lived.

The coin he'd offered wouldn't save the man, no. It might, however, allow him to pass his sufferings sooner, and perhaps also die happier with a full belly and a bottle of leftover wine. You could only do that much for a conscience, or you wouldn't survive in a city like Rasharwi—or any city, for that matter.

'Prosperity, over-population, and poverty go hand in hand,' Dee had once said. *'Keep too many rats in a cage you can't expand and they'll start eating each other. That's why the Salar needs to take the White Desert and Makena. Colonization, at any given place or time, arises from a shortage of resources and room. Or a fear of one.'*

The need for resources and room was why his Kha'gan had been raided and the reason he was here in Rasharwi. Logically, he should despise all Rashais, and perhaps also Samarrans, Khandoors, Cakorans, or anyone in alliance with the Salasar. Rasharwi, being the capital city, was filled with a great mix of those. It was also full of people of all races, shapes, and sizes who had helped him survive and suffered alongside him in the pleasure district. Hate wasn't easily applied for those who had to live without choices. You didn't get to pick a whole race to hate unless you were born with enough privilege to shit on people just because they were different.

He would, however, be expected to do just that in the White Desert. His people would call him a traitor for offering coins to Rashais. They would also, by law, execute him for having served anyone in Rasharwi if he ever set foot back on his own land. A fine evidence, that, of how close one could resemble one's enemies when blinded by hate and vengeance.

Going back to the desert was never going to happen. Hasheem shook himself free of the thought and gave three more coins to a woman, a kid, and another old man who wouldn't live through the night before rounding the corner. The street turned into a wider, cleaner one, leading to the cobblestone-lined bank of the Mardira. Across the canal, far back behind richly-decorated homes and large mansions, the Black Tower rose majestically in the dead center of the district, its five hundred torch-lit rooms twinkling like fireflies on a gigantic tree—only it was a mountain, composed entirely of obsidian. At the very top of the Tower, the brightest, most prominent display of light dancing against the pitch black sky was the residence of the Salar of Rasharwi, supreme ruler of the Salasar—the man who had ordered the raiding of his home.

It was a beautiful sight, anyone would say, and he might still have agreed had he not seen enough of what went on inside of the Tower. To Hasheem, who now lived most of the time in it with Dee, it reminded him of too many ugly things for such a word to be used. Court was court—it wouldn't have mattered if it were made entirely of gold. Blood could stain anything—only on obsidian, it wouldn't show.

The General's mansion was on the other side of the Madira, perched high on an elevated section of the bank for protection. Four soldiers guarded the entrance on his side of the canal. Six more patrolled its walls and gardens across the water. There would be more inside, of course, waiting to bring certain death to intruders who might try to break in or out of the compound. It could still be done, Hasheem thought to amuse himself, but it would take coordinated work of at least three men who knew exactly what they were doing.

A useless idea for another time, and for a different circumstance. He hadn't come to break into the mansion. He'd come by invitation from its master, for pleasure and for paid time.

A ferry was there to carry him across, guarded by two armed men who seemed to have been there for a while. It was standard procedure to make sure he was admitted as quickly as possible. Making the Silver Sparrow wait cost money. His standard fee, after all, happened to be charged by the hour.

One of the guards frisked him before allowing him on board. They didn't find anything, of course. He had come as an escort, not Dee's assassin. Killing a client on an escort job was off limits. It wasn't just bad business–it would end his career in pleasure once and for all. And since his value as Dee's apprentice had half to do with the information he could get as the Sparrow, while his fee as an escort had tripled once he became known as Dee's gold-ring assassin for the excitement it offered, keeping both jobs running professionally was crucial.

Such protocols had never been broken in his career, which contributed to the guards' quick decision to allow him on board. The Silver Sparrow of Azalea was a name that could get him anywhere, even into the most secure chambers in Rasharwi, for that reason. He had yet to be called to entertain the Salar, but his wives and children had been among his clients. The fees, of course, were always collected by Dee, which meant not a single coin could be missing—or late—even if you were a prince of the Black Tower. It was good business, and one only a suicidal fool would throw away.

The ferryman greeted him with obligated politeness as he stepped on board. You couldn't ask for more than that if you were a Shakshi slave in Rasharwi. Hasheem offered him a smile, asked him about life and family, and gave him two coins once he'd reached the other side.

The soldiers at the door made way for him when he approached. A steward who had been waiting to escort him inside inclined his head and offered to take his cloak. Hasheem handed it to him and followed the man into the foyer with a ritual slowness, making sure the exquisite white Makena silk of his tunic would be free from wrinkles when he arrived. Image was everything in his profession. You had to try to be desirable, presentable, to put yourself on display in any place and at any time, to hold value.

The steward led him up the stairs to the second floor, pausing in front of the door at the end of the hallway. He knocked twice, listening for a signal, before pushing it open. Hasheem thanked the man and gave him a silver coin before he entered. It was tradition, and a wise person buys favors when they can be bought.

The room was brightly-lit, with six golden hurricane lamps illuminating the intricately-woven crimson and cream carpet made from what appeared to be an exceptional grade of Cakoran wool. A four-poster bed with a red velvet curtain was propped against the wall on the left behind a set made up of a round table and four matching chairs. Next to it, the

General stood in a silk robe of deep crimson, nursing a cup of wine in his hand, waiting for him with poorly-concealed enthusiasm.

"I thought you would never pick up my offer," said the General, with the same authority in his voice Hasheem remembered—only now it was coarser, rougher, probably with age. It had been a while since they'd last conversed. Seven years, to be exact. "What kept you?"

The door closed with a click from behind, and Hasheem realized he'd nearly jumped at the sound. *Seven years and you're still afraid of this man,* he thought, shaking off the memories that still haunted him some nights.

"Inconvenience," he lied, heading to the table where the wine had been prepared and pouring himself a serving. He needed a drink. Some things, no matter how much time had passed, still needed to be dulled. "I don't come down much from the Tower." That was true. It took an hour to scale that mountain by horse, and the permission to do so required a day to obtain. Dee never left it unless he absolutely had to.

"It never ceases to amaze me," said the General, moving to stand in front of him at an arm's length away, "how you managed to land yourself in Deo di Amarra's care in so little time."

Hasheem put on an innocent smile, giving the man a ceremonious shrug. "Luck." In truth, luck had little to do with it. You didn't get anywhere with only luck in a city as big as Rasharwi. Around here, you licked the right boots, fucked the right people, killed some when necessary, and *sometimes* luck would get you somewhere. Money and power came at a cost, and those with a lot of it were never without blood on their hands—and he was, indisputably, the richest slave in the history of the Salasar. Though much of it was thanks to Dee's ingenious connections. By seventeen, his hands had seen more blood than most people's would in their entire lifetimes.

The General's hands had been one of those stained with blood, and judging from the way those eyes roamed over him, he hadn't changed much. It had been obvious, even when they'd run into each other by chance a year ago, and by the letter that had arrived soon after, what the man wanted. The sum proposed in that invitation was large enough to make Dee choke on his drink. You didn't offer to pay that much above the asking price unless you wanted something very specific.

The General took a step closer, his tall, beastly figure towering over Hasheem the same way it once had. He was a lot taller now than he had been at ten, but it didn't feel any different. He was still the same boy, looking up at the same monster back in Sabha seven years ago.

The same monster who had been the first to break him.

'The first time is always the hardest,' someone had said after he'd returned from the General's chamber, with two broken ribs, a twisted ankle, three long gashes on his thigh, arm, and back, and a dozen or so bruises. It hadn't gotten any easier after that, except that the pain had become more bearable with time. Most tortures lost some of their intended effects when one expected or got used to them.

But he had never, not once, gotten used to being in the same room with this man. He didn't think he ever would.

"Let me see you," commanded the General. Two familiar calloused fingers lifted his chin, tilting his face to catch the light.

Hasheem's skin crawled at that touch, despite experience, despite expertise, despite everything he had been through and accomplished in the past seven years.

"I thought you were pretty then." Those same fingers caressed his skin, traveling up his cheek. "Look at you now. The Silver Sparrow of Azalea. The most beautiful face in the Salasar. Tell me..." A thumb dug into his lower lip, pulled his mouth open. "...are these as skilled as they were then? Or even more so now?"

He ought to have bitten that thumb right off and shoved a knife down the man's throat. Instead, Hasheem found himself struggling to breathe, the convictions trapped inside suddenly paralyzing limbs. He should have said something to respond. Couldn't.

The General caught it, of course—he never missed those things. That was the point—the pleasure of torturing someone. He smiled. "Still the same frightened little boy, I see. All this time, and you still haven't changed." The same thumb, digging into his cheek, pressing into the inside of his mouth and against a tooth. "I wonder what kind of sound you will make now. Your voice," another hand tugged carelessly on the sash at his waist, pulling it free, "is very different."

His hand slipped underneath the silk, brushing over an old scar on Hasheem's torso just above his hip. He put on a mask of indifference as something twisted and turned in his stomach, trying to swallow the wine that was threatening to come back up as he did.

"I remember this," said the General, keeping his eyes on him. He liked to do that—to look at fear as it swallowed someone whole, to be acutely aware when and how the breaking happened. "And this." The hand drew a small circle before dipping down to another scar just below the first one.

Hasheem drew a breath and turned away toward the table, to the object that had been placed next to the wine before he'd arrived.

The wooden box gleamed in the flickering light of the hurricane lamps, and its imperfections from regular use stood out from the smooth, shiny black lacquer. The memory of what it contained was still startlingly clear in his mind. It paralyzed him for a second, before the thought of its contents being used on a certain someone washed away the numbness in his limbs like a flood, replaced with a rush of energy he'd just now forgotten he had.

"I am what you want me to be," Hasheem said, picking a smile, managing its delivery, and surprising himself that he could still accomplish the task given how shaken he was. "With what you're paying me…" He inched a little closer, his white tunic sliding against the General's robe, initiating a sharp hissing sound from both the fabric and the client. "We can talk," he whispered, feeling the General's muscles straining with each word from their proximity. "We can play." Brushing his lips now against the exposed flesh just behind the right ear. "Or we can fuck." It earned him the shudder, the heaved breath he needed. He said, pushing it further, "Not…necessarily in that order."

The General, eyes gleaming now as they always had when they caught him staring at the container—feverish and clouded with the desire to break, to conquer, to hear him scream—closed the remaining distance between them, forgetting completely the one thing he should not. "You remember it too, don't you?" he said. "It will be just like old times, I assure you. Perhaps even better, now that you've grown so much." The right corner of his lips lifted into a smile, one Hasheem had come to know by heart. He would be thinking now which one of those things to use first, and where. Which one of them would inflict the deepest pain and earn him the loudest scream.

So, Hasheem thought, *am I.*

The following bonus short stories of Muradi and Zahara are available in the e-book format of Obsidian:Awakening :

—With Or Without Your Clothes On—

—The Breaking of the Beast—

ACKNOWLEDGEMENT

As a mother and a wife before all else, I can't thank my children and my husband enough for their support while I took family time to write this book, without whom I would not be able to write love as I am now. To my parents who offered me the opportunity to study abroad and learn to write in English, and for having raised me to believe nothing is ever above my ability to accomplish. To my dear friends, readers, and amazing writers, Murjani, Natasha, and Del who have taught me so much and been the best friends I could have asked for throughout my writing journey. To Sergio, Jenny L. Gale, Julia, Clementine, and Isianya who have held my hands through writing Obsidian and been the biggest fans and support a writer could have asked for. To my editor Kyle who understood me so well and made editing this book a breeze.

Last but not least, this book is out in public at all because of every reader who decided to reach out to me to say how much they love this story, without whom I would have stopped sharing this book a long time ago and keep it to my grave unseen. You have all been a big part of my life and wherever this series goes, this is as much your story as it is mine. So thank you, with all my heart, for being on this journey with me.

ABOUT SIENNA

Sienna Frost is a mother, a wife, and a traveler who has spent a good ten years writing to entertain only herself and the next two decades sharing her stories online for free. Her previous works have been fan-translated into seven languages and shared around the world. Obsidian is the first book she has decided to publish due to requests from fans who have been following this story on the internet. She does not consider herself a writer. She writes and hopes to find readers who want to share her journey.

Sienna loves to talk to her readers. Visit her on Twitter with this handle: @Siennafrst or on Wattpad.com @siennafrost for more stories.

Also Available on Amazon:

Made in the USA
Middletown, DE
26 May 2023

31493973R00298